D0328771

GUARDIAN

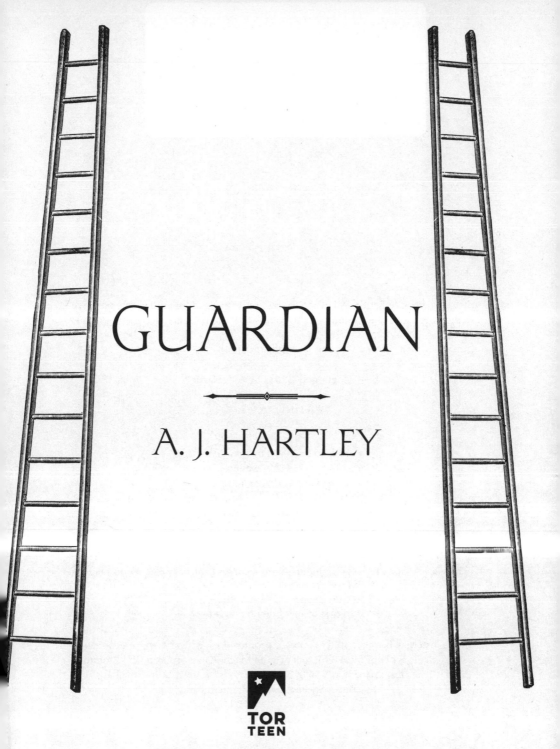

GUARDIAN

A. J. HARTLEY

TOR
TEEN

A TOM DOHERTY ASSOCIATES BOOK
NEW YORK

This is a work of fiction. All of the characters, organizations, and events portrayed in this novel are either products of the author's imagination or are used fictitiously.

GUARDIAN

Copyright © 2018 by A. J. Hartley

A Tor Teen Book
Published by Tom Doherty Associates
175 Fifth Avenue
New York, NY 10010

www.tor-forge.com

Tor® is a registered trademark of Macmillan Publishing Group, LLC.

The Library of Congress Cataloging-in-Publication Data is available upon request.

ISBN 978-0-7653-8815-5 (hardcover)
ISBN 978-0-7653-8817-9 (ebook)

Our books may be purchased in bulk for promotional, educational, or business use. Please contact your local bookseller or the Macmillan Corporate and Premium Sales Department at 1-800-221-7945, extension 5442, or by email at MacmillanSpecialMarkets@macmillan.com.

First Edition: June 2018

Printed in the United States of America

0 9 8 7 6 5 4 3 2 1

To Finie and Sebastian,
and to all who have to fight for what others are born to.

GUARDIAN

CHAPTER

1

DAHRIA FROWNED, SHADED HER eyes, and turned to where a long-tailed whydah with a crimson beak was calling from a thorn tree.

"What a racket they make," she observed, put out. We were sitting on the porch of the Willinghouse estate, sipping plumet juice chilled with the last flakes of ice bought from the peddlers a week ago and stored in the house's deepest stone-lined cellar.

"I rather like it," I said. There were lots of birds that never braved the smogs of Bar-Selehm, and it was easy to forget just how wild the land was only a few miles from the city center. Dahria rolled her eyes.

"Of course you do," she remarked. "Being almost feral yourself. I'm amazed you aren't rolling in the dirt with Grandmamma's hyenas. And you wonder why I don't want to be seen in public with you."

"I am not feral!" I exclaimed, eyeing one of said hyenas as it trotted past and gave us an unreadable look that made the hair on the back of my neck prickle. "City girl, me. Born and raised. Well, raised."

The Drowning wasn't strictly the city.

"But not raised well," said Dahria.

"That's a matter of opinion," I said. "And perspective."

"Oh yes," said Dahria, lizard dry, "I keep forgetting your years of finishing school up someone's chimney."

"You can see a lot of the world from those chimneys."

"What's that?" said Dahria, putting a hand to her ear theatrically. "Ah yes, I think I hear the not-so-stealthy approach of a lecture: The Hard Realities of Life in the Slums and Gangs, by Anglet Sutonga, steeplejack."

"You'd rather I'd spent my school years on embroidery and watercolors, no doubt?" I replied, equally arch.

"Now, there's an image to conjure with. The steeplejack urchin with a palette of paints and some fine brushes, instead of a bucket of . . . What do you call the stuff that holds the bricks together?"

"Mortar?" I said, wide-eyed. "How can you not know what mortar is? What did they teach you in those precious finishing schools of yours?"

"Not bricklaying."

"Or anything else useful."

"Not much call for mortar when taking tea with counts and duchesses in elegant withdrawing rooms."

"Well, it's a good thing someone knows what mortar is," I said, "else your elegant drawing rooms would be likely to fall apart and kill you all. And we all know what a great loss *that* would be."

"I didn't say I didn't know what mortar was," said Dahria, biting back a grin. "The word merely escaped my memory, it being something unbecoming to a young lady."

"Ah. That must be it. The word knew better than to sully your mind and fled."

"Quite right too," said Dahria, and then she laughed, and I laughed, and for a while we forgot that the world was falling apart at the seams.

WAS THAT OVERSTATING THE case? Perhaps a little, but I don't think so. We had known as soon as the newspaper began to scream about the so-called "Arms for Rebels" scandal that the ruling

National party was going to be embarrassed, since several of its highest-ranking members had been connected to the illegal supplying of the northern tribes with Bar-Selehm machine guns. What we hadn't seen right away was how quickly Norton Richter's Heritage party would seize the initiative, using the crisis in the government to push for more extremist policies. A revised version of Richter's Bar-Selehm First bill, minimally adjusted to allow small areas of the city to remain exempt, had been forced through, and many of the local black and Lani people would have to move out of white areas of the city by the close of the year. Willinghouse had led the Brevard party charge against the policy shift, but the law had been passed anyway, the Nationals caving to pressure from Richter's swaggering, uniformed bullies and voting en masse to approve. It wasn't yet clear how far this would all go, but there were elections on the horizon and the fear—which was widespread—was that there would be huge gains for the Heritage party at the Nationals' expense, and that a coalition government might well be in power by year's end, with Willinghouse's Brevard party stripped of what little authority it currently had. Worst of all, Prime Minister Benjamin Tavestock—a reasonable and occasionally decent man with whom I disagreed about everything—was considered ripe for the plucking, though who might take his position, I couldn't say.

It was unlikely to be an improvement.

"What are you thinking?" Dahria said suddenly.

"Nothing," I replied. "Why?"

"You were looking at me in that probing, impertinent way again," she said. "Like you were burrowing into my head to see what was inside." She paused, waiting for me to respond, and when I went back to looking at the garden, added a peremptory "Well?"

"You remember that abandoned vault they found under the bank near Mahweni Old Town?" I said. "The police cordoned off the area, and they sent military engineers in to blast it open in the hope of gold doubloons or something from the days of Captain Franzen."

Dahria screwed up her face. "What are you babbling about, girl?" she said. "Of course I remember. What has that to do with what we were talking about?"

"I imagine seeing inside your head is a bit like that."

"How so?"

"Very hard to get into and really not worth the effort."

Again the half flicker of a grin quickly doused in affronted outrage. "You work for my brother!" she exclaimed. "You're staff. I should thank you to remember your place."

"I bet you would, but I don't think it's going to happen," I remarked.

Now she gaped, her face full of mock indignation. The fact that she was a little less guarded around me might have come from the assumption that I didn't matter, that I wasn't truly a person in the way her society acquaintances were, but I didn't believe that. I thought it was friendship, closeness, even if that was something we rarely acknowledged aloud, and never in front of other people.

"I should have you horsewhipped!" she said.

"Probably." I considered my drink. "My ice has all melted. Shall we go in?"

She harrumphed. "I suppose so. Will this summer never end? I swear I'm sweating like a steeplejack."

"Hilarious."

"The underclasses are so thin-skinned," said Dahria with a mischievous grin.

"Maybe we should test how thick-skinned the landed gentry are," I replied, reaching to the small of my back and sliding my brand-new kukri from its sheath. "I've been wanting to test the edge of this blade—"

She made a breathy noise of panic and pretended to run away. I went after her, menacing her with the heavy, curved knife, till she squealed and ran giggling to the door, with me in mock pursuit.

The door slid open, and there was Madame Nahreem clad in formal black, roused by our noise, glaring at us. We stuttered to a silent halt under her imperious stare like naughty children caught out of bed. She didn't say anything. She just *looked*. Even in her regular clothes, her countenance with all its labored patience, exasperation, and thinly veiled disdain would have left us chastened for our frivolity, but in the complete and utterly unexpected mourning she had taken to wearing since the death of Namud, we felt young and stupid. We watched Dahria's black-wreathed grandmother walk silently back into the house.

"If she had been fifty years younger," Dahria whispered to me, "I might have found myself rethinking the nature of their relationship."

I gave her a shocked look, but for once she wasn't joking or being dismissive, her expression serious and sad.

There were codes of mourning for the upper classes, set periods and depths according to one's status and relationship to the deceased. Six months for siblings. Two for nieces and nephews. A year for a parent or a child. It was all set and officially agreed upon, violation of the code being a matter of great social scandal, though it was also (as Dahria was quick to point out) profoundly unjust. Men mourned their dead wives for only three months, while women were supposed to mourn their husbands for two or three *years*. But nowhere in the code did it suggest that aristocrats should mourn for lost manservants.

I had liked Namud a lot and grieved for his death, but those feelings could not take away the strangeness of Madame Nahreem's extensive formal mourning. Since Dahria had avoided her grandmother's house like the plague, she had known Namud no more than I had, less in some ways. Dahria's grief at his death—buried deep enough that you had to know the signs to see it at all—was almost as surprising as Madame Nahreem's, or would be to her white, city friends. Dahria was more careful about what she gave away in front of them.

"Whose is that coach?"

Dahria was gazing down the long, tree-lined drive to where the iron gates were being opened for a glossy black two-horse fly. I stood up and saw, squeezed in on either side of the driver, two white men cradling shotguns.

"Get in the house," I said. "Tell Madame Nahreem to alert the servants. We have unwelcome guests."

There was a gun room beside the library on the ground floor. There hadn't been much in it since Willinghouse's father had died, but there were still a few dusty hunting rifles and some ornamented pistols in glass-fronted cases. I moved inside, closing the door behind me and bolting it, before making for the gun room. If I was overreacting, I would live with the shame.

I emerged with a breach-loading carbine I had handled once before, my hands hastily relearning how to cock the weapon as I returned to the front of the house, wishing I had felt strong enough to choose one of the longer and heavier hunting guns. The staff had been mostly released for the day, and there were no more than a couple of maids, the cook, a kitchen lad, and a twelve-year-old Quundu footboy. I could rely on no one but myself to protect the house.

There was a small shuttered window that looked out onto the veranda, and I opened it, slotting the rifle's muzzle through and peering down to where the coach had pulled up at the foot of the entrance steps. The two armed men were already climbing down, one of them stepping back and opening the fly's side door. They moved efficiently, like men who had spent time in uniform, but though their eyes seemed to rake the house and grounds for any sign of life, the grip they maintained on their weapons seemed almost casual.

I hesitated. Something about this felt strange, stranger than a robbery.

I had, however, already chambered one round and was prepared to fire a warning shot when a tall, slim white man with jet-black hair and muttonchop side whiskers climbed out of the coach. I stared, doubting my eyes, but there could be no mistake.

It was Benjamin Tavestock, First Lord of the Treasury. The prime minister.

CHAPTER

2

THE NATIONAL PARTY WASN'T the enemy, not like the Grappoli
were or Richter's Heritage party, but they were the establishment
and had been for generations. People like me had little to thank
them for and a lot of reason to be suspicious of them, so I dithered,
rifle in hand, as Madame Nahreem rolled past me like a great black
battleship and began unbolting the front door. I gave her a doubtful look, expecting a torrent of disdainful abuse, but she merely
shook her head, then nodded to the window.

I looked.

Emerging from the plume of dust stirred up by the prime minister's coach was another carriage, one I recognized as belonging
to the estate. And another behind it, shabbier and unfamiliar. As I
watched, Willinghouse leapt down from the first one before it had
come to a complete halt and strode purposefully toward Tavestock,
touching his shoulder and motioning him toward the house.

Madame Nahreem gave me a meaningful look and said
simply, "Go."

I knew better than to ask why, and for once her tone was urgent, but not accusatory. She didn't want the prime minister, his
men, or whoever was in the third carriage to see me. My secret
association with the Willinghouse family and the Brevard party
was still intact, and it was important we kept it that way.

I took the carbine and broke into a trotting run down the long
central corridor and up the stairs to the bedrooms, listening as I
went. I had just reached the broad landing when I heard the click

of the door latch and the murmured greetings of the arrivals. Dahria was standing outside her door, her face tight and still as if she had been carved from ivory. Her eyes met mine, and I felt her anxiety and tension, even if I couldn't see them in her posture. When I took a step toward her, she raised a warning finger, listened for another moment, then said, "I must change."

She vanished behind her bedroom door, and I could hear her hastily putting together something formal and public should she be called upon to meet our unexpected guests.

Unexpected didn't begin to cover it. Willinghouse was the most vocal and conspicuous of the parliamentary opposition's young backbenchers, and the idea that the leader of the government would have anything to do with him outside the Parliament House was hard to imagine.

Of course, Dahria would find this all terribly boring. When her brother started one of his dinnertime rants, she would begin by rolling her eyes and end by threatening to leave the table if he couldn't discuss more pleasant subject matter. But Dahria found everything boring. It was part of her aristocratic deportment, passion of any kind being at best unseemly and at worst a kind of weak-willed collapse into barbarism, but sometimes I would catch a look in her eyes (hastily stilled), and I'd say that the real reason she didn't want us talking politics was because she was scared. If Richter and his Whites First cronies took over, she knew full well that Willinghouse would have a sign—if not a target—round his neck, and not merely because he was their political enemy. Dahria and her brother were both one quarter Lani, and while they might pass unnoticed among white people who didn't know them—Dahria in particular, since she had made blending into polite society her life goal—the family was well known in Bar-Selehm.

That however, sells Dahria short. If she was afraid, it wasn't entirely for herself. I'd have waged everything I owned on it

And it wasn't just fear, either. However much she worked to hide it, Dahria was, under that elegant, feline exterior, a creature of deep and powerful feeling. We never talked about it, but I was sure in my heart that it was true, and it was a good part of why I liked her, snobby, privileged, and tiresome though she frequently was.

Still, however dull she found political meetings, even Dahria would have had to acknowledge that what was happening at the estate today was nothing short of remarkable.

Which is why they are here, and not in town, I thought. This was a meeting, and one they didn't want reported in the press. Possibly one they didn't want members of their own parties to know about.

But a meeting about what?

For a second I loitered outside Dahria's room, but then another door downstairs clicked shut and the already muted voices dropped to almost nothing. I strained to hear more but was startled by the sharp barking call of an alarmed vervet monkey somewhere on the roof. I blinked and decided.

I walked quickly to my room, shoving the door wide and leaving the carbine on the bed, then turned on my heel and half ran back along the landing and down the stairs. At the bottom I made for the kitchens and found Mrs. Tarulli, the cook, busying herself over the stove with a kettle of water.

She gave me a sharp look as I came in, then went back to what she was doing, waiting for me to say something. Mrs. Tarulli was Lani, like me, and I had always felt a certain wary distance from her, as if she was suspicious of my presence in the house. Had it been up to me, I would have spent much of my time in the kitchens, helping out, watching her grind spices and roast meat, but Willinghouse had given me strict instructions not to interact with the staff of the estate. This too was a security precaution, but whatever he had said to explain my presence to them had not worked, and they regarded me as if I had somehow cheated or seduced my way into a place beyond my station. The idea embarrassed and annoyed me, but this was not the time to dwell on that.

"Where are the parlor maid's things, Mrs. Tarulli?" I asked, trying to sound less like a brat from the Drowning and more like the lady of the house.

"Her things?"

"Her smock and apron," I said. "Her cap."

"Over there," she said, nodding to a closet I had taken for a pantry, and adding, as an afterthought, "Miss."

I rushed to it, speaking as I walked. "Are you making tea for Mr. Willinghouse's guests?"

"Yes, miss."

"Good," I said. "I'll take it."

"You'll what?"

"I'll serve the tea," I said.

She was a small woman, probably fifty, but wrinkled and lined from the sun so that she could pass for half as much again. She frowned now and cocked her head in the Lani way.

"That's not your place, miss, if you don't mind me saying."

"It is today," I said, trying to sound sure of my authority.

"Perhaps if I consult with Madame—" she began, but I was already pulling the maid's smock over my head.

"I take full responsibility for the decision," I said, amazed by how much I managed to sound like Dahria. "Just set up the tray, and I'll take it."

I used the poor reflection in the steel of the oven door as a mirror, adjusting the maid's white cap as the cook made the tea, muttering to herself in wordless, musical phrases of displeasure. When she was ready with the stacked china saucers and teacups, the little jug of milk and plate of lemon slices, the nested teaspoons, the sugar tongs in their dish, and everything arranged immaculately on the silver tray like the crown jewels, I took it up and considered her doubtful face.

"How do I look?" I asked.

Her frown deepened, as if something was profoundly wrong with the world but she could not say exactly what, and replied with an uncertain shrug, "Like a maid."

"Perfect," I said, and stepped toward the door, the items on the tray rattling like teeth and coins. I dared not look back, and moved through the swinging doors with studied care. A satchel of tools and a hod of bricks, I could manage without breaking stride, but this study in the fragile niceties of elegant society left me moving at a snail's pace, sure that I was about to drop everything in a shower of fractured porcelain and scalding tea.

One of the men with the shotguns was standing outside the door to the withdrawing room where I had once taken refuge from a hyena. He became quickly attentive as I appeared, but lost interest immediately, chewing his lower lip and glancing away as if my very presence annoyed him. I tried to apear polite—I could not manage apologetic, even as a parlor maid—and hovered at the door, registering the grumble of male voices inside. When he just stood there, I shot him the smallest of expectant looks, and, with a sigh, he rapped gently on the door.

There was a sudden silence within while I stood waiting, and then the door popped open, and there was Willinghouse, looking red-faced and impatient, his eyes sliding from the gunman to me and widening slightly.

"Tea, sir," I said, eyes lowered, partly playing the politeness that came with the role, partly just avoiding his stuttering amazement as I slid past him.

I might not have been on close terms with the staff of the Willinghouse estate, but I had met plenty of servants in the past, particularly Lani servants. The one thing they always said was that servitude was the surest way to be invisible that humanity could manage. Unless you messed up, of course, in which case you became suddenly and glaringly conspicuous.

So don't, I told myself, taking my time as I crossed the embroidered rug and setting the tray down on a side table. The other gunman was in the room, but once the door closed again, his eyes slid away from me and back to the two politicians. I might as well have been a ghost.

The prime minister was perhaps a virile fifty, a little thicker about the waist than Willinghouse and lacking the younger man's spontaneous catlike energy. As I arranged the cups and saucers with deliberate slowness, the conversation recommenced. I risked a glance at the speakers just in time to find Willinghouse's bright green eyes watching me with something like apprehension; the sickle-shaped scar on his cheek stood out cool and pale in contrast to the heat in the rest of his face. I wasn't sure how much of that had been occasioned by my appearance.

Most astonishing, however, was the presence of the two other men in the room, one standing against the wall like a guard or a secretary, the other sitting with Willinghouse and Tavestock like an equal. They were both black.

They were young, too, no older than Willinghouse, who was in his late twenties and wore dark formal suits like the politicians, though the shirts beneath them were, instead of the white and cream, vivid oranges and reds blurring together as if dyed in cold water. They both had neat mustaches but were otherwise clean shaven, and the seated man wore spectacles. The studious, intent air they gave him could not mask his youthful energy, and when he saw the tea tray, he gave me a smile so grateful and genuine that I faltered, unsure how to react.

"Look, Willinghouse," said the prime minister, picking up the thought where it had been left, "it won't wash. My party won't stand for it."

"If you won't retract the racial identity provisions, I have to demand it," Willinghouse answered, sitting.

"You are not in a position to demand anything," said Tavestock.

"Frankly, Prime Minister, neither are you."

"I think you forget whose party is in power," said Tavestock with hauteur. "Mine."

"For the moment," Willinghouse answered. "And only by the slimmest of margins, which will almost certainly collapse in less than three months. You won't survive the election. You know it, sir. I am offering you an alliance that would circumvent that eventuality, but if you will not meet my terms—"

"Then I lose, and you get Richter," snapped Tavestock. "Hardly an ideal solution for either of us."

"No," said Willinghouse. "That is true. Then let us begin again."

I was pouring the first cup of tea, but it was all I could do to keep my eyes on the thin porcelain, the situation was so remarkable.

Willinghouse was brokering a deal with the Nationals to contain Richter! It was extraordinary, and for a moment, I imagined how Sureyna would react when I told her. No wonder they were meeting away from prying eyes. But who were the Mahweni, who, thus far, had not spoken at all?

"My party's faithful have no interest in female suffrage," said the prime minister. "And appointing black members of Parliament is out of the question. These are both Brevard party hobbyhorses! I will be accused of selling out all the National party represents. They'll have my head at the next available opportunity."

Black MPs and votes for women! I could barely pour straight, so astonishing was what I had just heard.

"Richter is coming for you, no matter what you do," Willinghouse retorted. "He's been pushing for greater ties with the Grappoli instead of improving relationships with the blacks and colored of the city for as long as he's been in Parliament! And he has friends in your own party, Ben, you know he does. Archibald Mandel, for one."

"Mandel is no longer a member of this government," said the prime minister.

"He'll be back," said Willinghouse knowingly. "Investment in Grappoli munitions factories won't keep him out of Parliament for long, not with the way things are going. Is that who you want in your corner? A man who profits from the weapons the Grappoli will one day use against us?"

"I may not have a choice."

"You can add friends from our side of the aisle to make up for those you have lost on the right."

"There are principles at stake here, Willinghouse," said Tavestock, drawing himself up ramrod straight.

"Maintaining a power base isn't a principle," snapped Willinghouse. "This is your chance to be on the right side of history! You think even your own party will regret giving women the vote in a year or two?"

"If the voting booths start stinking of essence of bergamot and lavender, I won't have a year or two."

"I think you're wrong. Half the city's population are women. You don't think that even those silent white ladies whose husbands vote National party don't secretly desire to join them? They may not be chaining themselves to the Parliament railings, as some of our more ardent sisters have done, but don't assume they don't yearn to show their political might."

Willinghouse was warming to his theme, drifting into what Dahria called his Rising Backbencher voice: a fuller, more modulated, more public sound than was strictly necessary for a private conversation.

"Yet when they get the right to enter those voting booths," said Tavestock sharply, "those *secret* voting booths, whom do you think they'll be voting for? My colleagues, the people their husbands stand behind? Or will their soft and gentle women's hearts lean more to emotional arguments about the poor and underrepresented made by your good self? And since you mention white women, let me add that I notice you aren't limiting the suffrage issue to them. You want black and colored women voting too! Yes, Willinghouse, I see your strategy. You think that if women get the vote they'll follow not the Nationals but the Brevard party in precisely the same way that you know that if we legalize blacks running for Parliament, they will stand for your party, not mine, and energize their people. You make it sound like your campaign is selfless and altruistic, but it's not, and we both know it. Black MPs and women voters will secure a Brevard party landslide, and you insult me not to admit the fact." He turned his head quickly, his face full of passion, to stare at me. "Could I have my tea, please? I feel like I've been waiting a half hour."

I flushed, having been caught staring. I wanted to say something about not wishing to interrupt, but I knew my place was to hide my face in shame and mutter an apology. And, of course, to pour his bloody tea.

I did so and might have fled the room thereafter, my cheeks burning, but the seated black man spoke, and I found that I could not move. His voice was gentle, unassuming, and unpretentious, his Feldish crisp and minimally accented, but it was the calm, amused deliberation of it that was so arresting. It spoke not just of intelligence, but of thoughtfulness. And power. Not the hectoring power of a speaker like Norton Richter, a bully on a platform, but the power of ocean waves that do not need to roar and crash to gradually erode the cliff side.

"Let me say, Prime Minister," he said, "that you persist in seeing the matter as one over which you have a choice. But this is not the case. Not in the long run. Justice will come to Bar-Selehm. Perhaps not this year or next, but it will come. The black people of this land will govern themselves. Women will make their own decisions, and if you do not give them the vote, they will take it."

Tavestock gave him a disbelieving look.

"A women's revolution? I think you will wait a long time before you see that," he said, shooting Willinghouse a grin.

"Perhaps so," said the black man. "But it will come. And when it does, the women and the blacks and the Lani such as your young servant here, and everyone else your government has oppressed, ignored, stolen from, and told that they were not real people with all the rights bestowed upon white men, will stand shoulder to shoulder against you. The only question is whether the future that comes after that will have a place for you in it. Some of my black brethren would see you all burn, and with good reason. I offer you peace through the sharing of power and resources among all our people. You turn such an offer down at your considerable peril."

It was a remarkable speech. I had never heard anything quite like it before and stood openmouthed. Even Tavestock seemed caught off guard, and he sat there, blinking like a newborn in the sun. At last he shifted in his seat as if the room had suddenly become uncomfortably warm and said, "Then it seems there is much to discuss."

The black man's reference to "your young servant here" had acknowledged me. The speech had been given to everyone in the room, as if we all shared equal stakes, but now that it was done, I seemed to be merely loitering. Willinghouse fixed me with a pointed stare and, reluctantly, I left the room.

How utterly maddening.

I went back first to the kitchen, then to my room, changed,

paced, and went to see Dahria. She had dressed for company, but I suspected she had wasted her time and told her so.

"There'll be no sipping sherry while you play old Belrandian melodies on the pianoforte," I said, slumping onto her bed. "Strictly a business meeting, and a secret one. The political landscape of the city is being reshaped down there, so naturally, our input is not desired."

"Thank goodness for that," said Dahria. "I can't imagine anything more tedious."

"Liar," I said.

"Oh yes," she replied, scrutinizing her face in the wall mirror. "I forgot how much better you know my mind than I do myself."

"I'm just more honest about your feelings than you are."

She gave me a quick look, sucking in her breath, as if I had said something thrilling, but her eyes narrowed cautiously as they fastened on me.

"What rot you talk," she replied languidly. "My dear steeplejack, you can't assume everyone cares about the things you do."

"I don't," I replied, feeling something of her excitement in the sudden flutter of my heart. "I'm not talking about everyone. I'm talking about you."

"Then let me rephrase the remark," she replied, eyes returning critically to her reflection. "You cannot make people care about the things you do simply because you think they should."

Whatever strangeness had just passed between us—the momentary hesitancy, the probing for confidences—it had gone. Though I did not understand why, I found myself very slightly hurt, and when I spoke, there was an edge to my words.

"One day you will find that pretending not to care because the people around you don't still doesn't make you one of them. It just makes you not really yourself."

She frowned. "When I have deciphered what that is supposed to mean, I will deliver a crushing riposte," she said.

"No doubt," I said, rising impatiently and going to the window. An eagle was circling the trees that lined the drive, and the vervets were shrieking their alarms again, scampering into the most tangled branches, where they knew the bird would not follow. "There are two black men in the meeting," I said, unable to contain my curiosity. "One of them speaks like . . . I don't know. A leader. A politician."

Dahria made a face and shook her head.

"Not whatshisname, the leader of the unassimilated tribes?"

"No. This man is quite different. Very much an urban black."

"Some rabble-rousing youngblood, no doubt," she said. "Morgessa is alive with them."

I shook my head again. I had heard the corner preachers and union leaders. This man was something different. I could feel it. But he was clearly not part of Dahria's world, so I changed tack. "Seriously, though," I said, turning back to her, "would you not vote if you had the option?"

"Cast my lot with thousands of others over some petty rules of law and policy whose effects I will probably never see? Stand in line in the streets with all manner of people like a street girl selling star fruit from a barrow?"

"You would," I said.

"I absolutely would not!"

"You would, and you'd be mad not to."

"My dear steeplejack, you think like all people of your social rank: that politics matters, that it shapes your life and the lives of everyone around you."

"It does."

"It may shape your life, but it does not shape mine. You have— forgive my bluntness—nothing, and so you depend on law and policy to make life fair and just. I don't need those things. I have money."

"All the more reason to use what power you have to aid those who don't!"

"I have no power, as you are fond of pointing out, and I don't want it. I wish, above all things, to be left alone. Not by *you*," she added hastily at the look on my face. The hurt had come back, if only for a second, but her remark dispelled it. "By the government! By tedious men who like the sounds of their own voices and wish to build their own pompous little empires with words and bills and elections."

"You confuse the process with the effect," I said. "You don't have to like politics to see that it does indeed shape your world—even if you do have money—and that of other people even more."

"Perhaps," she said. "But it is so very tiresome. See how even this short conversation has wearied me? I think I need a lie down."

"You are an insufferable old fraud," I said.

"Outrage!" she said, snatching up a decorative pillow and tossing it at me. "Insurrection by the masses!"

"It's not funny," I said.

She considered me for a moment.

"No," she said, looking at me with unusual tenderness. "I suppose it isn't. And if I thought my voting or otherwise showing interest in my brother's world would make a difference, then maybe, maybe I—"

A door banged shut downstairs. She broke off, startled out of whatever she had been about to say, and joined me at the window, where we watched Benjamin Tavestock and his two escorts as they marched down the steps toward their carriage.

"I assume," she remarked, "that we are witnessing what the politicians call an impasse."

CHAPTER
3

"**WHAT IN THE NAME** of all that's holy were you doing playing parlor maid?" demanded Willinghouse.

"You know perfectly well what I was doing," I answered. "I wanted to know what was going on."

"So you risked exposing yourself to my political enemies."

"Josiah!" exclaimed Dahria with faux outrage. "Such language! If you talk further about ladies exposing themselves, I shall have to leave the room for the sake of propriety."

"I didn't mean—" Willinghouse sputtered. "You know perfectly well—"

"No one pays attention to servants," I said. "Especially Lani servants. Everyone knows that. Your secrets are safe."

"These are delicate times," said Willinghouse, still fulminating, despite Dahria's amusement. "The slightest of matters might trigger the sort of calamity that could engulf the city."

"Did you make any headway?"

"What?" he said, derailed.

"With Tavestock," I clarified. "Will you be making some kind of alliance—"

"Don't even breathe the possibility!" said Willinghouse. "It really would have been better if you had not heard any of it, and if you go telling your little reporter friend—"

"I wouldn't do that, and you know it!" I shot back.

"You've done it before," said Willinghouse.

Dahria gave me a look. "He's not wrong about that," she said, clearly enjoying herself.

I had given Sureyna, my friend at the *Standard,* the occasional scoop.

"That was quite different," I said, flustered and covering. "I only did it when I felt she had earned the story. And you don't need to lecture me on importance and secrecy and delicacy. I may not be able to vote—for the moment—but I am not an idiot."

Dahria grinned and turned expectantly back to her brother, like she was watching a tennis match. Willinghouse scowled, particularly at that "for the moment" and then muttered his grudging agreement and a halfhearted apology.

"I don't believe you answered her question," Dahria prompted. "Did your little meeting achieve anything?"

Willinghouse blew out a long sigh.

"That remains to be seen," he said. "The conversation is far from over, but it is at least continuing, and that, I suppose, is something."

"Ah yes," she replied, rolling her eyes, "what politicians like best: more talk."

"If it leads to changes in electoral law—" Willinghouse began.

"You really think it might?" I cut in. "Women voters and black MPs?"

Such things seemed impossibly far off, particularly with Richter pulling the Nationals farther to the right.

"Not now," said Willinghouse. "Maybe not even soon. But eventually, if the city as we know it is to survive. It is, I think, the only way forward."

"Black MPs won't change anything unless there's also a change in voting districts," I said. It was well known that the constituencies with the largest black populations—Willinghouse's among them—were massively underrepresented.

"That will come too," he replied.

"When it does," said Dahria, "white rule in the district, including your benevolent leadership, dear brother, will end. Maybe not at once, but eventually, and everything you know will change, not all of it for the general good and certainly not for ours. You know that, don't you?"

For a second we both looked at her. The studied ennui and practiced wry amusement had fallen away, and she looked serious, thoughtful.

"I know," said Willinghouse. "But as I said to the prime minister: better to be on the right side of history."

Dahria eyed him thoughtfully but said nothing, so that I wondered, with a curiosity the intensity of which caught me quite unawares, what she was thinking.

I CONTINUED TO TRAIN with Madame Nahreem, though I had no specific task to perform for Willinghouse, occasionally working with the neutral mask but generally focusing on the Kathahry exercises, which combined strength and balance. Often she would do them in silence beside me, and there were surprisingly few she could no longer manage, despite her age. She was no more nurturing than before, but she was less critical and seemed to move from pose to pose with an abstracted numbness as if she was only half present, and when she was not exercising herself, it felt like her attention was elsewhere.

"I miss Namud," I said after one session.

She gave me a startled look, and her vague expression became carefully blank.

"Indeed," she said.

"I mean, I didn't know him as well as you, of course. I can only imagine what you . . . How much you must miss—"

"Do not presume to discuss my feelings with me," she said, indignant.

"I just meant that—"

"I have no interest in what you meant." Her face became granite hard. "If I want your advice or your sympathy on personal matters, *private* matters, I will request it directly. If, however, I do not, I would appreciate it if—"

"Yes," I said quickly. "I understand."

"Very well. Now, let me see you move from weancat to pine tree again. Your posture was sloppy, and the movement graceless."

I took a breath, swallowed back my retort, and moved carefully into the weancat pose.

"YOUR LITTLE SCRIBBLING FRIEND has been at it again," said Dahria, pushing a newspaper to me across the dining table that evening.

I looked up from my plate of chicken anduul—a hot, dry spiced curry with cardamom and lentils—and read the title in the bottom right corner of the second page.

GRAPPOLI PUSH ENDS

The story was, surprisingly, by Sureyna. I knew she had earned the respect of the *Standard*'s editorial staff, but it was unusual for her to be covering international news, and I read eagerly. It turned out, however, not to be an international news story at all, or at least, not the kind that came from foreign correspondents or war reporters.

Sources close to the Grappoli ambassador suggest that the recent Grappoli push across northern Feldesland has come to a complete halt. Troops have withdrawn and no further movement seems evident. Reports suggest that the Unassimilated Tribes have proved increasingly resistant, making incursions into Grappoli territory and assaulting travelers south of the desert. There have even been reports of Mahweni placing blockages on railway lines, attacking those sent to remove them, and generally disrupting traffic bound for Bar-Selehm.

I looked up, baffled. South of the desert meant close to the city. If the Unassimilated Tribes north of Bar-Selehm were attacking traffic so close, we were moving into a new chapter of local unrest.

"Can this be right?" I said.

"If the paper thought it was," said Dahria, shaking her head, "it would be screaming at us in three-inch capitals from the front page."

"Why don't they believe it?"

"The key is in that *sources close to the ambassador* stuff," said Dahria. "I think your friend has been talking to servants. Or to the ambassador's lady friend, Lady Alice Welborne."

"I don't think they are together anymore," I said.

"Exactly," said Dahria. "Lady Alice, never the keenest intellect in the city, is trying to attract attention to herself with rumor in the hope that she can whip up a reputation as a delightfully knowing socialite before the cream of Bar-Selehm abandon her to the fate she so richly deserves."

"Which is what?"

"What ladies such as Lady Alice dread most: being ignored."

"I'm surprised Sureyna would give her the spotlight," I said, considering the article. "She's not interested in being a gossip columnist."

"You think," said Dahria. "There's money in it, not to mention fashionable parties, concerts, the kind of exclusive clubs that wouldn't normally allow someone like her to darken the door—no pun intended."

My frown deepened, but I shook my head.

"No," I said. "Sureyna isn't interested in those things."

"Well, why should she be?" said Dahria with feigned agreeableness. "Why would a young black girl want wealth and power? Obviously nonsense."

"She wouldn't," I said.

"Everyone you know is so altruistic, have you noticed? Pillars of virtue. Except me, of course. Unless the saints and angels with which you surround yourself are actually more human than you realize, and would be quite happy to line their own pockets even if they let slip some of your high ethical standards in the process."

"You're wrong," I said, hoping it was true.

"Frequently," Dahria agreed. "Which is why I have no qualms thinking that my blessed brother will push only for unpopular but virtuous things like votes for women and black MPs against his own self-interest when he knows he can't possibly win."

"What do you mean?"

"Nothing," she said sweetly. "But I wonder just how hard he would fight for such things if victory were indeed in his grasp. So impressive, don't you think, to be the lone voice for selflessness and truth. It almost doesn't matter that he'll never actually win, will never have to deal with the consequences of victory."

"You think he doesn't really want women to have the vote or for the Mahweni to have more control of the country?"

"I think there's power of a sort in being seen to be the person who wants those things, even if you never get them, and when getting them might lead you to being less powerful, well . . ."

She let the sentence trail off and went back to her food, humming absently to herself and not looking at me.

I STRUGGLED TO FALL asleep that night, even though I did an extra exercise session and added a run before sundown so that my body was close to exhaustion by the time I got into bed. Usually, the run clears my head, but Dahria's cynical words circled in my mind, making my anger and anxiety leap like tongues of fire. I was used to the idea that the Grappoli were the enemy and that Richter and his Heritage party were at least as bad, but as I had shed some of the isolation I had felt as a worker in the Seventh Street gang, I had come to new ideas about friends and family and being on the side of right. Willinghouse, and his grandmother, Inspector Andrews, Captain Emtezu, Sureyna, some of the ladies of Merita, and my sisters, Rahvey and—in ways I could not properly explain—Vestris, stood with me on that side. Even Dahria had played her part for what I felt sure was right. The idea that their intentions were not what I assumed—hoped for, needed—bothered me, and I lay awake in the dark, listening to the sounds of the bush not so very far from the walls of the estate with increasing unease. When I woke, tired and irritable, the go-away birds crying their melancholy dawn chorus, I knew I had to get out of this place and back to where life made more sense, in the smog and hubbub of the city.

WHAT I HAD PLANNED as a retreat from the complexities of life with the Willinghouses proved hard to shake, however, and my announcement was greeted with declarations from both my employer and his sister that they also had to go into town, so we would

all travel together. I sat in the hot coach, dressed in the fusty waiting maid's dress and bonnet for propriety's sake, sulking in silence,
while Willinghouse pored over papers from his valise and Dahria
fanned herself. The long ride into town from the estate was always
stressful, since the area was home to elephants and one-horns, both
of which would reduce the carriage to kindling in a heartbeat, but
today I was doubly anxious to get out and slip away down the brick
alleys of Bar-Selehm and the streets I called home.

I was, I had realized that morning, angry with Dahria, who had
made me doubt her brother's motives and—therefore—the value
of my work for him. I had always been able to endure the unfamil-
iarities and irritations of my job because I had believed in its essential
rightness. The possibility that I was merely a pawn in Willinghouse's
political long game meant that such things would have to be re-
considered. While I didn't believe it, not yet, Dahria had created
the flicker of an anxiety I had not felt in months.

Perhaps I was not being rational, but she had spoiled it, my sense
of purpose, my life.

I hated her a little for it, and for the studied indifference with
which she had raised it, as if it were another mildly amusing curiosity, something about which she could be cynical and witty.

As ever. She was being glib about things for which she felt nothing.

I had gotten used to thinking that her distant posturing was
some aristocratic self-protection, that at heart she was someone
quite different, someone passionate and principled. Someone more
like me. That she might not be was more than a disappointment.
It pained me unreasonably, reminding me in some dull, unspecific
way of my sister Vestris.

In the stuffy dimness of the carriage, I could not meet Dahria's
eyes, thought they flicked toward me several times, watchful and,
as usual, amused.

We entered the city through Deans Gate where a pair of sentries waved us through without even looking in. As soon as we hit the cat-head cobbles of Fullerton Lane, I opened the door beside me and dropped to the street. Willinghouse looked up, startled, from his reading, but I didn't pause, walking briskly away.

I had, I reminded myself, no assignment, no mission, no mystery to unravel. I was, for the moment, free. What I would do with that freedom remained to be seen, but my plan was to visit my true friends: first Tanish, then Sureyna, then Captain and Mrs. Emtezu, and then—continuing my journey west, to the Drowning and my sister Rahvey.

My friends. The people most like me: not all exactly poor, but certainly not the landed gentry. My people. People I could trust.

But as I walked the streets of the Soot, where chimneys towered, belching their thick, caustic smoke into the Bar-Selehm sky, and I heard the ringing of hammers, the hiss, whir, and clang of steam-driven machinery, it all felt at once familiar and strangely distancing. All around were people working, because at this time of day that was what you did. That was what I had done once. But not now. A curious sensation fell upon me, and it was as if I had gone to the zoological gardens to see the animals, but here—instead of the iron bars of cages and enclosures—I was peering in through filthy windows and half-open doorways, spying into a life I no longer lived. Before I realized I had made the decision, my feet were taking me east, along Winckley Street and past the public library, where someone had pasted up a series of handbills for a traveling circus.

I paid them and my surroundings no mind. I had to return to see Willinghouse. Dahria had planted a question in my mind. I needed to ask it.

So I walked beside the embankment of the Flintwick railway station to the opera house and the Winelands Arcade, all the way to Hanover Street and Grand Parade. The Parliament House loomed over the streets with their lampposts and ornamental trees, a great, brooding domed building of elaborately latticed pink stone, which glowed like fire in the sunlight. There was scaffolding on the northwest corner where it looked like work was being done on some of the stone cornice and trim, but I didn't recognize the russet-painted wagon, and there was no one on the scaffold. I wasn't sure if Parliament was in session, or whether Willinghouse would be in his backbencher's office on the second floor, but that didn't matter. Whatever his schedule, he would make time for me. I would give him no alternative.

As I walked, I formulated the question in my head, trying to find words I would actually be able to speak.

Do you really want the things you stand for, or are they just banners to wave while you storm the government? Who do you really represent— your constituents or yourself? Are you chasing justice, or do you just want to be prime minister?

The very phrasing made me angrier, and my pace increased. I knew that my cheeks were hot and—bafflingly, maddeningly— I felt my eyes brimming with furious, unshed tears, but I kept walking.

I arrived to find the public doors closed and guarded. The House was in private session, and I would have to wait till they adjourned to ask my questions, if that was what they were. The more I turned them over in my head, the more they sounded less like questions and more like accusations. I lowered my bonneted head, not wishing to attract hostile looks from the various soldiers and police who were on duty, and made for the Brevard party offices. I couldn't get up to the MPs' chambers without an appointment, so I sat on a hard wooden bench in the lobby, head down, watching the comings and goings for signs that the politicians were back and scattering for lunches and meetings in the surrounding buildings.

It didn't take long for them to arrive. In their monochrome suits and close-fitting trousers, they looked like lapwings squabbling along a riverbank, and the lobby was soon full of their chatter. There was, however, no sign of Willinghouse.

I waited, but as the crowd thinned and Willinghouse still did not appear, I went back outside, meaning to return to the main entrance in case he was there. I did not want to miss him, but then, now that I was here I found that I did not want to ask my questions either. Or rather, I feared what he might say in response. If he so much as faltered, if I smelled his guilt as I might once have probed the mortar line of a chimney for damp, I would leave and never speak to him again. I would go back to being a steeplejack, a cleaner, a doer of odd jobs . . .

Better that than . . . what? A tool for Willinghouse's advancement? Something like that.

It was no wonder my heart was thumping like the pistons of the Thremsburg Flyer.

I had to fight the remains of the crowd on the steps of the Parliament building, and when I dithered in the flow, a guard called to me.

"No point going in now," he said. "Everything's finished."

"I know," I said. "I'm just . . . I have to see something."

"Suit yourself." He shrugged, half blocking the tide so that I could slip through and into the main entrance hall.

A few MPs were talking to each other or meeting with men I took to be lobbyists or delegates, but they were drifting out, and the great double doors to the main debating chamber had been closed. There was still no sign of Willinghouse, so I took a hard left and, at the end of a hallway, found a flight of stairs up to a long corridor floored with polished wood with marquetry trim. A pair of dragoons in ceremonial blues eyed me, their rifles at their sides, but they did not prevent me from moving to the little door that led up a narrower staircase to the public galleries.

I had been here only once before, but I found my way without difficulty, though it felt different this time, silent and abandoned, the chambers having a cathedral stillness and grandeur about them that made me feel small, and the hot little questions in my mouth seemed foolish and impertinent. I climbed the narrow stairs and opened the door at the top.

For a moment I thought everyone had left, the great domed debating hall below me seemed so big and empty. But then, apparently startled by my movement, Willinghouse looked up at me, his face pale and eyes wide. He was stooping over something, leaning his weight on the end of one of the silver-trimmed seats. He spoke, but I could not tell what he said, and when he moved, straightening up, I could see that there was another man lying faceup on the floor.

The man's starched shirt was soaked with crimson, his neck horribly gashed. As Willinghouse started shouting for help, even as the guards burst in through the lower doors in the House itself, I saw the knife in his hand and realized that the dead man at his feet was Benjamin Tavestock, the prime minister.

CHAPTER

4

A WHISTLE RANG OUT, long and shrill. It filled the air with a keening panic like the cry of the vervets when the eagle dropped on them. Doors banged, voices were raised in anger and alarm, and booted feet drummed on the hallowed floor of the chamber. The noise filled the great hall and echoed in the dome overhead like the tolling of a dreadful bell.

Up in the coloreds side of the public gallery, I dropped to my knees and hid. Not too long ago I had been reveling in my connection to the friends and family who were outside of Willinghouse's lofty sphere, celebrating my own lowliness. In this moment, with the political leader of the region bleeding to death only yards away and every policeman in the city rushing to this very spot, I could think of nothing worse to be.

You have to get out.

That, at least, was certain. I flattened myself up to the waist-high screen that ran along the front of the gallery and raised my head slowly and carefully till I could see down. It was a chaos of uniforms below—police and soldiers—shouting orders, running about, clearing a path for the doctor with his bag, who was hurrying in from the back even as they made a preliminary search of the chamber.

"Lock those doors behind him," shouted an officer in dress uniform, once the doctor was in. "Alert Black Rod, the Yeoman Usher, and the War Office. Summon the Fourth Harbor Rifles and the Second King's Own Light Cavalry. Secure the building with guards on every door. Lock down everything from Occupation Row to Cannonade. Now!"

As he bellowed that last word at the dithering soldiers, I scuttled back toward the door through which I had come, certain that I did not want to be found skulking up here, but I was only half through it when I heard the officer speak again, quieter but with no less cast-iron authority.

"Mr. Willinghouse, put the knife down very carefully or my men will open fire."

I froze.

For a second I could think of nothing and began to turn back, as if I could call down and explain. The horror of seeing that Mr. Tavestock was dead—or very close to it—had filled me with old fears for my own safety. That they would hold Willinghouse responsible had not occurred to me.

How inconceivably stupid of me. Of course they would treat him as the culprit. They had caught him red-handed. Literally. And there was no one else in the building.

Except me.

Get out! Get out!

In the sudden stillness below, I heard the faintest clink of metal followed by the officer's commanding voice.

"Stay on your knees please, sir. Hands on your head."

They were arresting him. He would be shackled and marched through the crowd of soldiers and police, his colleagues, his political friends and enemies, the gawkers straining to see, the reporters shouting questions . . .

I felt it all as if I could see it, and it pulled on me like a great chain coiled around my midsection and dragging after me, but I walked, quickly, lightly, almost doubled over, out through the door and along the sweeping hallway that circled the great hall.

They would be coming, the soldiers, swords and rifles at the ready. The city had just been plunged into the greatest crisis in decades. They would not hesitate to cut down anyone who did not comply with their orders.

I began to run, wishing I were wearing my own familiar boots, not the dainty shoes that came with dressing as Dahria's maid.

Dahria.

The thought brought me up short, and I almost stumbled, stricken by pained sympathy. How long would it take her to find out? What exactly would she be told? That her brother had found the prime minister's body? Or that her brother was a killer, a political assassin of the most insidious kind?

I regained my pace, conscious that my labored breathing and racing heart could not be explained solely by my exertion, and tried to force some order to my thoughts. If I went back the way I had come in, I would be stopped at the door and arrested. I had done nothing. They could prove nothing against me.

But. But. But.

I was a Lani woman in the halls of the mighty, a former steeplejack who now had money for reasons no one could explain. I may well have been seen with Willinghouse, with his sister; perhaps my picture would appear in the paper and someone would note my resemblance to a mysterious Istilian princess who had fled an exclusive club on the night of a society murder . . .

I could not be caught.

I kept walking, pausing only at a broad window on my left to look out and down to Occupation Row. People were running about. Even from here, three floors above, you could almost smell their terror, their excitement. If I climbed out of that window and inched round to a drainpipe or recess where I might slip down to the street, would anyone notice?

I hesitated, chewing my lip, torn between haste and caution. It was noon, and the sun was bright and high. There were no deep pockets of shadow on this side of the building, and even as I stood there in my agony of indecision, the police presence below seemed to swell like a river in flood. It was too desperate a hope to think I might escape that way unseen.

So I walked farther, listening for the inevitable dragoons as they searched and set guards on every part of the structure, and as I rounded the corner, I saw a door. It was small and insignificant looking, its varnish worn and cracked, and looked like it might be a caretaker's closet. It was also on my right, which meant it led back into the building, not out.

No use there.

I had almost passed it when I heard the brisk boots of the guards coming. I reached back and tried the handle.

Locked.

Of course. I looked toward the turn in the corridor, which the soldiers would soon round, but there was nowhere to hide. No swag of curtain, no conveniently bulky table, nothing but open hallway and imminent arrest. Or worse.

Fortunately, my hands were quicker than my mind. In the time it had taken to assess my lack of options, I had unclasped the ridiculous little purse that went with my servant's dress and slid out Namud's lockpicks and skeleton keys.

I had been practicing with them in the long, hot summer hours at the Willinghouse estate, so the choice of which to use was made by my eyes and my fingers, not my brain.

I slid a key into the lock, my face turned toward the sound of the soldiers, guiding it deftly by feel, holding the rod in the space between the tumblers and pressing very slightly, searchingly. I felt it, made an adjustment to the depth of the skeleton key, and turned.

The lock thunked softly and I shouldered the door open, closing it behind me again before I even looked where I was. There was a sneck on the inside of the door, and I latched it, letting go just as the feet reached the door and the handle turned.

I stepped back. The room—if that was what it was—was almost completely dark, the only light bleeding in from the threshold and lintel of the ill-fitting door. I kept very still, hands clasped and pressed to my lips.

"You got a key?" snapped one of the guards on the other side and only inches away.

"Me?" said another voice. "What am I, the janitor? No, I ain't got no damn key."

An irritated sigh.

"Stay here," said the first voice. "I'll go find one."

"Be quick. I'm not interested in tackling an assassin by meself."

"You won't 'ave to, mate. They've already got 'im."

"That Brevard MP? You reckon?"

"Figured he were movin' up in the world, weren't 'e?" said the first voice. "Stands to reason."

"Nah," said the other. "Kill the PM and 'ope he'll get the job when 'is party's not even in power? Don't make sense."

"Yeah? Tell you what, smart man, if we find anyone else 'ere, anyone other than Willing'ouse, I mean, drinks are on me tonight."

"All right. But be quick about it."

One set of footsteps marched back the way they had come, but the sentry on the door snorted and stayed on guard.

I was trapped.

My eyes were still adjusting to the dark, so I couldn't risk doing anything that would make a sound. Very slowly, I revolved in place, taking in my surroundings even as I listened to the thoughtless noises of the guard outside.

There were dusty shelves, boxes of tools, and discarded parts: an old handrail, a set of battered candelabra, a mildewed pile of upholstery fabric, and some cobwebby chairs. A long tea chest with leather handles sat on the floor beside me, and I briefly considered opening it up and climbing in, though I'd have to unstack the dusty books that sat on top of it first. I would fit. Just. But if the guards were even semiserious about their search, they would find me in a second.

I need a better option than that.

The room was deeper than I had expected, and though it was now little more than a junk room, it had once been more like rest space for a duty custodian. Eight feet from the door, beyond a stack of musty-looking books, was a tiled hearth and a tight little fireplace.

The room had been forgotten, rather than closed off, so it was at least possible that the chimney would still be open. I took a steadying breath and assessed my route to the fireplace. I would have to step over the books, but otherwise I could get there without making any noise, assuming the floor was sound. How silently I could get up the chimney, I had no idea.

The skirt and bonnet would have to go. I was wearing some of Madame Nahreem's gray silk exercise clothes beneath in place of underwear, and I could adjust my chemise enough that I wouldn't get arrested for indecency, should I reach the street . . .

I shook my head and began to unlace the infernal corset with one hand as I picked my way across the floor, ears open for the sound of the guard returning with a key. How long would that take? Maybe the confusion downstairs would buy me a few minutes, but maybe it wouldn't.

My crinoline was nothing like as large or elaborate as Dahria's, and it was easier to get out of than it was to get into. I stepped out of the cane loops gingerly, removed the petticoat, exposing my silk trousers, and navigated the stack of books, just as the guard outside the door blew his nose so loudly that I jumped. The books wobbled, but I stayed them with a swift hand, then climbed over and squatted on the dusty hearth, reaching up and in for the flue.

I figured that I was on the top floor of the building with only the dome over the main chamber reaching higher, so I shouldn't have far to climb to reach the roof. If I could get there and orient myself quickly, there was scaffolding on the northwest corner that I could use to get down. Turning my back to the fireplace, I sat on my heels and leaned back, ducking under the mantel and staring up into the blackness. A foot above my head was the iron damper, which was, unexpectedly, already open. I pushed my head through, kicking myself for not stowing my cast-off hat and skirt in the tea chest.

Too late now.

There was daylight a mere fifteen feet above me. My body leapt for it, seizing on the sheer physical fact of climbing as the only thing that had made any sense these last few hours. I found the rough handholds in the crudely mortared brick and pulled myself up in one strong surge from my arms. My half disguise felt clumsy in the tight square of the chimney, the sleeves snagging on the coarse, close walls, and I kicked an exploratory shoe, hunting for a foot hole.

It was a rash and thoughtless act, and when my foot found something solid and pressed on it, I realized too late that it was the damper above the fireplace. It slid with slow inevitability and rang out like a bell. The rattling of the door handle came seconds later, followed by the shouts of the men in the hall just as I reached the last yard of the stack.

Spitting cobwebs and bits of abandoned bird nests, I surged up into the air, clawing my way up the sooty brick as if trying to fly vertically into the blue Bar-Selehm sky. As I hauled myself out, I heard the crash of the door splintering in the room below, and rolled quickly away in case someone stuck their rifle up there and opened fire.

I was nestled between the angular brick of the roof and the slow curve of the great dome. I had to move fast if I was to find a way down before the guard breaking into the custodian's storeroom raised the alarm outside. I looked quickly around and saw, on the gray lead trim that ran around the base of the dome, a small clear footprint.

A bare foot, perfectly defined in fine white powder.

I turned to scan the dome, my eyes climbing the great half sphere to the gold finial and statue on the top, but I was too close to see either. I could see another footprint, however, not as complete as the other, but unmistakable.

I gazed up. There would be a maintenance hatch in the top of the dome, one that—it seemed—someone had used very recently. Someone small.

I stared at it wonderingly.

The footprint would have matched my own.

CHAPTER
5

SPRINTING BETWEEN CHIMNEYS AND the steeply canted roofs that surrounded the dome, I found the corner where the restoration work was being done. There was no one there, but the scaffold was still in place, and the masons had rigged a refuse chute out of sackcloth and large buckets with their bottoms removed. I barely even glanced down before I climbed in feet first. I was steeling myself for the descent when I heard a roof access door boom somewhere close by. I tucked my arms, pressed my legs together, and dropped.

It was almost a straight fall, and I accelerated fast. I nudged outward with my elbows until I got a little purchase on the coarse fabric of the chute, jolting them painfully as I went through another bucket join, but slowed myself just enough that the final fall into the back of the open wagon didn't break my ankles.

Still, I landed hard on chunks of fractured masonry and chipped bricks, tearing clothes and skin, and emerging slowly, covered in soot and brick dust. A white kid in the street sucking vacantly on a piece of peeled yellow fruit became a statue of terrified astonishment when his eyes found me, but then I was out and running clumsily, trying to shake off the pain in my legs and arms.

The crowds had moved toward the front of the building, leaving this corner about as quiet as I could hope for. I kept my head down and didn't stop running till I had made a series of sharp cuts to the left and right, which took me into the service alleys running between the grand homes in the northeast corner of the city. I hid for a while in a coal house behind a fancy restaurant, assessing my injuries and getting my breath back, then cleaned off the worst of the filth at a standpipe used for filling animal troughs. I looked absurd, half dressed in mismatched clothes, and those who saw me—turning sourly away as they did so—took me for a homeless person who had cobbled her wardrobe from other people's garbage. If I was very unlucky, I'd walk into a policeman who might charge me with begging or loitering or soliciting—the usual crimes thrown at young Lani women found in places they weren't supposed to be—but it seemed they had all been diverted to Grand Parade. I headed west, making my way to the back of Willinghouse's town home, which I entered by scaling the garden wall and using a combination of downspout and tarashla tree to reach the sash window of the back bedroom kept for guests.

I got in, I think unseen, shrugged out of my dirty clothes, and lay for a long moment on the counterpaned bed, feeling my heart slow and my mind race. Willinghouse had been arrested. It seemed impossible, but there was no doubt. He was going to be charged with murdering the prime minister, a charge so absurd I suddenly found myself ashamed that I had been poised to demand to know the purity of his political motives. Of course he would sacrifice his place in government for the people he represented. Of course he would share power with the Mahweni even if that meant losing some of it himself. And of course he would not kill the prime minister, a man with whom he had hoped to forge an alliance.

Anyone could see that.

But the words of the soldiers patrolling the halls inside the Parliament House rang in my ears.

Figured he were movin' up in the world, weren't 'e? Stands to reason.

Surely no one would believe that?

I had to speak to him. To Andrews. To someone. Dahria was in town, so she would eventually come to the house, but she would surely go to the police station as soon as she heard, and may not get back here till late. I had to find her. I had to start making sense of what was going on before it all slipped away. Again I felt a pang of guilt that I had doubted my employer.

Well, I would make it up to him now.

I left the room and went down to the kitchen, where I startled the elderly white butler, Higgins.

"I'm sorry, miss," he said. "I didn't know you were here." His eyes flashed over my bizarre mismatched clothes, but he was too much the dignified professional to acknowledge my state.

"I need some clothes," I said.

"Certainly, miss. I'll speak to the housemaid. Evening wear or—"

"Lady's maid," I said.

"Very good, miss," he answered, unblinking. "Perhaps you would like to avail yourself of the facilities while I summon the necessary garments?"

"Thank you, Higgins," I said.

He escorted me to the "facilities," collecting a decorative box of guest toiletries on the way. In twenty minutes, I was thoroughly washed and dressed to face the world as a Lani servant once more, complete with an ugly and cumbersome bonnet into which I piled my hair. I wore it as low as I could and kept my head down. I didn't know what I was going to do, but I couldn't risk being recognized by the parliamentary guards.

The butler showed me to the front door after giving my attire an approving nod.

"Higgins," I said on impulse, "by day's end, you will hear some distressing news about your master. Do not believe it."

The butler stiffened, then nodded fractionally.

"Very good, miss," he said, his face leaden. "I have no doubt that you will do your utmost to resolve matters."

We had never discussed my various duties, and I did not know how much he was aware of what I did for Willinghouse, though he had observed my odd comings and goings in various guises for months. I matched his stoic manner.

"You can count on it," I said.

It was wet outside. A sudden storm had rolled in, poured steadily for twenty minutes, and gone again, leaving the cobbles slick and steaming, the side roads muddy and puddled. Instead of retracing my steps along the back alleys behind the opera house, I took the main street to Hanover and south toward the Parliament buildings, but the way quickly became crowded with huddled bystanders as if every home, office, and emporium had disgorged its people onto the road as news of the calamity spread. I had seen widespread excitement and consternation in Bar-Selehm before, but never had the mood been so tinged with fearful alarm. It was thick in the city's thoroughfares like smog, caustic and nauseating. I could feel it creeping into my lungs with every breath, settling into my stomach, and churning it up like acid. Usually when dire events struck, the crowds' moods depended on their place in the city, but today the anxious looks, the hesitant whispered inquiries, seemed to come from society ladies, Mahweni laborers and factory workers, Lani street vendors, and men of every color and stripe. Whatever had happened, however awful, it had done what few things ever did in Bar-Selehm: it had united the city.

Against Willinghouse.

I heard his name hissed in fevered conversations on every street corner. The evening edition of the papers was an hour away, but the story was already out, and the guilty party charged in the court of public opinion. My churning stomach tightened still further.

I thought of the footprint I had seen on the roof of the dome. Someone else had been there, I was sure of it, though the sudden rain would have washed the print away.

Again my stomach roiled. The footprint might be the one thing in Willinghouse's favor, but it worried me nonetheless. If word of it reached the press, it wouldn't be long before it was connected to one of the region's favorite horror stories.

The Gargoyle.

I knew more about that particular nightmare figure than I would like. The creature had come to my rescue only a few weeks before, and it had had the ravaged face of my sister Vestris.

I pushed the thought down, gripping my little purse tight as I elbowed my way through the muttering crowd.

That was easier said than done. As the domes and towers of the Parliament House came into view, the throng thickened and the roads clogged. Carriages and flies were stuck in the congestion, their horses and orleks stamping and shaking their heads restlessly. Their drivers murmured and patted them, but if the roads weren't cleared soon, the tumult would be made more dangerous by stampeding animals.

The mood of mounting unease was also infecting the police, who were glancing at each other nervously, as they tried to contain the crowd, arms spread, their truncheons swinging from thongs around their wrists. For now. As tension rose, it felt like we were moments away from the officers wielding those batons more decisively. On the other side of the street, they were backed by pockets of dragoons with bayoneted rifles.

I wasn't going to get any closer to the Parliament House, but then maybe that wasn't where I should be going, anyway. The main police station was on Mount Street on the other side of Ruetta Park, but that was surely too far to be where they had taken Willinghouse. Given the military presence, perhaps they would have used the War Office, which was one of the city's original fortifications and still had its own garrison. If they had indeed stowed him there, I hoped there was no plan to move him to the police station, not with the mood in the streets as it was now.

The crowd's smoldering attention was on the Parliament build-ing itself. An expectant hush was spreading through them, as if they knew an announcement was coming, and some of those who were pushing to the front had notebooks clutched to their chests and pencils tucked behind their ears: reporters. Sureyna was prob-ably in the throng somewhere. I fought the tide back up Hanover toward the War Office, where a pair of decorative bronze one-horns stood on plinths above a pair of less decorative field guns. The guard on the perimeter had been doubled, and the sentries had shed their ceremonial air, looking ready for trouble. Two of them spotted me as I crossed the street, and as one swung his rifle round to half ready, the other raised a hand. It said, in no uncertain terms, *Stop*.

"The offices are closed," he shouted. "Clear the premises."

The noise of the crowd at my back was like the drag of the ocean, like the throb and scrape of machinery. I raised my voice opting, for once, for honesty. Of a sort.

"I'm attached to the Willinghouse family," I said. "I was sum-moned to see to my master's needs."

All right, not really honesty.

The soldier who had spoken hesitated and exchanged a word with his companion, which I couldn't hear.

"The prisoner has not been granted visitation privileges at this time," he said at last.

So he *was* there.

"I have documents requiring his signature," I improvised.

"You?" said the guard, his formal demeanor wrinkling with scornful amusement. "I think the Parliament secretaries can take care of any official correspondence."

"These are family matters," I said, pretending I hadn't noticed the change in his tone. "I am his private secretary."

"You a reporter?" said the rifleman, peering at me.

"A Lani reporter?" said his companion. "Come off it."

"Makes as much sense as some stray Lani bitch working as an MP's private secretary."

I bristled, glancing away while I swallowed down my fury, then said, "No, I am not a reporter. I am, however . . ."

I paused, words queuing up in my mouth, desperate to spill out and overwhelm them with my abused authority: words like *Inspector Andrews, Elitus* and *Merita, the Glorious Third Infantry Regiment,* and a host of other things I could not discuss publicly, no matter how wounded my pride. When I just stood there, the guard's half smirk blossomed.

"I reckoned as much," he said. "Be off with you, or I'll make you *my* private secretary and teach you some manners."

He leered, and his friend snorted with amusement, but their attention was suddenly taken by a police carriage drawn by four horses and escorted by a pair of blue-caped officers mounted on orleks. It had pushed its way through the crowded street, and as it came to a clattering halt, the doors kicked open. Inspector Andrews emerged, drawn and intense, and with him, between two other officers, was Dahria.

All her studied nonchalance and dispassionate amusement was gone. She looked exhausted, her eyes red-rimmed and her face ivory-blanched. Her gaze lighted on me, and her mouth opened as if she was going to cry out. We rushed toward each other, but at the last second, faltered, unsure of what to do. I wanted to throw my arms around her, but if she wanted the same, she seemed to check the impulse. For a moment we stood facing each other, the toes of our shoes only inches apart but our arms awkwardly, painfully by our sides. In the next instant, Andrews had strode over, his face dark and serious.

"Miss Sutonga," he said.

"I was trying to get in," I said, dragging my eyes from Dahria, "but—"

"Come with us, my dear," he said.

He flashed papers at the guards, who fell back warily, watching me with a suddenly hunted look that, in other circumstances, I might have enjoyed. As we walked silently across the forecourt beneath the great bronze rhinos, the one who had threatened to make me his private secretary came to a hasty decision and stepped forward.

"Miss, I'm sorry for my previous remarks," he babbled. "I wasn't aware that—"

I turned on him, drawing myself up, my face implacable.

"No. You are aware of nothing," I said.

His face clouded, unsure of whether I was offering him an olive branch or making a point, then he nodded earnestly and stepped back as I brushed past. I did not look back.

Instead, I hurried to catch up with Andrews and, just under my breath, said, "Someone was on the roof of the dome. I saw a footprint."

He gave me a quick look, and his pace stuttered.

"You were *there*?"

"I didn't see what happened. I arrived right after the . . . incident."

"And left via the roof?"

"Yes."

"Very well. I'll send a man up to look. In the meantime, Miss Sutonga, say nothing. You are Miss Dahria's maid, nothing more. Do I make myself clear?"

"Yes, sir," I said.

He looked embarrassed by my unusual deference, and smiled sadly.

"We will clear this business up—have no fear," he said.

I opened my mouth, then just nodded. Together we hurried to catch the others up, aware of the two sentries looking blankly after us.

PAPERS WERE SIGNED AND stamped. We stood in an imposing circular lobby and waited till more papers were presented and they, in turn, were signed, scrutinized, and stamped while policemen and soldiers kept a wary, watchful distance. Andrews did the talking for us, and neither I nor Dahria spoke, avoiding each other's eyes as if afraid of giving something away. At last we were escorted along a long, marble-flagged hallway and through a series of heavy doors, all guarded. Unlike the men outside in their crimson and brass, the soldiers here wore simpler uniforms of dull russet fabric with black belts and boots. They did not gleam like the ceremonial officers in their parade dress, but their rifles looked at least as functional, and their lack of grandeur gave them a purposeful air.

We passed a series of hallways with cells along one side, all faced with wrought-iron grilles and smelling faintly of metal and urine. There were few windows, and the place had a hard and uncompromising air to it that made me feel unaccountably guilty. Willinghouse was kept in a separate cell at the end of an otherwise deserted hallway made of whitewashed stone blocks. It too was faced with a floor-to-ceiling iron grille like the front of a cage, into which was set a door, though we were not permitted inside.

Willinghouse was sitting on a short wooden bench with his head in his hands, his jacket cast onto a barrack room cot with a single coarse blanket. He looked stunned. His dress shirt was speckled and smeared with darkening blood. Worst of all, he did not immediately respond when we arrived, looking up vaguely and glancing at us in turn before lowering his gaze to the stone floor once more.

"Keep your distance from the bars," said the duty officer, who was holding a pistol in his right hand as his left rested on the hilt of his saber. Behind us, two other soldiers stood, rifles unslung and held across their bodies, at the ready in case . . . I didn't know. In case we tried to break Willinghouse out by force, I suppose. There was nowhere for us to sit down, and we dithered, unsure of what to do or say. I felt like I had fallen into a nightmare and that the world as I knew it no longer had any relevance.

Willinghouse looked at us again, as if just remembering we were there, and his eyes lingered on me, then flicked to the guards with a hint of warning. He did not want our professional relationship to be revealed. I bit my lower lip. I would not be able to speak, and that meant that my friends would need to ask the right questions.

"What happened?" said Andrews.

Willinghouse looked miles away.

"Josiah," Andrews prompted, "what happened?"

Willinghouse sighed and shook his head.

"We had been talking," he said, his voice barely above a whisper, "Tavestock and I. Informally. Trying to reach agreement on . . . some matters. It doesn't matter."

"It might," said Andrews. "But what happened today?"

"We were in session this morning. He said he wanted to talk to me before question time this afternoon. Didn't want it to look secret, so he told me to meet him in the main chamber beforehand."

"What did he want to talk about?"

"He didn't say, but I thought that he was perhaps prepared to discuss some issues that he had previously said were off-limits."

"What issues?"

"I'd rather not say."

"Joss!" exclaimed Dahria.

"I can't, Dahria," said Willinghouse, looking at her, his green eyes blazing. "I'm sorry. If he recovers . . . It could . . . I don't want to damage his standing in his party by giving away confidences."

"I thought he wanted to talk publicly?" said Andrews.

"On his own terms, yes," Willinghouse answered. "But I don't know what he was going to say or whom he wanted to witness the conversation."

"What time did you go in?"

"When he rang. The morning session ended at eleven. Question time was scheduled to begin at half past twelve. I must have gone in around noon, maybe a few minutes after."

"Which was when he had asked to meet?"

"Yes."

"He rang?" said Andrews.

"There's a bell pull system. All the offices have one. He said he would ring when he was ready, so . . ."

"You can access those bells from the main chamber?"

"Yes. There's a switchboard just inside the main door. It's used to summon MPs for voting."

"And when you went in, what did you see?"

"Nothing at first," said Willinghouse, who looked more gaunt and haggard by the minute. "He had been . . . He was lying by the speaker's chair, but I didn't see him right away. I thought the place was empty, that he hadn't arrived yet. I went to my usual seat. I heard something, a groan or a sigh . . . I wasn't sure. I got up and walked to the center of the building and saw him beside the dais. On his back. His throat . . ."

His voice tailed off and his eyes looked blank, unfocused.

"Did the prime minister say anything to you? Anything at all?"

"Nothing. He tried to. I could see it in his eyes, but he could not summon the strength. Or his voice . . . No. Nothing."

There was a loaded stillness as the full horror of this registered. Tavestock had been unable to speak because his throat was cut.

"There was so much blood," Willinghouse mused, his eyes going to his own stained hands as if noticing them for the first time. "I tried to close the wound, but . . ."

"How long were you sitting before he made the noise?" Andrews pressed. "Come on, man. It's important."

"Not long," said Willinghouse. "A minute, maybe less. I got some papers from my case, but I didn't have time to start reading them."

"And you saw no one else in the room?"

Willinghouse shook his head emphatically. "I suppose someone could have been hiding," he said, almost hopefully. "I didn't look around. I went to him, but I didn't know what to do. The guards came in almost immediately."

"Did you look up?" I asked. I couldn't help it. I had to know.

Andrews gave me a sharp look.

"Up?" said Willinghouse, vaguely.

"The public galleries," I said, ignoring Andrews's hot stare. "The dome itself."

Willinghouse's brow contracted, as if he was trying to remember who I was, but he shook his head again, his eyes almost closing wearily.

"And you heard nothing?" I pressed. "Even when you first came in? Think."

One of the soldiers turned to look at me, frowning at my familiarity with the great politician.

Willinghouse began to shake his head again, then stopped.

"There was something just as I walked in," he said. "A click like a door latch or window."

"There are no windows in the great chamber," said Andrews, still eyeing me.

"Just a snap, like metal," said Willinghouse, musingly, as if trying to summon it back to his ears, his mind. "Louder than a door latch, somehow. It seemed to come from all around."

An echo resonating in the dome. There must be a maintenance hatch up there.

"Who knew you were meeting?" asked Andrews.

Willinghouse shrugged.

"He spoke to me privately," he said. "I don't think anyone heard. If he told someone else . . ."

Again the hopeless head shake, but before he had chance to say more, the door into the cell corridor crashed open and a uniformed policeman, broad and barrel-chested, his face pink and his whiskers gray, strode in, two more officers struggling to keep up.

"What is the meaning of this?" he barked.

Andrews turned to him, straightening up and stiffening.

"Commissioner!" he said. "I wanted to begin the investigation while the prisoner's memory was fresh."

"Have you been assigned to the case, Andrews?" the commissioner fired back.

"Not as of yet, sir, but since I have had some dealings with the accused—"

"Precisely, sir," the commissioner roared. "Some dealings! He's a *friend* of yours, man! You will have no part in this matter, do I make myself absolutely clear?"

Andrews blinked.

"I'm sure I could be a valuable resource for whomever you appoint—"

"Nonsense, man, you will have nothing to do with it. And what do you mean by bringing these women in here?"

"They are part of his family, sir," said Andrews. "I thought that—"

"You *thought*? When I want you to think, I'll let you know. Now get them out of here. I don't want to see your face until this matter is resolved."

"Commissioner, I strongly request that until the prime minister is able to speak of the matter, I continue to be involved—"

"Speak of it?" said the commissioner, his florid anger hardening. "He shall not speak of it, sir. He's dead."

CHAPTER

6

NEWS OF THE PRIME minister's death roared from every headline that evening, and the low rumble of unease that had suffused the city became a shrill mosquito whine. Regardless of race, creed, sex, or political affiliation, the crowds in the streets stayed, waiting to hear something that would comfort or explain, milling like anxious chickens during a thunderstorm. In the context of Tavestock's death, and with increased military presence on every corner, rumors were spreading that a black activist assassin had been caught, however much the War Office denied them and appealed for calm.

The government was in closed emergency session, all parties meeting separately and then together to determine a stabilizing course of action. This, at least, was what we were told. The late editions of the *Clarion* and *Standard* cut most of what had already appeared to give space to substantially new material, most of it gleaned from various parliamentary spokesmen. The ambassador from Belrand was assisting the government in the drawing up of plans to navigate what was already being called "the succession crisis," though it was made very clear that Belrand had no official say in what would happen next. Ever since the separation of the city from its colonial forebear a century ago, Bar-Selehm had been entirely self-governing, and while trade and military relations with Belrand remained cordial, their involvement was strictly advisory. The papers seemed unsure whether this was a good thing or not, championing our independence on one hand and worrying about our sole responsibility to fix the situation on the other.

Feeling pent up in the house, our silent pacing getting on each other's nerves, Dahria and I went out and roamed the streets to see for ourselves what was happening. The largely unified hubbub I had seen earlier in the city had already begun to fragment along racial lines. The wealthy whites had withdrawn, leaving their poorer brethren to rumble dangerously on the street corners, where they demanded explanations if only to know whose house to menace. The blacks were gathering in and around Mahweni Old Town. They were quieter, warier, waiting for this to be blamed on them and steeling themselves for what would follow. In the main square, two black men addressed the crowd, urging caution and patience. One was Kondotsy Furwina, the new head of the Unassimilated Tribes. The name of the other, a younger and more intense man who wore the clothes of the city but with deliberate splashes of color, I did not know, though I was astounded to realize that he had spoken to me once. It was the man who had met with Willinghouse and the prime minister at the estate yesterday morning.

Overwhelmed by it all, Dahria and I retreated to Willinghouse's town home, where we sat in drained silence at the dining room table, staring at cooling plates of roast duck, lost in thought. At last Dahria got up and went to the window, gazing out into the dusk to watch the lamplighters.

"The chancellor of the exchequer should take over," she said at last. "According to parliamentary procedure."

"Who is that?" I asked.

Dahria blinked.

"I don't know," she confessed, humbled by her own ignorance.

I got up and went to her, unsure what I was going to say.

The door opened, and Higgins, the butler, looked in.

"Forgive me," he said, as we broke apart like guilty children. "There is a young lady of the press to see you. Should I send her in?"

"The press?" exclaimed Dahria. "Absolutely not."

"She claims to be a friend," said Higgins. "She is a young lady of the Mahweni persuasion—"

"Sureyna!" I said.

"I believe so, miss," said Higgins.

"Then yes," said Dahria. "Send her in. And bring the girl something to eat. She's probably been out there all day."

Moments later, the door opened once more, and Sureyna came in. She dropped her notebooks and reticule on the table and folded me into a firm embrace not unlike the one I had wanted to give Dahria. I wasn't sure why I had not been able to.

"How are you?" she demanded seriously.

"As well as can be expected," I replied.

Sureyna turned to Dahria and, on impulse, hugged her too. Dahria stood motionless, her arms stuck awkwardly out, and said, "Well, yes. Quite so," until Sureyna stopped.

"He didn't do it," I said.

"Of course he didn't," said Sureyna, "but that's not a common or popular view outside this room."

"What do people think?" asked Dahria, smoothing her skirts.

"Well, I can't speak for all of them," said Sureyna, eyeing the remains of the cold duck, "but some are saying it's a Brevard coup, an attempt to derail the election they knew they were going to lose."

"That's absurd," said Dahria.

"Obviously," said Sureyna, her gaze flicking back to the table.

"Oh, for heaven's sake, girl, help yourself," Dahria added.

The reporter fell on the food like a starved dog. It was a mark of her distraction that Dahria said nothing about Sureyna's table manners.

"Sorry," she said. "I'm really hungry. This is very good."

"What have you heard?" I asked.

Sureyna swallowed.

"Nothing you haven't already heard, I suspect," she said. "Panic, mostly, and rumor. Willinghouse—sorry, *Mr.* Willinghouse—is the only suspect so far. There was a story about footprints on the roof, but the police didn't find anything."

"It rained," I said.

Sureyna's eyes got big.

"It was something to do with you!" she said.

"I saw the print," I said. "That's all. Someone got out through the dome just as Willinghouse went in. He found the prime minister's body moments later."

"Out through the dome?" said Sureyna.

"Presumably he had a rope," I said. I wasn't sure why I said *he*, but I did, avoiding their eyes and picking at a duck thigh. "There was no other way up, even from the public galleries. Must have come in that way. Scaled the outside of the building, then dropped through the dome access hatch down a rope and went out the same way. There was a refuse chute up to the roof, which might just have been convenient or might have been set up on purpose."

"Would have to be a pretty strong climber, no?" said Sureyna.

I shrugged, but there was no point denying it.

"I suppose," I said.

"Like a steeplejack?" said Dahria.

"Free climbing on a rope?" I said. "Not likely. We're mostly ladder types."

"The Gargoyle!" Sureyna said, eyes alight. "It has to be!"

Dahria gave her a strange look, but I stared doggedly at my food, saying nothing.

"Ang!" Sureyna pressed. "It must be! It fits the pattern of those Gargoyle attacks that made the papers a few months ago."

"This was indoors," I said, still not looking at her. "Those were all in alleys, and in some pretty dodgy areas. This is totally different. Breaking into the Parliament House and assassinating the prime minister? No. This isn't the Gargoyle." I could feel Dahria's eyes on me, but I forced myself to look thoughtfully nonchalant and said, "We need to find a political motive. If a skillful climber could do this, bypassing parliamentary security and timing it perfectly so that the blame would fall on Willinghouse, it can't be some random lunatic or disgruntled voter. It feels organized. That reminds me: there was repair work on the building's northwest cornice, but I didn't see anyone there and didn't recognize the wagon. Can you find out what company was doing it and who hired them?"

"Easily," said Sureyna. "You think this was a professional killing? That someone paid for it?"

"Yes," I said. "But who? The Grappoli?"

"Cut off the head of the city and exploit the resulting chaos by encroaching on our territory?" said Sureyna.

"Would it work?" I asked.

Sureyna cocked her head on one side, then waggled it doubtfully. "The Grappoli have gone quiet," she said. "Stopped expanding in the north and regrouped at home. If they were trying to exploit division in the city, something else has to happen. Right now, Bar-Selehm is as unified as I've ever seen it."

"Against my brother," said Dahria.

She spoke quietly, wonderingly, and there was a brittleness to her manner that worried me. The more Sureyna and I talked politics, the more distant she seemed, as if all her attention was on her brother's predicament. I looked at her now, registering her uncanny stillness, and I felt that, in spite of everything I had thought about her cynical detachment and her attitude toward Willinghouse, she was close to breaking down. Again I felt the urge to reach out to her, but whether it was Sureyna's presence or something else entirely, I could not bring myself to do it.

"Why are you writing about the Grappoli?" I asked Sureyna. "Hardly your usual job."

"Our foreign correspondents are missing," said Sureyna. "They haven't reported in for two weeks. We don't even know for sure where they are. There have been rumors of Mahweni resistance fighters impeding road traffic, even blocking railway lines. There's not much news getting into Bar-Selehm from the north right now. We're rather hoping no one notices."

My heart sank, but I nodded sympathetically.

"I'm sorry," I said. "But I understand the paper's silence. The last thing we need right now is a racial row in the city. Speaking of which, who is the man leading the Old Town rally with Kondotsy Furwina?"

"Young man with glasses? That's Aaron Muhapi. Born in Nbeki, son of a schoolteacher. Compelling, isn't he?"

"He is," I agreed.

"Get used to him," said Sureyna seriously. "He is the future."

I raised an eyebrow, impressed.

"If so, he's going to need help," I said, "and that means getting Willinghouse back in Parliament."

"Which will happen how?" said Dahria, politely. "He was caught, as the vulgar expression has it, red-handed. There are no other suspects, and the one possible clue we have was washed away in a storm. If this was engineered, if he was—as another vulgar expression has it—*set up,* then whoever did so has done a masterful job. He can neither prove the guilt lies elsewhere nor clear his name."

"He doesn't need to," I said decisively.

"And why not, pray?" asked Dahria.

"Because that's what he has me for."

I SOUNDED CALM AND in control, clear in my mind and sure of my course of action. In fact, I was none of those things. Willinghouse's arrest had shaken me badly, and though I would admit it no one, I had wept for the injustice of it and what it must be doing to him. I did not fully understand my dashing, irritating, powerful, but perpetually absent employer. I knew I liked and respected him, that he had saved me from Seventh Street and the Drowning, that he had placed trust in me when no one else had, and that he was dedicated to the good of the city and its people. I had worried about those last points, but I was resolved in my mind now. Willinghouse was a good man, and one day he might even be a great one, but that would not happen if his name were not cleared beyond the merest shadow of a doubt. Otherwise, if the police were incapable of proving his innocence, his potential for greatness wouldn't matter a damn. He'd hang for murder and treason.

I WAITED FOR INSPECTOR Andrews on the steps of the Mount Street Police Station early the following morning, huddled under a blanket like a beggar and rattling a rusty can. Dahria had gone back to the War Office, hoping to get another interview with her brother. I did not hold out much hope that she would get her wish or that she would learn much that was useful to me if she did.

"Penny for a lost girl?" I said, using the street slang that was supposed to work on the superior morals of the city's middle-class whites: one of those benevolent terms attached to prostitutes, drunks, and opium addicts.

His gaze slid off me at first, so I added, "Come on, mister. Help you catch a killer."

He peered at me suspiciously, and I, smeared with mud and coal dust, winked at him. His mouth fell open, and momentarily his face took on a look of panicked despair, as if Willinghouse's fall had already brought me to this deplorable state. I took pity on him.

"It's a called a disguise, Inspector," I said. "You'd think a policeman would have encountered them before."

He relaxed.

"Miss Sutonga," he said. "We shouldn't be seen conversing in public—"

"That," I whispered, "is why we're going to meet in the alley behind the tradesmen's entrance in ten minutes."

For a split second he just looked, then he nodded once and, for the appearance of the thing, fished a farthing from his pocket and flipped it to me.

"Most generous, sir," I called after him. "You're a gentleman and a scholar, you are, sir."

He did not look back, but went into the police station through the main doors, brandishing his papers to the guards as he did so. I sat where I was, still shaking the rusty can in which Andrews's farthing now rattled, for a couple of minutes, then got slowly up and drifted apparently aimlessly in the direction of Ruetta Park and the back of the building. Once out of public view, I dashed along the alley to the rubbish bins by a loading dock with a pair of blue painted doors, and waited.

Andrews arrived a few minutes later. He looked harried and pale, his eyes flitting about as if scared he was being watched.

"What is it?" he demanded, just this side of annoyance.

"I want to know the state of the case," I said, as if that were obvious.

"I don't know it," he snapped, "and even if I did—"

"You'd tell me, because I've earned it, and so has Willinghouse," I said.

He looked about to protest, but thought better of it.

"The commissioner is overseeing the case personally," he said. "I'm not sure why. Security, he says, which probably means he doesn't trust me or the other local inspectors to be objective. He's telling us nothing."

"You must have learned something from the beat officers? Has there been a house-to-house inquiry for witnesses to whoever was on the roof?"

"They found no footprint on the roof of the dome."

"Well, they wouldn't have, would they? It had rained by the time—"

"The guards saw no one up there. Neither did anyone in the street. The public galleries were empty, and the only person seen entering the building even close to the time of the killing was a young Lani woman dressed as a maid. You, I take it."

I grunted in assent.

"I thought so," he said. "They found your skirts in a storage room with roof access. Fortunately, the timing of everyone else leaving the chamber and Willinghouse going in, coupled with the coroner's report, suggests that the attack had already happened. They think you were just frightened of the guards and ran, so no one is looking for you. The bad news is that they clearly aren't really looking for anyone else either. Everything points to Josiah."

"That's nonsense."

"Perhaps so, but from a certain perspective, it is both plausible and—" He hesitated.

"What?" I prompted.

"Sometimes cases are determined not by absolute truth but by what will allow the world to go back to normal as quickly as possible."

My bitter laugh had a snarl in it. As a brown person in Bar-Selehm, I knew all about that. The newspapers were full of Lani and Mahweni who had been picked up for crimes based on the testimony of better-represented members of the city's community, and the less lucky ones, whose names rarely made the papers, didn't always make it out of the justice system. The most frequent casualty of crime in Bar-Selehm was absolute truth.

Andrews read my face but did not argue the point, so I moved past it.

"Have they suggested a motive?" I asked.

"Professional jealousy, an attempt to delay the government's redistricting policies—"

"That's absurd!"

"Of course it is. The only thing more absurd is the suggestion that he thought he might step into the prime minister's position himself."

"His party isn't in power!"

"I know that. They think he might have been trying to create a coalition with the Nationals to keep Richter and Heritage out. Tavestock wouldn't play ball, so Willinghouse killed him, thinking he could force the coalition by sheer personal magnetism in the resulting power vacuum. His star has risen of late."

"It's not rising now."

"Well, yes. Quite," said Andrews. "Look, Miss Sutonga, your employer's predicament is bleak indeed, but I feel sure that the one thing that he would not want is that he take you down with him."

I frowned, trying to make sense of the remark. Andrews held my gaze significantly.

"You think I should drop it?" I said, disbelieving. "You think I should leave him to whatever the police commissioner finds convenient in getting the city back to its daily business?"

"Of course not," said Andrews. "Josiah is . . ." He faltered. "But this is a deep and dark business, and at the moment I see no light at all. I am afraid for your employer, but I would not be doing my duty as his friend if I encouraged you to risk your life on so slender a prospect of hope."

I nodded, then looked him squarely in the face—something I wouldn't have been able to do before I began working for Willinghouse—and said, "I do not need your encouragement. My own sense of obligation will suffice. If I learn of evidence that will help his case and bring it to you, will you act on it?"

"I am not on the case, and the commissioner has made it quite clear that . . . But yes," he said, straightening up. "I will act on whatever you find."

I put out my hand. He blinked, considered it, then shook it decisively.

I RETURNED TO THE town home on Harrington-Clark Street to wash my face, but found the place in an uproar. Servants were bustling about looking panicked, one of the maids had clearly been crying, and even Higgins seemed jolted from his usually unflappable composure. With Dahria out and Willinghouse incarcerated, I could not understand what might have created such a frenzy of anxiety.

"The lady of the house has graced us with an unexpected visit," said Higgins, guardedly.

"Dahria?" I said. "But she's—"

"The *lady* of the house," said Higgins with careful emphasis. "Madame Nahreem."

CHAPTER

7

I GAPED. NO WONDER the place was in chaos. Willinghouse's grandmother hadn't been into the city for months, to my knowledge. I wouldn't have been surprised to find that it was actually years.

"My lady especially inquired after your whereabouts, miss," said Higgins. "Might I suggest that you join her in the withdrawing room as swiftly as your ablutions will permit? She has been waiting some time."

"For me? But I didn't . . . How was I to know that—"

"Nevertheless, miss," said Higgins, in the manner of a man putting down an explosive device.

"Yes," I said. "All right."

I had enough on my mind without being condescended to by Madame Nahreem, and I muttered to myself irritably as I used the bathroom downstairs to prepare for the audience, privately deciding that I would give the conversation no more time than it merited. I had better things to do. I would be polite, sympathetic, but I would not allow the old woman to monopolize my time.

Madame Nahreem, still in formal black, sat in the drawing room like an empress, glowering at the door as I came through it.

"About time," she said.

"I was speaking to Inspector Andrews," I said.

"The man who sent the runner to me last night," she said, a chill fury in her face. "That is to say, the man who informed me of my grandson's fate while you were . . . what? Out dancing with Dahria?"

The injustice of this overwhelmed all my studied courtesy.

"How dare you?" I shot back, standing tall as I could. "I have been working to learn as much as I could of your grandson's predicament so that I could do something about it."

"Such as?"

"Finding out the true circumstances of the prime minister's death!"

"And have you?"

"Not yet! Don't be ridiculous."

Madame Nahreem drew in an outraged breath, but she did not raise her voice. Instead she spoke in a tone of icy calm.

"I'm sure the executioner will give you as much time as you feel you need."

"If you are worried about how I spend my time, I suggest we waste no more of it in this conversation," I said, biting off the words, feeling the heat in my cheeks.

For a moment we glared at each other, then the older woman glanced away toward the window and said, "Sit down, girl. We have things to discuss."

The strangeness of this remark, coupled with the sudden weariness, which had drained all the anger from her face, was like a bucket of water on the fire raging in my chest. I focused on one of the padded, high-backed chairs and moved to it, feeling her eyes on me, and sat with the studied deliberation of the Istilian princess I had once been for her. There was a long, pregnant silence.

"Andrews says you believe there was someone on the roof of the Parliament building," she said with forced care.

"Yes," I said. "I saw a footprint. Bare. It's gone now, though, washed away, and no one else saw it."

"A bare foot," she said. "You are quite sure?"

"Of course, I'm sure," I said, my hauteur rising again. "It was made in fine powder or dust. Very pale."

"And the foot itself?"

"Small, like mine."

I said it warily, feeling a sudden and unexpected sense of unease. I wanted to be out there, climbing, looking, asking questions, not stuck in here with this maddening and imperious woman—

"What do you know of the Crane Fly?" she said at last.

Again, the unexpected nature of the question knocked me off-kilter, and I shot her a puzzled look.

"You mean the legendary Lani steeplejack?" I said. "Why?"

"Legendary, you say, but the Crane Fly was real enough."

This was bizarre. The Crane Fly was a collection of industry heroics. Tales of the highest work ever done in places ladders couldn't go. The fastest climb up the great smokestack in Riddley's coke yard. The saving of a whole gang's wages when an unscrupulous employee demanded three sets of chimney repairs be completed in only two days. They were stories for steeplejacks, and they had only a fraction more truth to them than the tales of the Gargoyle.

"Maybe he was real once," I said, "but so what? Most of it was probably made up, and when I heard the stories, they were already a half century old. If he was ever real, he's long dead by now."

Madame Nahreem's gaze which had fixed me like a butterfly in a case, suddenly grew vague, and she turned her face back to the window as though looking at something far away.

"No," she said. "The Crane Fly lives yet."

"You think he had something to do with Tavestock's death?" I said, incredulous.

She shook her head.

"No," she said. "But the Crane Fly wasn't merely a steeplejack. The Crane Fly had apprentices."

I made a face. "Today? In the city? I'd know."

"You didn't know the Crane Fly was real and still alive."

"I still don't," I said, defiant. "Should he be alive, he'd be more than just a myth. He'd have a real name. A face. You don't come into the city, so I wouldn't expect you to understand, but when you work here, you get to hear what people talk about, and I'm telling you, if he was ever real, he's moved away or died years ago."

"No, Miss Sutonga. She lives."

I had opened my mouth to say something, when the full weight of that pronoun hit me and I realized what I was being told.

"No," I said. It was more a breath than a word, and it wasn't so much a contradiction as the bursting out of an impossible idea. "*You?* You were the Crane Fly?"

"Long ago," she said. She smiled, a wan, sad smile, and when she moved her hand distractedly, it seemed to flutter, as if she was wrestling with some powerful emotion.

"Wait," I said, still trying to process the knowledge. "You were a steeplejack?"

"For many years."

"But in the stories, the Crane Fly was always male! No one ever said—"

"Does that surprise you?" she said, and the smile was real this time.

Of course it didn't surprise me that the best steeplejack the city had ever known had been a woman. It wasn't a detail that would survive as gang lore generations later. I considered her as if seeing her for the first time, and I knew she was telling the truth. She was in her eighties now, but she was still strong and alert, her body remarkably supple for her age, as I had seen when she performed the Kathahry exercises with me. I thought of her work in the neutral mask, and I could almost see her up on the ladders and the high scaffold where the vultures perch, gracefully moving along the top of a wall a single brick wide and with nothing to hold on to but air . . .

Yes, said my heart. Madame Nahreem was the Crane Fly. It made absolute sense.

She saw the realization in my face, then hit me with a question, like a fighter who goes for the throat when his opponent is already off-balance.

"And how is Vestris?"

I stared, my mouth opening and closing stupidly like a fish snatched from the river.

"She's dead," I said at last, knowing she wouldn't believe me, knowing that panic was leaking out of my every pore.

"She's not. We both know that. Namud knew it too. She is alive, though she is, I believe, somewhat changed."

I just sat there, paralyzed by fear and indecision as I tried to figure out how much the old woman knew.

All of it, said a nasty voice in my head. *She has known for weeks.*

"You will recall," she said, "the night the *Georgiana Maria* incident came to a head at the harbor, when Richter's men exposed the city's trafficking in weapons and slave labor—largely thanks to you and my grandson— several people died. There was a question about how one of Richter's thugs had met his end. He was a blond man called Barrington-Smythe, I believe. A killer, and a cruel one at that. As I have pieced the story together, he gave chase to a group of refugees, women, and children. You went after him, but in the ensuing melee, he was killed by a knife to the throat, a single, swift slash from behind."

She let the image hang in the air between us. I remembered it in all its horror, but could say nothing.

"It was a singular and professional attack," she continued, her dark eyes boring into mine, "ruthless, you might say. You had good reason to hate him, to fear him and what he would do if he survived that hour. But I do not believe you killed him, not like that, coming so decisively from behind. It is, perhaps, to your credit that I cannot see you doing it."

"I did," I said, my voice cracking. My mouth and throat were dry. I swallowed, then said it again. "I did. I killed him. He deserved it."

"Perhaps he did," she answered, her expression unchanged. "But if he had earned his death, he did not receive it at your hands, did he, Miss Sutonga? Not when someone else was on hand to take care of it for you."

I went back to saying nothing. She knew everything, or thought she did, but I saw no reason to confirm her suspicions.

"The method of attack," she went on, "matches others in the city. People killed from behind with a razor to the throat, people who also, perhaps, had earned their deaths and were dispatched by what witnesses came to think of as a kind of avenging angel, one they mapped onto another old steeplejack legend and nicknamed the Gargoyle. A fanciful, even romantic appellation, wouldn't you say? We know her by another name, don't we, Anglet?"

"No!" I blurted out, tears filling my eyes.

"Yes. There is nothing to be gained by denying it. I am sure you feel . . . conflicted about your part in your beautiful sister's trans-formation, your hand in making her what she has become. If it is any consolation, I understand. I share your feelings."

"What does Vestris have to do with you?"

Madame Nahreem smiled the slow, sad smile again.

"Oh, Miss Sutonga," she said. "Let us not pretend. You know I trained her. You know she left me and became something quite different and dangerous."

Namud had warned me that there were things I did not know that concerned me, but the fact that Madame Nahreem was still unwilling to explain herself was a shock. The fact that I had also kept secrets from the Willinghouse family did not help.

"Yet you chose to train me," I said. "Her sister. Why?"

"It was my way of helping your family."

"It didn't work out with Vestris. Why would you try again?" The words came out almost as an accusation. The question had been rubbing at me for weeks now, like an itch I couldn't reach, but one that worsened dramatically over time. Now something hot burned in my chest. Tears burst from my eyes and ran down my cheeks. "What are we to you? Toys? Tools you use to pretend that you are still just a Lani steeplejack yourself? Is that it? This is how you play at being an ordinary person instead of the Great Lady of the House? Or are we just the Crane Fly's last great performance?"

She shook her head, but for once she could not hold my gaze. My furious and unanswered questions still in the air, I fled from the room and slammed the door.

CHAPTER

8

I RETURNED TO GRAND Parade determined to do something, anything, that would take my mind off my conversation with Madame Nahreem, but when I got to the great ornamental facade of the War Office and the Parliament House, I could think of nothing, and found myself pacing back and forth, sure that I would eventually attract the attention of the watchful guards. If I was right about a climber using the dome to enter and exit unnoticed by the sentries, I was stuck with the problem of how he had gone unseen by the people outside.

The attack had taken place at lunchtime, when the area thronged with visitors foreign and domestic. It was the busiest time of day for the neighboring shops and cafés, let alone the MPs, police, and soldiers who would have been teeming around the building. It was impossible that no one had seen somebody climbing up and down the walls of the great Parliament House. A quick escape via a hastily erected masonry chute, I could see, but entering from there would have been far too conspicuous. Then there was the attack itself, timed too perfectly with Willinghouse's arrival to be coincidence. I was missing something.

Having walked purposefully along Hanover Street, I cut down a quieter road of offices housing the civil servants, diplomats, and other lesser officers of the great governmental machine, and my puzzlement swelled like a sugar grub, laid by its mother just under your skin as you sleep. It ate into me, burrowing deeper and deeper, getting ripe and fat off my uncertainty. The Parliament House was a block to itself. It adjoined nothing, and the closest building was forty or fifty feet away.

The chute was sheer inside, and the scaffold covered only the corner of the roof. So the assassin must have scaled the city's most conspicuous and secure building unseen in broad daylight.

It couldn't be done. I spat on the pavement and stared at the towers and dome from below, feeling the grub in my belly chewing its nest out of my flesh.

"Oy!" said the inevitable dragoon across the street, glaring at me. "You planning on putting down roots? This is a secure area. Move along."

"What's going on?" I said, emboldened by his attitude.

"Gotta pick a new PM, haven't they? Nothing to do with the likes of you, though, is it? So like I said: move along."

DAHRIA RETURNED IN A foul temper, after waiting for hours to see her brother only to have the meeting denied by the Commissioner's Office. When she heard her grandmother had come from the estate, Dahria proclaimed she had a headache and was going to take a sleeping draft. Shortly afterwards, I left the town house in something close to my steeplejack clothes and a pair of sturdy work boots, a set of which I kept at the house for just such an eventuality. I rode the Flintwick underground to Atembe and then headed south through the Numbers District to the Weavers Arms on Bridge Street, avoiding the darkest and narrowest alleys but staying, for once, on street level.

I found Tanish in the backroom, nursing a pint of porter and telling tall tales to a huddle of boys even younger than him. I kept my head down until I was sure Sarn wasn't on hand. I had no wish to remind the Seventh Street gang, which the older boy now led, that I was still alive and working in the city.

It was a mark of Tanish's improved standing in the gang that he did not wait anxiously for a moment to get away when he saw me. He dismissed the younger boys, put a booted foot on a chair at his stained table, and pushed it out for me, simultaneously pulling out a clay pipe and packing it with tobacco, pleased with himself. Some of this was doubtless a performance for my benefit. There was no question he seemed older than his thirteen years, and I felt a conflicted pang at seeing him: glad that he seemed to be thriving, yet saddened that he had left behind some of the wide-eyed innocence I had known when he had been my apprentice.

"Hi, Ang," he said, putting a match to his pipe and puffing to get it going. "You must be having an interesting day."

He knew who I worked for, but I trusted him to keep that information to himself.

"You could say that," I said.

"But you've come to see me," said Tanish shrewdly, "which means . . ." His eyes lit up. "Willinghouse is innocent, and you're on the hunt. Excellent."

I couldn't help but match his grin.

"Can't put one past you, can I?" I said, part flattery, part impressed affection.

"You want my help," he said, all his studied languor falling away like a dog catching a scent. "What do you need?" Before I could answer, he glanced up to where a harried-looking barmaid was clearing tankards, tapped his mug with a finger, and shouted, "Two more, Jenny, yeah? When you've got a minute."

He was cocksure, in his element, and again I felt the tug of mingled pride and sadness. I had spent my first months out of the gang worrying how he would survive without me to protect him from the hard corners of the world, but he had toughened up quickly. Matured, I supposed, though it was impossible not to feel a sense of loss at the transformation.

"I'm looking for a climber," I said. "A young boy or a woman, feet no bigger than mine. Someone skilled on a rope who works barefoot."

"Barefoot?" said Tanish. "In the city?"

Bar-Selehm may once have been a land of grass and sand and warm, flat rock, but it was now a place of cobbles and concrete, scattered nails, fractured brick, and broken glass. No one worked barefoot in the city.

"So you're looking for someone really, really stupid," said Tanish, musingly.

"Well," I said, "I'm looking for a specialist."

The barmaid slopped a couple of mugs onto the table, and Tanish gave her a fractional nod of acknowledgment.

"Cheers," he said, taking his and sipping from it.

"Cheers," I agreed. "It's good to see you."

He looked at me over the rim of his mug, and there was something cautious and skeptical in his eyes that I hadn't seen before. He knew my feelings toward him were conflicted, even if he didn't understand why. Feeling suddenly transparent, I took a long swallow of the dark, thin beer and found an unexpected honesty.

"I missed that," I said, considering the porter.

"Don't get a decent pint in your fancy digs, eh?"

"Not often," I admitted.

"What do they give you?" he said, genuinely curious. "Like, claret? Porto?"

He said the words as if they were foreign terms whose meaning he could only guess at.

"Something like that," I said. "Water, usually."

Tanish made a face. "I wouldn't drink the water round here if my life depended on it," he said. "Got bits in it. And worse. A week ago, right? One of the new boys had a bottle of water he was swigging from up on the scaffold, and it was brown. Like, thick, dark brown. Swear to all the gods. Said he'd got it from the pump on Third Street, but I reckon it came from the river. Things living in it. We're working the candle factory in Evensteps, and there's a bloke there who drinks this nasty, black oily stuff—"

"So this climber I'm looking for . . ." I prompted.

"Right. The barefoot bloke."

"Or woman."

"Yes. Not sure. I can ask around."

"Don't know that that's a good idea," I said.

"Why, what did he do?" Tanish replied, but the answer came to him almost immediately. "You think he bumped off the PM? Cor! Really?"

"It's possible," I said. "And keep your voice down."

"Still," he said, his excitement fading, "steeplejacks don't go barefoot. You want, like, one of them black unaffiliated thatcher guys, maybe, but they don't work up high."

"Any new gangs in town, Mahweni, maybe, or rural Lani?"

"Nah. Maybe a few journeymen have come in from the sticks, but who would hire them for real steeplejacking? I can check on the Jewel, but even the Tsuvadas wear boots." The Jewel was the great suspension bridge, which was still unfinished, and on which half the steeplejacks in the city had worked at some point, myself included. The Tsuvadas were Lani from the mountain towns a couple of hundred miles north of the city where the tallest structures were trees. They only came for seasonal jobs, Tanish was right. Even they didn't work barefoot. He sipped his beer and mused aloud. "Who would use just a rope instead of ladders and scaffold? Mad, that is. Show-offy."

I nodded and drank, slipping into the familiar comfort of being in this place with him. There was something else I had to ask, but I was avoiding it, and for a moment I wanted to stop time, so that I could stay here, not think about Willinghouse or Tavestock and the over-pressurized steam boiler that was the city itself. And Vestris. I wanted to think about her least of all, but that was not an option left to me.

"Tanish," I ventured, "have you heard anything more about the Gargoyle lately?"

He gave me a quick inquisitive look and a wary grin, like I might be setting up a joke.

"Thought you didn't believe in the Gargoyle?" he said.

"I don't. Not as such. But I'm curious about . . . anything, really. There were some attacks, which some people attributed . . ."

"Weeks ago," he said. "Nothing since that night on the docks. A few sightings, rumors really, but no attacks. Why do you . . . ?" His eyes got big as dinner plates. "You're looking for a climber who might have killed the PM, and you're asking about the Gargoyle?" he gasped, thrilled and delighted.

"I told you to keep your voice down," I hissed, lowering my head so that he drew instinctively closer. "I don't think . . . Not really. I just have to consider all possibilities."

"PM killed by Gargoyle," he murmured, trying the words out like he was reading a newspaper headline. "Blimey."

"You are not to say a word about this, Tanish. You hear me? If I see it in the papers, I'll know where they got it."

"Just an idea, ain't it? You can't blame me if someone else thinks up the same—"

"I can, and I will," I said, with a warning glare. For a couple of seconds, he held my eyes defiantly, but then he wilted, aging backwards till he was my little boy apprentice again.

"Fine," he scowled. "But it's a stupid idea anyway. The Gargoyle hasn't attacked anyone in ages."

"You said there have been sightings."

"There's always been 'sightings,'" he said, "but you know what most of them are: too much beer and not enough brain. Someone scared of the night or looking to get some of that fear into someone younger and stupider. You've said so yourself a thousand times."

"I have, and you're right. But a few months ago you convinced me that there was something to the stories after all. The papers said the monster killed at least three and was seen by a lot more. Then what? Did the Gargoyle just disappear? What are people saying? Anything new?"

He had been trying to play it off as something childish that he'd grown out of, but he knew me a little too well and could feel my nervousness, my dread. I had to know what people knew, or thought they knew, because amongst all the strangeness and half truths, one thing was certain: I was going to have to find my eldest sister.

Tanish shrugged, but his eyes stayed on mine. His casualness was an act. He had caught something of my fear, like when you touch the stanchion of a girder bridge as the train rolls overhead and the rumble of the wheels and gears above you goes through the steel and right into your heart so that for a second you are the engine.

"It's probably nothing," he said after a while, "but some of the little 'uns were working Semmerline Terrace, switching out chimney pots and cleaning the flues, you know, and they said . . . I mean, it's stupid, probably nothing . . ."

"What did they say, Tanish?"

He was getting anxious, and I didn't think it was because he was worried I'd think his story stupid.

"Well, they said, that . . . You know how the Inns of Court has those five angels standing on the roof, the statues with wings and spears and whatnot?"

"Yes."

"But there was another one on the end which is missing, right? Fell down years ago and never got put back."

"Yes."

"Well, they say, that if you stand up on Semmerline Terrace with your back to the Dyer Street cement factory, you can see the Inns of Court right over the rooftops. You can see the five angels."

"And?"

Tanish licked his lips and said, "Sometimes there are six."

SEMMERLINE TERRACE WAS THE last opulent street on the east side of the city in sight of the river, and all the way on the other side of Old Town. By the time I got there, the lamps were lit and the streets deserted as evening turned to night. It was the dividing line between all that was fashionable and exclusive to the north and the industrial clutter to the south, where the factories and warehouses clustered along the northern bank of the Kalihm as it flowed into the sea. As if to prove its hold on the socially elevated realm it faced, the Terrace seemed to be in a state of constant refurbishment, and barely a day went by when there wasn't a team on scaffolding and ladders painting, repointing masonry, planting ornamental roof gardens, or adding decorative trim in accord with the latest architectural fashion. It was a half mile or so southeast of the Inns of Court, and I went there first to test whether the young steeplejacks' story could be true.

There was no scaffold rigged, but the gang's ladders had been stowed around the back, carefully chained and padlocked. Not that I would need them. The stonework all over the front of the three-story houses had been studded with brass accents a few feet apart, each one a well-fashioned ornamental pinecone that stood a couple of inches proud of the masonry. They were as good as a ladder.

Somewhere below on the back side of the terrace I caught the sounds of laughter and shouting, but it wasn't directed at me, and eventually moved slowly off toward whichever pubs might still be open. I squatted on the ridgeline and turned to the northwest. In the distance I could see the bright, hard radiance of the Beacon shining out over the Finance District and giving a little spangle to the colonnades and statues as far south as the Martel Court. The Inns of Court, which stood between them and me, were largely dark, save where their own gas lamps picked out a little pearly silver on the stone and ironwork. The statues on the roof were not individually lit and were visible only as pale, ghostly shapes against the dark sky.

There were five, as I had expected there to be. Their attitude was not visible to me now, but I knew them well enough. Tanish called them angels, but they were figures from the mythology of justice, metaphors in stone and bronze proclaiming the city's essential rightness in defiance of all the evidence in the streets below: two white—tall and godlike, two black—wild and strong—two Lani—draped in fluttering saris. It was one of the city's rare monuments to its entire population, though whether the high-minded sentiments of the architect and sculptor were enacted by the business conducted below was a matter of debate. The missing figure on the end—one of the Lani angels—had fallen from its niche some thirty years ago, I was told, though I didn't know what had happened to it. Some of the city's older statues were held together with iron rods slotted through the stone. When they rusted, the pieces fell apart, which was probably what had happened to the sixth angel. Nowadays they dipped the iron in molten zinc.

The shouts from below came again, nearer this time, and I slid down the slope of the roof so I wouldn't be visible even as a silhouette. A Lani woman skulking round by night would be viewed with considerable suspicion. With Willinghouse in prison and Andrews keeping a low profile, I could not count on my ability to slip out of an arrest. I waited, listening, and again the sounds seemed to move off.

Nothing to do with me, I decided again, but I waited a while longer before moving to a position from which I might climb down. I had seen all I needed. The steeplejacks might have been making things up or been caught in their own fearful imaginings, but their story was at least plausible. You could see the plinth on which the sixth angel had once stood from here.

I had thought of the angels as figures of justice and—by association with the folklore surrounding the Gargoyle—vengeance. I recalled in the northern religion, angels were also guardians, protectors with flaming swords watching over places, but also over people. That might be a better association for those that kept vigil over the city. Or at least I would like it to be.

I stood on the edge of the roof, poised to turn and begin working my way down bit by cautious bit. In the last second something caught my eye and I hesitated, staring back across the roofs toward the Inns of Court. It was dim out there, the building and its statues mere shadows and grayness in the thin light of the gas lamps below, but there could be no doubt.

There were six angels.

I RAN THROUGH THE night, making a hard beeline for the elegant formal buildings of the Inns of Court. I thought of the unvisited clock spires and pinnacles and tower rooms that dotted its roofline. All good hiding places for someone unafraid of heights. I had used the Martel Court on the opposite side of the square in just such a fashion on several occasions. Bar-Selehm loved its extravagant and imposing skyline, particularly in the grander parts of the city where it gave the eye a much-needed respite from the clutter of chimney stacks. Once built, though, the city didn't do much with its lofty architectural features. They were turned over to the steeplejacks, vultures, and bats that haunted the higher reaches of the town. That these niches above might also be home to the creature known as the Gargoyle seemed to me perfectly plausible.

So I ran, but I also chose the shadows and the alleys that would keep my approach least visible. Reaching the Inns of Court, I looked to make my ascent to the roof on the northwest side of the building. That way, if someone was up there on the angel's plinth, I would come at them from behind.

I wore the kukri that I habitually carried. Heavy as an ax, it served as a tool as well as a weapon, and if I was caught, it would not get me into the same legal difficulties as a pistol, but as I began to climb, it felt clumsy and inadequate. I suddenly realized that I had spent so much mental and physical energy reaching this moment that I had given no thought to what might happen next. If the person up here—assuming it was a person and not a trick of the gloom—was no one I knew, I might escape without incident. Or I might find myself in a fight to the death. It was unlikely that anyone up here at this hour was merely an upstanding citizen taking in the view.

And if it *was* someone I knew? That seemed even less clear.

I was climbing using the sharp prominent edges of the stone blocks, but it was finger and toe work: safe enough if there were no distractions, deadly if there were. I felt with the steel toecaps of my boots, pulling myself up step by step like a fly on a water pitcher, and I hoped to all the gods that there was no one waiting at the top. A well-placed kick would be as sure as a bullet between the eyes.

I waited, breathing, feeling the strain in my arms, my body taut as piano wire, and then I sprang for the top, three fingertip grabs, three precise stabs of my boots into the grouted gap between the blocks, and I was up. I rolled over the cornice and onto the roof as silently as I could.

There was no one in sight.

I stepped carefully, hugging the pitched roof in the center, every sense alert for movement, peering cautiously round the corner toward the rear of the building. I could see the backs of the five angel statues, their bronze swords and spears held like talismans.

The sixth was slightly smaller but just as still.

The figure was wearing a long gray hooded cloak and was standing, like the angels, gazing out toward the river and beyond. Not taking my eyes off the living statue, I reached back and drew the kukri from its sheath.

It did not move, and only the faintest stirring of the wind in its robe distinguished it from the statues lined up beside it. I straightened up and took three long, silent steps toward it, feeling the weight of the heavy, curved knife in my hand. After two more steps, the figure turned fractionally toward me, and though I could see no face within the shaded hood, I knew it had seen me before it turned back to the cityscape below.

I waited but, when nothing happened, began walking again till I was only twenty feet away.

"Hello, Ang," said Vestris. "I wondered when you would come."

The voice was odd, slurred and muffled strangely despite what sounded like careful enunciation. It was neither the voice of my sister as I had known her in my youth nor the animal snarl of the Gargoyle creature she had been when I saw her last.

"It is remarkable up here, is it not?" she said. "So much beauty and ugliness together. So much life and death."

"I don't see death," I said, still holding tight to my kukri.

"But you know it's there," she answered, still not looking at me. "Everyone does, though some are better at not seeing it than others. I would have thought the poor, the disenfranchised would all see it quite clearly, and you perhaps most of all."

I wasn't sure if that was an accusation, but I said nothing. This was strange. I didn't know what I had expected, but it was not this.

"I am alive," she said. "Which would come as a surprise to a lot of your friends, I suspect. But if I take a single step forward, the kind of step I take all the time on solid ground, out into the air, all that life—the pumping blood, the thought, the feeling—it all goes away in an instant. It is remarkable, is it not, that we are so extraordinarily fragile?"

"That's why we take care to stay alive," I said, as if we were making conversation while cooking Papa's supper.

"Indeed," she said. "And I have taken more care than most."

She turned to me then, and pushed the hood back.

It was almost her. The beauty I had known, but which had been so blasted when I saw her last, had made some small gains on her face. Where her skin had been gray and patchy, she had become brown and smooth once more. Her bald, skeletal head was regrowing its hair, if unevenly; a short bob of glossy black now reached where her collar might be. It was not unbecoming. Her eyes were the same as ever, deep and powerful, but her cheeks were still hollow, and I could tell from her speech that she had lost most of her teeth. However else she reclaimed her former health, they were gone forever. She managed a dry smile at my reaction.

"You have recovered," I said, unable to contain both my surprise and my conflicted feelings. Vestris was my sister. She was also a killer, and while her most recent victims had been the rough justice of a vigilante, not all her victims had been guilty of anything.

I worked for Willinghouse because of a boy called Berrit who would have been my apprentice if he had not fallen to Vestris's knife.

"In part," she said. It was amazing how much weight, how many mixed and competing meanings she could pack into those two simple words. It seemed, judging by the way she returned her gaze to the city spread out to the south, that I wasn't the only one with conflicted feelings.

Or the performance of them.

Yes. Vestris, I reminded myself, had been a consummate liar and manipulator for many years. I should be on my guard.

"You came to ask me something," she said. "What is it?"

"Three things, actually," I replied, refusing to be cowed by my sister's recapturing of some of her old dignity.

"Let me tell you before you ask," she said.

"I see no reason for playacting—" I began, irritated by her composure, by how easily she took charge.

"First, no, I did not kill the prime minister," she intoned, eyes still fixed on the dark middle distance. "I would not be surprised to learn that he merited such an act. Most politicians do, in my experience, but I did not kill this one, and I do not know who did."

I believed her instantly, which was probably foolish, but in the moment, though I barely knew her at all anymore, I felt sure she was telling the truth. I felt an unexpected sense of relief, as though she had removed a burden I hadn't known I was carrying.

"Your second question is, I think, more difficult," she said musingly. "You want to know why I helped you a few months ago."

"Yes," I confessed. "And more generally why you changed."

She laughed at that, making a strange soft-edged coughing sound.

"Because I changed," she said.

I scowled, dissatisfied.

"Because I went through death and out the other side," she said, not laughing now, "and the process broke me apart, showed me what I was, what I had become. Because surviving meant deciding to live for something, to be something, and I found I could not muster the energy to return to what I once was. Not that that was ever a possibility. Bar-Selehm prefers its society mistresses to have teeth and hair."

The starkness of the truth embarrassed me, and I looked down.

"Do you remember me as I was before I left the Drowning?" she asked. "When you were a girl, I mean. When it was just you, me, Rahvey, and Papa. Do you remember me as I was then?"

She had turned to gaze out over the city again, but I suspected it was because she could not look at me, and her voice was strained with emotion. She sounded more than sad. She sounded desperate.

"Yes," I said. "Of course. You were beautiful and kind—"

She gasped and bowed her head.

"Kind," she echoed, as if it was a word whose meaning she had forgotten. "Kind. I wonder. But thank you. I am glad you remember something more than . . . this." She gestured vaguely with her hands toward herself. Then nodded thoughtfully, saying nothing for several seconds before looking up again. "Your other question, I cannot answer," she said.

"Why not? What other question?"

"You want to know why Madame Nahreem, old spider that she is, hired you after she had so failed with me."

"There's no reason you would know that," I answered, mustering a little defiance, though I did not bother to conceal the fact that she had indeed guessed what my next question would be.

"I didn't say I didn't know," she said, turning to me again. "I said I won't tell you. She must tell you herself. It's time. When she does, I will be here, waiting for you."

"What makes you think I'll want to speak to you again?"

She turned to me then, and her composure was cracked with grief and longing. Her eyes swam, and her smile was full of knowing and loss and sadness.

"Oh, little Ang," she said, her voice almost breaking. "I will be here."

CHAPTER
9

WHEN I GOT TO the town house, Dahria was in bed and Madame Nahreem was gone.

"My lady did not feel her presence here aided her grandson's position," said Higgins. "She has left some money for legal expenses and instructions for word to be sent to her if there are any developments."

"She went back to the estate?"

Higgins nodded.

"My lady finds the noise and smoke of the city quite unsettling," he said.

"No doubt," I said, with just enough hardness that the butler's forehead tightened for a second with puzzlement or concern, but he did not pursue the matter.

Unsettling, I thought. I bet she finds it unsettling, being back here where she was once a lowly steeplejack working the towers and chimneys of the great filth that is Bar-Selehm, instead of being the lady of a sprawling estate under a clear blue sky, her tame hyenas playing at her feet . . . I had half a mind to go after her, to demand the answers she had held back at our last interview. But I couldn't. Willinghouse needed me here, though how I was going to help him, I had no idea.

"There is something else, miss," said Higgins, looking—as far as was possible within his customary butlery composure—uncomfortable. Actually, the word that came to mind was *shifty.* "You have a visitor."

"At this hour? Who?"

"The lady says she is your sister."

I gaped. Vestris had beaten me home? Why?

"Shall I show her in," said Higgins, clearly in uncharted waters, "or will you join her in the withdrawing room?"

"I'll go to her," I said. "She's alone?"

"She is indeed, miss. I served her tea while she waited."

My hand was on the door handle before I had fully processed the implication of what he had said. Vestris may have known various secret routes over the rooftops of the city, but it wasn't plausible that she had arrived in time to take tea before I got back. I opened the door just as I realized the truth, a truth almost as hard to believe.

Rahvey was sitting stiffly in her Cloudsday finest in an overstuffed armchair, looking deeply uncomfortable. The relief on her face as I came in was raw and touched with desperation.

"What is it?" I said, panic wiping away all social niceties. "What's happened?"

"It's the girls," she said. "They are sick."

"What? Sick in what way?" I said, caught completely off guard.

"I don't know. *Sick*. Throwing up. Running to the toilet. Burning up. Tired. Really tired, like unable to stand up. Headaches. And then, this afternoon, some of Aab's hair fell out."

Aab Samir was a deaf girl who played with my sister's daughters.

"They are all sick?"

"Not Kalla," she said. "Not me. Not yet. But the children. And Bertha, though she is not so bad."

Bertha was the black teacher I had hired to teach the Drowning girls when she wasn't working in the factories downtown.

"Why are you telling me?" I said, flustered. "You need a doctor!"

"The one who visits the Drowning doesn't know what it is. I thought you might know someone else . . ."

Her face showed defiance and shame and desperation all at once.

"I don't," I said, "but I'll find someone."

"Thank you," she said, as if I were some white lady from whom she had begged a crust. I scowled at her but then, to her amazement, opened the door and yelled into the hall.

"Higgins! Wake Miss Dahria, prepare the carriage, and summon the family doctor."

The butler, to his credit, did not hesitate.

I'm not sure what Rahvey thought would happen, but she seemed bewildered by the speed with which we got ready and took charge. Within twelve minutes, we were in the carriage, Higgins—a revolver tucked into his belt—riding on top with the driver. In sixteen, we had collected the doctor, and in under forty, we were in the Drowning. There we left the coach and picked our way along the winding dirt tracks down through the shanties that sprawled along the riverbank.

Mendelson, the white doctor, wore a black top hat and gray muttonchop side whiskers. He was closer to sixty than fifty and carried a capacious bag black as his suit, filled with instruments and phials of medicine. He gathered what information he could from Rahvey who, overawed by so grand a gentleman, had to be continually nudged and prodded to say more. He was kind to her, a fact that probably unsettled her as much as the evening's other strangenesses. I said nothing, but watched the equally silent Dahria, who stared at nothing, lost in her own thoughts.

Higgins had a shuttered lantern with a bulb of decent luxorite behind a directional lens, and he walked beside my sister, eyes on the weedy ground for the mambas and puff adders that plagued the area at this time of year. The sick girls had been grouped together at the edge of the constantly evolving village, huddled under a makeshift tarpaulin tent. Another child had been added since Rahvey left, so that they now numbered ten. They all attended Bertha's classes, and I braced myself for being blamed for whatever contagion had come upon the settlement.

The place smelled sour, unwholesome, and the sight of the children—Aab and Rahvey's girls in particular, pale and sweating, listless and moaning in discomfort—struck through my heart like a fine spear. I saw Jadary tossing in between waking and sleeping, horrified by how thin and aged she looked. Radesh lay next to her, watching her sister, her face drained but her eyes wide and scared.

"You should have brought me earlier," I said, as if I were an expert.

"Didn't want to bother you," said Rahvey. "What with . . . everything."

I looked at her quickly.

"Yes," I said. "Of course. Well. Let's see what the doctor can do."

The elders were there, watching silently, and the old priest from the monkey temple was leading some of the parents in prayer. Florihn, the midwife, had brought bread and water to the sick, but she evaded my eyes and consulted with the doctor in a manner that was both professional and respectfully subordinate, keen to show she had made no mistakes. There was nothing for me to do. Feeling useless, I hung back and left them to it.

"I'm sorry I woke you," I said to Dahria. "I don't know why I did. Company, I suppose. Not a very good reason."

"Good enough," said Dahria, taking my hand and squeezing it gently.

At this rare sign of affection, I gave her a startled look, conscious that I was blushing, but she was watching the doctor moving from bed to bed, her serious face lost in shadow.

"WELL?" I SAID TO Dr. Mendelson, as soon as he had finished his ministrations.

He pursed his lips and shook his head, dissatisfied.

"I have made them comfortable for now," he said, "given them something to bring their temperatures down, but I confess I am at a loss. At this time of year and in this place, I would stake my reputation on malaria, except . . ."

"Except what?" I said, as he mused to himself.

"The hair loss. The deaf girl is not the only one. The other symptoms, the fever, weariness, vomiting, and diarrhea, all might be explained by malaria. But hair loss . . ." He shook his head again. "I need to monitor them. I will find a place to stay here tonight."

I stared at him.

"Don't you have other patients who need you in town?" I asked. I did not say *white patients,* but that was what I meant.

"Colds and various versions of 'the vapors,'" he said. "Nothing that can't wait or be treated by someone else."

"Thank you, doctor," I said, meaning it.

"It's my job," he replied, almost brusquely, as if I had questioned his ethics. "I'll send for a tincture of quinine tomorrow. I have almost used up all the supplies I had on hand."

"I'm sure the Willinghouse family will reimburse you for your time and any necessary—"

"I have no doubt," he replied quickly. "Assuming the Willinghouse family has not had all its assets frozen by morning."

"I hope it will not come to that," I said.

"As do I," he remarked, giving me a frank look. "As do I."

It occurred to me only later, as Dahria and I made our return journey to the town house, that he had not asked my name or how I came to be there. He had promised to keep us informed, and we had left in a cloud of futility, painfully aware that there was nothing for us to do. With neither the doctor nor Rahvey riding in the carriage with us, there was ample room for the butler, but he retook his place on the driver's plate, though whether that was a matter of professional decorum or pained embarrassment at the situation we had left behind, I couldn't say.

It was a long, dark ride to the house, and neither of us was in the mood to talk. As Dahria slept, or pretended to, I focused on what I might do the next day to help Willinghouse. In this I was about as productive and useful as I had been in the Drowning, and on our arrival, I went to bed feeling not so much sad as lost and out of my depth, as if the world were crumbling around me and there was nothing I could do to stop it.

BUT SOMETHING CAME TO me in my sleep, or in that drowsy half-awake state in which I spent much of the short, anxious night. Not a plan, exactly, but a course of action that might be the beginnings of a plan. With nothing better presenting itself, it would have to do.

At first light I went to the kitchen to rebuild my maid's attire, complete with demure cap and apron borrowed without explanation from the hooks by the door. The burly Lani cook looked up from the stove and grinned at me.

"Rasnarian goat curry tonight," he said, either not noticing or not caring that I was helping myself to servant clothes. "Your favorite."

It was too—the first meal I had eaten in the house the night Willinghouse's men had brought me there, and I thought about it as I walked all the way over to the Parliament House in the gray light of the morning. I waited only ten minutes before the stream of servants and other menial staff began to file dutifully in through the tradesmen's entrance round the back. I chose a Lani girl of about my age dressed in similar attire and attached myself to her at the tail end of the line.

"Good morning," I said. She gave me a look of sleepy surprise, and I said, "I'm Zora. I'm new."

"Bindira," she replied instinctively then, thinking better of it, added with a smile, "Bindi."

"Hello, Bindi," I said, as if with great relief. "Have you worked here long?"

"Just over a year," said the girl.

"Oh, good," I said. "So you know what you are doing."

"What section are you working in?"

I had gotten as much as I could out of Dahria about the internal workings of the government buildings, but she hadn't been very knowledgeable, and this was all going to be somewhat improvised.

"Government canteen," I said. "Preparation and service."

"Which?"

My first mistake.

"They hadn't decided when I was hired," I said. "Said they'd send me where I was required."

"You were sent by an agency?" said the girl called Bindi, taking a couple of shuffling steps closer to the door as the line inched forward.

"Weren't you?" I said, sensing another error.

She made a face and shook her head emphatically.

"Everyone is hired through central staffing," she said. "Security. They must be shorthanded."

"I think so," I agreed, seizing the possibility. "It's only a temporary position. More's the pity. It must be nice to know you have a secure occupation."

"It's all right," she said, with a noncommittal shrug. "They work us hard and the money is *kanti,* but it's safe and steady, so long as you keep your nose clean and don't upset the Gentlemen."

"The MPs?" I clarified.

She nodded.

"I'm in light housework," she said. "Dusting, cleaning, making up the fires in the winter. Keep myself to myself as much as I can. Less likely to get in trouble that way. One girl in service tipped a flagon of sack over one of the Gentlemen in his cabinet office last week! She was dismissed and on the street before they had cleaned it up."

"Expensive accident," I said, trying to sound shocked.

"Oh, I'm not sure it was an accident," she said, giving me a furtive look. "That particular Gentleman needed a cooling off. Scandalous, he is. But that's the way of things. He gets handy, and she loses her position. That's why I like dusting. Less chance of having to deal with anybody who might not like what I do. I had one once who followed me round, criticizing. It was all I could do not to hit him with my mop. But that's not how you get ahead, is it, walloping your betters?"

"It sounds like *betters* might be overstating the case," I said, eyeing the guard on the door. I wasn't entirely sure what he was going to demand of me.

She laughed at that.

"Overstating the case!" she repeated. "What an odd way you have! Quite fancy. No wonder they made an exception with your hiring."

I was clearly spending too much time with Dahria. Her attitude rubbing off on me would only lead to trouble.

"Blimey," I said, overcompensating. "This line don't 'alf move slow. What are they checking?"

"Work papers, of course," she said. "You not got any?"

"Said I'd get them at the end of the day," I invented.

"They won't let you in without papers," said Bindi wisely. "Security."

I had feared as much, but I had a second line of attack. I fished in my purse and drew out a creamy envelope inscribed with copperplate script.

"Cor!" said Bindi, impressed. "What's that, then?"

"My letter of reference," I said, like they were the crown jewels. Dahria had drafted it herself and signed it in the name of Lady Alice Welborne, the rich debutante who had been romantically entangled with the Grappoli ambassador. It was a risk, but Alice was such an intellectually flimsy creature, a girl with no interest in anything beyond fashionable parties and suave entertainments, that I thought the possibility of her being known by anyone in government was very remote. Her actually being there in person was impossible.

When it came to it, the guard just scowled at the letter, then thrust it back at me.

"Not work papers," he said.

Bindi shot me an anxious look.

"I was told they weren't ready," I said, playing up my Drowning accent, "but they would be processed in the course of my workday. Is that a problem?"

"Not unless you want to get paid," said the guard with a sour smile. "Won't make a farthing till your paperwork is filed. Still want in?"

"Yes, sir. Most certainly."

"Your funeral." He shrugged, turning his gaze to the stragglers who had hurriedly joined the back of the line and checking the clock on the wall pointedly. "One more minute and I'm closing this door, whether it costs you your position or not," he announced warningly to the girls. The latecomers blushed and looked down, bobbing little curtsies, though they shot each other gleeful looks once they were inside. One of them couldn't have been older than the sick girls I had seen the night before.

And still knows more about how this place works than you do . . .

Perhaps so, but I had a steeplejack's poise and a spy's nerves, I told myself. I thought of the neutral mask, but its calming effect was derailed by the image of Madame Nahreem telling me that she had once trained my sister Vestris.

Focus. Like you're on a high ledge. One false move—

I turned to Bindi.

"Which way is the canteen?" I said.

"Government or opposition?"

I cursed inwardly. It had never occurred to me that the ruling party would dine separately, and I made a mental note to berate Dahria for paying so little attention to what her brother did all day.

"Government," I decided. I didn't know what I was looking for yet, so where I began was of little consequence.

"Then I can show you," said Bindi. "The Gentlemen's Sitting Room is just down the hall, and that's my first stop. Got to pick up my supplies."

I had never seen such silent labor. The corridors rang with the feet of parlor maids, cleaners, footmen, and guards, but no one said a word. The place thrummed with an industry so careful and efficient that it felt military, and an odd part of me thrilled to it, as if I was—however illicitly—part of something bigger than myself, something grand. I kept my eyes front and matched Bindi's brisk but careful pace so as to not draw attention.

The rear halls were stone flagged and cool at this time, giving way to ceramic tile and eventually wood as we pushed deeper into the building. We had entered at street level, but the official entrance at the front was atop a flight of imposing stairs, so that the lobby and the primary meeting rooms and offices were all on the floor above the hive of servants where we were now. A labyrinth of back stairs and passageways allowed the staff to go into the upper rooms without cluttering the hallways or exposing the human machinery that kept the building functional. The difference between the two floors and the means by which one reached them was monumental. Bindi led me up one nondescript staircase that doglegged back on itself and out through a plain door into a broad and elaborately carved stone hallway carpeted in crimson and gold. It was still quiet at this hour, but as the day progressed, it would be a thoroughfare for the most powerful men in the land.

White men. Downstairs there were at least as many blacks and Lani as there were whites, but up here, where it counted—

"Through there," said Bindi. "Report to Mr. Shyloh, the chief steward. He'll give you your instructions. My lunch break is at eleven. If yours is in the same slot and you want some company, meet me at the Rainbow Courtyard. It's nice there. Benches and so forth."

"Thank you," I said.

"Good luck. And mind yourself. They'll be watching. First day and all."

I nodded, and she went into an adjoining room with glass-paneled doors, turning the handles as if she were afraid of waking a sleeping child inside.

I watched her go and thought quickly. Reporting to this Shyloh character as she had suggested would mean I would have to do some more creative lying just to stay in the building and could still be dismissed for not appearing in any employment records. Even without anyone spotting my subterfuge, I might find myself scrubbing kitchen counters or mopping floors under the watchful eye of a guard. All day. Learning nothing.

I walked in the direction Bindi had indicated to me, trying to appear as if I knew where I was going. I passed a side table with a tray and a half dozen used glasses, then picked it up and carried it, so that it looked like I was doing something. The heavy, sound-muffling door at the end of the hall led to the back of a kitchen complex with access to a series of discrete canteens and private dining rooms. The place bustled with activity. Men and women chopped vegetables and stirred pots, while maids brushed and scoured and mopped around them, all under the watchful eye of a suited white man with an austere look and iron-gray hair.

Mr. Shyloh, almost certainly.

As I came in, he consulted a clipboard and spoke to a middle-aged black woman, who promptly scuttled away as he surveyed the kitchen like some medieval lord inspecting his troops before battle. I turned my back on him quickly, set the tray down on the first available surface, and left by the door I had come in by, desperately trying to communicate a sense of knowing purpose.

"You!"

I hesitated, considered just walking away as if he weren't talking to me, but it was impossible.

"You, girl by the door!"

I turned slowly, shamefaced. The chief steward glared at me like an elderly lion.

"Come here, girl," he said.

I took a breath and crossed the kitchen toward him.

CHAPTER
10

"**WHAT DO YOU MEAN** by putting that there?" the steward said as soon as I was close enough that he didn't have to yell. A few glances shot in my direction then flicked just as quickly away for fear of getting involved. "I will not tolerate laziness. You don't do your job, then someone else has to do it for you, and wastes time they could be spending on their own tasks."

"Yes, sir," I said, sensing that this was a familiar speech.

"Used crockery and glassware go on that counter there by the sink," he said, extending a long, bony finger. "Move it, before I dock your wages."

"Yes, Mr. Shyloh. Sorry, sir."

I picked up the tray and walked in the direction he was pointing, but he peered at me and my heart sank.

"Who are you?" he demanded.

"Please you, sir, I'm new. Zora, sir."

"I didn't hire you," he said, flipping the pages of his clipboard. "Which section are you in?"

"Please you, sir," I said, inserting a little curtsy as I had seen the girls at the door give, "my paperwork was incomplete, so I was assigned to help Bindi in the Gentlemen's Sitting Room."

"Bindi?"

"Bindira," I said, wishing I knew the girl's last name.

"Assigned by whom?"

"Please you, sir, I didn't catch the lady's name."

"Lady? Mrs. Winterborne?"

I saw no guile in his face. He didn't look the type to use trickery when he could simply command.

"Yes, sir," I said. "I think that was it."

He sighed irritably. Mrs. Winterborne—whoever she was—had apparently crossed him before.

"Then you've brought this to the wrong kitchen," he snapped.

I made to pick it up again, but he waved me away and turned his attention back to his clipboard.

"Never mind that now, girl," he said. "Get back to work."

For the smallest part of a moment, I faltered, hardly daring to believe my luck, but when he fixed me with his stare and said simply, "Well?" the spell broke, and I left. I did not look back till I had retraced my steps all the way to the sitting room where I had left Bindi, who was now dusting earnestly.

She turned as the door closed behind me, and her eyes widened.

"What are you doing here?" she hissed. "You get lost?"

"They sent me to help you," I said. "Didn't have a space for me on the kitchen roster. Said I would get under their feet."

"Mr. Shyloh sent you to help *me?*"

"Not by name exactly," I conceded. "But your section, yeah. You couldn't use a hand?"

"Course I could!" she answered, grinning. "Never had a helper before. Give us a hand with this top rail. You're taller than me."

She flipped me the duster, and I got to work on the painted wooden molding that ran around the door frame.

A day of mindless, menial, and frequently backbreaking work began. I confess that as a steeplejack, and later as whatever I became under Willinghouse, I hadn't thought much about the sheer tedium and relentlessness of being a cleaner, but I learned a good deal about it over the next few hours. We moved from the Gentlemen's Sitting Room and dining hall, to a series of offices and committee rooms, dusting, sweeping, sponging and brushing upholstery, taking up rugs and carpets for beating, tidying desks, polishing wood and brass, and most vitally, mastering the art of discreetly vanishing the moment "someone important" arrived. It was exhausting, and though there was a kind of dull satisfaction in the completion of tasks that required more effort than skill, it felt like a maddening waste of my time.

Willinghouse was sitting in jail, the prime minister was dead, and I was emptying litter baskets and making the smallest of small talk with Bindi. Used to working alone, the girl seemed glad of the company, though a silence would descend upon her like a cage whenever someone else arrived. But the more we talked, the more it became clear she had nothing useful to tell me and I, increasingly frustrated, felt a pang of guilt for misleading the girl.

We took our lunch, purchased at the staff canteen, in the Rainbow Courtyard Bindi had mentioned. As she had said, it was a lovely spot, a kind of oasis in the formality of the Parliament House: small and enclosed on all sides by the tall brick walls and elaborate stone tracery of the windows. There were indeed benches, and young orange trees in planters. Their fruit hung like lamps on the boughs, making the whole place fresh and fragrant.

"I can't believe they are letting you work with me," she said, between mouthfuls of a surprisingly good egg salad sandwich. "I'm getting through everything twice as fast."

"Twice?" I said, with a doubtful smile.

"Well," she confessed. "Almost. I'll miss you tomorrow, that's for sure. I hope they don't have us lugging boxes and so forth around again."

"Boxes?"

"Oh yes. Every time there's a change in secretarial staff, crates of new belongings arrive, and who has to shift them? Us. Books, I understand, but paintings? Mirrors? I mean no disrespect, of course: doubtless they are doing worthy work for the city, but some of these chambers are better furnished than most people's houses! Statues and lamps and who knows what! This last time there was a tea chest so heavy it took two of the footmen to move it, carrying it up on their shoulders like a coffin!"

She shook her head in disbelief, and I made the sympathetic noises that seemed to be expected of me, until something about the word struck a chord in my memory.

Tea chest.

"When was this?" I asked.

"Two days ago."

"The day the prime minister was . . ."

"Yes," said Bindi, "but we're not supposed to talk about that."

"What time?"

She shrugged. "First thing," she said. "Shyloh—I mean, Mr. Shyloh—says, 'Get that thing upstairs!' and me and Mashari Tula start to pick it up and nearly break our spines. 'Oy!' says Mashari—to Mr. Shyloh! Honest to all the gods—'Oy!' she says. 'We can't shift this. What's in it? Lead bars?' And he comes over like he's about to give her a flick behind the ear, but as soon as he touches it, he sees what we mean and has to get two of the biggest lads from the cellar team, one of them was this big fella who looks like—"

"Where did they take it?" I inserted, already guessing the answer.

"What? Upstairs. Top floor gallery, up *four flights of stairs*, mind, and shoved it in the Roll Closet. Took them half an hour, and it wasn't even something the Gentlemen were going to use! I mean, had it been going to a cabinet office or something, I could have understood it. That would mean it was important. But to lug the thing around just to bung it in a cupboard no one ever goes in? Where's the sense in that?"

Where indeed?

SINCE BINDI WAS AHEAD of schedule, I asked her to walk with me, figuring that two maids, one of whom was known, would be less suspicious than a single one who wasn't. She could also get me a key to what I had taken to be a mere top-floor janitor's chamber.

"Do you have to sign for it, or ask someone?" I wondered aloud.

"Nah," she said, sounding remarkably like Tanish. "The Roll Closet is filed as Non Secure Space. Practically disused. That was why it was so weird, making those lads carry a chest all that way . . ."

There were still guards all over the building. One of them winked at us as we passed. Bindi giggled. I gave her a look, and she shrugged.

"What?" she said. "So long as they keep their hands to themselves, I don't mind it."

We went via another of the building's ubiquitous back stairs and found ourselves on the familiar circular gallery that ran around the base of the dome. There was no sentry on the closet door, though it was locked. Bindi opened it, then stood aside, watching me uneasily. I hadn't been able to come up with a good reason for why I wanted to see that tea chest, and her attitude to me had shifted. She was quieter now, more watchful, and though I don't think she was afraid of me, and she said nothing, she had started to wonder who I really was.

The tiny sitting room-cum-closet was as I had left it, with one important difference. The stack of dusty books that had been sitting on top of the tea chest was now lying in a scattered heap behind it, as if someone had raised the lid without bothering to move them first. The lid appeared to be latched, and I wondered how Bindi would react to my forcing the lock, but when I ran a finger around the edge of the lid, it came up easily. Indeed, the latch on the outside appeared to be strictly decorative, the lock having no internal mechanism.

The latch on the *inside* was another story entirely.

It was a simple thing, a pair of hooks easily folded down but strong enough to make opening the chest from the outside impossible without breaking it. They proved my hunch accurate. The box had been heavy because there had been someone inside it.

It was empty now, but as I shifted it in the low light from the doorway, I saw the smudges of footprints, a mingling of white and black powder. One of them looked like chalk and would, I was fairly sure, match the print I had seen on the dome outside. The other was soot from the chimney I had used to get out of here on my last visit, and that was almost as telling as the stack of books so carefully positioned on top of the tea chest when I had been here last and now thrown in disarray on the floor.

The person who had killed Benjamin Tavestock had gone in and out of the great chamber through a portal in the top of the dome. But he or she couldn't get on and off the roof in the middle of the day unseen by the crowds which surrounded the building. The killer had been carried into the building in a box, stowed up here until the moment was right, when he or she went up the chimney, onto the dome and down a rope, knife at the ready. When he was finished with the prime minister, moments before Willinghouse came in to find him, the killer had gone back up the rope to the roof, then down the chimney and back into the tea chest to wait out the alarm. That meant that he or she had still been in there when I took refuge from the guards in this very room and unwittingly used the same chimney through which the killer would escape after the sun—and the search—had gone down.

I considered the room. For all its dust and debris, it had once been quite grand: the fireplace had an elaborate stone surround, there was intricately carved chair, shoe, and crown molding all round the room, and the cupboards on the walls—one large, one very small—were finely inlaid.

"Why is this called the Roll Closet?" I asked.

Bindi shrugged.

"Used to be a proper office, before they gave it to the janitor, I mean. Seems odd to have a proper office up here, doesn't it?"

"It does," I said.

Roll Closet, I mused, wondering what sense of *roll* was meant.

Roll like a map or parchment? Or roll like roll call?

That sounded more like it, because that meant a record of votes. The office had been assigned to someone whose job it was to track votes in the house? But then why up here and not in the main chamber? You couldn't see or hear . . .

I considered the inlaid cabinets, and an idea struck me. I clambered over an abandoned desk piled with boxes and pulled the smaller cabinet door open.

But it wasn't a cabinet. It was a tiny window, no more than a foot across. It had no glass, but the hatch door opened easily and silently, and through it I could see the main chamber below, empty now, but with a stained patch of carpet where Benjamin Tavestock had lain. A hundred years ago perhaps, some governmental officer had sat up here to tally the score when the House voted. The hatch was too small for even a child to crawl through, but it provided the perfect vantage point from which one might watch a show of hands.

Or a murder.

An idea occurred to me. I closed the little hatch and opened the larger cabinet beside it.

It contained dozens of labeled rings.

Bell pulls.

So that was how the killer had ensured that Willinghouse had arrived just in time to take the blame for Tavestock's death.

"What?" said Bindi, considering me with mounting wariness as I set to scouring the inside of the long, coffin-like box and emerged with a card that had been slotted into a purpose-built bracket fastened to the timber.

I read it.

"Mr. Johannes Kepahler, Purveyor of Finest Luxorite, Crommerty Street."

Well now, I thought. *Isn't that interesting?*

"Who are you?" asked Bindi suddenly. "What are you looking for?"

I gave her a reassuring smile and said simply, "Justice."

WE HAD MADE IT all the way down to the back stairs and hallways of the lower level when we caught the sound of a confusion of raised voices, some of them clearly angry. We rounded the corner and found the previously deserted lobby packed with both serving staff and MPs, all under the watchful eye of some uneasy-looking dragoons. The suited parliamentarians were mainly shouting at each other, some dismissively gleeful, some outraged. The servants looked mainly baffled and worried, none more so than the daunting figure of Mr. Shyloh, who was trying to make himself heard above the hubbub.

"Return your aprons and any cleaning supplies or other equipment to the kitchen stores!" he was saying. "Black and Lani only. White staff, you can stay and work as usual."

I gave Bindi a quick, startled look to see if this was some routine procedure I had not been told about, but it was clear from her face that she was as confused as I was. Seeing that this was no time to be reticent or worried about being recognized, I shoved my way closer to the steward and said, "Mr. Shyloh? What is going on?"

He turned to me, but his eyes slid over my face, distracted and—I was certain—upset.

"All black and colored staff are to leave the building at once," he said. "New security protocol. Turn in anything you don't own in case you can't come back."

"Can't come back?" blurted Bindi, shocked. "I work here. I need this job."

"Not anymore you don't," said the chief steward darkly. "Or at least not until you see a post to that effect in the evening papers."

"What about our wages?" said Bindi. "We haven't been paid this week!"

"Termination has been backdated till the end of last month," said Shyloh. "I'm sorry. There's nothing I can do."

"How is this legal?" I demanded.

The word caught the chief steward as bleakly comic, and he gave me a hard look.

"When you can change the law," he remarked, "*legal* is whatever you want it to be."

"The government passed this?" I said, incredulous. "When?"

"This morning," he said, too dazed by the proceedings to wonder why he was bothering to bandy words with a maid he didn't even recognize. "Closed session of the newly formed coalition government on emergency security measures."

My blood ran cold.

"Coalition?" I managed.

"For the good of the city," said Shyloh, with undisguised bitterness. "A new coalition of the National and Heritage parties, under the leadership of our new prime minister, Norton Richter."

CHAPTER

11

THE EFFECT OF RICHTER'S new leadership was instantly apparent, and not only because the streets around Parliament were
packed with uniformed, and frequently tearful, black and Mahweni
serving staff wending their ways home. They moved like sleep-
walkers, like people stunned out of consciousness. It was also ru-
mored that the House was already debating making the redistricting
plans that Richter had pushed through effective immediately, so
that many of the local blacks and coloreds would have to leave their
current homes and take up residency in Nbeki, Morgessa, or on the
south bank of the river. How this was supposed to happen, where
they were all supposed to go, and how they would maintain their
current employment in the city, no one seemed to know.

Or care.

Not the men who were making this happen, at least. Not the
Heritage party faithful and those Nationals too scared to stand
against them. The world seemed suddenly hard, unfeeling, and de-
void of hope. Bindi wept openly in the street, not knowing where
to go, what to do, or how she was going to tell her aging mother
that she would be bringing home no wages this week or for the
foreseeable future. I put an arm around her awkwardly and told
her everything would be all right, something would come along,
a job, some kind of justice . . .

I didn't believe it. Not in that moment. I said it because she
needed someone to, but I didn't believe it, and I found that I suddenly missed Willinghouse's energy, his moral certainty more than

ever. I had no choice but to press on with my investigation, though my faith that it might help was itself a kind of pretense, something else I didn't really believe.

A demonstration—mostly black but with a few Lani and still fewer sympathetic whites sprinkled in—had begun in Ruetta Park. I could hear their chanting as I approached Crommerty Street and found that I was looking directly at the back of a makeshift podium where speakers with bullhorns were gathering to address the crowd. Among them, fiery and earnest, the obvious leader approving hastily painted signs and banners, was the young man Willinghouse had met with at the estate and Sureyna had identified as the activist Aaron Muhapi. Marching toward the protesters was a unit of fifty armed dragoons with fitted sword bayonets. I scanned their faces and, noticing that they were all white, wondered if some executive order akin to the banishing of the black and colored servants from Parliament had been applied to the military as well.

Things were moving very fast. If no one put the brakes on soon, who knew where we would be in a few weeks? Or what we would be.

I moved closer to see how big the crowd really was, and as I neared the rear of the podium, Muhapi happened to turn and see me. He was in midsentence to someone, but even as he continued to talk, his brow furrowed and his eyes held me. It seemed impossible that he had recognized me, having seen me only once before, and as a Lani maid, but he clearly had. He smiled in my direction and then, as his brain found where he had seen me, frowned again. He broke off his conversation and crossed the park toward me.

"You work for Willinghouse," he said. "Yes?"

I had to remind myself that by *work* he meant "serve tea," not "gather information for by hanging off rooftops."

"Yes, sir," I said.

"Aaron," he said, extending his hand.

"Anglet," I said on impulse. His was a face you wanted to trust. "You are making a speech?"

"Until they move me on, yes," he said, smiling. "Always I am making speeches. There seems," he went on with a self-deprecating smile, "so much to talk about."

I returned his smile.

"Is Mr. Willinghouse bearing up?" he asked.

"The police will not let me see him," I said.

"No, that does not surprise me, and I doubt I can help you there. My relationship with the police is . . . rocky. Should you find a way to communicate with him, let him know that I will do what I can to aid his release."

"You think him innocent?"

"Do you not?" said Muhapi.

"I know he is," I said. "And I believe he has been deliberately positioned to take the blame for someone else's crime."

"Then we agree perfectly. Come. Let me introduce you to my wife and my colleagues."

"I can't stay," I said. "I have . . . things I must do. I'm trying," I began, unsure why I needed him to understand things I normally kept to myself, "to help. In my own way."

"That is all we can do," he said. "Use what talents, what opportunities you have, and I will use mine."

"I wish I could stay to hear you speak," I said, meaning it.

"I feel sure," he said, giving me an appraising look and a satisfied nod, "that you are with us in spirit."

"I am."

"Good. Excuse me," he said, turning and seeing the expectant faces of the men and women at the podium, one of whom I recognized from his visit to the estate. "I must go, but I hope to speak to you again. Find me."

"I will," I said.

He hurried back, just as I heard his name announced through the bullhorn and a shout of appreciation came up from the crowd. Muhapi bounded up the steps onto the stage, embraced the man who had spoken his introduction, and took the bullhorn from him.

I really did have to go, had things to do, but I hesitated as he welcomed the audience and thanked the previous speakers. He paused, and the crowd fell silent with anticipation, and then he said, "Someone once told me that if a black man wants to scare a white person for a moment, all he has to do is draw a gun." He let the observation hang in the air, and a murmur of assent went through the crowd. "But when you do that, you confirm in the white man's eyes what you are and all you are capable of. He wants to think you are an animal. A barbarian. Because that makes him feel better about himself, his culture, and what his people have done to ours. Show him the gun, and you scare him, but you also prove in his head why he needs more and better guns, why he needs the police to be white, why he does not need to believe you when you say that you did not mean to point the gun at him or that the gun is not yours. When you have the gun, you are the black man he wants you to be, the black man he needs you to be, and you become his fantasy, his nightmare. And I say *become*. Because when he treats you this way and you respond with understandable rage, he is in your head, telling you what you are, so that you start to believe him.

"But this is a lie. What the white man wants, what he needs from you are his problems, not yours." The crowd stirred at this. I heard voices shouting, "Yes!" and I felt a stirring in my breast, a quickening of my heart, as if I was seeing something that had always been there, but never understood before. "You are your own person. The white man does not own you, does not define you, does not say what you are worth. You do that yourself. We do that. We celebrate what we are, our beauty, our intelligence, not just our strength and our righteous anger."

The crowd swelled beneath him, and Muhapi's voice grew in power and conviction so that they did not miss a word.

"So I say this: if you want to scare a white man for longer than it takes him to call the police, read a book. A book about yourself, the things you love, the things that make you feel, the things that make you want to live another day, the things that make you a complete and glorious person. This is what scares him! And if you want to terrify him, tell him that you didn't just read the book, you *wrote* it! Then join with your black brothers and sisters, your Lani brothers and sisters, and with all people—including those white men and women who will recognize you as equals—stand beside them, shoulder to shoulder as fellow human beings, and sing your uniqueness, your specialness, and your common humanity!"

The crowd roared. The sound of their voices ringing in my ears, I walked away, feeling that there might yet be hope for the world. But before I got completely out of earshot, I saw a shiny black carriage parked on the street corner. Its emblems had been draped with fabric, so that the coach might pass as a cab, but the harnesses on the horses were fine polished leather with brass hardware unlike any I had ever seen on a public vehicle. The window on one side was open, and a man was sitting motionless, leaning out to listen to Muhapi's speech. He wore a hat pulled down around his brows, trying to be inconspicuous perhaps, but his focus on the speaker had undermined the attempt. He was turned toward the square, his eyes were closed in rapt attention, and the soft light of the late afternoon fell full on his face.

It was, I was almost sure, Count Alfonse Marino, the Grappoli ambassador.

CROMMERTY STREET AND I were old friends, though I had not visited there except to cut through for months. It was among the wealthiest and most exclusive shopping districts in the city, and its core establishments all dealt in luxorite. I checked the address on the card I had taken from the tea chest in the Parliament House and swept my eyes over the brass numbers fixed above the lacquered doors. Kepahler's stood midway along, two doors down from Ansveld's, which had been central to what I now thought of as my first case for Willinghouse. The memory of that came flooding back now as I walked the well-maintained sets of the street in the low light and declining heat of the early evening. It seemed so long ago that I had been poking around here, relaying my information to then Sergeant Andrews, a timid Lani steeplejack unsure of her place in the world, but certain that it wasn't among the elegant customers of Crommerty Street . . .

So much had changed since then, but other things—things well outside my control—had not, and I was unsurprised to see the WHITES ONLY sign in Kepahler's window, stamped in metal as if to show the world how deeply the sentiment was held.

I considered my options. Involving Andrews was impractical and would show what little hand I had to whoever might be watching. I could send Dahria, but while she might once have found such a mission a diverting adventure, her mood now was so hopeless that it would feel insensitive even to ask. But not all the luxorite dealers on Crommerty Street had signs like Kepahler's in the window. I walked back down the road and glanced in Ans-veld's window, where a familiar middle-aged man sat behind the counter with a set of luxorite lenses around his head and a jeweler's loupe pressed to his eye. He was such a welcome sight that I tried the door before I had truly made the decision to go in.

Ansveld Jr. was a pink-faced man in his late thirties who was be-ginning to spread around the region just above his waist. He looked up at the tinkle of the bell, but it took a second for his eyes to refocus on me and another for recognition to dawn. His smile was positively radiant with joyful surprise.

"Well, well, well," he said, rising and extending a hand to greet me. "Anglet Sutonga. Woman of mystery. To what do I owe the pleasure?"

I shook his hand, feeling slightly overwhelmed by the genuine-ness of his pleasure. Even now, after all I had done in the last six months, I was unused to being welcome. Ansveld—I did not recall his first name, if I had ever been given it—was one of the few people outside Willinghouse's special sphere who had some idea of what I did, though he had proved the soul of discretion. The case I had worked had involved his father's death, a matter on which I had managed to shed some light, and he had been most appreciative.

"I wondered if you could tell me a little about one of your neigh-bors," I said.

"Absolutely," he said, positively thrilled by the possibility. "Is it inappropriate to inquire to what it pertains?"

"Let's say it's a matter of the very highest import," I said, match-ing his mood and giving him what I knew he wanted.

He clapped his hands together with glee like a child.

"Excellent," he said. "Which of my naughty rivals in trade has earned your scrutiny this time?"

"Johannes Kepahler," I said.

Ansveld's eyebrows floated to the top of his head, and he mused aloud, "Really? Kepahler, eh? That is most interesting. What do you want to know?"

"It's a simple matter, actually, and I would ask him myself but . . ."

He nodded sagely. "Not all my neighbors are quite as welcoming as I try to be here at Ansveld and Sons."

"Indeed. I have a box that seems to have belonged to him. A tea chest, to be precise. I'm trying to determine how it came to be where it is now."

Ansveld's enthusiasm flagged a little.

"A box?" he said.

"A tea chest. Yes."

"And you want to know . . ."

"If it's still his. If he loaned it to someone. Or threw it away . . ."

Ansveld drooped still further.

"I have reason to believe it was involved in a serious crime," I said.

"Really?" he said, perking up. "Well, now. Let me see how I can help."

"Are you close to Mr. Kepahler?"

Ansveld gave his head a decisive shake, like an orlek shrugging off flies.

"I'm afraid we move in somewhat different circles," he said. "My father knew him a little better, but Mr. Kepahler and I share neither friends nor beliefs, and that rather keeps us apart."

"You don't see eye to eye politically," I probed. My gut sense of Ansveld had always been that he was more liberal than his elevated social position might lead you to expect.

"Absolutely not," he said. "Though that will not help you learn anything further about this mysterious box."

"And you haven't seen such a box in the last week or so?" I tried. This was starting to feel futile.

Again, a defiant head shake. "Sorry."

"What about friends," I said, changing tack. "Does Mr. Kepahler have a lot of visitors?"

"Only customers," said Ansveld. "He does not live on-site, so what he does in his free time, I couldn't begin to guess."

"You don't like him," I said.

"Not especially," Ansveld confessed. "It may sound odd coming from one in my line of work, but the man is a snob and—if the two might be yoked together—a barbarian."

"In what way?"

"Little things. He is a man of wealth and privilege, but no education. His taste in luxorite, as in all things, is gaudy, unsophisticated. He comes in from time to time, to see what I have and to keep some kind of private score. He flouts his sales, brags about how cheaply he bought things and how expensively he sold them on. He mocked me once for reading. I had a book behind the counter. Oh, he thought that was most droll! 'Books are to be sold,' he said, like it was wisdom. Philosophy. Odious man."

I smiled with understanding, liking Ansveld better, even though I knew this was leading nowhere.

"He bought something from me a couple of weeks ago," he added. "Odd purchase. A piece of luxorite carved into the shape of a rabbit, couple of inches high. Pretty in its way. Would have been worth an absolute mint if it were new."

The light luxorite produces softens dramatically over time in ways that significantly reduce its value.

"Yellow?" I asked.

"Beyond that, I'm afraid. My father, when he thought we might still sell it, called it orange, but it was really a dull red. I can't imagine what Kepahler wanted with it. I overcharged him quite outrageously, but he didn't so much as quibble!" he said, his victorious grin turning into a disappointed shrug. "He must have had a particular collector in mind. It never appeared in his shop window."

"Is there a rag-and-bone man who comes through here?" I asked, redirecting the conversation. "Someone who might have given him a few pennies for the box?"

"Rag-and-bone man?" said Ansveld, smiling again. "On Crommerty Street? My dear young lady, they'd beat him off with sticks."

"Garbage collection, then?"

"Round the back, every Plainsday. But I wouldn't see what he had put out." He stopped abruptly, sitting up. "There he is now!" Ansveld exclaimed, pointing through the window to where a tall, lean man with a supercilious expression was crossing the street. "I'll call him in."

He was moving across the store to the door, driven by his dislike for the man, ignoring my sputtering doubts.

"Kepahler!" he called.

The tall man span on his heel and glared hawkishly at him.

"What do you want, man?" he said. "I have an appointment."

"You had a box," said Ansveld, his face hard, like he was squaring up to throw a punch. "What happened to it?"

"Box? What box?"

"A tea chest."

I had sidled toward the window to watch surreptitiously, but Kepahler saw me and gave me a derisive stare.

"Yes, I had a tea chest," he sniffed. "What of it? It's gone now."

"I was going to make you an offer for it," said Ansveld, improvising.

"For a tea chest? What the devil for, man?"

"Where is it now?"

"Donated it, with some other lesser items," he said grandly.

"To whom?'

"What business is it of yours? It was only a tea chest. You can buy a dozen just like it at any market."

"I wanted that one."

"Well, that's too bad, though I confess your disappointment gives me a little pleasure. I take still more," he added, giving me a pointed look, "in knowing that my donation went toward building a brighter future for Bar-Selehm."

On that note, clearly pleased with himself, he stalked away.

I frowned after him, disliking the man even though I had not understood his parting words.

"What did he mean?" I asked. "Building a brighter future. How?"

"A jab at your expense, I fear," said Ansveld, closing the door but still scowling after his rival. "They say brighter, but they mean whiter."

"They?" I said.

"The Heritage party," said Ansveld, giving me a dour look. "Kepahler is an active member. Organizes fund-raising drives and the like. I'm afraid he donated your tea chest to the organization led by that cretinous bully, Mr. Richter. Or rather—and it pains me to so abuse the title by attaching his name to it—*Prime Minister* Richter. Kepahler probably has Richter's ear, thanks to his connections to that old snake Mandel."

"Archibald Mandel?" I said. "The former secretary for trade and industry?"

"The very man," said Ansveld, bleakly. "He was, you might recall, an acquaintance of several here on Crommerty Street, including my occasionally misguided father, and was—I'm sure of it—up to his eyes in that business at the Red Fort. Managed to slip his snakish neck out of the noose at the last moment, though, did he not? Very much a fixture at Heritage party gatherings, these days, is Colonel Mandel. You want to watch out for him, Miss Sutonga. If he is in any way connected to what you are investigating, I think you should proceed with extreme caution."

CHAPTER
12

KEPAHLER'S LINK TO HERITAGE was proof of nothing, but it was a link, and one that made a kind of sense. It felt indirect, however, a vague and minimal step forward, and I found myself thinking both of Willinghouse languishing in his cell and Rahvey's children, steadily worsening while I inched my way through a mystery that had nothing to do with them. I needed to approach the matter from a new angle.

I found Tanish at the Evensteps Candle Factory, where the gang were finishing a day doing some routine repairs and painting, inside and out. The area smelled of the slight sourness of the river, but here that was almost masked by the warm, honey-sweet beeswax aroma of the candle vats.

"You feeling all right?" I asked him.

"Never better, why?"

"When was the last time you were in the Drowning?"

"Two, three weeks, why?"

"What about your schoolwork?"

Tanish had been sitting in on Bertha's classes. He rubbed his face and looked guiltily away.

"Tanish?" I pressed.

"Been busy," he said. "Work. Can't just keep walking out on the gang, can I? Need the money. And when's the likes of me going to need reading and math?"

"Is that *your* opinion, or Sarn's?"

He shrugged. "Both, maybe."

"Tanish!" I sighed. "You don't want to do this kind of work all your life. It's too dangerous, and it pays next to nothing."

"Like you'd know," he muttered, looking away.

"Meaning what?"

"We don't all have rich blokes who fancy us," he said. He regretted it immediately and looked chastened.

"Willinghouse doesn't *fancy* me," I said. "It's good work. Useful work. You know that more than anyone."

He glanced down, then nodded quickly.

"Rahvey's girls are sick," I said.

He looked up again, concern in his young face chasing away all the adolescent pretense. "What's wrong?"

"Not sure yet. Maybe malaria."

Tanish's lower jaw fell, but he said nothing. He didn't need to. Malaria was the city's biggest killer.

"Who's sick?" he managed.

"Not Kalla, but Jadary and Radesh. Aab too. Most of the girls in the Drowning."

"Should I visit?" he said.

"I think they'd like to see you, but don't get too close."

"Why is it just the girls?" he said.

I hadn't thought of that.

"Good question," I said. "I'm sure the doctor is wondering the same thing, but I'll ask when I see him. Thank you. And I have another job for you. Worth a few shillings if you can help me out."

He recovered something of his former nonchalance. "Yeah?" he said. "What do you need?"

"A cove called Kepahler," I said. "One of the luxorite merchants on Crommerty Street."

Tanish raised his eyebrows. This was higher-end stuff than he was used to from me.

"What about him?" he said.

"I want to know where he goes and who he talks to," I said. "I don't need a strict schedule, but if he is visiting places other than his shop and his house, I want to know about it. Deal?"

"Deal," he said. "This about Willinghouse?"

"Maybe," I said. "I'm not sure yet."

"They're saying—"

"Trial hasn't begun yet," I said, cutting him off. I didn't need to hear the gang's speculations on how long it would be before my employer was hanged as a traitor.

"Might not be a trial," he said.

"What do you mean?"

He flipped open the evening edition of the *Clarion,* pushed it toward me, and tapped the lead story with his finger.

MUHAPI DETAINED, said the headline. I read hurriedly, anxiously, but there wasn't much more to it than that. "After addressing a crowd in Ruetta Park this afternoon, Aaron Muhapi, black activist, was detained by security forces in accord with new provisions to the Laws and Ordinances of the City of Bar-Selehm passed by the coalition government. At the time of going to press, it was not clear how long Muhapi and similar revolutionary elements could be held."

I looked up, dazed by what felt like a shift in the earth beneath my feet.

"You want to watch yourself," said Tanish. "I don't think your powerful connections are going to help if you get in trouble. The opposite, in fact."

He looked worried, doubtful, so I nodded and managed a smile.

"I'll watch my step," I said.

"Right," he agreed quickly. "And, Ang?"

"What?"

"Your sister's kids. Aab, Radesh, Jadary, and the rest. They going to be all right?"

"They have a good doctor looking after them, so, yeah, I hope so."

He nodded, but the smile didn't quite reach his eyes, as if he knew we were both sidestepping what might yet be a very dark reality.

I WOULD HAVE GONE back to the Drowning even without the conversation with Tanish, but now the need to see my sister's children again burned hot within me. I didn't really want to spend money on the underground, not knowing if my income from Willinghouse would ever restart, but the lamplighters were already out, and I didn't fancy walking through the west end of town alone after dark. The city had an urgent, manic feel, as if things that had been simmering unsaid and unacted upon for years were now coming to the surface. Richter's ascent to the highest office in the land had unleashed something foul that had been too ashamed to show itself before. Now there was scrawl in chalk and paint all over the town: WHITES FIRST, LANI OUT, BLACKS GO HOME. And worse, of course. Much worse. I used to fear pickpockets and deviants, drunks, gangs, and traffickers above the snakes and spiders that were always around. I still did, but now I got to add the fine, upstanding white citizens who saw the rise of Heritage as a cue to stop pretending that blacks and coloreds were real people.

I was safer on the train. I counted the coins in my purse to be sure I could make it back and wondered how awkward it would be to ask Dahria for money.

Pretty awkward, I decided, *but I may have to swallow my pride and do it anyway.* It might even amuse her, which not much else had done lately. I smiled to myself, then remembered where I was going and why.

It was dark by the time I reached the Drowning. That slowed

me down, since there were no street lamps out there, and I didn't want to step on anything lethal. Inside the first makeshift huts and tents, a ring-tailed genet went skittering over a corrugated iron roof, the sound so loud and echoing that for a moment I thought it was something much larger, like a baboon or even a weancat.

The sick tent was dark and quiet. Rahvey came to meet me, looking flustered.

"Where's the doctor?" I asked.

"He went for more medicine."

"Quinine?" I said. "Is it helping?"

She shook her head, and I saw something in her face that was more than grief and worry. She looked gray and hollow.

"You're sick," I said.

"It's nothing," she said. "I have to stay with the girls."

"Why is it just girls?" I asked, remembering Tanish's remark.

She scowled and shook her head, as if I were being willfully irrelevant.

"It just is. Girls are weaker, I suppose," she said.

"Not in my experience," I remarked. "Men just like you to think that."

"Don't start," she said.

"No," I replied. "I'm sorry. I just . . . The boys don't attend Bertha's classes, right?"

"No. They work. Why? You think they caught something off her?"

I gave her a quick look, and it was her turn to look abashed.

"I didn't mean . . ." she began, but abandoned the thought, looking suddenly weary and desperately sad.

"The classes still happen down by the river, yes?" I said.

"You think it's something they caught down there? Something in the water, perhaps?"

"Perhaps," I said. "I don't know."

"No," she said, not unkindly. "No one does. But it is getting worse. Three more children today, and one of the women who has been bringing them food."

"Can I see them?"

"The doctor said we shouldn't let anyone go in who doesn't need to be there. Not till he knows how you catch it."

I hung my head, eyes squeezed shut, feeling defeated.

"I'm sorry," I said.

"Not your fault."

I wasn't sure she really thought that. If Bertha or the classes were at the heart of this, then maybe it *was* my fault. Those had been my idea. I had set them up to try and improve the girls' chances later in life.

Nicely done, I thought, bitterly.

"Your friend is here to see you," she said. "I told him to wait at the temple. You know, for safety."

"Tanish?"

"No, the Mahweni."

"*Mnenga?*" I said, astonished. "He's here?"

"Came for you. A few of them. Not sure it's good, having them around the Drowning. Not what with everything that's happening in the city. People might not understand."

She avoided my eyes, her tone caught between shame and defiance.

"I'll find him," I said, my heart a little lighter at the prospect. "I'll come back soon."

"I know," she said. "What they are saying about Willinghouse—"

"It's not true," I said.

"No. I thought not. Will that matter?"

I wanted to sweep the question away with something certain about truth and justice, but the words stuck in my throat.

"I don't know," I said.

She nodded thoughtfully, as if this was no more than she had suspected. "Funny," she said, with a bleak smile. "You wouldn't know it to look at him, but I suppose he really is a Lani after all."

With that she returned to the heart of the tent where one of the little bodies was retching into a bowl in the dark.

I FOUND MNENGA IN exactly the spot I had known he would be, the place only yards from Papa's memorial stone, where I had first met him. He was not alone, but he embraced me as if he were, beaming and whispering his pleasure at seeing me as I clung to him, tears running down my face. I wasn't sure why I was weeping. I suppose I felt safe with him, even with others watching warily, and all the feelings I had been holding back, the rising sense of failure and calamity burst out as soon as he folded me in his arms.

I had expected the others to be his herder brothers, but they were not, and though it was too late for self-consciousness, I stepped away from him with a sense of having stumbled into something wholly unexpected. There were two older women and another man, all in their sixties; a striking, high-cheekboned woman in her late twenties; and a boy about my own age. They were all black and wore the woven colorful skirts of the Unassimilated Tribes with rich collars, belts, and necklaces of beads. The women were bare-breasted and had their hair piled in narrow basket-weave towers on their heads. The young man carried a hide shield and long assegai spear, while Mnenga himself had three of the shorter kind they called *iklwa*. They regarded me with frank interest but absolute composure and dignity, so that I was embarrassed, as if I had inadvertently stepped into the presence of royalty. Perhaps I had.

They were sitting formally and incongruously on what I first took to be a pair of long couches, but then saw were trunks not unlike the tea chest by which the assassin had been smuggled into the Parliament House. Behind them, steaming softly, were a pair of oxen with horns a yard or more across, and the cart they pulled. This was not simply a visit from a friend who missed me. This was a delegation.

"These are from my village," he said, indicating two of the three elders and rattling off their names so quickly that I did not catch them, "and these are from another village. She is a kind of princess," he said, nodding to the younger woman.

"And the young man?" I asked.

"He is a guard. Not important," said Mnenga, promptly grinning and translating for the others. The boy laughed, but the others' smiles were small, restrained. "He is my cousin."

"What are you doing here?" I asked.

"We came to talk. To many people. But we wanted to see you first."

"Why me?"

"We have something to show you."

He turned and spoke to the others in his own language, and they rose and led me in sad and silent procession to the oxcart where another long box lay. Between them, they lifted it down, saying nothing, their manner and dress lending the whole a stately and formal quality that unnerved me a little. I gave Mnenga a sharp look.

"What is it?" I asked, not sure that I wanted to see inside.

"We found him in the mountains."

"Him?" I said. "Who?"

The other man had worked the buckles free of the straps that held the box closed, and now he raised the long lid. The man inside was white, casually but respectably suited, and in his forties. His body had been decked with wildflowers, presumably by them.

I did not know him. He was dead, and there was a small rusty stain in the center of his breast where the shirt had a straight cut perhaps an inch across.

"Shot?" I asked.

"I do not think so," said Mnenga. "Look."

He made a gesture, as if asking the corpse for permission, and then unfastened the two shirt buttons closest to the stain. The blood was crusted around a slit-like hole that matched the cut in the shirt. It was thicker than a conventional knife blade, and the dark discoloration around it looked like a bruise. There was no scorching, no powder burns, and no cauterization, such as might have been caused by a hot bullet.

"A spear?" I asked, nodding toward the one he carried.

He shook his head fervently, and I began to guess why they had come to me. They did not want to be blamed for a white man's death.

"Spear tip is wider," he said, knowing what I was thinking.

I nodded, then turned the hands. The fingertips of the right were blackened with something like ink, and the palms had no calluses.

A professional man, then, not a laborer or farmer. But not a businessman or politician either, judging by the suit. His shoes were solidly made but not designed for bush walking, and their soles were badly worn. A city man, but not a rich one. I touched his cold cheek and felt stubble: not beard, exactly, but what a man gets when he does not shave for several days.

"Where did you find him?" I asked.

"Near my village," he said. "If we had not found him, the hyenas would have taken him."

I nodded, trying to look grateful but wondering why this was my problem. I had enough to think about.

"My people are afraid of your police," he said.

"Yes," I said. "I know. Did he have anything with him? A bag? Suitcase?"

Mnenga shook his head.

"That makes no sense," I muttered, knowing that I was being sucked into the mystery of the thing. "A city bloke out in the brush with no luggage? Did you check his pockets?"

"Yes. Nothing," said Mnenga, apologetic. They were all watching me earnestly as if I was about to do something remarkable that would somehow make this all right.

"That means robbery, or suicide," I said. "No weapon found with him, though, so robbery. No signs of wear on his trousers that suggest he was riding, and again the shoes would be wrong. So he was out in the bush on foot. Who would . . ."

I didn't finish the sentence. Instead I opened the flap of his jacket and felt inside, first one side, then the other. The interior pockets were, as Mnenga said, empty, but I felt the glossy fabric of the lining, working around the back and trying to ignore the face of the dead man.

"Lift him," I said.

Mnenga and the young man half rolled the corpse, and I quickly smoothed my hands over the inside of the jacket till I found the bulge I was looking for. I drew my knife and slit the silky material just enough to peel it back and produce a slim packet sown into the lining of the jacket for emergencies. I opened it and found what I had expected: a few pound notes, a single gold sovereign, and a carefully folded paper. It was the personal credentials of a man identified as Arthur Besland, and the top of the paper was embossed with a familiar masthead, which read *Bar-Selehm Standard*.

I had found Sureyna's missing foreign correspondent.

CHAPTER

13

THE NEXT MORNING, I went to see Andrews at the police station by myself. Mnenga's companions clearly did not wish to enter the city, which came as something of a relief. I did not want to have to explain to the women that they would have to cover up or be arrested for indecency. Even in the Drowning, people would stare. I told them that a police ambulance would come to take the body to the morgue and then I left them. I suspected that they would stand watch over the coffin until the police were in sight, but that the officers would find the body of Arthur Besland alone.

I did not speak to the inspector, but left a note for him saying exactly where to go and included the journalist's papers. That task complete, I went on foot via Javisha to Szenga Square and the ornamented facade of the *Standard*'s offices. I met Sureyna in the lobby, loaded down, with her reticule over her shoulder so she could manhandle a large cardboard box of books and papers, writing utensils, and other miscellaneous bits and pieces. Her face already matched my mood. I had been thinking all the way over how to say it, worrying my approach, since I did not know how well my friend had known the dead man, but now that it came to it, I could think of nothing to present but the unvarnished truth.

"Your missing correspondent was Arthur Besland?" I said.

"One of them, yes. What do you mean was?"

"I'm sorry, Sureyna. He's dead. Mahweni from near Mnenga's village brought his body to the city. By now it will be on its way to the morgue. His belongings were not with him, but this money was sewn into his jacket. I assume it belongs to the paper."

I waited for her to set her box down slowly, and handed it to her.

"How did he die?" she asked dreamily. She did not look like she was going to weep, but she seemed off-balance.

"I'm not sure. Stabbed, I think. He was out in the bush, but he was not killed by an animal. I'm sorry."

I'm not good at consolation. Other people's sorrow makes me awkward. Sureyna nodded vaguely.

"Were you good friends?" I tried.

She shook her head. "I only met him a few times. I don't think he was pleased that the *Standard* hired me as a reporter at first, but he complimented me on the Elitus story. But no. He was always away. A good reporter. I had hoped he might be a mentor to me one day, but I suppose . . ."

Her voice trailed off, and she looked suddenly lost.

"I'm sorry," I said again, meaning it. "We'll get to the bottom of it. You'll be able to write a tribute article to him, an obituary or . . ." She was still shaking her head. "What?" I said, frowning at the box she had been carrying. "Sureyna? What's going on?"

"You saw who Richter appointed to take over the newly created Security Department?" she said.

"No. Who?"

"Colonel Archibald Mandel," she said in a leaden tone, laying it all out as if every word had significance, all of it bad, "former secretary of trade and industry under the Nationals and late of the Glorious Third Infantry Regiment."

That wasn't just her usual perfect recall that made her sound like a newspaper report. She didn't like him, and with good reason, though neither of us had met him in person. Mandel was the man Ansveld had warned me about, the man who had run the Red Fort, or rather turned a blind eye to what Major Gritt did in his name, and he had an ugly reputation among those he did not consider his equals. I knew he had been connected to Richter, both by racial politics and industry connections: Richter and his secretary, Saunders, must have dealt with him all the time, given his background in the steel industry.

I remembered the man from a picture I had seen the day I met Emtezu: Mandel was an austere—if slightly absurd—military man with a handlebar mustache and a monocle. He had extricated himself from the business over the faux luxorite cave when their plans had gone awry, leaving his co-conspirators—including Vestris—to take the blame while he went into quiet retirement.

"But Mandel was in disgrace after the Red Fort business!" I said. "He resigned from politics over his shares in Grappoli munitions factories."

"Well, he's back," said Sureyna. "I'd say it was less disgrace than public embarrassment. Apparently the Nationals think he's paid his debt and is, as they put it, *what the times require,* which is their usual way of justifying ethical violations. Given his military background and knowledge of government, he was, apparently, an easy pick for this new security division the Heritage leaders have dreamed up. I suspect his former National party cronies are just glad to see a familiar face in Richter's inner circle. They go along with it all, but they're afraid of him and his goose-stepping supporters."

"What does 'head of security' even mean? We have police, army. Why do we need another security force?"

"Not clear yet," said Sureyna, "but it has people scared. Richter says it's a way to unite the existing branches, but it sounds more like a way for the prime minister's office to control what the police and military do more directly, and it allows the creation of a civilian militia, whatever that is. I've heard several generals are unhappy about it, and there's a group of police inspectors who have written a letter of protest to the commissioner, but that won't make any difference."

"Willinghouse said this would happen," I said. "That Mandel would make a return to politics. But what does this have to do with you?"

"The colonel remembers me," she said, looking utterly forlorn. "My writing, I mean. I don't know what he said, or how much it's part of a more general shift as the *Standard* faces a new political reality, but . . ." She shrugged sadly, a gesture that made her look younger than she was. "The paper doesn't feel that they can maintain the appearance of objective political journalism with"—and here she was quoting—"*a staff whose members belong to those groups that are most conspicuously hostile to the present administration.*"

"What does that mean?" I demanded.

She sighed.

"I've been fired."

CHAPTER

14

I MADE A HALF move toward her, but she, knowing how easily I was embarrassed by hugging and the like, shook her head, and when I stood there trying to find the words, she cut me off saying, "I know. But I'm more angry than sad, and that makes it easier."

"So what will you do now?" I asked, finding my voice again.

"The *Standard* said I could have my old job back, selling papers on the street," said Sureyna. I had taken the cardboard box from her, and she was walking doggedly with her reticule at her side, her eyes fixed on the road ahead.

"Will you take it?"

She snorted. "Never," she said. "Unless I can't find anything else."

She shot me a wan smile, and I returned it. Principled defiance is expensive when you have no food.

"Any ideas?" I said.

"One. This."

She nodded to a run-down-looking block of little shops frequented by the more affluent city blacks, and at a haberdasher's in particular. I gave her a quizzical look, but she kept walking, jutting her chin toward the second story where a pair of posters were hung in the narrow windows. They read simply THE CITIZEN.

"Not exactly the *Standard*'s status," she said, "but a good circulation among my people."

The Citizen was the free newsletter of Bar-Selehm's assimilated Mahweni.

"Are they hiring?" I asked.

Sureyna shook her head.

"So why are we—" I began.

She unfastened her tied-back hair and teased it into shape. It made her look quite different.

"They haven't met me yet," she said.

"Well," I conceded, "I'm betting *The Citizen* doesn't have many journalists who worked at the *Standard*."

"You'd be surprised," she said. "Some of my colleagues—*former* colleagues, I should say—used to ghost for *The Citizen*. It's a decent paper. You coming in?"

I considered the shop with its all black clientele.

"You think I'm welcome?" I said.

"I think you're confusing us with the other blokes," she said, grinning as she pushed the door open.

I blundered after her, levering my way through the door with the corner of the box, and wondering, given the state of things in Parliament, what the future of *The Citizen* looked like. Pretty bleak, I would have thought. And short.

The paper's offices might welcome me, but the paper itself had never had much to say about the Lani population. I had seen it rarely, and then mainly used to wrap fish down the Branmoor Steps chippy. The Seventh Street boys, who rarely had any time for or grasp of politics, had viewed it with suspicion, and had relied on the *Clarion* for their news. *The Citizen* always seemed to lead with accounts of demonstrations and detentions, though it was also a headquarters for social programs created primarily for the city's blacks. The latest headlines trumpeted the arrest of Aaron Muhapi after a peaceful protest. I put Sureyna's box down and considered the portrait of Muhapi's earnest and intelligent face in the middle of the front page as Sureyna introduced herself to the staff.

There were three of them, two women and a man, all in their

thirties or thereabouts. They had all looked up with curiosity verging on alarm when we came in, but had relaxed as soon as they saw who we were. Or who we weren't. One of the women wore heavy glasses on a leather thong around her neck. The other wore a yellow shirt that set off the darkness of her skin. She was looking at Sureyna and her overstuffed bag of papers doubtfully.

"So," said Sureyna, matter-of-factly. "My name is Sureyna Nbotti, and until about an hour ago, I was a journalist at the *Bar-Selehm Standard*. Now I work for you."

I stared at her. The eyebrows of the woman in yellow crept low on her face in puzzlement, while the other woman's did the opposite.

"Have you spoken to someone at the newspaper about employment?" said the man, as if he might have missed a crucial piece of information.

"I haven't," Sureyna said. "That's what I'm doing now. And I'd say that the *newspaper* could use me." She considered the current issue, a roughly formatted single sheet of paper folded in half, nothing like as professional as the *Standard*.

The woman in yellow, affronted at the implication, said, "I'm afraid we have no openings in the writing department at this time. You are welcome to leave your contact information and some samples of your work—"

"Which of you is *the writing department*?" said Sureyna. The woman in glasses began to raise her hand slowly, but Sureyna pressed on before she could say anything. "I just got fired not because of what I can or can't do, but because the paper I worked for doesn't want to look too black in case people don't take them seriously. That means you have a one-time offer. Hire me, and I'll produce some samples of my work right now, and you won't need ink, because I'm gonna write in fire. You hear what I'm saying? I'm going to write, and my words will be like an earthquake that will shake the government to its foundations. I'm going to write so you won't even have to read it. You can just hold the paper up to your head, and you'll hear it singing."

Sureyna was nothing like my height, and standing in front of the newspaper staff, she looked little more than a child, but her eyes were shining, and her arms and fists were locked with such force that they trembled in the loaded silence that followed her speech.

"Sounds like you should give that girl a job," said a familiar voice from the stairwell behind us.

Everyone turned in that direction and saw two black men, one supporting the other, who was limping badly and had one eye swollen shut. It was Aaron Muhapi.

The newspaper staff leapt to their feet to help him as the aide from the Willinghouse estate meeting got him up the last of the steps.

"What did they do to you this time?" said the woman in yellow.

"Oh, you know," said Muhapi, smiling hollowly. "They took offense to some of the things I said."

"Bastards," said the man.

"It's not so bad," said Muhapi, "though I'd be lying if I said I wasn't surprised."

"Richter has given the police new powers," said the aide to the room in general. "Nothing official, of course, but the word has gotten through. No one is going to look too closely at what happens to a black activist."

"You made a speech!" exclaimed the woman in yellow.

"I suppose that was enough," said Muhapi. "Now, if you wouldn't mind, I'd really like to sit down." A chair was moved out into the room for him, and he settled into it heavily, wincing. "That's good," he said. "That's what I needed. So I see *The Citizen* is expanding its staff? That's excellent too." He was putting a brave face on it, trying to redirect the conversation off him, but he was clearly in pain.

"We don't have the funds to hire a new—" the woman in yellow began.

"How much do you need?" I said.

"You think you can supply enough to pay a reporter?" the woman shot back with undisguised skepticism.

"Miss Anglet is a woman of resource," said Muhapi.

"You know these people?" said the woman in yellow, taken aback.

"I know everyone," said Muhapi, grinning. "Now, I'm afraid the police broke my spectacles, so I'm going to need to get some new ones. Could someone run down to Vetch Street and tell Mr. Saltzberg that his best customer needs his services again?"

I watched them, the way they deferred to him, the concern in their faces.

"What will you do now?" I said.

"I am hoping that I can get some new glasses," he said, with a slight twinkle. "But . . . that is not what you meant. I will keep doing what I always do. Speak. Ask questions. I have been promoting an idea for a small university for black and colored students where they can study their cultural history and literature so that they don't always feel pushed to the side of their own lives."

"I don't think now is the time," said the aide. He said it to Muhapi, but he seemed to consult with the women with his eyes, as if this was something they had discussed before. "They took you off the street. They beat you!"

"This is how the game is played," said Muhapi wearily. "They have taken their turn, and now it is mine."

"The rules are changing, Aaron," said the aide. "Richter has changed them."

Muhapi gave him a long look, then smiled at me and Sureyna.

"Peter worries too much," he said.

"So does your wife. And your son," said the aide.

Muhapi's look was longer this time as though a blow had landed and taken some of the fight out of him, though he recovered soon enough. He nodded. "Yes," he said, "and for my part, I would like to make the world they live in a little better. A little fairer. I do not think that is too much to ask or to risk for."

"They will beat you," said Peter, and there was more than worry in his face. There was devotion. Love.

"Better that than I sit to the side of their world smiling," said Muhapi, "telling them everything is all right and that our hopes, our lives do not matter. I will not be some sideshow entertainer, some *minstrel* for their amusement, and I will not be silent. I cannot be."

That last he said almost sadly; he had no choice in the matter, and it pained him.

"Now," he said. "About those spectacles."

I LEFT SUREYNA AT the *Citizen* offices to discuss the terms of her employment further and returned to Grand Parade outside Parliament, gazing up at the dome and thinking about Willinghouse. Since he had been arrested, we had heard nothing from him, except what the papers hinted about the matter coming to a hasty trial. I didn't like the sound of that. Richter's arm had grown remarkably long since his installment in the prime minister's office, and each new edition of the *Standard* contained developments that would have been shocking only a few days ago.

Perhaps they still were. It was unclear to me what the whites in the city thought of the new regime, though many had cheered Richter and his Heritage party on. Now? I wasn't sure. I thought all but his most ardent supporters had felt a tremor of anxiety at how quickly he had seized control and the firmness of his grip thereafter, but what did I know?

I wandered toward Winckley Street where the boy who had

taken Sureyna's old job was selling papers to a fevered crowd and, on impulse, bought one. The headlines seemed to grow shriller by the day, and tonight's was no exception.

PM EXPANDS SECURITY POWERS. CANCELS ELECTION.

I stopped where I was and read hungrily, my stomach knotted.

> In an unprecedented move, Prime Minister Norton Richter today announced that, given the heightened tensions in the city, the upcoming general election would be postponed for a minimum of six months. During this time, according to Jebediah Saunders, Mr. Richter's private secretary, the police and military would have significantly greater freedom and authority to act in the best interests and preservation of the city.

I stared dazedly across the street to where a ragged Lani boy was pasting flyers for the traveling circus I had seen advertised earlier, and I wondered once more what was happening and how we could possibly slow it down. Bar-Selehm was becoming a circus itself, juggling truth and justice from hand to hand with clowns on every corner—comic and somehow menacing—while our politicians engaged in some kind of high-wire act as the rest of us looked on dumbly . . .

High-wire act.

My brain snagged on the phrase like driftwood in reeds. I stared at the poster, its garish text and its images of clowns, elephants, and vaulting gymnasts. What had Tanish said about the barefoot climber? It wasn't just expert, it was *show-offy*. Theatrical. It wasn't what a steeplejack would do, scaling a rope with no boots on and a knife between his teeth. No chance.

But it was just what a circus performer would do. I crossed the street, dashing recklessly between a pair of dragoons on orleks and a horse-drawn fly whose driver yelled at me. I tore one of the posters from the Lani boy's hands.

"Oy!" he said. "What's your game?"

I ignored him, focusing on the all-important text.

One Week Only!
Messrs. Xeranti and Guests
Exotic and Death-Defying
World-Famous
Traveling
CIRCUS!

Nbeki Park.

"You never seen a circus before?" said the boy derisively. "Where've you been?"

I flipped him a farthing, which he caught expertly, then I walked toward the town house, my mind racing.

CHAPTER

15

THE COMPLEX OF TENTS and sideshow wagons that was the Xeranti traveling circus had been set up in a dusty, poorly maintained park in Nbeki, a low-rent district nestled by the river just inside the city's western wall. It was home to those laborers and factory workers who made just enough to stay out of the south side shanties, but not enough to live in Morgessa or Thornhill, a hardscrabble place, but one that looked after its own, black and white. It was one of the few places in the city where both races—with a scattering of Lani thrown in—lived side by side in compact row houses with relatively little friction. Though the park was a frequent staging ground for demonstrations and political rallies, it wasn't uncommon to see all the city's racial populations standing and listening together, united by the thing they had most in common: poverty.

That said, should all the new segregation laws pass, Nbeki would likely find itself packed with blacks forced to move away from the center and east of the city outside Old Town. The outnumbered whites might well abandon their old class allegiances with their Mahweni neighbors and—if they had the money—move into the leafier and more desirable residences Richter's law had opened up to them. Willinghouse had held forth on the subject many times. "Division and conquest along lines of race instead of income," he called it. "The most insidious of the Heritage party's stratagems."

For now it retained its patchwork culture. Trim northern churches with steeples side by side with the blue minarets of

Bashtara Koresh, ancient Mahweni ancestral shrines, and vibrant Lani temples. One store sold pickled fish, sheep cheese, and white bread, while the one beside it sold five different kinds of rice and would grind fresh spices while you waited. The one next to that was a Baswan butcher, its hooks hanging with goat and antelope flesh, the owner sitting cross-legged on a cushion, puffing on a water pipe. During the day, the narrow, cobbled streets were quiet, but when the factories let out, Nbeki turned into a place of music and food and raucous conversation. It was, I supposed, as good a place for a circus as any.

Dahria was less convinced.

We took the underground to Great Orphan Street via Atembe at six o'clock, riding in a first-class carriage, perhaps to maintain a sense of decency for as long as possible. I wore the maid's outfit I had patched together at the town house, and Dahria had opted—at my insistence—for the plainest and most ordinary frock she possessed. We had enough on our plate without her announcing her wealth to every footpad in the borough. She had a twin-shot pistol in her purse, though I had told her it should stay there unless her life was in real jeopardy.

"I am going to a circus in Nbeki with a steeplejack," she muttered dryly. "I don't have enough bullets."

"Best not shoot them, then," I replied.

She had insisted upon coming and then complained about every detail of the trip. She had spent much of the day trying to get an audience with either her brother or with the police commissioner who had undertaken the investigation of the prime minister's murder himself, but she had been shut out at every turn. As a society lady, she was accustomed to getting what she wanted, and if wealth and status didn't solve matters to her liking, her brother's name usually did. It was one of the painful ironies of her present situation that that particular trump card made it categorically certain that she would not get her wishes. In other circumstances, I might have thought the lesson useful.

As it was, I pitied her, not just for her anxiety, but for her guilt. I saw our earlier conversation in her face every time she looked at me, the shame that she had doubted her brother's political motives. She didn't say it, but I felt it keenly: a sense that—at least in her mind—she had, by indulging her familiar and comfortable cynicism, misjudged Willinghouse, betrayed him, even. It was a fact, of course, that nothing that had happened had actually proved her skepticism wrong, but her brother's being laid low, abandoned by his party—who seemed to want nothing to do with him in case he turned out to be guilty—had jolted her out of her former complacency. The brother whose principles and high-mindedness she had always mocked had, in falling from his public pedestal, somehow stepped up to another in her heart.

None of this made her any happier about attending "a low entertainment in some squalid tent surrounded by pickpockets, cutthroats, and foreigners." Or so she said. In fact, in any other circumstance, I think she would have secretly delighted in this taboo excursion far from the fashionable emporia, coffeehouses, and music rooms of Bar-Selehm's society districts.

The park was located between the complex of alleys known as the Sparrow Islands and the shambles, which stank of animal blood day and night all through the summer. It was usually a brown, grassless area with wilting, water-starved trees, which turned to ankle-deep mud after a downpour, a place of bonfires and refuse, jackals and carrion birds. Homeless people slept under the trees, their mangy dogs on ropes, at least until the coppers came and moved them on.

Not now. Nbeki Park was transformed. We could hear it a block away—rolling music from a crazed hurdy-gurdy or pipe organ, barkers, their voices amplified by bullhorns, bells, cymbals, and drums, plus the cheers and laughter of a great crowd of people, all rising above the drone of steam engines. The area was wreathed in fragrant smoke like the incense that pencils the air around a temple, and among the scents of sandalwood and jasmine hovered the mouthwatering tang of roasted meat. Closer, you could taste the edge of the coal smoke and metal in the air, the slightly fetid aroma of bodies, animal droppings, and rotten fruit, which the incense couldn't mask completely. It smelled of life and danger, of strange, exotic things that would thrill and delight and horrify. I caught Dahria's eye, and a half smile flickered around her lips before being hastily doused, though she couldn't hide the spark in her eyes.

The circus had come into town by train and had, according to what Sureyna had told me earlier that afternoon, taken two days to set up. There were half a dozen tents on each side of the square and twice as many caravans, all hung with glass and ribbon and bells. Many of these looked like the living quarters of the workers and their families. Others sold food, drink, and trinkets, while some hosted games of skill and chance, sideshows, fortune-tellers, snake charmers, and miniature zoos, all fronted by outlandishly dressed hawkers advertising the strangeness and rarity of their offerings. It was like stepping into another country, romantic and a little bit frightening. All around, brightly colored signs directed us to the "Big Top," the garish red and gold tent in the center, which dwarfed all the other structures in scale and magnificence.

It was round, near enough, and impossible to ignore. I had scanned the various sideshows with their magic tricks, fire breathers, and puppet shows, but had seen nothing that involved climbing. With a thrill of foreboding, we paid a handful of pennies and went inside.

"Colored section over there," said the white ticket boy to me.

I hesitated. There were provisions in the theaters, orchestra, and opera house for nonwhite servants to sit with their masters and mistresses, but in lower entertainment, no exceptions were made to city ordinances. The music halls went so far as to have "blacks only" shows, but that could also get them into trouble for, if you can believe it, *discrimination*. "Whites only" shows had no such problems.

"She's with me," said Dahria with an imperial stare, so that the boy faltered.

"Not up to me," he managed. "It's the law, ain't it?"

"I believe the matter is at the discretion of the individual venue," said Dahria.

"There you are, then," said the boy, thinking this let him off the hook.

"Exactly. So she will be sitting with me."

Realizing this forced him to take responsibility for defying her, the boy looked wildly around for someone who outranked him. When no one presented themselves and Dahria continued to stare in that way of hers that could make marble statues want to crawl away, he sputtered, "Well, all right. But if anyone complains, she's out."

"We will meet that eventuality should it arise," Dahria replied, not giving an inch. She gave me a half look, but her next words were clearly meant for him. "How the lower orders love to vaunt their status! I wonder if ants and worms are so carefully authoritarian?" She stalked past him, and I hurried in her wake, torn between amusement and irritation.

There was seating on tiered wooden benches on all sides of the central ring but the back. It was stuffy inside, dim except for the stage, which was lit with torchlight that gave a smoky quality to the sawdust- and animal-scented air. I felt like I was entering the temple of some strange, mystic sect to watch a sacrifice. The crowd, like the region, was mixed and raucous. Though I glimpsed a little cadre of gentlemen and their well-dressed ladies slumming it with a pair of dragoons for escort, Dahria's dull finery outranked everyone else's; even my maid's attire put me socially even with the bulk of the audience. As showtime approached, I felt a rising sense of anticipation, which listed into anxiety, though I could not be sure why beyond the obvious. We were out of our element, both of us, and in a place frequented—if we were right—by killers who would surely know who we were.

I wished Dahria had selected a more face-concealing hat: something with a veil, perhaps . . .

Suddenly, there was a burst of applause and a roar from the crowd as a pair of curtains parted on each side of stage, new torches leapt into flame, and an unseen brass band burst into strident life. A pair of marble-white horses pranced into the ring, ridden by what looked like Lani women arrayed in gold and sprouting broad wings from their shoulder blades. The brown of their skin had a curiously orange hue, which made them strange, radiant in the torchlight, and the feathers of their wings had been treated with silver bright as chrome, so that they looked like figures from ancient scroll paintings of angels.

The crowd gasped, and their simple pleasure at the spectacle was interwoven with something like awe, as more and more resplendent and curious figures joined the parade. In addition to the horses, there were orleks, a troupe of clothed monkeys—one with a comic suitcase—and an ebony goddess wearing little more than spangles, holding a pair of black weancats on leashes. Even the orleks were exotic, being not the usual black-and-white-striped variety but what they called Wilderheld orleks, whose paler parts were a strange blue-gray.

There were red-skinned acrobats and jugglers, a fire breather, and a strong man who wore close-fitting blue robes. More horsemen—

some of them shooting rifles and pistols, which they spun improbably from hand to hand. A stream of mongooses followed each other single file, leaping through hoops. Last came an elephant with an austere-looking man staring us down from its back.

He was the only categorically white man in the company, but he retained the curious foreignness of the rest. He wore riding boots, jodhpurs, and a braided military-looking jacket over a bare, muscled chest, and as the rest completed their laps of the ring and filed out the back, he slid effortlessly down the elephant's trunk and strode haughtily to the center of the stage. He bore a long coachman's whip, which he cracked ceremoniously, and then stood with his arms akimbo, casting an imperious stare on the audience until they fell absolutely silent.

"Ladies and gentlemen," he began. I had expected a booming, autocratic showman's voice, but while we heard every word with perfect clarity, he spoke softly, relying upon us to strain our ears. "Welcome to the traveling home of Messrs. Xeranti and their esteemed guests. You are most fortunate to be here, for tonight we will show you wonders!"

You could feel the audience leaning forward in their seats, every eye fastened on the curious man with the unplaceable accent. It struck me that I had no idea where they were actually from. The Lani and black performers all seemed to be wearing extensive theatrical makeup and wigs, so that their true ethnicity was impossible to guess for sure. The circus people might all have been local, but they knew that part of their appeal came from seeming foreign and mysterious.

And so it was. Every act was as much art as it was skill, and each had its own unfamiliar flavor, hinting at magical places far away. Each time the performance moved toward its climax, the audience was left openmouthed not by simple dexterity or cleverness but by something entirely unexpected that made the whole feel mystical, dreamlike. The pretty assistant had to be in the last box, but when that too was destroyed by the elephant's crushing foot, she emerged smiling and unscathed from somewhere else. The scarred, blindfolded knife thrower did not just miss the lady spinning on the wheel, he cut the ropes that held her up so that she slid free just as the wheel itself burst into flames. Tricks seemed to go wrong, animals seemed to break loose, but all turned out to be just part of the act. Even the clowns—in yellow face paint with elongated, lizard smiles—were tricksters rather than buffoons, using sleight of hand and other misdirection techniques so that every joke seemed finally to be on us rather than them. It was mesmerizing and made you doubt your mind and senses.

And then the trapeze artists came on, and I knew I was looking at a killer.

He was small, maybe Tanish's age or a little younger. His head was shaved, and his skin was painted a bilious green so that he looked like a water demon from some Mahweni folktale. He ran up the rope. There was no more suitable word, though my mind tried to reject it. He put one foot, pale with chalk dust, onto the knotted cord, seeming to grip it between his toes, and then raced up hand over hand, foot over sure, secure, and above all, rapid foot. He was at the top in less than three seconds, moving like a mongoose. I stared, gaping. I had been climbing most of my life, but I would not have believed that possible. In that moment, I realized I had seen enough.

Dahria sensed my response and turned to look at me as the crowd applauded, but I was already leaving my seat.

"What are you doing?" Dahria demanded.

"Have to get backstage," I said.

"It's the middle of the show, you mad creature! How do you think you are going to do that?"

A fair question, but one I did not stay to answer.

It was an occupational habit that when I was inside any structure for more than a few moments, I would find myself considering its highest reaches, imagining how I could get up there to perform cleaning or repair jobs, wondering about how much scaffold I'd need to erect, whether I was better approaching from the inside or the outside, where I could see ledges that were wide enough to stand on, moldings and other handholds that would bear my weight. I had done it in Parliament, I had done it in the opera house, and I had done it in churches and temples of every denomination in the city. So I had spent the moments before the circus began reflecting upon the big top from the perspective of those who had to erect it—tightening its many ropes and cables, securing necessary pegs high above where the audience now sat—and generally scrutinizing the physical architecture that kept the whole thing from coming crashing down and stifling all who weren't crushed by the timbers.

I had no plan, but I didn't have to pause to consider my route. I couldn't get backstage via the ring because everyone would see me, and the various exits were covered by toughs making sure no one snuck in without paying. I had no way of knowing how heavily they were guarding the stage door itself—or whatever you would call the equivalent in a huge tent—but I had seen enough expertly wielded guns and knives among the cast to know that any resistance at all might be lethal.

I fought my way out of the row of spectators, all agog and gazing up to where the high-wire act had begun, and up the tiered aisle to the back of the big top. Instead of a single pole in the center, which would have taken up room in the performance ring itself, the tent was supported with six separate poles, each as thick as the trunk of a full-grown malbanta tree, and with the same naturally smooth surface. They were angled in toward the stage so that from outside the big top looked like a ring of a half dozen peaks. The poles were connected at the top, not just by high tensile cables, but by a series of rickety gantries from which lanterns hung around the stage. More importantly, from shoulder height, they were set with climbing spikes all the way to the top. Those tops had been quite visible before the show began, but now that the lantern height had been adjusted and some clever mirror devices were focusing them into the central area high above the ring, the gantries were so dim that they were almost invisible. If I could get up there in the shadows, I could use those gantries to get to one of the other pole stanchions that slanted down through the rear canvas and into the backstage area.

As the crowd oohed and cheered the trapeze act, I looked quickly about and, when I saw no sign that the various guards and ushers had noticed me, slipped hurriedly out of my skirts and bonnet, revealing the close-fitting shirt, trousers, and work boots that were my steeplejack attire. Then I began to climb the rear pole. The "rungs," which alternated to the right and left side of the pole every few feet, were wooden dowels driven into the main spar and just long enough for a handhold. I was used to a vertical climb up walls and chimneys, so the angled ascent was disorienting, and I had to remind myself to keep my body central on the main shaft: too much swing as I climbed hand over hand, and I might lose my footing. Eyes front, I left the ground and the audience beneath me and scaled the sixty or so feet.

I had been humbled by the way the boy climbed the rope, and I felt the urge to race up just to prove to myself that I was as good as him. It was a stupid impulse, especially on this unfamiliar, canted structure, and I bit it back, thinking of Madame Nahreem's mask, pushing away any conflicted feelings about the lady herself, and focusing on the rhythm of the climb.

At the top I made a cautious transfer onto the gantry, a wire and lattice affair not designed to handle a lot of weight. It shifted under my boots, and I took hold of the side cable to steady myself, looking down at the brightly lit performers and upturned audience faces through the smut of the torches. There were three performers out there in addition to the rope-climbing child, two men and a woman, though the youngest seemed to be the star of the act. They all had the same sickly green colored skin, which made them strangely reptilian as they performed their aerial acrobatics, swinging from one high platform to the other, throwing and catching each other to the gasps of the crowd. The catwalk on which I now squatted was some ten feet above the highest point of their elevated stages, but I felt sure that even in the gloom they would surely see me if they looked directly at me, so I kept very still and watched.

They moved with grace and ease, as comfortable in the air as fish in water. Each leap, each somersault, each catch, ended with a haughty flourish, like preening turacos displaying in the mating season. I doubted the plainspoken and understated city folk had ever seen anything quite like it.

I would wait the act out, I decided, as close to invisible as I could be, and as soon as they finished and the lights shifted, I would move along the gantry to the rear slanting spar, and make my way down into the backstage area. What I would do then, I wasn't sure. Speaking to the child seemed reckless and pointless, but getting a name—posing, perhaps, as an enthusiast hunting autographs—meant I might have something I could take to Andrews. Perhaps I could learn whether the boy had been seen with anyone local, or whether he had come into money lately . . .

The crowd below was quiet, focused in their attention, so the sudden roaring bark at my shoulder was doubly shocking. I skittered instinctively away, feeling the gantry shake and sway under me, as the first baboon leapt from the pole I had ascended, its teeth bared. It was a big male, only twenty or thirty pounds lighter than I was, its shoulders and hindquarters hulking as it stared me down. There were at least two more coming up after it. It seemed that the circus did not rely exclusively on human guards.

The baboon roared again, and I felt the eyes of the trapeze artists lock onto me. Then it attacked.

CHAPTER

16

BABOONS ARE POWERFUL ANIMALS, fast, strong, and as comfortable in treetops as they are on the ground. The cleverness of
their hands is matched only by their intelligence, and I had grown
up knowing that they would watch humans for hours, learning
their routines so that they could get into their houses to steal food.
More than cunning, they were capable of a ferocity that verged on
savage. Twice in my youth, they had killed children in the Drowning; even faced by big men, they were fearless and dangerous
fighters who knew how to work as a team. I had heard stories of
them killing leopards and weancats, and I had responded by staying as far away from them as I could. A baboon is a wolf with hands.

This one—the fur of its mane and shoulders standing on end so
that it looked even bigger, close-set eyes fixed in its long, black dog-
like face—snorted, showing long pale fangs, and charged. I scrambled backwards, eyes locked on the creature, knowing I couldn't
outrun it but with no other choice than to try. As I ran, feeling the
nauseating yaw of the gantry beneath me, I realized that the trapeze gymnastics had stopped. For a wild moment, I considered
leaping from the catwalk and taking my chances on the aerial plat-
forms, which at least had ladders to the ground, but I knew that
the baboons would match and better any jumping or climbing skill
I might use.

I made it six or seven yards before the baboon leapt. It hit me in
the small of my back, strong hands grabbing me by the neck and
shoulders. The impact sent me sprawling forward. Astride me,

the animal clawed at my head, and I felt, trampling on my fear, a squirming revulsion that made me cry out. I felt its long muzzle buried in my neck, its dagger-like teeth worrying at me, looking for a grip. The momentum of my fall had rolled me to the very edge of the catwalk. I scrambled to hold on, feeling the flesh tear under the monkey's claws. As I fought against falling, the baboon was roughly unseated and almost thrown clear. For a second it hung by one arm from the gantry, and in that second I got back to my feet and ran a few more steps. The rest of the pack came at my heels, whooping and barking like creatures of death and nightmare, as the audience below turned to look up at what they probably thought was part of the show.

At the end of the gantry, I turned to face them, kicking wildly at the closest. The big leader was back up on the catwalk now and fighting its way through. Two new ones were bringing up the rear. More than enough to tear me apart. I reached for my kukri, realizing too late that I had left it in the town house because it showed too much through my absurd maid's dress. I was defenseless.

There was nowhere to go but down. I practically vaulted onto the great slanting pole that reached through the torch smoke behind the stage, knowing I would never make it with the troupe coming after me. I did it anyway, clambering wildly down, reaching blindly with my feet, not daring to take my eyes off the baboons as they began their effortless, loping pursuit. They came down headfirst, staring at me, their black lips snapping back to show their teeth. I kept going, punching at intervals, to slow their attack.

It almost worked. Despite the ease with which they climbed down, they didn't want to be knocked off and seemed to hold back. I realized that as soon I reached the ground, they would inevitably drop on me. There was blood in my eyes from where the big male had caught me and worse cuts on my back that I couldn't see. The closest one was still coming. Babbling with fear and dread that it would reach me, touch me, I climbed down another ten feet, dropping dangerously past several rungs and feeling myself almost roll off the canted beam. The baboon thrust its head down till it was mere inches from mine, screamed, and snapped its jaws. It filled my vision like a black lion, and suddenly I could stand it no more.

I let go. I had no idea how much farther I had to descend, how long and lethal the fall. I simply could not bear it any longer. I dropped, half rolling through the air as I fell.

Ten feet.

Twenty.

I had not reached the canvas panel separating the performance ring from the backstage, so I landed hard on my back in front of the baffled audience. That saved my life. While there was no safety net below the trapeze, the floor had been heaped with lumpy and irregular mattress-like pads faced with canvas. They puffed sawdust from the seams as I thumped into them. I sank through, the air momentarily driven from my body, but my spine and limbs intact. I would be cut and bruised in the morning, but knowing it could have been so very much worse, I almost laughed.

Then I processed the hush, the patter of uncertain applause, and the ominous thuds on the pads around me as the baboons dropped to attack. Someone in the audience screamed.

The sound was contagious. It spread through the big top like fire. People were getting to their feet, shouting, running, panicking. They did not need to be told that baboons at close quarters could be lethal.

I rolled woozily, feeling the pain awaking in my back and shoulders, and wiped the blood from my face, but even as I did so, I scanned the stage area first for the baboons, and next for the trapeze artists. The animals, though far from spooked by the crowd noise, were watching the uproar in the seats with cautious interest as if deciding what to do next. The green-skinned performers were talking to each other in frustrated whispers. Except for the boy. He was looking directly at me.

His eyes were wide, his mouth set firmly shut, and in his face there was fear and recognition. He knew who I was, and before I could do anything else, he ran.

As the ringmaster strode into the ring, calling in his commanding voice for order in the house, I went after the boy, who had ducked through a flap into the backstage area. I ran cautiously, testing my bones, but though the ache in my back was swelling fast, the only sharp pains were from the baboon's teeth and claws. The tented area behind the big top was a maze of square, dirt-floored chambers, part greenroom, part storage. I weaved round colorful boxes with trick panels, racks of costumes, weapon stands, and crates of animal feed, but the boy was fast. His green-hued feet and shaved head stayed agonizingly out of reach, and then he was diving under another flap of the tent and was gone. I hesitated just long enough to be sure he wasn't waiting on the other side, knife at the ready, then got down on my belly and slithered through after him.

It was darker here, the canvas walls closer so that the space felt less like the main circus and more like the corridors of a sideshow, a makeshift gallery . . .

But a gallery displaying what?

The air smelled heavily of soil and animals, and after my encounter with the baboons, that gave me pause. I wasn't sure what the residents of Bar-Selehm would pay to see that they weren't already accustomed to, and I wasn't sure I wanted to find out. Not alone in the dark like this, anyway. For a second, I stood quite still, and in that moment, I heard the distinct snap of a lock, then the groan of a cage door used to staying firmly shut.

And then came a deep chuffing breath from something big. It wasn't a thousand miles from the bark of the baboon, but it was deeper, and it resonated in the chest of an animal much, much larger than any monkey. I took an uneasy step back toward the flap I had crawled under, but even as I did so, a large shadow came round the corner in front of me.

It was bigger than me. Much. It turned, leaning into what little light remained, and I sucked in my breath and held it. An ape, but far bigger than any I had ever seen, its head high, almost conical, its arms massive. It rested on its immense knuckles, and I felt its eyes on me, as it stretched the vast expanse of its shoulders, filling the narrow hall like a cloud. At first it seemed black as night, save across those shoulders where the hair seemed touched with silver, but then it moved its face into the light and I gasped. A name from books drifted back to me, a word loaded with legend and horror.

Xipuku.

It was something between a mandrill and a gorilla, a massive, hulking beast with a red muzzle and a bright pink line along its nose set improbably in a silver-blue face. The buttocks showed the same garish colors, but the rest of the animal was black as night, save its calculating yellow eyes. They were creatures of the mountain rain forest, and I knew them only from stories.

I couldn't move. I couldn't even think. I had been ready to fight the baboons, even if I knew they would overwhelm me, because I knew them, and however much they frightened me, they were familiar. This was different. This was a distillation of all the strength and strangeness of the circus, a creature I had barely believed in but that had the strength of half a dozen men, and could—quite literally—rip me into pieces like I was paper.

It stood no more than five yards away, breathing, watching me. Who knew what horrors it had been through in the past at the hands of the circus folk, how it had been captured and kept, what it had been fed? Who knew how deeply it had come to hate people and what it would do to them now that it had the chance?

Outside I heard the rush of footsteps as the circus emptied, the outraged voices of audience members who wanted their pennies back, the shouts of sudden argument, and I saw that the xipuku heard too. It took two rolling steps toward me and grunted again, longer this time, following the noise with a series of panting breaths that raised the hair on the back of my neck. Another step, and it was close enough that I could see its nostrils flare as it inspected me. Tears rolled down my face, but I still could not move. It reached toward me, took another hopping step, and with a kind of gentleness, pushed me aside and lay flat on the ground, one finger raising the canvas flap I had crawled under, so it could peer out.

I stared, disbelieving, and then, with an extraordinary effort of will, I moved a fraction. The xipuku's eyes flicked to me with mild interest, then returned to whatever it could see outside. I took a step away, then another, my eyes still fixed on the colossal beast, the leathery soles of its feet exposed like an infant, unconcerned. Two more steps, and I was round it and moving through the dim canvas passage. I turned the corner, to where the cage sat, fetid smelling, its gate hanging open, and then, unable to think of whether it was a good thing to do or not, I ran, a desperate, sprinting dash through the gloomy corridor with its darkened tanks and cages of who knew what, and out.

I emerged at a flat run, tripping over the prone, green body of the boy climber. I recovered from my fall and rolled him onto his back, revealing the triangular-tipped throwing knife that was buried in his heart.

The child assassin was dead, and with him, any hope that I might turn my one discovery into information that might free Willinghouse.

CHAPTER

17

I TRIED TO REVIVE the boy, but it was too late. I called for help, and when none came—the crowds all being out front—I went looking for Dahria. I found her sitting primly on a bench at the north end of the park, where she had, apparently, been preparing her opening line.

"First the opera house, now this," she remarked. "Are there any forms of theatrical entertainment you haven't disrupted by falling from the ceiling? The baboons were a nice touch. Most dramatic. Though I fancy the circus owners may be less enthu-siastic—"

"The boy is dead," I said. "I went after him, and someone killed him."

Dahria looked momentarily abashed, then frowned. "Why kill him and not you?" she said. "I mean, I'm glad they didn't, but if they were trying to stop you learning anything from him . . ."

It was a good point, one I hadn't considered till now.

"Because if a Bar-Selehm citizen is killed by a foreigner with a traveling show, there'll be an investigation?" I tried.

"Whereas if one of their own is killed . . ." Dahria mused, agreeing.

"I suppose we'll find out."

"You want to go the police?"

"To Andrews," I said. "He'll take us seriously, and there's no clear link to your brother's case, at least as far as the police are con-cerned, so no one will stop him."

I thought of the dead boy, of the baboons, and the xipuku in the sideshow, and all my aches and pains came back to me like weariness or grief. Dahria leaned in and pushed my hair aside with one hand tenderly.

"You are bleeding," she said. "We should get you to a doctor."

Her closeness, her kindness flustered me. I could smell the fragrance she brushed through her hair.

"Later," I replied deliberately, drawing away so that I would not lose myself in the moment. "The boy . . ."

I didn't know what to say. I had been so caught up in my own dramas that the weight of the child's death was only just beginning to register. He might have been a killer, but he had also been younger than Tanish. He had been an instrument used by someone else and discarded as soon as he became troublesome.

I could not have known this would happen, and it was hard to feel deep remorse for the death of a killer, however young he might have been, but if I had not gone after him, he would still be alive, and that was something I was going to have to live with.

I found that I was angry. I had been played like one of the gullible fools who got lured into the cardsharps' games, tricked. So had Willinghouse. Indeed, so had the whole city. Someone had arranged all this.

So find them.

"Are you all right?" said Dahria, breaking into my reverie. "You are crying."

"I'm fine," I said. It wasn't true. Not yet. But it would be. The tears I wiped away were hot.

"I see you have managed to lose another of my maid's dresses," said Dahria, deliberately not looking at me. "You must be the patron saint of the city's homeless women."

"What?" I said. Numbness was descending on me.

"Nothing," she said. "We'll take a cab to the police station."

ANDREWS RETURNED WITH US to the circus site, but his questions produced nothing. The trapeze boy had taken ill, said the other members of the company, almost word for word, and had decided to leave the organization. His parents—the trapeze group had been a family act—were annoyed, but his work had not been entirely satisfactory, so they had raised no objection. There were plenty of other agile little children keen to learn the secrets of show business . . .

It was both maddening and bizarre.

"There's nothing I can do," said Andrews. "They aren't citizens of the city, and they deny a crime has taken place. No one will support my holding all of them based on your testimony, and in a few days, they'll be gone."

"Then you were right," said Dahria to me. "They killed him because it would make less fuss than killing you."

I didn't want to think about that, but knew she was right. For a moment she looked exhausted, worn out with whatever Dahria had in place of emotions. She squeezed her eyes shut, then got to her feet.

"I'm going to wait outside. Someone might recognize me. And besides," she added, wrinkling her nose, "I have smelled enough circus to last me a lifetime."

I watched her go, but her concern reminded me of something.

"He knew me," I said to Andrews. "The boy. I saw it in his face. That's why he ran. He must have seen me at the Parliament House. He may even have still been in the tea chest when I was hiding in the Roll Closet, watching me through a crack. Or maybe he saw me on the roof by the dome. Either way—"

"Roll Closet?" said Andrews.

I told him all I had learned while posing as a cleaner in the Parliament House.

"So someone got him in and lured Willinghouse to the crime scene," Andrews mused. "You say the boy was killed by a throwing knife?"

"Yes. A broad blade with a weighted, triangular tip, like those the showmen use in the circus."

"Then we are not done," said Andrews, grimly. He made for the strutting ringmaster. "I want to speak to your knife throwers," he said.

"We are busy. Your little friend caused us a lot of trouble tonight," he said, eyeing me with cool dislike.

"Perhaps you'd like to show us your immigration papers instead," Andrews said levelly.

"You can't touch us," said the ringmaster. "We have letters of support and invitation from some very powerful people."

"I don't doubt it," said Andrews, "but I am confident that they would prefer not to be drawn into this sordid little matter. Fetch your knife throwers. Now."

"What people?" I said, sitting up. Andrews had commandeered one of the caravans for his interviews. He gave me a blank look. "With international tensions being what they are, it can't be easy to travel across borders like the circus is doing, but he says they have letters of support from powerful people. Which people?"

Andrews nodded thoughtfully and made a note. I would have said more, but at that moment, the tent flap was flipped imperiously aside and the knife thrower strode in. During the performance he had been wearing a flamboyant red coat, which made him look wide-shouldered and imposing, but without it, he looked lean and efficient, his arms sinewy strong. He had an elaborate black mustache, which ended in waxed twists, and long, deep scars on each cheek, so perfectly balanced that they looked deliberate, decorative. He might have been a storybook pirate from some distant land. His glossy black hair trailed down his back like a mane, and his skin was a rich rusty brown, much closer to red than my own. He smelled of sweat and drink, and something else I couldn't place, and he wore knives: a dozen of them in an amazing variety of shapes and sizes, all in perfect, custom-made scabbards attached not just to his belt, but to his thighs, his chest, the sleeves of his buckskin shirt, even high up his back.

Andrews eyed him warily. "Would you mind laying your weapons on the table, please, sir?" he said, in his polite but unyielding policeman's voice.

"Not weapons," muttered the man, deftly pulling the first knife from its sheath. "The tools of my craft. Nothing more."

Like the ringmaster, the knife thrower's accent was strange, not quite like anything I had ever heard, and I had no idea where he came from.

"What's your name, sir?" said Andrews.

"Blogvitch," he said, "Blogvitch the Magnificent."

"So 'the Magnificent' is your surname, is it, sir?" said Andrews, archly.

The knife thrower glared at him. "Just Blogvitch," he said.

"Very good, sir," said Andrews, who was putting on a master class of being unintimidated by a suspect. Blogvitch was still engaged in the time-consuming process of unsheathing all his knives. They included something like a kukri, though more curved, some knives that were more like darts with needle points, and a pair of throwing axes with broad, sweeping heads that I hadn't even noticed. But the one that matched the knife I had seen in the climbing boy's chest was simpler, the blade long and leaf shaped, heavy at the swollen tip, but with a keen edge that ran all round, and a triangular point. The weight of the tip, I realized, designed to make it fly point first, would leave a wider slit than a conventional knife, and I found myself thinking of the body of Arthur Besland, late of the *Bar-Selehm Standard*. Andrews caught my eye, and I nodded inconspicuously. Having been recognized once already, it was probably vain to keep a low profile, but there was no point drawing attention to myself. Blogvitch had eyes for no one but Andrews and the uniformed constable who sat beside him, his truncheon pointedly across his lap.

"Are any of your weapons—sorry, your knives—missing?"

"No," said Blogvitch.

"Does anyone in the circus own similar knives?"

"These were made specially for me. Balanced the way I like. They fit my hands."

"I'll take that as a *no*," said Andrews. I wasn't certain if he was trying to annoy the knife thrower or if he just found his showmanship annoying. "And when did you last see . . . What was the boy climber called? The one who died?"

There was a fractional pause before Blogvitch said, "No one died. There was a boy in the trapeze company, but he left tonight. His name was Sardish."

"And he left tonight."

"That is what I said."

"Because he wasn't happy with his wages," Andrews said, as if this were agreed.

Another hesitation.

"No," Blogvitch answered. "He was sick."

"That's right," said Andrews, as if it was all coming back to him now. "Odd though that, no? When I feel sick, I go home early, maybe take the next day off. I don't quit and leave town."

"He was weak," said Blogvitch. "Foolish. A child. I don't know why he left. He was not good at his job. Maybe he knew that there was no room in the circus for the weak and sickly. Knew that a replacement would be found."

"So he left," Andrews concluded. "But I heard that he was actually quite good. A skilled climber. Pretty good with a knife himself, by all accounts."

Again the cautious pause before Blogvitch's answer.

"He did not use knife in the act."

"And when he wasn't onstage?"

"I know nothing of his life. He was a child. I never spoke to him."

"But you were seen talking to him in town a few days ago," said Andrews, as if mildly surprised. I looked at him. Either this was information he had not shared with me or he was fishing. "Someone saw you with him. Seeing the sights, were you? The witness was quite sure. I think you would agree that you have a distinctive— even *magnificent*—appearance."

Blogvitch smiled, and not at the backhanded compliment. It was a hastily doused smile, and that meant that it was real and he knew the inspector was bluffing.

"Your witness must be mistaken," he said. "Blogvitch stays in the circus. He does not see sights."

It was Andrews's turn to hesitate. He considered the knife thrower thoughtfully, then closed his notebook.

"The witness must have been mistaken," he said.

Blogvitch waited patiently, flexing his fingers, but he knew that the interview was over.

"Will that be all, officer?" said the ringmaster once the knife thrower had been dismissed.

"No," said Andrews, clearly dissatisfied. "Send me the boy's parents."

The ringmaster managed to shrug with only his eyebrows, and left.

"This doesn't feel right," said Andrews, leaning forward. "What's going on here?"

"Foreigners," said the constable knowingly. "Weird bunch."

I gave him a disbelieving look, but said nothing, and for a few minutes, we sat in silence, until Sardish's family were shepherded into the tent. They were still wearing their strange green makeup, and they sat in stiff silence, like creatures not from another country, but from another world entirely. As Andrews made the introductions and asked some simple, clarifying questions, I studied them. The father was lean and angular, perhaps thirty or thirty-five. The mother was a little younger, though it was hard to say since they were all completely shaven, and the effect—combined with the luminous, painted skin, made them oddly ageless. The daughter was about my age. In the stage light she had seemed exotic and beautiful; up close she was ordinary looking at best, but lithe and strong as an eel. Her bilious lime-green makeup had been carefully and recently retouched, and her eyes looked pinker than was normal.

Had she been weeping?

As Andrews asked his questions and was given monosyllabic denials and the same word-for-word explanations about the boy's illness and decision to leave the company, I watched her. When the knife thrower had flexed his fingers it had been a deliberate and faintly threatening show of just how uninterested he was, but as she did something similar, it was unconscious, anxious even. I wondered if Andrews had noticed.

"So he will have gone where?" asked Andrews, who was losing patience.

"Home," said the father.

"Which is?"

"Sorry?"

"Where do you live?"

"Raspacia," said the father.

"*Raspacia?*" Andrews echoed. "That's the other side of the world! What are you doing here?"

"We work in circus."

"Well, obviously! But I mean . . . Oh, never mind."

They sat like statues, and eventually he waved them away, muttering that he'd be in touch. When the ringmaster returned, Andrews gave him the same chilly brush-off.

"Then if your officers are concluded with their most important inquiries," said the ringmaster with the kind of obsequiousness you weren't intended to take as genuine, "and you might see your way clear to vacating the premises, we do have some rather important matters to address. Work never stops in the circus."

WE REJOINED DAHRIA AND rode back toward the town house in the police carriage, an annoyed Andrews drumming his fingers on the doors, saying nothing, not speaking until we were sitting in the dimly lit drawing room of the silent house.

"It was one of their own who died," he said. "Why does no one care?"

"The sister might," I said. "If she is a sister."

"I thought the same thing," said Andrews eagerly. "No resemblance between any of them and no emotion that the boy was dead. We have only their word that any of these people are who they claim to be. Raspacia, indeed! If they are from Raspacia, I'll eat my hat."

"Why lie about where they are from?" asked Dahria.

"Part of the show, isn't it?" said Andrews. "What does the poster say? Foreign and exotic, right? But why continue the illusion after the audience has left?"

"Unless the police are the audience," I said. "Did you see the way the knife thrower reacted to your claim that he had been seen in town? He had been worried about everything you had said so far, careful, you know. But not that. Why?"

"Because he hadn't been in town with the boy and knew I was lying," said Andrews.

"Or because you said he was distinctive, easy to recognize," I said.

"He is, rather," said Andrews.

"But that's all hair and makeup. You could smell it on him, the greasepaint. I noticed the same smell when the trapeze family—if they are a family—came in. I'll bet a thousand pounds that his skin is not brown and that that ridiculous mustache and the pirate mop hair all comes off when he goes to bed at night. If he went out into the city without what is effectively his costume, he could wander completely unnoticed and absolutely unrecognized. That's why he knew you were lying."

Andrews nodded thoughtfully, but the point did not raise his spirits.

"We still can't touch them. They claim there was no crime, and without a body, we can't prove otherwise."

"Raid the place," I said. "It has to be there."

Dahria shook her head.

"You'd be wasting your time," she said. "The circus I saw is a study in illusion and misdirection. If they can make a live woman disappear and reappear in front of a thousand spectators, they can hide a body. And if they don't feel like hiding it, they have hungry weancats and lions at their disposal. Please make me say no more on the matter."

"If the boy was indeed Tavestock's killer and there are other people at the circus involved—" Andrews began.

"He is," I inserted, "and there are."

"Then why are they still here?" the policeman concluded. "They could easily leave the city and vanish. Why remain where they can be watched and interrogated?"

"Because they aren't done," I said.

"Meaning what?" said Dahria, looking alarmed.

I shrugged.

"I don't know," I said. "But the murder of the PM doesn't feel like an isolated event, and not just because Willinghouse, Richter's fiercest opponent, has been conveniently implicated in the crime. Something larger is at work here. It feels . . . orchestrated, like the circus itself. Lots of sideshows and individual performances, but only one pot that all the money goes into, one mind at the center making it all work. If they aren't leaving town yet, it's because there's something else they have to do. Given what they have already achieved, we have to assume it's something big, something very bad for Bar-Selehm. I can feel it. Behind the smoke and mirrors, there's a serious threat to the life of the city itself."

It was a mark of the sense of panic, which seemed to be increasing by the hour, that neither of them contradicted me, and as I looked into their faces, I was sure they felt it too.

"There is something else," said Andrews, eyeing Dahria. "I received no notice from the commissioner, but I have it on good authority through internal channels that your brother's trial will begin tomorrow."

"Tomorrow!" Dahria gasped. "How is that possible? There has been no word of it in the papers."

"Nor will there be," said Andrews gravely. "Not till a verdict is recorded. He's being tried not just for murder, but for treason, and that means the entire process will take place behind closed doors. The *Standard* will be allowed to cover the proceedings for the look of the thing, but their reports will be heavily censored and discontinued entirely if they stray from the party line. Richter's people favor the *Clarion* anyway and will feed them their own version of events, so that the *Standard* won't dare risk losing their old monopoly on such matters. I fear," he added, darker still, "that the matter will move very quickly."

"How quickly?" said Dahria. She looked badly startled.

"Word inside the police station says that the investigation, such as it has been, has turned up nothing to mitigate your brother's apparent guilt. I would not be surprised to see the whole thing concluded in no more than a couple of days."

He did not need to elaborate on "concluded." They were probably readying the gibbet even as we spoke.

"I am sorry," said Andrews. He looked almost as lost and hopeless as we did, and he clearly felt a sense of failure, which was unjust. Dahria recognized the look in his face and nodded, suddenly her old self again, for his sake: unyielding and perfectly composed.

"None of this is laid to your charge, Inspector," she said. "You have been a good friend to my brother and a fine officer. You have done all you could. Others must take over the matter from here."

He nodded gratefully and excused himself, leaving us sitting alone in silence. I watched Dahria in the gloom, as her carefully erected restraint crumbled and, for the first time in my life, I saw her weep. She muttered my name in a kind of desperate trance, leaning into my arms, and sobbing bitterly. I held her, feeling my own tears mix with hers as our cheeks pressed together, and for several minutes, we sat there unspeaking. I doubt either of us had shared so intimate a sadness before.

CHAPTER

18

"ARE YOU SURE YOU want to do this?" I asked Dahria as we gazed up at the elegant white frontage of the Heritage party headquarters, its flagpoles flying both the Bar-Selehm standard and the black and red lightning fist of the party faithful. I had visited the doctor on Dahria's insistence to have my wounds tended right after breakfast, but that hadn't taken long at all, and it was still early.

"I most definitely do not," she replied. "But what choice have I?" She looked at me, but it was not a real question, and eventually, seeing the desolation in my face, she smiled softly. "Come along, Ang. It may not be as bad as all that."

The fact that she'd called me by my real name suggested that it was exactly that bad, but I nodded and steeled myself for what would follow.

The white guard on the door—and he *was* a guard, uniformed in gray with shiny black boots and the Heritage armband worn above the pistol holster on his belt—was unimpressed by us and disinclined to let us in, doubly so when Dahria said she was there to see Richter.

"The Lord Protector does not take visitors off the street," said the guard derisively.

Lord Protector was a new one on me, but I managed not to show the disdain I felt for the title. Dahria did not give an inch.

"Tell the prime minister that Josiah Willinghouse's sister is here to see him," she said coolly, handing him a cream-colored calling card from her purse.

The guard hesitated then ordered us to wait outside while he consulted with his superiors. Dahria looked affronted, but there was nothing to be done, so we stood there as instructed. Out in the street, people passed by, glancing toward us. Dahria turned her back on them, but her face burned all the same. At long last, we were showed in to an antechamber where Jebediah Saunders, Richter's weasel-ish private secretary, gave us a scornful look and said, "The Lord Protector is in a meeting and is very busy. If you will wait in the room at the end of the hall, he will join you when he has a free moment."

Dahria managed a stiff smile and a minute nod, then turned in the direction he had indicated. I followed, my head lowered, glad, for once, of yet another maid's outfit, hastily cobbled together from the town house stores. We were running out of them, but since the staff had been temporarily dismissed because they could no longer legally live in the east end of the city, that didn't much matter.

"Impertinence," Dahria murmured as we walked.

There were several maids and footmen around, but they were all white, and no one spoke to us. Nor, when we had let ourselves into the room to await the *Lord Protector*'s appearance, did anyone come to offer us refreshment. We heard distant voices, the occasional closing of doors, and brisk footsteps in the corridor outside, but no one came. While the clock on the mantel wound slowly on, we sat, saying nothing. An hour passed. Then another.

"This is deliberate rudeness!" said Dahria, getting abruptly to her feet and beginning to pace.

"Yes," I said, though being less accustomed to people dropping what they were doing to serve me, I was less concerned with the impropriety than I was with the waste of time. I could be doing something—anything—more useful than this.

"Maybe he won't come at all, and this is a kind of bitter joke.

Perhaps his cronies are sitting in some other room even now, smoking cigars and laughing at the Lani mongrel sitting fruitlessly alone while her brother is arraigned for execution."

"You're not alone," I said. "And your brother will not be executed without a trial."

"Of a sort," she said. "One guaranteed to reach the verdict they want."

I couldn't argue with that and wouldn't insult her by trying.

Ten more minutes passed and, after a few furious, rustling circuits of the room, Dahria settled herself in a chair again, her eyes fixed on the clock. I watched the windows, wondering how dark it would become before we were seen or we abandoned the mission and went home.

The door cannoned open without warning, and Norton Richter strode in. He wore the gray trousers and high boots of his followers, but his silver-trimmed jacket was black, which made the red of the armband even more strident.

"Miss Willinghouse, I believe," he said, reading it off the card Dahria had presented at the door, as if he didn't know who she was. Or didn't care. We both rose automatically, but he waved the courtesy away and settled into one of the available armchairs. His eyes never came to me at all, as if he couldn't see me. "I'm a very busy man, so I would appreciate it if you would say what you have to say swiftly."

He was in his fifties, slim and fit, his face carved from stone or— more likely, given the industry that had made his fortune—welded in steel. He had an abrupt manner of speaking and a perpetual sneer ghosting his eyes and mouth, as if he could not quite believe how poorly the world was populated. In the case of Lani and black people, of course, he meant that literally and remorselessly, but a version of it haunted all his dealings, acting as if he were a kind of minor god doomed to walk the earth with lesser mortals.

"I have come about my brother," said Dahria, taking a direct but pleasant tone that must have pained her.

"Out of my hands," he said. "The man will have his day in court, and that's all there is to it. Now, if you don't mind—"

"You are a man of considerable influence," Dahria persisted. "If you were to intervene on his behalf, to show mercy, I am sure it would endear you to a great many people who might otherwise—"

"Endear?" he echoed contemptuously. "My dear young lady, I care not a jot for the opinions of the idle and degenerate. The opinions of those who matter to me, I have already. If there is nothing more—"

He got abruptly to his feet. For all his stuffy indignation, he could not completely conceal the fact that he was enjoying himself. He made my skin crawl.

"Perhaps there is something I can offer that might alter your position," Dahria ventured.

I gave her a quick, panicked look, but Richter's scornful smile only expanded.

"I have no base appetites, Miss Willinghouse," he snapped. "My heart is pure as steel. You would do well to keep such *offers* to yourself, lest you soil what is left of your reputation."

"You misunderstand me," she said quickly. "I propose a trade. My brother's life, for information."

Richter's confident swagger stalled for a moment, and his face tightened. He was both skeptical and intrigued.

"What kind of information?" he demanded.

"On my brother's activities," said Dahria. "His plans, his party, his friends."

I stared at her aghast.

What is she doing?

"Leave us," Richter commanded, not so much looking at me as turning slightly in my direction but keeping his eyes on Dahria.

I dithered and gave her an anguished look.

"Do as the prime minister says," she said, playing the aristocrat once more. "I believe I am quite safe in Mr. Richter's company."

I had no alternative but to stand, execute a clumsy curtsy, and leave the room, trying not to show the revulsion I felt at being so close to him.

I DIDN'T KNOW WHERE to go. Even more than that night at Elitus, I felt that I was in the belly of the beast, the very heart of an organization that despised me, my family, my friends, and all I stood for. Indeed, I did not need to stand for anything, to espouse any position or doctrine, for the Heritage party faithful to despise me. My very existence was enough.

So I moved along the hall, looking for somewhere to wait for Dahria where I could hide for however long her desperate interview took. Behind me, I heard footsteps and turned in time to see a pair of uniformed men emerge from a side chamber. Not wanting to have to justify my presence—my existence—I tried the closest door handle and, finding it unlocked, slipped hastily inside.

Like all the rooms I had seen in the Heritage headquarters, it was an elegantly appointed room furnished in the northern style and hung with portraits of Belrandian kings, generals, and politicians. I selected an overstuffed wing chair beside a shuttered hatch in the wall and had almost sat down when I realized I was not alone.

Seated in another wing chair, its back to the door, was a familiar man in a fussy blazer quite different from the uniform gray of the Heritage faithful. It was the Grappoli ambassador.

"I beg your pardon," I said, bowing, partly to hide my face. "I did not realize the room was in use."

"No reason you should, my dear," said Count Alfonse Marino, smiling, his black, crystalline eyes twinkling playfully.

He was as I had seen him before, slick and polished to the point of oiliness, slightly overfed, well-manicured, and languid. The plate beside him was covered in fine crumbs, and there was a scent of curry in the air that almost masked the woody, citrusy aroma of what I took to be the ambassador's hair tonic.

"No need to leave just yet."

I faltered, unsure what to do or say, my old diffidence return-ing with a vengeance. "Sit," he said. He had an insinuating croon of a voice. If a well-indulged and aging house cat could speak, this was what it would sound like. "I take it you are escorting a guest?"

"Yes, sir," I said, emphasizing the Lani lilt to my voice. I was still standing. We had met twice before, but on one occasion I had been heavily disguised and on the other he had not seen me properly in the shadows. I did not think he would recognize me, but if he did, the consequences would be dire indeed.

"I thought as much," said the ambassador. "Mr. Richter sur-rounds himself with people who look like he does." He grinned knowingly, as if this were a minor peccadillo, but then added, "I've never really understood why. He thinks white culture—white *people*—are corrupted by the very presence of blacks and, frankly, people like you. Do you have an opinion on the matter?"

"I'm sure I don't know, sir," I said, with difficulty.

"You are discreet," he said approvingly. "A good thing in a lady's maid. But you must have an opinion on the subject. Come. Sit. And tell me. I will not hold it against you or your mistress."

I settled cautiously into the chair opposite him, as he seemed to wish, and then pretended to wrestle with the question he had posed. I thought of the night I had seen him in his carriage, unnoticed in the dark, listening to Aaron Muhapi speak.

"I don't concern myself with politics, sir," I said.

"No," he said. "I don't suppose you do. But politics concerns you, whether you like it or not."

A strange thing to say, especially coming from the mouth of the Grappoli Empire, and doubly so in this of all buildings. Afraid I would give away too much, I said, "Do you like it here, sir, if you don't mind me asking? In Bar-Selehm, I mean."

"I do," he said, his brow clearing as if a warm breeze had blown through a cold room. "I love it here. The city is so . . . vibrant! That is the word, yes? Rich and full of life."

"Yes, sir," I said. "That is the word."

"The art and culture here . . ." he began, but faltered, looking suddenly wistful.

"You mean the art from Belrand?" I probed. I didn't know what I was doing. The conversation felt surreal, like something I might dream, but I did not want to let it go.

The ambassador waggled his head on his neck: *not exactly.*

"Belrand is a wonderful place, have no doubt," he said. "So is Grappol. All of Panbroke is a wonderful place." He waved his hand as if to suggest that this was all self-evident but also uninteresting. "But Bar-Selehm is different. Special. Yes. I love it here."

Again there was something complicated in his voice, as if he had come to a realization that saddened him, but his eyes fell on his empty plate and he managed a smile.

"Samosas," he said. "I could eat them all day. They are a Lani delicacy, I believe. Curried meat or potatoes and chickpeas in crisp pastry. I buy them on the street and bring them with me. They warm them up for me here, though I am afraid Mr. Richter does not approve. They are quite delicious. I cannot get them at home."

Again the smile faded, and he gazed at his hands, frowning.

"I agree," I said, keen to revive the conversation. Something about it puzzled and intrigued me. "Bar-Selehm is a wonderful place, a special place, and much of what makes it special comes from its people. White people. Black people, assimilated and unas-similated. Lani people like me, and others who do not clearly fit into any of the other boxes. This is what makes the city what it is—"

I heard and cursed the clumsiness of my remark before I saw it in his face.

"Well," he said, rising suddenly, and smoothing his waistcoat, his face dark. "This has been most pleasant, but I fear I am needed elsewhere."

I considered him, trying to decide if it was worth apologizing but, not sure what it was I was attempting to achieve, and knowing I had already overplayed my hand, I let it go.

"Your servant, sir," I said, rising and curtsying quickly.

"Indeed," he said, turning on me and nodding. "Quite so." He hesitated, then something crossed his face and he frowned. "Have we met before? You seem—"

"Never, sir," I say flatly. "But then, how could we have? Your people and mine interact so . . . infrequently."

"That is true," he said vaguely, not satisfied by my answer, but then propelled down an avenue of his own thought that seemed to trouble him.

"But you are needed elsewhere," I reminded him.

"Indeed," he said again. "Quite so."

He clicked his heels together in the typical Grappoli way and gave me a short nod, which was, I thought a mark of his momentary disorientation. So formal a farewell would normally be reserved for social equals, not Lani maids.

Before he could turn, the door snapped open, and an elderly white man stepped through. He wore a monocle and had a graying mustache which stuck out at waxed angles almost as far as his side whiskers.

Archibald Mandel.

My breath caught, as if a cold hand had closed around my throat, and I stared. His eyes moved from the ambassador to me and fixed me with a stony glare.

"Who the devil are you?" he demanded.

"Miss Willinghouse's maid, if it please you, sir," I said, remembering at the last second to lower my eyes and drop into a swift curtsy.

"It doesn't please me," he barked. "Not in the slightest. What are you doing, Marino? We're waiting for you. Didn't Saunders tell you?"

"I was on my way," said the ambassador, trying to banish the strange, wounded expression that had been on his face a moment before.

"Well, get a move on, man," snorted Mandel. "We didn't bring you over so you could make idle chat with some Lani baggage." I stiffened but kept my eyes down. "Frankly, I would have expected a man in your position to have more refined tastes."

Then he was gone, and I was left staring so hard at the door he had closed behind him that I could have set it aflame with my eyes. I had all but forgotten the ambassador until he bustled over to the door, put one hand on the handle, and turned it.

Then he stopped and, for a second, just stood there, the door still closed in front of him. Without looking round he said, "I am sorry." And then he was opening the door and vanishing into the hallway.

DAHRIA FOUND ME TEN minutes later. We left in hurried silence, but as soon as we got into the street, I turned on her.

"Well?" I said.

"I don't know," she said. "I was vague in my promises. He expressed interest, said he would delay a verdict in Joss's trial, but how long I can stall him without giving him any real information, I don't know."

"You shouldn't trust him," I said. "No matter what you give him, he thinks of your brother as a mortal enemy."

"He's right to," said Dahria. "But he's not sure about me, and that gives me an advantage."

"You are going to go back?"

"When I have something to give him, yes, and you will be coming with me, so get your devious little brain to work on some plausible lies."

"That's a very dangerous game, Dahria," I said.

"Not to play it means that my brother's life will terminate at the end of a rope in a matter of days," she said.

I could not argue with that.

As if to drive the point home, the evening edition of the *Standard* was out by the time we wended our way back through the streets, and Willinghouse's name was all over the front page. **CONSPIRACY!** screamed the headline in such bold type that at first I thought I'd picked up a copy of the *Clarion* by mistake. I tried to fold it under my arm where Dahria wouldn't see it, but she held out a gloved hand.

"It doesn't help me not to know what they are saying about him," she said.

I handed the paper over, and we huddled together to read the cover story.

Sources close to the office of the police commissioner have revealed that former prime minister Benjamin Tavestock visited the remote country house of his accused killer, Josiah Willinghouse, the day before the assassination. More remarkable still, they were apparently joined by none other than the infamous black activist Aaron Muhapi, who was recently detained by police for incitement to revolt and causing a public disturbance. Investigations are also probing links between Willinghouse, Muhapi, and those unassimilated Mahweni tribes that have been harassing trade and travel routes north of the city. Officers involved in the case are wondering if Willinghouse, whose trial is scheduled to begin tomorrow and will be covered exclusively by this newspaper, is the center of a larger conspiracy against Bar-Selehm. The assassination of the prime minister may be only one step in a larger plan to destabilize the government in preparation for a black uprising. In response, the new prime minister, Norton Richter, has ordered that black members of the police and armed forces stand down until the crisis has passed. Their arms and weapons must be made available to a civilian militia to be orchestrated by ranking members of the Heritage party. . . .

Dahria said nothing. There was nothing to say. Silently, I slipped my arm into hers and drew her to my side as we paced the sidewalks back along the streets north of the opera house. It felt good to be so close to her, and I felt a pang of guilt that a part of me was enjoying the new bond we had forged, since it had emerged from so terrible a situation. But there was no denying it. She needed me, and I could not pretend that that did not give me pleasure, however much the sweet was touched with bitterness. We walked briskly, so that we would be home before the curfew patrols came out. If they saw me, I'd be arrested, and while Dahria was used to passing as white, that seemed unlikely to protect her now.

CHAPTER

19

THE TENTED AREA WHERE the sick children lay had twice as many beds now, mostly just blankets on the ground. More of the girls were losing their hair. They lay tossing vaguely in a kind of constant, uneasy slumber broken only by sudden staggerings to the designated latrine. The place smelled sour, the air rank with vomit and other body odors. Most of the new beds had been filled with those who had most ministered to the children, Rahvey and Florihn included.

"It seems to be contagious," said the doctor, who was looking pale and drawn in stained shirtsleeves. He rubbed his temples as if they pained him. "I am not sure how much longer I can stay out of bed myself."

"Here?"

"To go elsewhere risks spreading the disease," he said. "I fear that leaving is not an option, though staying is . . ." He gave me a wan smile.

"You think they are going to die?" I said, horrified that everyone seemed so much worse than when I was here last. I'm not sure if I expected the doctor to be encouraging or simply evasive, but he was neither.

"I'm amazed it hasn't already started," he said. "A matter of hours now, I suspect, for some of them."

I stared at him, aghast.

"Which?" I managed to ask, though the question seemed offensive in my own ears. He knew I meant my family.

"The ones who first showed signs of infection," he said, knowing he was confirming my worst fears. "The deaf girl first."

"Aab?"

"I'm afraid so."

I scanned the groaning, heaving bodies on the ground and found her, tiny, doubled up, and still. She may have already been dead. I picked my way through toward her, feeling a strange and unnerving dizziness as I got closer, as if my fear was overwhelming my balance. I dropped into a squat beside her and ran my fingers through what was left of her hair. Pieces of it came away in my fingers. Without that wild mane, she looked skeletal, her head small and smooth, the skin starting to flake away. She looked like something not altogether human, a goblin child or . . .

A gargoyle.

I blinked, then leaned in and parted her lips. Her breath smelled stale and rancid, and the slim gash of her mouth showed raw pockets in her gums where two of her teeth had been.

I stared, my mind racing, then seized the sleeping girl's hands and turned them over. Her finger ends and palms were red and blistered. Burns.

I had seen such injuries before.

"Aab!" I said. "Wake up! Aab!"

The girl barely stirred. I turned quickly to the bed beside her where Jadary lay, lost in her own trance-like sleep. I grabbed her hands and studied them, but other than the patchy skin, which they all seemed to have, there was no sign of the scalded redness.

"What is it?" said the doctor, hurrying over.

"I don't think it's a disease," I said, my attention back on Aab. I shook her, speaking her name with gentle insistence. "Aab! You have something or you found something. Something strange and shiny . . ." She couldn't hear me. I shook her again.

The doctor was asking questions I couldn't answer, so I asked him one instead.

"These burns on the fingers," I said. "Do any of the others have them?"

The doctor shook his head.

"She had them from the start," he said. "I assumed she was playing near the stove or helping cooking. They are not symptoms."

"They are," I said. "The first and most important."

"Then why don't the others have them?"

Jadary stirred. I ignored the doctor and gave her my attention, calling her from sleep.

"Jadary! It's Auntie Ang."

The girl's eyes fluttered and opened vaguely.

"Here," I said. "I'm here."

Her eyes closed again, but she smiled distantly as if at something in a dream.

"Jadary!" I said, giving her a shake. "I need to know something. It's very important. Aab had something. Something shiny. Maybe a secret thing she kept to herself. Have you seen it? Do you know where it is?"

The girl's face slid softly into confusion and then her eyes opened again. Her mouth moved, but no words came out and then, just as she was about to drift back into sleep, her eyes went to Aab beside her and moved deliberately to a little burlap purse half buried in the covers drawn tight around her shivering body. I reached for it, pulled it open, and emptied the contents onto the ground.

There was a notebook full of childish scrawl and some drawings, notes presumably from Bertha's classes. There was a soft toy that might have been a home-stitched monkey. And there was a roughly fashioned metal egg with strange luminous panels of what looked like smoked glass.

I picked it up gingerly, half expecting it to be hot. It wasn't, but I knew immediately that this was the source of the contagion. I could feel it in my head, my guts.

"Where did she get this?" I demanded.

Jadary looked scared, shrinking away from the hardness in my face.

"You're not in trouble," I said. "Neither is she. But I need to know where she got it."

"Voresh!" the girl whispered, her eyes full of dread. "She said the Voresh brought it. Saw him down by the river. He left it." She broke off, coughing. Aab still lay unmoving, but as I started to move away, Jadary seized my hand in her frail and tiny grip. "He came back, the Voresh. Here to the sick camp, Aab said. I didn't believe her. But then, last night, when everyone was sleeping I thought I saw . . ."

"What?" I said. "What did you see?"

Her eyes filled, and she squeezed them shut, as if locking out a memory, so that the tears broke and ran down her face.

"I saw the Voresh," she managed. "Here! Moving between the beds. Hunting. I closed my eyes and pretended to be asleep. When I looked again, he was gone."

"What did he look like, Jadary?"

"Like a Voresh!" she said, and I knew from the fear and exhaustion in her face that I would get no more.

"Thank you. Rest now," I said. "You will be fine. So will Aab."

As we moved away, the doctor, who had been watching, silently touched my sleeve.

"You shouldn't promise them health when you can't deliver it," he said, not so much scolding as advising.

"I can," I said. He was about to contradict me merely, but he saw the certainty in my face and the question in his mouth turned into something else.

"What is a Voresh?" he said.

"A Lani myth," I said. "A goblin man. One of the armed sentries of the underworld."

"A hallucination brought on by her fever?"

"I don't think so," I said. "Search the camp for more of these," I said to the doctor. "There is somewhere I need to go."

"What about the children?" he said.

I paused and looked around me.

"If you don't find any more of these, and they make it through the next few hours, I think they will be all right."

I DIDN'T REALLY KNOW that. Teeth wouldn't grow back, even if hair would, and who knew how much other damage had been done affecting things below the skin. Vestris had survived, but she was not whole, and there was something insidious about the device I had stowed in my satchel that felt worse than the cave where I had left my sister to die half a year ago. How that could be, I didn't know, but I knew who could tell me.

I took the underground all the way to Flintwick, staying away from other passengers as best I could, then ran flat out to Crommerty Street and Ansveld's shop. By the time I got there, I was nauseous with more than anxiety. The device in my bag was poisoning me. I could feel it. I slammed the thing onto the counter, speaking rapidly about what I feared it was and the damage it could quickly do.

"If I'm right," I said, "I need a way to contain it or seal it away where it cannot harm anyone."

Ansveld Jr. considered me seriously, then unsheathed a luxorite lamp and placed the object under one of his large lenses.

"Oh my, yes," he said. "I can feel it. Most unpleasant."

He turned the rough metal and glass almost-sphere in his hands, then reached for a fine screwdriver. He worked it into position, then gave it a twist. The egg popped open, splitting into two pieces. Inside, bright, hard and tinged very slightly with emerald green, was a chunk of what I had once thought was luxorite.

"So there's more," he said, musingly. "Or is this from the same source?"

"I don't know yet, but we need to find out how to stop it from doing whatever it does to people."

"Indeed," he said, "though I feel we have already made progress in that direction."

I was about to demand what he meant, when I realized that I felt it too. The noxious effects of the brilliant fragment of crystal had already dulled.

"Curious," he said. "Unless I am very much mistaken, the housing functions as a kind of magnifier. Not for the light of the piece, but for its other less wholesome properties."

"How could smoked glass do that?" I said, peering at the intricate filigree of metal parts, all carefully bonded around the irregular fragments of glass.

"How indeed?" he said, wonderingly. An idea struck him, and he snatched up a headpiece with a series of colored lenses, which he slid into place over his eyes, experimenting with each as he considered, not the greenish diamond-like light source, which he had already slipped into a metal box with a black velvet lining, but the roughly welded housing. "Ah!" he said at last. "Fascinating. I see . . ."

"Mr. Ansveld?" I prompted.

"Yes, Miss Sutonga. What a remarkable young lady you are," he observed, smiling. "Always full of surprises. This is most intriguing. You see, the green luxorite fragment is like those we saw before, quite possibly part of the same batch and from the same cave, and

I'll wager it has the same properties. If you are exposed to it for a long time, it will make you sick."

"But this made people much more sick and much faster than last time," I said, "though the crystal is tiny."

"Because," he said, pleased with the discovery, "what looks like glass in the housing around the crystal, is not glass at all, but very old luxorite. The real stuff, mind, not your faux green toxic variety. It seems to work as a lens, multiplying the strength of the stone inside many times over, and beaming it out in all directions. What you have found, Miss Sutonga, is a weapon. A kind of noxious bomb."

"Old luxorite?"

"Of the kind recently purchased from me by my unpleasant neighbor," he said significantly.

"Kepahler!"

"The very same. Now, I'm not a naturally suspicious person, Miss Sutonga, but until you walked in here today, I would have been prepared to go to my grave believing ancient luxorite has no practical use or commercial value, and anyone purchasing it was a crank. But now . . ."

"It can't be a coincidence," I concluded for him.

"It seems highly unlikely," he agreed.

"All right," I said, nodding at what felt like progress. "But first: this toxic luxorite, how do we make it safe?"

"An excellent question. I wonder if whoever made this had the answer?"

I shook my head. "How could we know?" I asked.

"Do you know much about photography, Miss Sutonga? A faddish thing, being popularized by the newspapers now and a little hobby of mine." As he spoke, he turned to the cabinets behind him and rifled through them, producing some small dishes and glass jars of fluid from a medicine chest. "Some time ago a friend of mine, a colleague in the luxorite trade with a similar interest in photography, you understand, chanced upon an interesting discovery. He found that luxorite—the real stuff, I mean—will darken an unexposed photographic plate even when its light is completely shielded by almost all substances. Quite fascinating. The mineral seems to stream through the majority of materials as if they are not there at all. Isn't that remarkable?"

"Yes," I said, shortly. "But how does that help us here?"

"True luxorite casts its light, and whatever else is in there, at all times and through most substances, but it is quite harmless," he said, apparently missing my impatience, as he measured out liquids and swabbed the outer metal of the egg. "Now your green, venomous variety—we really should give it a proper name—does, I'm guessing, something similar, but whatever it radiates is lethal to human beings. Now if I were trying to use such a substance to nefarious ends, I would begin by finding a way to protect myself from the core toxin, and the first thing I would try would be the one substance which shields those photographic plates from the strange, invisible effects of shaded luxorite."

He pulled the glass stoppers from two bottles, one of which smelled sharply of vinegar. The other was labeled SODIUM RHODIZONATE. He mixed the contents together, and then took the swab he had used to rub down the surface of the egg and immersed it in the liquid.

"The metal casing is simply iron," he said, "but whoever put it together protected himself from the mineral inside and left, I hope, a trace of . . ." He considered the liquid, then smiled, as it turned pink. "Lead." He clapped his hands together in delight, and grinned at me. "I believe I have a suitable piece of foil in the back."

He was gone less than a minute, returning with a square of

charcoal gray metal thin as paper into which he placed the fragment of green luxorite, folding it tightly and evenly.

"There," he said. "Quite safe. Though I suspect that this is only part of whatever mystery you are trying to unravel."

"Thank you," I said, almost hugging him with relief, which would have been as inappropriate as it was out of character for me. "One more thing. Last time we spoke, you mentioned Colonel Archibald Mandel."

"I did."

"You warned me to stay clear of him."

"Before he became the architect of the Bar-Selehm police state," said Ansveld with grim amusement.

"You said he knew your father and that his politics were . . ." I hesitated, seeing the way Ansveld shifted uncomfortably in his chair.

"You are wondering about my father's politics," he said.

"I'm sorry," I said. "I'm trying to gauge exactly what kind of threat Mandel represents, and I thought perhaps you might know because . . ."

"Because my father was a racist?" said Ansveld. He held my eyes, and there was a sudden coolness in the room as the silence blossomed. "There is no other way to say it," he conceded, "and the answer, I'm afraid is yes. A good old-fashioned Bar-Selehm racist of the unapologetic kind, the kind Mr. Richter has made respectable again."

"And Mandel is the same?"

"Worse."

"How far would he go . . ." I began but could not find the words to end the sentence.

"To rid the city—to rid the *world*—of blacks and coloreds?" Ansveld concluded for me. "How far would a farmer go to eradicate rats and cockroaches? Colonel Mandel was always a dangerous man, ruthless and manipulative, and he always had powerful friends. But now, with his so-called *Security Force* on hand, and whispering into Richter's ear . . . Yes, Miss Sutonga, I would be very wary of him indeed, and I would believe nothing below him when it came to people who did not share the color of his skin. Nothing at all."

CHAPTER

20

THERE WAS A NEW curfew for nonwhites in the city, which meant that you could be locked up for being out after sundown unless you could prove you were either working or on your way—by a very direct route—to or from your place of employment. I was used to not attracting notice, but I couldn't afford to lose a night's investigation by being tossed into some stinking cell, so I went over the roofs wherever possible, approaching the Inns of Court from the northwest via the elegant curl of Long Terrace. I watched the Martel Court and other civic buildings from behind a marble statue of a self-righteous Justice to ascertain the city's increased security forces weren't around before making my final approach. I say "the city" but it wasn't, not in my head. It was Richter. Everything that was happening to the city was at his urging, cheered on by Mandel and his Heritage party cronies and facilitated by the spinelessness of the Nationals. Some of the latter were probably secretly delighted to watch the government make this hard turn to the right, but others were closer to the Brevards ideologically. They just didn't have the guts to stand up and be counted.

I scaled the walls as before, all fingers and toe caps, up the grout lines between the stone-block facing, pulling myself onto the roof. I moved cautiously, not because I expected there to be guards, but because there was something eerie about the six stone angels up here in the dark and silence. Particularly since one of them was my sister.

A guardian angel? Or simply an angel of death and vengeance?

I didn't know how often she stood up here, how long she held her strange, watchful vigil, or why. It made me wary, and I realized that I had begun to suspect that the injuries done to her by the false green luxorite had affected more than her body.

Vestris did not turn to greet me, but she seemed to sense my presence, though she waited till I was almost close enough to touch her before she spoke.

"If you pushed me now," she said, as if pondering some abstract philosophical problem, "I would not be able to stop you."

I hesitated, unsure how to respond, then said simply, "I would not."

"No?" she said musingly. "No, perhaps not."

I didn't ask why she thought I might push her to her death. I knew. We both knew. There were things in her past for which she would never be able to completely atone. I would not kill her for them, of course.

Of course.

Though I thought of Berrit often . . .

"Did you take tea with the spider?" she said.

A cold chill of alarm ran through me, and I felt the hair prickle on my neck before I remembered that she had used that word before to mean Madame Nahreem.

"Not yet," I said, recovering my composure. "I came to ask you something."

"Then ask," she said, seeming to lean out over the abyss, as if contemplating one final step into nothingness and death.

"The false luxorite cave in the mountains," I said. "Was that the only source, or were there others?"

"The cave where you left me to die?" she said, almost wistfully.

I swallowed and licked my dry lips.

"Yes," I said.

"That was the only place we knew of. Why?"

"I found another piece, here in the city."

She turned to me then, the wind rustling the light hood of fabric around her unearthly face, her eyes smoldering inside its dark folds like coals.

"That isn't possible," she hissed.

As she spoke, she seemed to shrink slightly, drawing herself into a crouch, like an animal poised to spring, and her mouth opened. I took a step back, afraid, but she stayed frozen in that attitude as if she was indeed the gargoyle for which she had been named.

"It's true," I managed. "Someone took a piece to the Drowning. Magnified it with true luxorite so that it made the children sick. Rahvey's girls . . ."

For a moment, Vestris just stared, and then she crouched lower and leapt forward on all fours like a baboon. I shrank back against the stone, fumbling for my kukri, but she went right past me without so much as a backward glance, trotting along the very lip of the roof, and then dropping over the edge.

Coming back to myself, I took a few hurried steps to the brink and looked down; she was crawling like an insect on the face of the building. Her black eyes found me, and she hissed again, before continuing her descent. At the bottom, she leapt into the shadows of the street and loped away at considerable speed, so that a moment later, she was gone and I was left alone. As I stood there, lost in confused thought and a dreamy, unplaceable fear, the thought dawned slowly on me that if anyone happened to look up to the roof of the Inns of Court, they would think me the sixth angel. The thought chilled and hardened within me like molten iron, and I wondered again what that meant.

An angel of death and vengeance, or a guardian?

THE MORNING PAPERS ANNOUNCED that, in late-night session, Richter's coalition government had pushed through a series of laws in the interests of "National Security" that included orders of removal for all nonwhites from the east side of the city along a line slashing up from the Ridleford pontoon bridge up to Deans Gate. Blacks and coloreds were given two weeks to move. Effective immediately was an order that all nonwhites carry papers of employment at all times should they cross over into the designated area, and that those papers could be demanded for inspection by law enforcement or by members of the new civilian militia.

I had already seen this so-called "civilian militia" on patrol. The organization—too grand a term for a uniformed gang that served as the armed wing of the Heritage party—had no training or experience, and their qualifications were limited to a shared ideology. They had been around for a while, skulking in the corners and prowling like jackals around party rallies, tapping truncheons into their hands and leering meaningfully, but they had been few, regulated by real law enforcement, and generally despised. They were thugs and bullies playing at soldiers, poor whites looking for someone other than themselves to blame for their low standing. Now, however, they were legitimate and respected, a breeding ground for the politicians, generals, and leaders of the future—according to the recruiting handbills that had suddenly appeared all over the city. They were still thugs and bullies, but now the leash that had kept them in check had been taken off, and people—including white people, even including those politicians, police, and military who were not so high in the esteem of the Heritage party—were afraid of them.

The black community's response to the new laws and the increased powers of the militia was instant and predictable. Within hours of the news, a massive rally had been orchestrated, and a group thousands strong, led by Aaron Muhapi and his entourage, marched on Szenga Square—a beautiful tree-lined park well inside the designated whites only area.

I was in that entourage. I didn't know the songs and chants, particularly those that had old Mahweni words in them, but I walked, eyeing the watchful members of the so-called civilian militia, swaggering in their high boots and unearned uniforms. When we reached the designated place where the platform had been raised, I watched Muhapi take the stage, and I listened.

"So here we are," he said, facing the crowd, his eyes blazing. "On this spot where we have been for generations, a place we have endured all manner of hardship, injustice, and exploitation at the hands of our white oppressors. It has been a kind of game, and we have played our parts in the hope that if we showed willing, if we were compliant, if we agreed to their terms and went along with their rules, our voices would be heard, our freedoms and rights would be addressed. And we have been patient. We have watched the sun cross the sky over this great city, much of it built by our hands, thousands and thousands of times, waiting for change. And now change has come, but it is not what we expected, not what we were promised by our leaders. We stand here where we have been for hundreds of years, and we are told that simply being here, standing on land that was once ours and ours alone, is no longer allowed. Blacks and coloreds who have lived and worked here must now move away, and their return to this area will be regulated at the discretion of the white man.

"My friend Peter, Peter Vincenti, a great friend to me and the Mahweni people, tells me that the rules of the game have changed, and he is right. We would have liked to debate those rules, to sit with the leaders of the National-Heritage coalition government to argue our case, but that opportunity has not been provided. Our people have been huddled into pockets so that our representatives— some good men of the Brevard party—have even less power than they used to. Our districts will have populations of tens of thousands, mostly black and colored, to each member of Parliament, while white districts contain mere hundreds or less. For decades we have been promised greater representation, a louder voice in the political process, but what do we have? This change of the rules is one more broken promise, one more step away from equality for the black and colored people of this city. We have, as I say, been patient. We have trusted and waited in spite of right and justice on our side.

"Well, no more. This is our land. The cobbles we stand on, set by our hands, and ground roamed for a thousand years by our ancestors, belong to us as much as the white men who have passed these laws, and if they want us to move off them, they will have to make us."

As the crowd thrilled to his energy, his rage, he turned to face the Parliament, and he was not talking to the assembly anymore. Now he was talking to Richter and the government.

"You call us beasts. You say we do not merit full power sharing. You ban us from our native lands, from our places of work, and you strip us of our voice in a Parliament that you have shown to serve only your interests. You ban us from our streets, from our very homes with immoral laws passed by an unelected government led by a racist. Did you think we would go quietly? Did you think we would smile and nod and accept the old lie that you know best, that you are protecting us from ourselves, that your version of culture proves you to be our moral betters? Did you think we would skulk away like beaten dogs? You were, as you have so often been, wrong. We. Will. Not. Move."

And they didn't. For three hours they sang and chanted, listened to speeches about what should be done and not done, and the white dragoons watched from the sidelines but did not intervene. There were, perhaps, two or three thousand people in the crowd, too many for the soldiers to engage safely, though I saw no weapons among the assembly, and for all their defiance, they were surprisingly contained, almost placid. When night fell and the meeting broke up, it did so with a sense of something achieved, and the mood was satisfied, even hopeful.

"We will do it again tomorrow, and the day after," Muhapi remarked to Peter, his aide. "And we will keep doing it until these absurd laws are abandoned."

"And if they aren't?" said Peter, who seemed more cautious than his charismatic friend, less buoyed up by the success of the rally.

"Then we are going to be busy," said Muhapi. "Come, Peter. This was a victory. A peaceful protest of such size, and not just made up of Mahweni. They cannot ignore such protests forever."

"I hope you are right," said Peter.

"I am," said Muhapi. "I have to be, for all our sakes. Now, you may be determined to be miserable, but I want to celebrate. You will come to my house, and we will grill meat and drink wine. Miss Sutonga and her friends will join us, yes?"

It was impossible to refuse him in this rare ebullient mood, and I knew Sureyna wanted to go along, so I nodded.

"Good," he said. "You can meet my family. And I believe we have some mutual acquaintances."

I gave him a quizzical look, but he just smiled and nodded to where two black men stood in serious conversation, one lean and rangy, almost unrecognizable in city clothes, was Mnenga. The other, bigger in the chest and shoulders, but also unfamiliar in civilian dress, was Captain Emtezu.

I stared at the strangeness of seeing them together, but I did not have to ask why they were here, and a part of me had known Mnenga would seek Muhapi out. The assimilated and unassimilated Mahweni were testing some new alliances in the light of recent developments, and while Emtezu had kept his politics to himself for the sake for the uniform he wore, that too had become moot. He surely did not intend it, but Richter was driving together people who had circled each other warily like lions for decades. It was good, I decided. Almost good enough to take my mind off Willinghouse, who seemed curiously irrelevant to all this progress. The idea pained me, because I knew he would have been here, talking to the crowd, shaking hands and throwing whatever personal and political muscle he could behind Muhapi's movement. It seemed unfair that it was all happening without him.

"You wish Willinghouse were here," said Muhapi, looking at me shrewdly.

I gaped at him, amazed—not for the first time—at the way the man seemed to read my thoughts, but opted for simplicity in my answer.

"I do," I said.

"He will be soon," said Muhapi. "Do not despair. We sent a powerful message today."

"A political message," I said, "yes. But politics alone will not free him. That will take evidence."

"Which you will find," said Muhapi.

"You are very confident," I said.

"Today, yes," he said. "I am." He laughed. "This was a good day, and there will be more. See? Even Peter is smiling."

"Mr. Muhapi—"

"Aaron, please."

"Aaron," I said, "forgive me if this is an impertinent question, but do you know Count Alfonse Marino?"

"The Grappoli ambassador?" said Muhapi. "I have seen him at social events, but I don't believe we have ever met, no."

"What kind of social events?" I asked. It seemed unlikely that Muhapi moved in the same circles as the Grappoli ambassador.

"It's quite funny, actually," he said. "There is a club in Morgessa called the Black Ibis. Music mostly, but also some drinking and dancing. All quite sedate, refined even, but very black. Particularly the music, and the clientele."

"You saw the Grappoli ambassador there?" I said, amazed.

"Twice!" said Muhapi, amused. "He sits in the corner, wearing street clothes. Keeps his hat on indoors and wears spectacles with ordinary glass in them. A kind of disguise, I suppose, but everyone knows who he is. He doesn't talk to anyone, just sits and listens to the music and drinks brandy. Tips well, I'm told. Always picked up and dropped off by private carriage. A funny thing, isn't it, the world?"

"It is indeed," I said.

We walked all the way to Morgessa, Muhapi talking animatedly about his plans for what they would do tomorrow and the day after. I walked with Mnenga who, in his city clothes and stately movement, felt like some foreign dignitary, an ambassador, perhaps. It occurred to me that, in a way, he was. Though the elder dignitaries were not with him, the young woman with the towering hair who he had said was a kind of princess was. She was wearing a long rust-colored dress that fitted her like a sheath. She still wore her beads, but the dress made her look elegant, sophisticated, and I realized that at first I had taken her for one of the city blacks. For reasons I could not pinpoint, the thought unsettled me.

"Where are the others you came with?" I asked him.

"Meeting with Kondotsy Furwina at his home, which," Mnenga added, with a sideways smile, "I believe you once attempted to burn down."

"That was under his predecessor," I said, making a face at him. The incident he was referring to had occurred when Sohwetti was head of the Unassimilated Tribes. "Why wasn't Furwina here?"

"Because alliances between the assimilated and unassimilated Mahweni make the city nervous," he said.

"So what are you trying to build?" I said.

"An alliance."

He shot me that big, open smile of his, and I couldn't help laughing, though I knew he was playing with fire. We all were.

The black population of the city has always been a little larger than the white, which is why the electoral districts were so carefully constructed to reduce the power of their vote, something Richter's redistricting plans would only intensify. Though the Unassimilated Tribes outside the city had nothing like the coherence and identity the city Mahweni had, there were a lot of them. If they were to combine with the black population of the city itself, they would be a formidable force.

This was, Sureyna had explained, what made the redistricting so dangerous. The whites thought they were stripping their black neighbors of power, and they were, but they were also closing off the Mahweni's legal options. I knew very well what happened to people who felt that they could no longer achieve what they wanted, what they *needed,* under the protection of the law: they stepped outside it. Should Richter make the black vote meaningless, then the Mahweni would look to other possibilities, and a union between city blacks and the Unassimilated Tribes could mean only one thing: civil war, or its threat as a bargaining card.

"They are saying that the Unassimilated Tribes have been attacking railway lines north of the city," I said. "Stopping mail, cargo, and passenger trains."

"Who has been saying this?" said Mnenga. It wasn't a real question, and he was still smiling, though his amused look was weary.

"The papers," I said, knowing how lame that sounded.

"The newspapers who have fired their black and Lani staff?" said Mnenga. "The newspapers who now have their stories approved by a government censor before printing them? The newspapers who have yet to produce a single reliable witness or photograph that supports these claims of tribal sabotage and intimidation?"

"Yes," I admitted grudgingly.

"I thought so," he said.

"'Sabotage and intimidation'?" I echoed.

"What?" he said.

"You speak Feldish much better than you suggested when we first met."

He laughed, then caught the slightly wounded look in my face and realized what I was thinking: that he had misled me on purpose about his role in the politics of the region. He frowned.

"I have been practicing," he said, then smiled kindly. "And I have had some good teachers."

I returned his smile, then turned to see the young Mahweni "princess" appearing at his side as if she had been looking for him. Mnenga said something to her in his own language and she smiled first at him, then at me.

"My Feldish is not good," she said. "Sorry. Mnenga tells me about you." She smiled and nodded to suggest that he had said good things.

"Thank you," I said. "I'm sorry, I didn't catch your name."

She looked momentarily puzzled then said, "Ah. Yes. I am Lomkhosi."

"I am pleased to meet you," I said, wondering why that did not feel entirely honest.

"Ang!" called a voice. I turned to find Sureyna hurrying to catch up with me, her eyes alight. All around us black, Lani, and a handful of whites walked together, talking excitedly, sharing ideas and plans, radiating energy like sunlight. "Isn't this wonderful!" she breathed. "Can you feel it? It's like . . . hope."

MUHAPI'S WIFE, SAMORA, TOOK over the festivities once we reached their large but simple Morgessa house, throwing open every room and ordering her husband to stay away from the great pit barbecue, which was already hot and smoking in the backyard. Their son, Hlumelo, who was six, was charged with offering juice and wine to their guests, a task he undertook with great solemnity, winning the hearts of all who looked on him. Suddenly it seemed the house was packed with dozens—perhaps even a hundred— people, all laughing and talking, marveling at how Samora was able to provide for so many, and as a group of black men and women broke into song, accompanied by a pair of drums and a stringed instrument whose name I did not know, the whole completed its transition from political meeting to party. When Samora—a solid, businesslike woman who was wearing her hair in the traditional piled manner of Mnenga's village elders—began to dance, the tension of the last few days seemed to burn away.

"A remarkable thing," said Captain Emtezu, appearing beside me, "the power of food and music."

It seemed like a very long time since I had spoken to the captain, and uncharacteristically caught up in the mood of the moment, I embraced him like a favorite uncle.

"I didn't know you knew Muhapi," I said, once our pleasantries about his family were done.

"Everyone knows Aaron Muhapi," he said, watching the man arguing playfully with his wife to the delight of several bystanders. "I am more surprised to see you here, but I suppose I should not be."

"What are you doing now, since . . . ?" I wasn't sure how to phrase the question and left it dangling.

"Since I was stripped of my weapons and sent to sit behind a desk organizing supply lines?" he said, unable to keep the bitterness from his voice, though he smiled still. "Precious little. Mostly, I am waiting, though I am no longer sure what I am waiting for. I thought it was reinstatement and rejoining the barracks with my men but now . . ." Again he scanned the assembled crowd. We were outside, watching as the men bickered over whether the skewers of impala flesh were thoroughly roasted and their wives made fun of them. "Now I am not sure. Something is coming, but I am not sure what. I fear I may yet need my rifle again."

I watched Mnenga dancing with Lomkhosi. She looked beautiful. Radiant. Mnenga could not take his eyes off her. I took a breath that was almost a gasp, then looked quickly away.

Emtezu sipped his wine. "And you?" he said.

I pulled myself back to the conversation, thought of Willinghouse, and shook my head vaguely.

"I don't know," I said. "I am doing . . . what I can. I'm not sure it will help."

"Sometimes," he said, "the effort is all. Muhapi says that when we all try, the world moves on its axis and suddenly impossible things can happen."

I smiled. "Do you believe that?" I asked.

"I don't know," he replied. "But I do not need to believe in the end to make the attempt."

I nodded, watching the dancing people again, caught between elation and a deep sadness. Back in the house, someone shouted. Then another. I thought it was a laugh at first, but then heads were turning, and alarm spread through the crowd like a herd of wildebeests spying a lion.

"What was—" I began, but then the door into the house was kicked open and I saw the grim-faced white soldiers with their rifles and truncheons. At the front was a captain in a red tunic. Emtezu stepped toward him, but another soldier drew a pistol and leveled it at his face. Emtezu faltered, hands raised, babbling his rank and number, but the officer ignored him, scanning the crowd.

The music stopped, and there was a sudden, terrified silence as the officer spotted Muhapi, standing watchful, expectant by the wall of the yard. Peter was beside him, and as the officer took another purposeful step, two more dragoons coming with him, Peter's hand dropped to his pocket. For a split second, I saw the butt of a pistol in his hand, but then Muhapi reached out, his movement quick as a striking snake, stilling him, pushing the gun back into his pocket.

"Am I a thief," said Muhapi to the soldiers, "that you come for me in the night? You could have come for me today in the square. Breaking into my house, disrupting my family, my friends—"

"Aaron Muhapi," said the officer, unflinchingly. "I am arresting you on charges of sedition, distributing banned literature, and organizing an illegal gathering. Come with me."

Muhapi considered him as if weighing his options seriously. Without taking his eyes off the officer and his men, he said, "Very well. I will come and I will come quietly, and my friends and family will, on this occasion, do as I ask and not interfere." His eyes flashed to Peter, and he managed a smile for his aide's benefit. "I am a man of peace. Do me the honor of respecting my wishes."

Peter was very still. At last, his jaw tight and his eyes full, he nodded.

"Have no fear," said Muhapi to the room in general. "All this means is that they are taking us seriously."

He paused only to hug his wife and son, the former strong but strained, the latter confused, his eyes on the soldiers.

"Well then," said Muhapi. "It is time."

And with that, he followed the soldiers out, leaving the house stunned and silent, the only sound coming from the crackling of the fire whose smoke was still sweet and heavy with the aroma of roasted meat. My eyes moved over the stunned faces and found

Samora. She looked, in spite of the people offering her their con-
dolences mixed with their sureties that all would be well, curiously
absent. She stood in a way that made her seem completely alone; I
felt that I was seeing right into her heart, where there was nothing
but profound grief. It was as though she had already seen the future
and had found it to be a blasted landscape of loss and the absence
of hope.

CHAPTER
21

"WHAT AM I GOING to tell Richter?" said Dahria, looking up from the paper that heralded the start of her brother's closed-door trial. "I promised him information in return for his slowing proceedings. If I can't deliver—today—it will be too late."

I had been mulling the same problem, and my answer was risky.

"We invent something," I said.

"He'll know."

"Not if we make it sound good."

"He'll know eventually."

"Maybe. But we're just trying to buy time."

"Till what? You've been investigating, or whatever it is you do, and you have no real evidence. If we stall Richter with bad information but can't derail the trial, he will make sure it goes all the worse for Joss."

"How much worse can it go, Dahria?" I said. "He's accused of assassinating the prime minister! You understand, don't you, that there can be only two possible outcomes of the trial: either he is acquitted or he is hanged."

"So we have to give Richter real information," she said, shrinking away from the bleak reality in my words, as if it was something grotesque she didn't want to look at.

"Not if it disrupts the activities of your brother's friends and allies," I countered, "and certainly not if it leads them to prison or worse. He wouldn't want that."

"I'm not sure we have the luxury of honoring his wishes," she said.

I was about to say something pointed and hurtful about her being cavalier with her brother's principles because she had none of her own, but I saw the desperation in her blanched face, the unsteadiness of her usually unflappable hands, and I relented.

"We need a delay," I said. "That is all. We know your brother is innocent, so the truth must be out there for the finding. I'm close. I'm sure of it. Perhaps we can get him to agree to a delay of only a day or two."

"Perhaps," she said doubtfully.

I had already strained my optimism as far as it would go. I could promise no more.

"Yes," I said. "It might prove crucial."

"And if it doesn't?"

"I don't know, Dahria. I don't have all the answers or all the plans. All I know is that we try what we can, and if that doesn't work, we try something else."

She sat, hung her head and sighed, but when she looked up again she seemed resigned to follow my lead.

"Tell me what to say to Richter," she said.

"What he wants to hear," I said. "He knows your brother was talking to Muhapi, whom they have already taken into custody. The papers are alleging some conspiratorial alliance between the assimilated and unassimilated Mahweni, and have already printed reports of tribal attacks on roads and railway lines north of the city."

"I thought Mnenga said none of it was true?"

"He did, but that doesn't matter. Richter and his friends want it to be true. They want to feel that there is a black threat to the city and that your brother was involved in it. Richter would love to try your brother not just for murder, but for treason, exposing the entire Brevard party as enemies of Bar-Selehm who are allied with Mahweni savages."

She stared at me.

"That sounds like a very dangerous card to play," she said. I nodded, my mouth dry. "Once we raise that possibility, it might be a very difficult ship to stop."

"I know," I said.

"They won't just believe it. They'll jump on it," she said, her face full of warning. "It will be the propaganda coup of the century. It will end white resistance to Richter, his government and his policies in a heartbeat. You think the black and Lani population have it hard now, wait to see what happens to them if Richter proves collusion between my brother and the Unassimilated Tribes in an attempt to destabilize the city—proves it based on fake information supplied by me! It will be the end of everything!"

"I know," I said, my voice very low.

"How sure are you that you will be able to bring enough evidence to save my brother and stop whatever destruction this will start?"

I thought, not about the case and how much or little progress my investigation had made, but about how few alternatives there were that might save Willinghouse's neck.

"I'm sure," I said.

She gave me a searching look, so that eventually I turned away, feeling transparent, but at last she said, "Very well."

THE DETAILS OF THE plan were picked from conversations with Mnenga and from Sureyna's impeccable knowledge of what the *Standard* had been printing since she left. I think it helped to take her mind off Muhapi's arrest; the event had merited no more than a few lines at the end of a story on page two, which also implied Aaron had been pulled in for being drunk in the street. She burned with cold fury all the time now, and when I explained our plan to her, she gave me a worried look.

"They will use this against us," she said. "Even when they know it isn't true."

"Then we need to win a more decisive victory so they can't," I said.

"Victory," she said bleakly, shaking her head. Mnenga put his large, sinewy hand on hers and smiled at her.

"I trust Anglet," he said.

Sureyna seemed irritated by the remark's naïveté, but in the end she just shrugged and nodded.

"What do you need to know?" she said.

"Every report of unassimilated tribal aggression north of Bar-Selehm cited in the last month, and what sources supplied the information."

She rummaged in her overstuffed bag, pulling out old newspapers and a map of the area, which had been folded so many times the creases had worn through until the whole was like a collection of separate squares loosely taped together. She pushed them over to me, but instead of looking at them herself, she half closed her eyes and began scanning that remarkable memory of hers. Mnenga gave me a look.

"And what do you want from me?" he said.

"Something much harder," I said. "And probably quite dangerous. You will need to get the support of the other villages."

"I can do that," he said simply.

"You don't know what I want yet," I said, marveling at his faith in me.

"We know who our friends are," he said.

I held his eyes, then Sureyna's eyes snapped open, and she spoke.

"I know what you need."

"Go on," I said.

"Willinghouse has family connections here and here," she said, pointing at the map, areas north and west of the city. "His grandfather owned silver mines on land bought directly from Unassimilated Tribes. Both areas have been connected to recent acts of sabotage, though to be honest, I don't think there was anything to them. They came third hand through Arthur Besland, the reporter whose body you brought."

"You want to invent another story supposedly sent in by Besland?" I said. "What if they know he's dead?"

"We backdate a report," she said. "Make it sound like it got lost in transit."

"What would we put in it?"

"Depends what you want it to do," she answered, eyeing me. I had been cagey about what I was up to.

"Something that will describe a gathering of Unassimilated Tribes on Willinghouse family land," I said.

"A gathering?" said Mnenga warily. "What kind of gathering?"

"Hunters," I said. "A raiding party. Men with spears and—"

"An army," said Mnenga, his face hardening, his eyes fixed on mine. Sureyna whistled in wary disbelief.

"You want to create a fake threat to the city," she said. "Why?"

"Because Richter will believe it," I said. "Because it's what he has been praying for, and because while he verifies it and packages it to share with the Bar-Selehm population, he'll make sure Willinghouse stays alive."

"And you want the *Standard* to pass this on to him?" said Sureyna.

"Not at first," I said. "I want the tip to come from Dahria."

Sureyna's eyebrows hovered just below her hairline, then she said, "Eventually the papers will weigh in. They won't confirm the story, however much they want it to be true, unless they think it's right. They might be in the government's pocket, but they'll want evidence."

"That's where Mnenga comes in," I said, turning to him, conscious that he had said nothing since I floated the idea. "He gets some of his people to be seen in the area." I waited, but he sat there saying nothing, and eventually I spoke. "I know it's asking a lot."

He laughed, a short, hollow laugh. "Yes," he said. "It is."

"Just a glimpse, Mnenga!" I said. "A few men with weapons. We make sure they get seen, then they get out of there before anything—"

"Before the real army comes," he replies flatly. "The Bar-Selehm army, with rifles and machine guns."

"Your people will be gone by then," I said.

"Perhaps," he said. "But maybe the dragoons will move quickly. Maybe they will move by train and by horse. Even come up the coast by boat. And then maybe they will come looking for my people. And then what, Anglet?"

"I know it's risky—"

"But not your risk," he said. "Not Willinghouse's risk. My risk. My people's risk. For what? For whom?"

"It's not just about saving Willinghouse," I said, surprised by how bad this all sounded now that I had said it aloud, how much it sounded like I was using him, and I realized how much it sounded like I was choosing Willinghouse over him.

Again.

But it wasn't like that. Not really.

Sureyna was watching me, chastened and embarrassed as if she had stumbled on something painful and intimate, while he just looked . . . sad. Disappointed.

"No harm will come to you or your people," I said. "I promise."

"You don't know that," he said. "You can't."

"I can if we do it right," I said. "A few people seen together dressed as a raiding party who move quickly from place to place so that they are seen in different areas. A few well-spaced campfires whose smoke can be seen from a distance."

He watched me thoughtfully, tipping his head on one side.

"My people are good at hiding in the bush," he said. "They have to be."

"And white people can't tell one Mahweni warrior from another," said Sureyna, "so no one will realize they are seeing the same handful of blokes."

I gave her a disbelieving look, but Mnenga nodded and laughed.

"This is true," he said.

"Fighting racism with racism," said Sureyna. "Interesting."

"By the time word gets back to the city, your people will be long gone," I said, seeing the conviction building in his face.

"How many do you think we need?" asked Sureyna.

"A dozen?" I suggested. "Two dozen?"

Mnenga shook his head, and for a moment I thought he was going to shut down the whole plan.

"At least two hundred," he said. "For people to believe it. And it's safer to move in larger groups where there are one-horns and weancats."

I gazed at him gratefully.

"You will not regret it," I said. "I promise you. If we can save Willinghouse, I will make sure that he knows what you did."

"I know," said Mnenga.

"Right," I said, squeezing my eyes shut for a second to refocus my thoughts, then studying Sureyna's ragged maps. "Where do we need to make our imaginary army appear?"

Sureyna leaned in.

"Here and here," she said, pointing to parcels of Willinghouse's land some fifty miles north of the city. Both were close to a freight line.

"You said these were silver mines, yes?" I said. "That suggests armed escort for cargo. Is there anything that will be less well protected? I don't want Mnenga's men stumbling into security guards with guns."

"There's a coal mine here," she said, indicating a spot a little farther west. "The Lilac Roller. Mostly disused now, but Willinghouse still owns the land, and some of it has been fenced for grazing. That might be a good spot. Not well protected and far enough from the railway line that armed support will take time to get there. Sound good, Mnenga?"

"Yes," he said. "This is good."

"Ang?" Sureyna prompted. "You all right?"

But I barely heard her. My fingers went unthinkingly to the double-headed coin I wore on the thong around my neck, and when I blinked, tears ran down my cheeks.

"Anglet!" said Mnenga. "What is it?"

Sureyna took my hand and gazed, mystified, into my shocked face, but when she implored me to say what had caused the sudden change in my mood all I could say—whispering vaguely, recalling the word like I was quoting something from a dream—was "Atonement."

"YOU KNOW WHAT YOU are going to say?" I asked Dahria, as we made our way back to the Heritage center. It was two hours since my conversation with Sureyna, the conclusion of which I had resolved to bury as deep in my heart as was humanly possible. I imagined myself standing on the highest chimney in Bar-Selehm, writing the truth out on paper, then wrapping the paper around a stone and dropping it down the barrel of the chimney like I was casting a coin into a well.

An unwishing well.

I swallowed, wiped away my tears, turned my face into the hot sun, and got on with things, because that was what you did. In this and this alone, the very poor were like the very rich. You did not indulge your feelings. You bit down hard, you strangled sentiment, you said nothing—absolutely nothing—and you continued.

So. There was work to be done, and I set out to do it, though we had been turned away from the Parliament building by the Saunders rodent, Richter's private secretary.

"Of course I know what to say. Stop asking. You're making me nervous."

We kept walking in tense silence.

"I can go over it again if—" I began.

"I may not live by my wits, swinging from roof to roof like some overstimulated monkey, but that doesn't make me a moron," she shot back.

"Sorry," I said. "It's just that Mnenga—"

"I know all about Mnenga."

"And his people—"

"And his people," she replied. "Now, shut up and let me concentrate."

As it happened, her attempt to prepare herself mentally for the interview was premature. Richter was annoyed.

"What do you mean, coming to see me in Parliament?" he snapped as soon as we were shown in. "Are you stupid, woman, or were you just trying to embarrass me?"

I felt Dahria stiffen beside me, but for once she swallowed down her pride.

"I am sorry, sir," she said, "I did not think—"

"That, madame, is self-evident," said Richter. He enjoyed the power he had over her. I could tell. For all his previous dismissal of the idea that he might want anything from a beautiful woman, I sensed that he enjoyed humiliating someone like Dahria precisely because of who she was and what she looked like. "I hope the information you have to offer me has been better thought out than the manner in which you chose to deliver it."

"I hope so, sir," said Dahria, hating him.

"Well, let's hear it, then," he barked, checking his pocket watch. "Haven't got all day."

"Well, sir," Dahria began, "I think this will be of interest to you, and I hope that you will agree that it is worth commuting my brother's trial—"

"I'll be the judge of what your information is worth," he snapped. "Out with it, woman. I have no patience with the roundabout politenesses and small talk of your class. Say what you have to say and get out."

"Yes, sir," said Dahria, faltering but trying to regain her composure.

There was a ghostly tap on the door, and a moment later it opened, revealing Saunders, apparently newly arrived from Parliament. Richter looked up expectantly and extended a hand toward Dahria, silencing her as if she were an unruly child. The slender private secretary stooped and whispered in his ear like a bird hunting for seeds. Richter's face went from puzzlement to calculated amusement.

"He's here now?" he said.

"He is, sir," said the secretary.

Richter rose and said to Dahria, "Wait here." His supercilious gaze lingered on her just long enough to see if she would dare express outrage, then he turned toward the door. As he opened it, I realized that with the secretary's entrance, I had caught a woody aroma, which had blown in with him from the hallway. Not just wood. There was a citrus note there too.

Hair tonic.

The ambassador was here again. But Richter's manner was curious. I stepped toward the door after him, but the secretary stopped me with a look.

"Where are you going?" said Saunders. I might have been a mangy dog.

"My mistress's conversation with Mr. Richter is private," I offered.

"I think you mean the prime minister," said the secretary. "Or the Lord Protector. Either one is acceptable."

"Yes sir, sorry sir," I said.

"Very well," he said, stepping aside. "Wait in the kitchen."

As Saunders settled behind Richter's desk, looking Dahria up and down in a manner that managed to be both leering and contemptuous, I stepped into the hallway just in time to see a door click shut. It was the room where I had seen the Grappoli ambassador before. I walked toward it, but the door was heavy and I could hear nothing of the conversation from within. I stopped entirely, but it made no difference, and I knew that were I caught, I could not possibly claim I thought this was the kitchen. I dithered, trying to remember what I had seen in the room when I had been there last. An internal chamber. There were no windows at which I might eavesdrop and no chimney that might carry some of the dialogue in the unlikely event I could find a vent higher up. There was nothing I could do. I should do as I was told: find the kitchen and wait patiently for once.

The kitchen.

An idea struck me. This was an old building, and I was sure there were servants all over the place, though they were kept out of sight and mind even more efficiently than at the Parliament House. The people who met here wouldn't want to be constantly interrupted by servants offering to clear glasses or make up the fires.

Last time I had been inside the room, I had noticed that the ambassador had been sitting beside a shuttered hatch in the wall and that he had recently eaten a plate of samosas, which had been served hot. In the absence of scurrying servants, that could mean only one thing.

A dumbwaiter.

I checked that there was no one watching me, then set off for the kitchen as fast as I could without running.

CHAPTER

22

I FOUND THE STAIRS down to the deserted kitchens and larders, making sure I kept a good sense of my position in relation to the rest of the house, and chose a shutter on the kitchen wall beside the gas-fed oven. I raised it and stuck my head into the dumbwaiter shaft. It was no more than that: a square hollow that ran up to the higher floors, hung with pull ropes and with metal runners set into the shaft walls like vertical railway lines. The little wooden platform that ran on them was dimly visible two floors up.

I wasted no time, unfastening my skirt so hurriedly that it tore a little, then pulling myself backwards into the chimney-tight shaft and feeling the walls for hand- and footholds. Leaving the skirt in the bottom, I climbed the ten or twelve feet, which I was almost certain, put me behind the shuttered hatch in the study where Richter and the ambassador were now talking.

I could hear them already, Richter clipped and haughty as he had been to Dahria. The Grappoli ambassador, by contrast, sounded quite unlike himself. Instead of the suave purr I associated with him, he sounded brusque, cornered. I adjusted till I felt sure of the brackets my boots had managed to find in the shaft wall, then pressed my ear to the frail hatch screen.

"And I think," Richter was saying pointedly, "that the balance of power in this relationship of ours has changed quite considerably, and you would do well to remember that. I'm not some minor minister who has to kowtow to you anymore, Alfonse. Your military masters understand that, even if some of your politicians don't."

"Which means what, Norton?"

"It means, among other things, that you address me as Prime Minister or Lord Protector," said Richter coldly, though I felt sure that this was another conversation he was enjoying.

"Very well, *Prime Minister*," said the ambassador, "though I would remind you that my allegiances are not to your government but to the vast and expanding Grappoli Empire."

"Are they?" Richter demanded. "Some rum tales about your after-hours entertainments have come my way, Alfonse, and I can't help wondering if your superiors would be as mystified by them as I am."

There was the merest shadow of a hesitation, but it was enough to tell me that when the ambassador said, "I'm sure I don't know what you are referring to," he was lying.

"I'm sure you don't," said Richter, and though I could not see him I knew he was smiling like a cat. "Just see that you remember who your friends are, or the next few days might prove very difficult for you."

"Don't you dare threaten me!" the ambassador returned, though his defiance felt hollow.

"Let's call it less a threat and more an observation," cooed Richter. "Now. Unless you have something important to tell me, I suggest you leave. You've been seen around here too much. Use the drop box like we agreed, and don't interrupt me."

"You are speaking to the Willinghouse woman again?" said the ambassador, sounding both curious and perturbed.

"I am indeed," said Richter, and I could hear it once more, that thick, liquid pleasure in his voice. "It is quite delicious to see one's enemies so utterly discomfited, doubly so when they have no idea just how complete their failure is about to be."

"It's too fast," said the ambassador, recovering some of his former dignity. "You are overreaching yourself, Richter. You are making mistakes."

"Like trusting you, you mean? I think not. I am surprised at you. Clumsy and stupid though you are, made lazy and fat with your so-called duties—all those embassy parties and rich dinners that you are pleased to call work—that you have learned so very little about the world and those who make it turn. Watch and learn, Alfonse. Watch and learn. Oh, and call me anything other than *Prime Minister* or *Lord Protector* again, and I'll have your credentials revoked and put you on the next train. I suspect that your superiors will be most disappointed, and that they will show their displeasure by sending you to run some stinking Quundu prison on your northern borders. Don't think I won't. Do not assume past dealings will soften my vengeance if you turn against me. I swear on the very skin I call holy, you cannot conceive the terror of having me as an enemy."

He had begun the speech calmly, but as his passion grew, his volume dropped, so that by the end, he was whispering, and I had to press my head to the shutter to catch the words. They chilled my blood.

I did not move until I heard first Richter leave, then—slower, the chair creaking under him as he left it, the ambassador. I climbed down, spent a moment listening to the silence of the kitchen, then clambered out and put the infernal skirt back on.

TRYING TO LISTEN IN on Richter's conversation with Dahria would have been pointless and likely to get me caught, so I sat in the silent kitchen with my hands clasped in my lap demurely as maids came and went, turning what I had heard over and over in my mind, and cursing myself that I had missed the beginning of the conversation. All I had was a sense of the mood, of a relationship that had shifted drastically and recently, though what had prompted the change I couldn't say. What was clear was that Richter wasn't done. Not by a long way.

Something is coming. Something big. Something new.

When Saunders summoned me to join Dahria in the lobby, I moved with reluctance, sure I would learn more if I could find a reason to stay, but that was not an option. I was a servant, which meant I went where my mistress went. I let us get two whole blocks from the Heritage building and did a careful scan to see we weren't being followed before asking how it had gone.

She shrugged, a vague, hopeless sort of gesture.

"Did he believe you?" I asked.

"Enough to look further into it," she said.

"That was to be expected," I said. "The story will stand scrutiny."

"Perhaps," said Dahria, seeming not really to care one way or the other.

"This is good, Dahria," I said. "It's progress."

"If he does what he promised," she said.

"You don't think he will?"

"For a while," she said. "Which I suppose is all we can hope for."

I watched her, but she didn't want to say anything else and had taken to rubbing her temples as she did when she had a headache. In truth there was nothing more to say. The delay she had mentioned was indeed all we could hope for, and though I didn't want to admit it, I knew it wouldn't last long.

"Did you learn anything from the ambassador?" she asked. I had told her of my spell in the Heritage dumbwaiter.

"Not sure," I said, then shook my head and added. "No, not really."

She nodded as if this was to be expected. "Not going very well, this, is it?" she said.

I ESCORTED DAHRIA BACK to the house on Harrington-Clark, but found the butler shutting the place up.

"I'm afraid we have been given our relocation orders," he said. "It will take several days to find somewhere suitable, but I have, for now, booked you into an inn in Morgessa."

"Morgessa?" said Dahria, not so much outraged as genuinely surprised, as if she hadn't thought it would really happen.

"Yes, miss," said Higgins. "You will find your grandmother there waiting for you. She came to town to visit your brother, but was not granted an audience."

Dahria's face closed up as tight as the shuttered house, and I looked away, my mind racing. I had not had time to prepare what I would say to the old woman. Perhaps if I could find a little privacy when we arrived . . .

But that was not to be. Dahria and I met Madame Nahreem in the street, en route to the Atembe underground station.

She read the discovery in my face the moment she saw me. A grayness slipped over her like a shroud. She stood in the street as the crowds jostled her, looking at me, all her studied neutrality drained away so that she appeared as she was: old and tired, spent like a stub of candle. I saw no value in delaying the conversation, even if neither of us wanted to have it.

"You should have told me," I said.

"Yes," she answered, humbled, the only time I had ever seen it in her. "I should."

"Told her what?" said Dahria, confused and slightly alarmed by her grandmother's chastened manner. "Grandmamma? What is this about?"

The old woman seemed to age further, to shrink in on herself as if she might collapse into the folds of her black sari and crumble to dust.

"The Lilac Roller mine," I said.

Dahria's brow contracted in bewilderment, then she shook her head.

"What about it? It's closed."

"Yes," I said. "Because of an accident two and a half years ago."

"A shaft collapsed," said Dahria, remembering. "So?"

"Some miners were trapped," I said. "Others went in to look for them, but the collapse spread, and though the miners who had been trapped were found alive, those who went in after them were not so lucky. Three men died."

"I don't understand," said Dahria. "I mean, that's very sad, but what has this to do with us?"

"You own the mine," I said, the tears starting to my eyes again, my face suddenly hot.

"Well, yes, but mining is dangerous work and sometimes there are accidents," said Dahria.

"Particularly when safety standards are not followed to the letter," I said.

Dahria opened her mouth, but shock stole from her whatever indignant words she was going to speak, and she turned to Madame Nahreem.

"Grandmamma, is this true? Father ignored safety protocols, and that led to the collapse?"

There was a long and loaded silence, uncanny in the bustling street, and then Madame Nahreem nodded. "It was oversight rather than deliberation," she said, "but yes. Your father was sick and anxious about his political career. He was not paying the attention he should to his properties outside the city. The safety foreman was negligent, and your father did not know about it till it was too late, because he did not look closely enough. I could see it. At the time, before the accident, I knew. I could see he was not engaged with his holdings, and I should have known what would happen, but I was concerned for his health, so I said nothing. I did nothing."

It sounded like a speech she had constructed over long, hard nights of brutal self-scrutiny. Dahria stared at her, leaning back slightly as though she needed more distance to focus on her face, but then she shook her head again in confusion.

"Why are we talking about this now?" she asked. "Why is Miss Sutonga interested?"

"Because one of the miners who was killed," said Madame Nahreem, "was Ang's father, and I wish with all my heart, with every piece of my being, that that were not the case."

CHAPTER

23

I SPENT THE NIGHT alone with my thoughts and was, for once, glad to get out into the street the following day with a sense of things to do. Tanish, when I found him, was relieved to hear about Aab and the others, whose conditions had stabilized almost as soon as the strange device had been removed. Though he didn't realize it, he had brought me relevant news. Needing something of a distraction from the Willinghouse family, I was glad of it.

"So this Kepahler cove," he said. "Might be the most boring bloke in town."

"You tailed him?"

"All over the city, and not a lot of fun was to be had in the process, I can tell you. Three full days I've been following him, and he hasn't been to a show or entered a single boozer. Lunch at the same fancy restaurant serving rubbish food—trust me, I've begged there—one meeting over with his Heritage pals—more fancy rubbish—bed by eleven every night, and the rest of the time either behind the counter of his own shop or trawling for new stuff elsewhere."

"Where?"

"Other dealers, jewelers, goldsmiths, and pawnbrokers."

"High end?"

"The ones he does himself," Tanish nodded, tearing off a strip of naan and folding it into his mouth. "But he bought stuff from a couple of street rats that absolutely wasn't, unless it was nicked."

"What kind of stuff?"

"Couldn't tell and didn't want to look too nosy, you know? Bits of glass, maybe, gemstones. Didn't seem what you'd call precious, not by the way they was being handled."

"Could it have been luxorite?"

"Nah. No shine."

"Really old luxorite?" I pressed. "Old enough that it's barely even orange and you'd have to be in total darkness to see it glow?"

He frowned, then shrugged. "Could have been, I suppose. Some of it definitely looked sort of brown. Yeah," he decided. "Very possible."

I nodded, but I already knew this.

"Did you see him carrying any of this stuff when he went to his Heritage meeting?"

"Nah," said Tanish. "Most of it was pretty small. Could have fit in his pockets. But he got quite a lot, so if he took it all to them, he'd need a bag of some sort, and he never did. Only time he went out with a briefcase was when he went to the smithy."

I nodded absently, disappointed at how little this was producing, then that last word struck me.

"Smithy, like a goldsmith's shop?"

He shook his head.

"The goldsmiths and jewelers are all up near Saint Helbrin Street," he replied, chewing. "I mean an honest-to-God blacksmith's behind the Hunter's Arms."

"Smithy Row?" I said. "What was a fancy gent like him doing up there?"

"I asked myself the very same thing," said Tanish wisely.

"And did you get an answer?" I said, forcing myself to be patient.

"As a matter of fact, I did," he said, pleased with himself. "Bloke by the name of . . ." He paused to check a scrap of paper with penciled capitals scrawled on it. "Eb Harding."

"Kepahler bought something from Mr. Harding?"

"Sort of. I mean, again, I didn't get a good look and didn't stick around to ask questions after one of the yard lads spotted me: didn't take kindly to *Lani street trash mucking up our neighborhood, and now Richter's in power we don't have to put up with the likes of you no more—*"

"Tanish?" I prompted.

"Right," he said, returning to the matter at hand. "Like I said, I couldn't really see, but it looked kind of like a helmet."

"A helmet?"

"Or a colander. Sort of. Weird shape. Big. Metal, but with loads of little holes in it. Sparkled a bit in the light. Like one of them stained-glass windows you see in the white churches, but not with nearly as much glass. Maybe not so much a helmet as a big lantern. Does that help?"

"Yes, Tanish," I said, rooting in my purse for a few coins. "That helps."

TANISH'S TALK OF THE smith's malevolent yard boys gave me pause. Considering Kepahler's sympathies, it was hardly surprising that he dealt exclusively with whites of a particular stripe, and it seemed likely that any attempt to get information out of them would prove at best unhelpful and at worst seriously hazardous to my health.

I needed to find out who had commissioned the luxorite device— *devices* if Tanish's reconnaissance had been right. The one that had plagued the girls in the Drowning had been much smaller than the one this Harding character was building now. Which made the one that had nearly killed Aab and Jadary what? A test? A dry run?

Try out the weapon in the Drowning because no one will take any notice of a few dead brown kids? Decrease the Lani population of the city as you test out your weapon: two birds, one stone . . .

The thought turned my stomach as if the false luxorite were working on me.

We'll see about that, I thought.

But how was I supposed to find out if this was a sick project of Kepahler's own devising, or if he was involved in something larger? And if he was, who was pulling his strings? I knew there was a Heritage connection, but was it more than a shared philosophy of hate, and if it was, how could I prove it?

I thought about paying Tanish to take up a permanent stakeout on the Harding smithy, but he had already been seen, and there was no one else I trusted who could go unnoticed in the gritty industrial alleys of Smithy Row. I would have to do it myself, and decided I would have a better chance of seeing what clues the place might yield at night.

Smithy Row lay a few blocks east of Szenga Square and south of the theater district, in the slummy construction yards of those businesses that hadn't scaled up to full factory size. Here the workforce relied more on muscle than on steam: old crafts that didn't generate the kind of product bulk that would benefit from the automation provided by the Numbers District, the Soot, and the great chimneyed sheds on the south bank of the river. At their best, they offered a kind of hand-craftsmanship that was as much art as it was labor, particularly in wrought-iron ornamental gates and railings custom-made for the shops and houses to the north and east. But alongside such places were those whose output was simpler and more utilitarian, and who only stayed in business—clung to it, in fact—because their particular product had not yet been snapped up by the city's great steelworks.

I thought of Richter's own factory and wondered—if there was a Heritage connection to the device used to poison my sister's children—why he had not made the metal shell himself. Perhaps he wanted to maintain what politicians called "plausible deniability," particularly after his part in the scandal involving the machine-gun-mounted armored tractors. It had taken weeks in court to verify that his works had been commissioned by people within the government and that he had acted "in good faith"—a phrase inaccurate in every way except, alas, technical meaning.

But then maybe it was simpler than that. Richter dealt in large-scale steel. The device I had seen was small and irregular, better suited to a jeweler than a producer of railway tracks, girders, and rolled steel sheet. Though the thing had no aesthetic appeal, it had taken time to weld a frame around all those tiny fragments of ancient luxorite, and however insidious its purpose, it had been the work of a craftsman, not a factory.

By day, Smithy Row rang with hammers beating out their rhythms on anvils and bellows blowing air through the hot coal, but at night it was eerily quiet. It smelled of ash and soot and metal, a tang you could taste in the back of your throat. I squatted on the roof of the Hunter's Arms, watching for signs of life beyond the fox-headed fruit bats and a lone, skulking jackal rooting through a garbage pail.

I was at the back of the houses and shops in a narrow, unlit alley. Reaching into my satchel, I plucked out an expensive flashlight with a luxorite source and a mirrored lens, which I had purloined from the town house, and carefully rotated its screw cover till a narrow beam of yellow light shone out.

Each of the houses had a front drive for goods haulage closed by heavy iron gates. Harding's was the third on the left of the row, an untidy place with mounds of coal and barrels of scrap iron all over the place. It was surrounded by a brick wall whose mortared top had been set with fragments of broken bottle, but there was no guard dog, and I made it over quickly and unhurt. The main structure was both house and storefront, but the windows showed no lights, and I set to exploring the yard where the work itself was done. There were two complete forges, each with anvils and matching sheds. The latter were padlocked, but I was getting good with Namud's picks and had them springing open in under a minute each, holding the narrow flashlight between my teeth. Both contained tools and boxes of work in progress or abandoned. In one was a heavy cabinet with large storage bins. The lock on this was trickier, and I labored on it for several minutes with my tools, listening to the night with mounting irritation. I didn't want to leave signs I had been here, but if I couldn't open the lock soon, I would have to set to work with my chisel. I took a breath, inserted a different tension wrench into the lower part of the lock, and started over, working the pick all the way to the back with my right hand, and applying a little pressure on the wrench with my left. When I felt the rear pin rise and hold, I pulled the pick back and did the same with the next, maintaining my half turn on the wrench. Two more, and it finally popped.

I pulled the broad cabinet door open, realizing too late how loudly it creaked on its hinges. On the top shelf was what looked like two sets of full body armor such as you saw in pictures of knights from ancient times, complete with face-covering helmets, all of a dull gray metal I'd wager was lead. Lined up on the shelf below were three of the roughly welded luxorite devices, each as big as my head. Each had an elaborate shutter mechanism fitted with dozens of little metal flaps, all connected to a single lever. I pulled it experimentally, and they opened like the spines of a bush porcupine, revealing panels of brown luxorite that glimmered softly in the darkness, a dull, smoky glow like a poor candle behind a thick amber shade.

Three of them!

This was bad, but presented with the fact of my discovery, I wasn't sure what to do next. Taking them with me, even if I could carry them, would only delay the danger and would expose my investigation while revealing nothing about who was involved beyond Kepahlcr.

Go to the police. Find Andrews. They can force the truth from both the smith and the luxorite dealer.

I closed the shutters on the device, shut the cabinet, and locked it. I was out in the yard again when I heard the door of the house slam.

CHAPTER

24

FOR A MOMENT I froze like a roach in lamplight, staring back toward the house, where someone was opening the gates to the drive. Dimly revealed in the soft glow of a gaslight across the street, I saw what looked like a high cart or wagon drawn by a single horse. I snapped the padlock hasp over the shed door latch with clumsy fingers and caught a snatch of unintelligible conversation on the air, as I hastily turned the flashlight hood. The world went dark. They had been gruff, male voices, low and, at least for now, showing no sound of alarm.

I ducked round the back of the farthest shed, feeling my way in the blackness, not daring to sprint across the open yard to the wall over which I had climbed in. There was no real cover there, and I would be seen by anyone who stepped away from the shed, so I reached up the timbered wall as quietly as I could, grabbed part of the frame, and pulled myself up. From there I dragged my way onto the pitched roof and rolled onto my back, listening. When nothing happened for a moment, I walked my elbows a few inches and risked a cautious look down, peering through the night to the pearly glow in the street. I could see that the wagon was russet-colored and that the horse drawing it had a strange blue tinge to its striped face.

Wilderheld orlek.

It was the circus people. It had to be.

I remembered the taciturn knife thrower who had, I was sure, ended the life of his boy accomplice and then denied it with no trace of emotion. I flattened my spine to the roof once more, my heart pounding. Only then did I remember the wagon too. I had been in it. It had been parked outside the Parliament House the day Benjamin Tavestock was murdered, part of the little tableau of equipment designed to look like there was repair work on the building but that merely provided an escape for the assassin via the makeshift refuse chute.

Another sideshow . . .

I heard more voices, then footsteps coming closer and a rattle of something metallic.

Keys.

"In here," muttered a voice.

No one answered. I pocketed my darkened flashlight silently, and put the heel of my hand on the butt of the kukri in my waistband, not daring to draw it for fear that even that whisper of sound would draw their attention. I kept very still in case the smallest shift would set the roof creaking, watching the sky above the yard leap into ruddy light as one of them brought an oil lamp to show the way. My guess was that there were at least three of them. Maybe four. I let go of the kukri. Fighting my way out was not going to be an option.

I heard the click of the padlock and wondered desperately if I had left any sign of my presence, relieved that I had not recently bathed. Soap smelled—not much, but enough. I heard the door open and close, but I had no idea if they had all gone inside, so I still couldn't move. If I made a run for it now and there was some lone sentry out there, perhaps someone skilled with a throwing knife, I was as good as dead.

So I lay where I was, listening in the dark, my back flat against the warm, pine-scented timber of the shed roof, and no muscle in my body stirring. I didn't hear the cabinet lock turn, but I heard the creak of the door and some muffled words exchanged below me. I felt the rumble of their movement, even their inaudible conversation resonating through the boards of the shed and into my spine. There was a grunt and a gasp, which might have been exertion as one of them picked the heavy devices up, but I had no way of knowing, and then they were leaving again.

I listened for the noise of the locks, but none came, just footsteps and the sound of bodies moving, labored this time.

They're taking the devices, I thought wildly. *You missed your chance!*

But there was nothing to do but wait. I heard the clank of the gate, another snatch of conversation, still more distant now, and the sound of the strange blue orlek's hooves on the cobbles as the carriage turned and moved away. Even then, I waited to be sure, listening, and when I finally rolled and dropped into the yard, I hesitated before running for the wall.

The shed was still open. I could make out the door hanging there. Not so very strange, I supposed, that Harding would leave it like that, but just odd enough to make me look inside. I pulled the flashlight from my pocket and, once I was inside and safe from the view from the house, I rotated the lens cap.

A fraction of a second before the light came on, I knew what I would see. You don't notice, not usually, especially in the light when the color is so much more compelling, but blood has a smell, sharp and coppery and brimming with alarm.

It hit my nostrils just before the luxorite beam hit the body of the smith. He was lying on the ground, eyes and mouth open in astonishment, the life quite gone from his face, and a familiar wound through the center of his rib cage.

I MADE FOR THE Mount Street Police Station, though it was too much to hope that Andrews would still be there. The point, as it turned out, was moot. As I came down, Javisha, a policeman, stepped out of the shadows on the corner of Winckley Street and seized me by the scuff of the neck.

"Where do you think you're going?" he sneered, twisting my face up to his so he could make doubly sure what I was. "Not supposed to be out round here, are you? New laws we have about your sort, or can't you read the papers?"

"I'm going to the police station!" I said.

"That you are," he replied with grim amusement.

"I NEED TO SEE Inspector Andrews!" I protested.

"Oh, do you indeed?" scoffed the policeman as he shoved me through the cell door. There were four other women already inside, three black and one Lani. "Anyone else you'd like to speak to? The Lord Archbishop, perhaps? King Stefan? The lead cellist of the Bar-Selehm Symphony Orchestra? Tell you what: you wait here, and I'll go get some paper so I can make a list."

"Funny," I said.

He slammed the cell door and I turned, meeting the blank faces of the other women, who were sitting in sullen silence on a pair of benches. The other Lani woman was looking at the floor, her eyes red from crying. One of the black women met my eyes, held them, and when I gave her a cautious nod, smiled unexpectedly and returned it.

I sat beside her, and she gave me a sidelong look.

"You wanted to see a policeman?" she said.

"A particular policeman," I said. "Yes."

"Only white policemen left."

"I know."

She leaned back a little, as if to get a better look at me.

"You asked to see a white policeman?"

"Yes," I said. "I have met him before."

She shook her head and looked at the woman beside her.

"This one is crazy," she observed conversationally. The other woman considered me, nodding.

It was going to be a long night.

ANDREWS DIDN'T COME FOR me. The three black women and I took turns napping on one bench, coming to a silent, mutual agreement that the Lani woman, who sobbed quietly to herself all night, should get the other bench. I tried to console her, but she turned her face away, ashamed of being there. It awoke a sleeping anger in me, and when morning came and the duty officer arrived to take our names for filing, I didn't trust myself to speak.

The inspector, it turned out, knew I was there. He intercepted me as soon as I picked up my bag—which, fortunately, had not been searched—walking quickly through the lobby as I stalked ahead, furious.

"I couldn't come," he said. "My position is shaky enough as it is. I'm being watched. The last thing I needed is to be associated with a young Lani woman picked up for breaking curfew."

"So long as you're all right," I said darkly.

"I couldn't have done anything, anyway," he protested. "Things aren't like they were. I don't have the power I had before. Willinghouse is in jail pending—"

"And you are doing what about that, exactly?" I said, turning on him.

"I haven't had any good leads—" he began.

"The circus was a lead," I said. "You should have arrested them."

"On what charge? They denied the boy had been killed, and we had no body and—

"For the killing of the prime minister!" I exclaimed. "You have *his* body, don't you?"

"And no evidence that there was anyone with him except Willinghouse!"

"You have *my* evidence," I shot back. "I saw a footprint on the roof. I swore to you I'd seen it. Or is that not good enough anymore?"

"For me, yes, but not for the commissioner."

"Because my skin color makes me blind? A liar?"

Andrews looked away, his lips pursed. He could think of nothing to say. I stared him down, and at last he hung his head.

"These are bad times, Miss Sutonga," he murmured.

"Worse times," I said. "They were bad before. For some of us. You just didn't notice."

He looked at me then, and the truth of the remark seemed to register slowly.

"So I am beginning to see," he said.

I nodded. It didn't make sense to take my anger out on him.

"You need to go to Smithy Row," I said. "A place called Harding's. You'll find some odd armor and a body there."

"What? Whose?"

"A metalworker hired by Heritage sympathizers to create a toxic device."

"What?" said Andrews again, dazed.

"The wound in his chest is the same as the one that killed the boy climber."

That seemed to focus his mind. "You think it was the knife thrower," he said. He must have been wearing the strange leaden armor for protection against the false luxorite; in it, he would make as good a Voresh goblin man as any in Lani legend.

"I'm almost sure," I said. "I also know how the boy killer got inside the Parliament House. The evidence is circumstantial, but if you ask the right people—"

"No," he said, suddenly sure. "Your word is good enough for me. I'll assemble a team of constables and you and I will return to the circus to make some arrests."

"Will the commissioner authorize such action?" I said, taken aback by his sudden certainty.

"The commissioner can go hang himself," snapped Andrews. "I can do this on my own authority and explain myself later. Wait here."

IT TOOK NO MORE than twenty minutes for Andrews to gather his team of armed officers. They were, like all the active police now, white, and several of them gave me appraising looks.

"Yes?" demanded Andrews of one of them. "Is there a problem, constable?"

"No, sir," said the officer, dragging his eyes from me to the inspector. "But . . ."

"Yes?"

"Wasn't she in jail last night?" said the policeman, caught between embarrassment and genuine confusion.

"She asked for me and was ignored," said Andrews, drawing himself up.

"Oh," said the constable, not really sure what this meant but sensing the kind of professional danger he needed to get away from. "Very good, sir."

I rode in the lead coach beside Andrews with two other officers armed with truncheons and revolvers as we followed the underground line to Atembe, then down to Great Orphan Street and the Hashti temple. We could see the big top almost as soon as we entered Nbeki, but the closer we got to the park, the more obvious it was that something had changed.

It was quiet, an ordinary morning, without any of the oily bustle generated by the sideshows and their strange, foreign staff. The reason became clear as soon as we entered the park. The big top, its vivid red and gold striped canvas flapping in the breeze, had a desolate and faded air, and felt not exotic and exciting, but tawdry and cheap in the flat morning light and the silence. The sideshows, caravans, carts, games, exhibits, and animal cages, the steam organ, the hawkers, and roustabouts, were all gone. Litter blew through the abandoned big top, and without the aromas of sweet and unusual food, the rutted, dung-heaped ground held none of its former mystique.

The circus, it seemed, had left town.

THAT AFTERNOON, I WENT with Dahria and Madame Nahreem to see Willinghouse, playing the lady's maid once more, a role to which my stony silence was well suited. Dahria watched me, not knowing what to say; my father's death hung between us like a curtain, making us separate, alone, even as we walked together. Sometimes she would catch my eye, and her face would freeze with the stunned pain you feel immediately after being slapped. Her upbringing had not given her the words to navigate her feelings, let alone mine, so she said nothing, fidgeting with her purse and parasol like a child before giving a recital for which she had not practiced. If I hadn't been so paralyzed by my own feelings, I would have felt sorry for her. As it was, I was almost relieved.

But only almost, because those similarities between the poor and the rich I mentioned earlier were only almost true. We did not handle emotion well, but that superficial resemblance just concealed how different we were. Indeed, though I had come to like Dahria, the news of my father's death in her family's mine was a measure of the gulf between us, a marker of her extraordinary wealth and privilege. It somehow also showed the extent to which my family were, as we had always been, little more than tools. That Madame Nahreem's solution to the problem of Papa's death had been to hire first Vestris, and then when that unraveled, me, employing us, as if a little money would compensate for our loss, left me cold. The fact that I didn't know what I would have preferred did not make me feel better.

I imagined Papa's broken body being drawn up from the black depths of the mine and being inspected by—whom? Willinghouse senior? Madame Nahreem herself? I wondered if my employer had also been there, a keen young man still a student at Ashland University College, Ntuzu, who had not yet set out upon the meteoric political career that had ended days ago with his arrest for murder. He sat before me now, his usually sharp and focused face glazed with hopelessness. They had moved him on the third night, stowing him in a secure cell in the bowels of the Mount Street Police Station a corridor or two over from where Aaron Muhapi was being held. The room was almost identical to the one in which he had been imprisoned in the War Office, a blank, whitewashed brick box with bars across the front and a sliding wooden screen door that afforded him a little privacy. We were made to talk to him through the bars.

Or rather, Dahria and Madame Nahreem were. I was a servant and not expected to talk at all. Not that there was anything to say. Willinghouse was disheveled, unkempt, but he didn't seem to notice and regarded us with the kind of blank, absent expression that reminded me of the men you saw stumbling out of the opium dens in the docklands.

In truth, the fact that his grandmother and sister were licensed to speak seemed of no particular use. As we sat there, moving between stiff silence and stiffer questions about his well-being and laundry needs—it began to feel like a kind of cruelty. As Dahria didn't know how to talk to me about my father's death, so neither she nor her grandmother knew how to talk to Willinghouse about his own impending execution. After a few minutes, the interview began to feel like the corpse viewing the night before a funeral, except that the dead man was sitting upright.

The closest thing to real communication occurred when Willinghouse's slow gaze found my face and, after acknowledging the bored and burly constable who was chaperoning us, asked simply, "Anything?"

I looked down, defeated, then met his eyes once more and shook my head. Dahria gave me a searching look, and I knew what she was thinking. I might not have firm evidence, but I had certainly made headway. Was I simply reluctant to show my hand in front of the watchful policeman? Was I resisting the impulse to give him false hope? Or was I punishing him for his part in my father's death?

I wasn't sure.

I did not blame Willinghouse for what had happened to Papa, but it was inconceivable that he had not known about it. Dahria lived in a bubble, and it was easy to believe that her grandmother had not confided in her, but Willinghouse worked with Madame Nahreem. His sphere was more public than her secretive spidery machinations—or had been until he hired me—but there was no possibility that they had not discussed the matter.

He had known. I was sure of it. He had known, and he had decided not to tell me, and I was suddenly less sure that I wanted to see him released.

CHAPTER

25

THAT NIGHT THE CITY burned literally and metaphorically. Parts of it, at least. Richter's new civilian militia, decked out in Heritage party uniforms and carrying flags and torches, marched on Old Town and staged a demonstration in the ancient Mahweni Square that had been the original heart of the city before the white conquest. Some of those torches were then stuck through the letter boxes of shops and houses where blacks still lived and worked. The program of speechifying and singing of suitable anthems was punctuated with breaking windows and a handful of beatings administered to dissenters. The police presence watched but did nothing, and the following morning, the few remaining blacks emerged from their shops looking stunned and frightened, their belongings crammed into bags and boxes, which they manhandled into carts. The so-called Resettlement Day was still a week away, but it was, they said, only a matter of time, and a lot could happen before then, none of it good.

In the morning, I visited Rahvey and her family—a considerably quicker trip into the Drowning now that we were living in Morgessa—and was surprised to find Dr. Mendelson completing his rounds.

"I thought they were better?" I said.

"They are," he replied, "much. But I'm less sure than I was about the source of the contagion."

"We found it," I said. "The device containing the green luxorite. They started improving as soon as we removed it."

"It seemed so," he replied, riffling through the compartments of his bag and frowning. "But similar cases are emerging inside the city walls. Faster onset and more severe symptoms. I have to consider the possibility that the disease is spreading through human contact."

"There are new cases? Since when? I've heard nothing about this."

"No," he said, with a grim smile. "But since the new cases are all in Nbeki, that is to be expected."

His meaning was plain. Sickness in a primarily black area of the city was not considered newsworthy.

"They began yesterday," he said. "Same lethargy, same nausea, even some hair loss. I might not have given the matter a second thought had I not seen the same thing here."

"Yesterday!" I said.

He nodded gravely. "I anticipate the affected persons will show the most extreme symptoms we saw here within another twenty-four hours." I stared at him, and he nodded once more. "Yes. The strain seems even more virulent."

"But it's not a disease," I said. "It's not spread from person to person. There must be a device like the one we found."

"I still can't account for how that device caused the effects we saw," he said. "A crystalline mineral that makes people sick? I have to consider more conventionally plausible medical explanations."

"Where are the worst cases?"

"I told you: Nbeki."

"I mean where exactly? Which streets?"

"Right in the center."

"And diminishing the farther you move away from that area?" I prompted.

He shook his head. "That's why I think my previous diagnosis was wrong," he said. "It's all over the area, and it's not clearly more intense on any particular street."

I thought furiously. It could not be a coincidence. The same symptoms meant the same cause. I leaned in to see his list, and—somewhat grudgingly—he permitted me.

"What do the asterisks by their names mean?" I asked.

"They don't actually live there," he said. "Just staying there short term."

"Wait," I said. "That's it. Nbeki is one of the areas designated for black and Lani according to the new government rules."

"So?"

"So the area is suddenly awash with people who are just moving into the area, people who are taking up residence with friends and relatives, moving from house to house so that they don't overstay their welcome as they wait for a more permanent solution."

He considered this and conceded the point. "So if there is a device—or devices—its effects might be confused as people move around the area," he agreed. "But unless the device itself is also moving, there should still be a clear area of strongly affected people."

He pulled a well-thumbed book from his bag and scanned a list of names and addresses beside which he had scribbled case notes in pencil, using an index finger to work through the list, flipping pages as the pattern began to emerge. He rummaged in his bag some more, fished out a roughly folded street map, and pored over it, checking the list of addresses and muttering names under his breath.

"It's as I said," he concluded, jabbing a finger at a blank square surrounded by streets. "The epicenter of the infection is here: Nbeki Park. By God, you're right," he remarked. "The other severe cases are all people who have recently moved in."

Nbeki Park, I thought. *Of course it is. Everything points back there.*

"I believe," the doctor remarked, "that at the moment, there is a circus there."

"There was," I said. "It's gone now, though no one saw them leave."

The doctor gave me a curious look, and I realized with a start that—to both our surprises—he was waiting for advice, even instruction.

"Go to whichever hospital officials you trust to put the health of people above all other concerns," I said. "Move everyone out of the affected area. Tell anyone you meet there—especially the union bosses and factory owners—to help spread the word."

"Everyone? That's thousands of people!"

"I'll find the device and disarm it, but it's working fast, much faster than the one we found in the Drowning. Minutes could make a difference in fatal exposure."

"Where should I take them?"

"The Drowning is safe now, but . . . No. They should stay in the city. The Nbeki device might not be the only one, and it only makes sense to move the people to areas that will not be infected."

"Such as?"

I chewed my lip, then decided.

"Something is coming," I said. "I feel it in the air. Something is coming now. Move everyone east."

"To the Soot? The Numbers District?"

"No," I replied. "I wouldn't be surprised if those places were targeted too. Move them all the way east, as close to the ocean as you can get and still be in the city."

"But that's . . ."

"Government Center, the Finance District, and the most upscale residential area in the city," I agreed. "Yes."

"But, the districting regulations? Almost everyone who is sick is black or Lani."

"Yes," I said again. "Isn't that interesting?"

He gave me a baffled frown that creased his forehead and tightened his eyes, but as the implication of what I had said registered, his face slackened and opened up, till he was staring at me with shock and horror.

"Go to the police," I added. "Ask for an Inspector Andrews and have him meet me in Nbeki Square. He may need armed support."

NBEKI WAS UNCANNILY QUIET for the time of day, even as the doctor and his local outriders got the word out and the people started locking up and moving north across the railway lines into Morgessa and points east. Though I was soon swimming against a tide of swathed and sweaty people, there was a dull, airless quality to the place as if all sound had been sucked from it. It stank already of disease and despair, a scent I associated with the Drowning. Detecting it here inside the city walls filled me with a nagging sense of urgency or alarm, like an impala that feels the eyes of the weancat on her.

By the time I reached Nbeki Park, the area was deserted. The circus was gone, but the big top itself still stood gaudy and derelict, its canvas flapping, its flags streaming. The emptiness of a place built to be stuffed with hordes of noisy people made it all feel dreamlike.

And then there was the effect of the green luxorite.

I could feel it as I got closer. Half a mile north, I had thought I was imagining that faint prickle of something in my skin, the occasional stomach slosh of nausea, but down here, in sight of the great tent, it pressed on my head, chest, and gut like motion sickness. With each step, the dizziness increased, and I felt my breakfast stir in my bowels, as if I had eaten living things. I pushed through the tent flap and into the cavernous arena, and the feeling spiked so that I had to steady myself, wishing I had stolen some of the leaden armor from the dead smithy's shed. I moved into the silent ring where the sandy earth had been pounded by horse and orlek hooves, cheered on nightly, and again I felt the strangeness unique to an empty theater, a space you have caught not being what it was born to be.

Or maybe it's more than that.

I was being watched. I would almost swear it. I forced myself to turn unsteadily, one hand clutched to my belly, the other outstretched to help balance myself as I rotated, scanning the rows of empty benches and chairs.

There was no one. And I was getting worse. A few minutes like this, and I wouldn't be able to function. If I collapsed, I'd die: slowly perhaps, miserably, but it would happen. The magnified false luxorite was turning my body into a seething acidic swamp.

Have to find the device.

It could be anywhere, and the only way I had of determining if I was near to it—like the blindfold game we had played as children, where everyone shouted depending on how close to the treasure we were—was by monitoring the nausea meter of my own body: the sicker I felt, the closer I was.

Not encouraging.

I tried to reason the thing through. Whoever planted the device didn't want it found, so they would put it somewhere inaccessible where a beggar wouldn't stumble on it hunting for discarded food. I wondered wildly, and disconsolately, if it could even be buried— in which case I'd never find it in time—but chose to cling to the idea that the device's toxic effects would be muted if the luxorite panels were covered, even if the material blocking them wasn't lead.

So, inaccessible, but also in the open . . .

I looked up.

From the highest point of the big top's great center hung a

helmet-sized lamp on a chain. As soon as I saw it, I knew it, and felt its steady poison streaming directly at me. I also knew I couldn't reach it, not without ladders. It was suspended from the very center of the big top, under a sheltered hole in the canvas that allowed the smoke and smell of the show to escape, and there were neither poles nor guy cables within twenty feet of it. There was, however a single rope not unlike the one the boy climber had used.

I was used to ladders and scaffold, not to freehand rope climbing, but I took it in both hands and tested it against my weight. All at once the effects of the green luxorite, combined with all that gazing upward finally overcame me. The tent ceiling swam, I slewed drunkenly to one side, then the other, and collapsed facedown in the sandy earth. When I tried to get up, the nausea tugged more powerfully than ever, and I leaned over and vomited into a hoofprint in the dirt.

For a moment I stared blearily at the spattered ground, miserable with the seasick swilling in my guts and the fuzziness in my head, only just resisting the urge to dig my hands into the sand to hold on. As I stared, I realized that the depression in the earth into which I had been sick was not a hoofprint at all. It was bigger than I had thought, and marked with four deeper impressions along one edge.

Knuckles.

I considered it, my slow brain trying to make sense of what I what I was looking at, what I remembered from before, and just as a picture appeared in my head raising the red flag of alarm, I heard the low chuffing cough of the great beast the circus people had left to protect their property.

Xipuku.

CHAPTER

26

THE GORILLA-LIKE CREATURE WAS, it seemed, even bigger in daylight, the bright, unlikely colors of its face more vivid and full of fire. Its yellow eyes were locked onto me, and it sidled as if tracing a rough circle around me, moving from knuckled fist to knuckled fist, suddenly baring its massive teeth in yawning threat, in case I considered drawing my kukri and taking my chances in a fight.

That would be absurd. The creature would shrug off my attack and hurl me into the audience like a rag doll. If I was lucky. If I was unlucky, it would bite me hard enough in the neck to all but sever my head, or simply take hold of my limbs and pull me apart. The xipuku were not local creatures, being confined to the mountain rain forests in the center of the continent, but they had been a favorite horror story of the Seventh Street gang, who had hoarded the boys' adventure broadsides they found or stole like they were luxorite. I knew all too well what the beast was capable of.

Keeping the rest of my body as still as I could, I reached for the laces of my right boot and unfastened them without taking my eyes off the almost luminous face of the animal. I gripped the heel and worked my foot out as the xipuku took another long and watchful sidestep. Then the same with the left boot. Then the socks. If I ran, the animal would come after me, would be on me in one leap. So I would do what I had been trained to do, though I had only a slender cord for a stairway. Without breaking the eye lock I had with the xipuku, I moved my left hand around until I brushed against the hanging rope and grabbed it.

I got slowly to my feet, feeling my head swim again, using the rope to haul myself upright. The creature became very still, gauging what I was doing, and it struck me that it was not immune to the effects of the green luxorite above us: its fur looked ragged and patchy, and it was drooling long, phlegmy strings. As it watched me gather the cord around my hands, it swayed as if it felt some of the same dizziness I did, though it was clearly much hardier to have lasted this long already. A man living this close to the source would have been dead by now. None of this made it less dangerous, of course. Maybe the opposite.

Still unsteady, head throbbing and stomach churning, I hooked the first two toes of my right foot around the rope as I had seen the boy do, then lifted my left higher and did the same with that. I took the first "step" up the rope, fighting the way the whole thing began to swing as I clawed for purchase with my toes, conscious also that the xipuku had stopped skirting me and was coming closer. My only option was up.

So I climbed and got another ten feet before my stomach cramped and I vomited again. Instinctively I twisted my head away so that I wouldn't get it on myself and nearly lost my grip, so that I had to just hold on for a second, knowing that the feeling was getting worse all the time. My only asset was speed, which was the one thing I dared not risk, not up here on a rope, and not with the xipuku prowling below me. At least it couldn't come up. The cord was too slim for its massive bulk . . .

But it might pull you down.

The idea stopped me again, and I risked a look. The creature was considering the rope. From here it was all hulking shoulders and a mounded black head, which suddenly twisted up to see me, the red and blue in its face as startling as the makeup of a clown. It stood up, gripping the rope, and for a moment, that movement alone seemed to halve the distance between me and it, so that I scrambled higher.

Ironically, it was easier to climb with the xipuku holding the cord, anchoring it, so that it was like scaling a pole, hard and un-yielding. I looked up again. The device was hanging from a chain only fifteen feet above me. I was weakening all the time, succumb-ing to its noxious qualities, but I was getting closer. I repositioned my feet, took another long vertical step, then another. My head was thick, my strength failing. My stomach felt like I was seesawing from wave to cresting wave on a stormy ocean, but I knew I had to keep going, though every yard intensified the awful sensation.

Three more steps, and I might reach the lever for the lead blinders.

Two.

One.

I reached a weary hand out and clawed at it till I snagged the lever, setting the luxorite device swinging. Tears ran down my face as I tried again, catching it and flipping the shutters closed.

The throbbing in my head stopped almost immediately, but the nausea and weariness would take time to pass, more time, perhaps, than I could hang on. I unhooked the device and hitched it to my belt, knowing full well that the xipuku was waiting for me at the bottom and able to do exactly nothing about it. I looked up again. The rope ran all the way to the roof of the big top, to the vent in the outside.

Ten more feet.

My body protested, but I pulled myself up, feeling the stiff, warm breeze flowing through the gap at the top. I reached it, leaned across through the hole in the canvas and pushed my head and shoulders through. For a second I was holding on to nothing, inches from sliding back through the hole and falling to the sandy ring below, but then I was out in the air and trying to slow my sliding roll down the sloped angles of the big top. I saw flashes of smoggy sky and Nbeki rooftops, and then I was scrabbling for a handhold on guy ropes as they whipped past, as I tumbled over the roof and fell the last twelve feet to the weedy ground.

The luxorite device slipped out of my hands with the impact and popped open, and I lay on my back, all the other feelings of sickness suddenly overwhelmed by the simpler pain of falling. For a moment, I couldn't move or think. It might have been a minute before I gingerly began isolating the pain and testing my body for serious damage.

My right side had taken the worst of it, and I feared I had broken a couple of ribs. My cheek was cut, but my arms, legs, and shoulder felt whole, if bruised. I was about to laugh with relief when the shadow of the xipuku fell across my face. I tried to get up, but my body cried out in agony, and I couldn't twist far enough to draw my kukri.

The creature loomed over me, its eyes misty and its red muzzle dripping. It extended one massive fist, and I shrank away from it, as much as my sickly and battered body would let me, hiding my eyes. I felt rather than heard the massive beast moving close to me, and then I was scooped up, limp and bloody, and pulled absently into the creature's arms. Stricken with terror, I opened my eyes and saw the animal looking away from me, and dimly I heard voices.

People were gathering.

I turned as much as I dared and saw, among the huddle of gawkers, a uniformed squad in blue.

Andrews.

The xipuku set me down and revolved to face them as rifles leveled and pistols raised.

"No," I said. "It's sick. It's not going to—"

But my words were lost in the roar of gunfire.

CHAPTER

27

I WOKE IN SAINT Auspice's hospital, a dressing on my face and my ribs strapped. There were three other people in the ward. The only one awake was an elderly black woman who eyed me over the top of a hefty, religious-looking book.

"Sister Beth!" she called, watching me as if I might make a run for it. "She's awake. The new girl."

A young Mahweni nurse looked in, then came to my bedside and took my pulse, checking it against a clockwork device she wore upside down on her apron front.

"How are you feeling?" she said.

I shrugged noncommittally, feeling the tightness of the bandages with even that small motion, but said, "Better, thank you."

"Good," she said. "You'll be wanting something to eat."

I started to say that I didn't but found that wasn't true.

"How long have I been here?" I asked.

"Just since yesterday."

"Yesterday?" I said. "What time is it?"

"Almost lunchtime."

"I've been asleep almost twenty-four hours?" I said, aghast. Anything could have happened in that time. I threw the bedclothes back, but the nurse replaced them.

"I'll fetch the doctor," she said. "Have something to drink."

She poured a glass of water from a jug and put it in my hands. I looked at it and waited, counting the seconds, feeling the woman across the ward watching me from her bed.

I needed to get out of here.

The doctor arrived minutes later, with Andrews in wary tow. He watched me too. I felt like a bomb everyone thought might go off at any moment.

"You did well," said Dr. Mendelson. "Probably saved a lot of lives. And your own injuries, in the circumstances, are minor."

"I have to go," I said.

My voice sounded cracked and strained. I took a sip of the water and moistened my lips.

"I'd give it a day or two," said the doctor.

"I don't have a day or two," I said. "I've already been here too long."

"You were exhausted. That kind of exposure, up close to the device . . . You have to rest."

"So I rested. Now I leave."

"Not yet," said the doctor. "I want to run some tests."

"Listen, Ang," said Andrews, "I'm sorry to have to say this—"

The inspector looked haggard, but I was in no mood to soothe his feelings.

"You didn't need to shoot it," I said.

"What?" he said, momentarily confused.

"The xipuku," I shot back. "You didn't need to kill it. It wouldn't have hurt me. It was used to people, and it was sick and . . . Wait. What were you going to say?"

Andrews looked down, his brow furrowing, and in that moment, the ward door burst open and Sureyna came in.

"Is she awake?" she said.

The doctor nodded, and Andrews opened his mouth to speak, then thought better of it and took a step backwards, allowing her access to me. I shifted painfully so that I could see her properly and every thought went out of my head as I took in the expression on her face. Her eyes were red and wet. She was ashen with shock and grief, and the hands in which she clutched a ravaged copy of the *Bar-Selehm Standard* trembled visibly.

"What?" I said, dreading her answer, my mind racing.

They accelerated Willinghouse's trial or passed a new set of laws . . .

"He's . . ." She tried, but could not find the words.

I stared at her, watching as all other emotions gave way to a sudden and overpowering sadness while Andrews and the doctor seemed to recede, their faces lowered ominously. Something terrible had happened.

"What is it?" I said again. "Tell me!"

Sureyna sank onto a chair and rocked forward, burying her face in her hands and clamping her hands over her mouth as if to hold back the wail that boiled out of her. Tears ran down her face, and she crumpled as if stabbed in the gut.

"Sureyna . . ." I began, but then I saw the newspaper headline.

Her tears had already spilled onto the paper so that it tore as I pried it from her hands, staring in horror.

> A police spokesman confirmed this morning that, apparently despairing of his failed political ambitions, noted black activist Aaron Muhapi hanged himself in his cell overnight. . . .

As my own tears started to fall, I heard myself saying, "No. He wouldn't. It's a lie."

BUT IT WASN'T. OR not entirely. In under an hour, the news that Aaron Muhapi was dead was everywhere. *The Citizen* confirmed it through black orderlies who had seen the body after he had been taken to the hospital, but their report also confirmed the lie I had recognized instinctively. He had not hanged himself. He had been beaten. Everywhere. It had begun with the soles of his feet, the small bones broken with truncheons, but it had progressed to more visible areas. The blow that killed him had partially crushed his skull.

The cover-up had been halfhearted at best. Richter's government stood by the official suicide story, using it to imply not just the innocence of the policemen who had beaten Muhapi to death, but also the inherent moral weakness of the dead man and the failure of his political movement. But privately, according to Sureyna's journalist friends, they didn't seem to mind that the truth had leaked out, as if they assumed it would scare Muhapi's supporters into silence and passivity.

I didn't think it would. In my mind's eye, I saw the fury in Peter's face; the disciplined righteous devastation of Muhapi's grieving widow, whose awful premonitions had all come true; the sorrow and anger of all who had stood peacefully behind the man at *The Citizen*, at his rallies; those who had danced at his house and delighted in his little boy . . .

Blood would run in the streets like rivers before they took this news silently, passively. But then perhaps that was what Richter and his cohorts wanted too, an excuse to bring the race war they so longed for to Bar-Selehm once and for all.

Richter was prime minister. Willinghouse was in prison. The Brevard party was in retreat, and the one man likely to unify the blacks, Lani, and moderate whites—a good, intelligent and charismatic man with a wife and a young son—had been beaten to death by a regime that felt so secure they did not even care that everyone knew. The city—my city—was collapsing. I held my tear-streaked face and drew my knees up to my chest, breathless with weeping, hugging myself and rocking back and forth like I did the day my father died.

I had failed, and all was lost.

CHAPTER

28

AGAINST THE DOCTOR'S ADVICE, and with no sense of what I was supposed to do next, I did go home, or what passed for home: my lodging house was still, mercifully, just west of the redistricted line. I wished Dahria were there waiting for me, and though I'd known she wouldn't be, I was still disappointed to get home and find the place empty. Why had I wanted to see her so badly? I was not entirely sure, and the question confused and upset me. My desire to be close to her in the midst of all that was happening, lost as it were in the spell of her, was perplexing, and I went upstairs with a still greater sense of distress. Resolving to consider the matter no more, I took medicine for the pain, knowing it would make me sleepy and—combined with the lingering effects of the luxorite poisoning—I found that by the time I got to my room, all I wanted to do was rest.

A nap, I thought. An hour at most, and then I would wake rested and think through what had to be done. If there was anything . . .

But I didn't nap. I slept for three hours and would have slept considerably longer had it not been for a distinct tapping at the door around the time the evening lamplighters had begun their rounds.

I drew the bedclothes to my chin, trying to climb out of my weary sadness, at least for form's sake. Perhaps the maid needed to know if I would be leaving the room so she could clean.

But when I got up and opened the door, it wasn't the maid. It was my landlady, Mrs. Topesh, looking about as excited as her carefully restrained demeanor would allow. I stood to attention, feeling—as I always did in her presence—like a guilty child.

"I'm sorry, Mrs. Topesh," I babbled. "I thought it was the maid. I'm sorry to be in bed so early but—"

"You have guests," she said. Mrs. Topesh did not like guests, particularly when they were unannounced, but while I might have expected her manner to be frostily formal, there was something cautious and watchful in her manner, which was almost impressed. "They insist upon your immediate attention."

I frowned, and my confusion was chased by panic. I had made no secret of my presence at Muhapi's rally and the party at his house that followed. As I had not hidden my association with Dahria. Yet the authorities—if that was what Richter's goons now were—had insufficient knowledge of my investigation or other secret activities to want me arrested. Muhapi's death had proved that. Still half asleep and drained from everything, the words came out before I could stop them.

"Am I in trouble?"

I heard myself, the defeated, hopeless childishness, and I felt absurd for ever thinking I could make a difference in this awful place. Mrs. Topesh looked at me as if startled. Instead of scorn, her face melted slightly, and she managed a weak smile. For a second, her eyes sparkled, and something of her rigid manner softened.

"No, my dear," she said. "No more than the rest of us, though that, I fear, is not saying very much. Now, get dressed. Your guests—whom I have ensconced in the withdrawing room—are most insistent."

I nodded gratefully, but with that last sentence, she had recovered her usual poise, and she merely inclined her head a fraction before slipping soundlessly out.

EVEN IN MY HASTE to see who had come to visit me, I paused to pick up the early edition of the evening paper from the side table in the downstairs hall. Several related stories dominated the front page under the heading

UNASSIMILATED TRIBES MASS FOR ATTACK!
TROOPS DEPLOY TO MEET MAHWENI THREAT

So it had begun. My eyes flashed over the smaller print—eyewitness accounts of hundreds, even thousands, of Mahweni bush warriors less than fifty miles north of the city, their certain connection to Willinghouse's attempted coup and to "the disgraced black activist leader, Aaron Muhapi, who killed himself yesterday." The warriors had surely been trying to starve the city of news and supplies during the past few weeks by attacking trade convoys and railway lines as they prepared their all-out attack on the city. . . . Their allies in the city, professing disbelief over the police account of Muhapi's death, had clashed with the civilian militia in rioting all over the city. . . .

It was all wrong. All nonsense. And my plan to buy Willing-house a little time had played right into it, feeding Richter's thirst to spill the blood of Mahweni, whether they were of the city or of the Unassimilated Tribes.

For a moment the news drove all other concerns out of my head, and I pushed the door to the withdrawing room open with no idea what to expect on the other side. I instantly understood Mrs. Topesh's strange, awed mood, because the people waiting for me—seventeen-year-old Lani steeplejack that I was—formed as strange and uneven a group as Bar-Selehm had seen in many a year.

Inspector Andrews, in uniform, sat on one ladder-back chair with Captain Emtezu on another beside him. Emtezu was dressed not in the patrol or combat attire, which had been confiscated, but in the dress uniform he kept at home. Opposite him was Madame Nahreem, draped in an austere black sari. Beside her, playing the elegant—and seemingly white—aristocratic lady about town, was Dahria, in resplendent mauve with matching parasol. And next to her was Mnenga, in formal tribal robes, sitting beside Lomkhosi, her breasts demurely covered, but still bedecked in beads, her hair raised in the same sculpted tower as before. Watching them warily from his position, cross-legged on the floor, was Tanish.

I stared, but only for a second, then I thrust out the paper I had brought with me from the hall and said to Mnenga, "What are you doing here? You need to get your people out of there!"

"That is done," he said. "My people had moved west before this was printed."

"Very well," I said, relaxing a little. "But why aren't you with them?"

"Because he has news," said Madame Nahreem crisply, her usual self. "Be quiet and listen."

"What is it?" I said, dragging my eyes off her and staring at Mnenga, feeling the tension in the room mount.

"I said my people were not responsible for the attacks on the railroads, on the trade convoys or on the journalists," he said. "Now we know who was. There are Grappoli troops ten miles from the city and moving toward you. Hundreds. Maybe thousands. They will be here by moonrise."

"The deployment of the white garrisons to the northeast has left the city largely undefended," said Emtezu, "and Mnenga's tribal contacts"—he nodded to the Mahweni woman, who inclined her head seriously—"say that a fleet of Grappoli war vessels were sighted off the western coast moving south toward the cape a week ago."

"So they will attack from the south as well?" I asked.

"I don't think so," said Emtezu. "If they came by ship, it doesn't make sense to disembark on the cape and march a hundred miles north, risking discovery with every step. With the city as poorly protected as it is, I think they will sail round the cape, up the east coast, and into the city via the river mouth."

I stared at him, aghast.

"What about the coastal defense batteries?" I said. "There are guns overlooking the bay. They would shred a navy that tried to enter the city that way."

"The forts north and south of the river mouth went strangely quiet last night after reports of a strange contagion gripped them," said Andrews. "The green luxorite devices were not merely a way to target the blacks and coloreds. They were designed to bring the city to its knees."

"So we tell the garrisons what we know," I said, "get in, find the devices before the Grappoli ships arrive."

"The silence from the forts suggests more than sickness," said Emtezu. "I think the enemy has already exploited the weakness of the soldiers."

Mnenga had taken to whispering translations into Lomkhosi's ear as we talked. She nodded, earnestly.

"You think the coastal forts have been taken by the Grappoli?" I exclaimed. "How? If troops had come into the city we would have seen—"

"Not ordinary troops," said Emtezu. "We got uneven civilian reports saying that strange people had been seen scaling the walls of the Ridleford fortress. No shots were fired. If there's any truth in it, I think we are dealing with specially trained soldiers skilled in assault tactics, climbing, hand-to-hand combat."

"Troops who were already in the city," said Andrews. "In disguise."

I gaped, and the truth hit me at last.

"The circus," I said sitting down heavily in the room's only unoccupied chair.

"I'm afraid so," said Andrews. "They may even be using those damned baboons."

There was a long, stunned silence and then a tap came at the door. It opened, and Sureyna peered in.

"I was told you were in here," she said.

Mnenga managed a smile, but the rest of us were still in shock.

"Any news?" Andrews asked her. It seemed my lodging house had—unknown to me—become the heart of some new resistance movement. Sureyna shrugged disconsolately, but before she could say anything, and as if to prove my previous thought, the window onto the flower beds outside rose, seemingly of its own accord. A slim brown hand reached in, and before we knew what was happening, someone was climbing up, through, and in.

A veiled and hooded someone.

Vestris.

She looked . . . embarrassed, almost ashamed of herself, her face low, her eyes on the floor, her hands adjusting the ragged robe, which was both cloak and hood. Madame Nahreem got unsteadily to her feet, one hand clutched to her heart, staring at my sister as if she were a specter from beyond the grave. Vestris saw her and became leopard-still, as if poised to flee. Or strike. The room was suddenly charged with the weight of things unsaid.

"You were right," said Vestris half turning to me, but her eyes still on Madame Nahreem. "Someone has been in the cave. Part of the concrete poured in to seal it was cut away. The opening has been hidden, but it's undeniable: someone has been inside."

Even without Madame Nahreem's prior association with her, Vestris's appearance, ragged and otherworldly as it was, had given the meeting a dreamlike quality from the moment she had clambered in. Andrews leaned forward, peering at her, the wheels in his head starting to turn.

"This is a steeplejack friend of mine," I said. Vestris caught my eye quickly, then looked down. Tanish, putting the pieces together, gaped.

"How did they find the cave?" asked Mnenga.

"Who is *they*?" said Andrews.

"They didn't find it," I said. "Not this time. They have known about it for months. Am I right?" I almost called my sister by name, but I saw the way Andrews was watching her and held it back. There would be a time for Vestris to answer for her past deeds, but it was not today.

"Mandel," she said. The word came out as a snarl, grotesque and laden with malice. The man who was now head of Bar-Selehm's security forces had betrayed her after all, though she was not alone in that. Emtezu rose slowly to his feet, and his face was hard and dark with anger. Mandel had once been his commanding officer. No one knew better than Emtezu what the man was capable of.

"Where is he now?" said Emtezu.

Andrews shook his head, but Sureyna spoke up.

"I know where he will be," she said, snatching my copy of the *Standard* from me and turning to the second page. She laid it on the coffee table where we could see it, reciting the text from memory. "Prime Minister Richter's inaugural diplomatic celebration will take place this evening at eight o'clock on the private yacht belonging to Count Alfonse Marino, Grappoli ambassador. The governmental party will include senior cabinet members and head of state security, Colonel Archibald Mandel. Light refreshments will be served as the vessel makes its way east of the Ridleford pontoon. Once in the bay itself, a fireworks display will commence from the deck, allowing a magnificent perspective of the pyrotechnics over the city."

There was a stunned silence as everyone made sense of this.

"My God," said Andrews. "The ambassador is going to sail the core of the government right into the mouth of the Grappoli fleet! The yacht will be boarded, and the prime minister and his inner circle will be taken prisoner. The administrative and legislative heart of the city will fall before a shot is fired!"

"We have to alert the government right away!" said Dahria.

"I'll report to my garrison HQ," said Emtezu, heading for the door.

"No!" I said, loudly. "Everyone just . . . be quiet."

There was another heavy pause, and they all stared at me.

"We have not a moment to lose," said Andrews.

"No!" I said again.

"We really don't have time—" Andrews began, but Dahria elbowed him in the ribs.

"Let the girl think," she muttered.

I did, the puzzle pieces swirling around in my head and then slotting into place.

"I thought we were dealing with two threats to the city," I mused aloud, looking at no one. "One from inside—Richter, Heritage, and their attempts to suppress the black and colored population by any means they could use, including a deadly toxin. One from outside—the Grappoli attack. But they were always part of the same thing. Richter and his government aren't about to be snatched by an unexpected Grappoli attack fleet. He is about to meet his Grappoli allies and hand them the city."

CHAPTER

29

"NO!" SAID ANDREWS. "SURELY not?"

"Richter always said the Grappoli were white Bar-Selehm's racial allies. He has always preached appeasement and alliance between the city and the Grappoli, an alliance against all the nonwhites in the region. This is to be his masterstroke, achieving both unity with the Grappoli and the banishment or destruction of the blacks and coloreds in one fell swoop."

"The city won't stand for it!" said Dahria.

"The city won't have a choice," said Mnenga. "Who will defend it?"

"Most of the regular army have been sent north of the city to meet a threat that doesn't exist," said Emtezu, "and most of the black people in the city are still recovering from the effects of the green luxorite. Richter's militia are virtually the only armed men in the city, and they will do what their leader tells them to."

"Then we've lost," said Andrews. "There's nothing we can do."

"If my brother were here—" Dahria began.

"He's not," said her grandmother. "Another fragment of the resistance conveniently swept out of the way."

"If he *were* here," Dahria persisted, "he would insist there is always something we can do, even if it feels impossible. Even if you cannot hope for success, the act of resistance is sometimes all you have."

"Aaron Muhapi would say the same," said Sureyna. "And so do I."

"Good," I said. "Then we will resist, whatever the hope of success. We will stand for the city we love, the version of the world we love, for right and for justice. Yes?"

"Yes," said Emtezu.

"Yes," said Mnenga.

"Yes," said Dahria.

"How?" said Andrews.

I smiled at him, suddenly struck with a disarming sense of compassion for them all, for their sadness, their desperation.

"We gather our forces," I said, pushing into the next sentence before Andrews could turn his obvious skepticism into words. "You reach out to the police you know you can trust. Mnenga, you put your warriors between the Drowning gate and the Grappoli soldiers coming from the west. Emtezu, you gather every black and colored soldier sent home by the recent ban and get what weapons you can, and we try to retake the coastal fortresses. Sureyna—"

"I will alert Peter and as many of the city Mahweni as can walk," she said. "They are very angry. They may not have weapons as such, but many have axes and wrenches, boat hooks and hammers—"

"So do the Lani," said Tanish. "I'll bring the gangs from the Soot and Numbers, the Drowning too if I can get word to them. They might not all get along, but if they have to pick between fighting each other and fighting the Grappoli? No contest, is it?"

I nodded with gratitude, then continued.

"We will need to disarm the other devices that have put the remaining garrisons out of commission. They will be located in high, unobtrusive places, so perhaps I should—"

"I will take care of them," said Vestris. I gave her a look, but her eyes burned with a fury I dared not contradict.

"I will go with her," said Madame Nahreem. "I am not the Crane Fly I once was, but I can still climb." As Tanish's jaw dropped, the two women eyed each other for a moment. "And besides," said

Madame Nahreem, speaking with an entirely unfamiliar lack of command that was almost humility, "there are things to say. Things owed." For a moment her face seemed to ripple with barely contained distress, but then Vestris inclined her head infinitesimally, and the old woman's mask slid back into place.

"And you?" said Mnenga. "What will you do?"

I pulled my eyes from Vestris's almost feral face and thought for a moment, hoping some other option would present itself, but I knew what was left to me. There was a polite tap at the door, and Mrs. Topesh appeared, dignified as ever, with a wheeled trolley loaded with porcelain cups and saucers.

"Forgive me for taking the liberty," she said, addressing me and my motley assortment of visitors, "but I thought your guests would appreciate some tea."

I couldn't help laughing, and when she gave me a bewildered look, I said, "Mrs. Topesh, you are a good person."

"Well," she said, coloring, but standing tall, "at times like these, if we can't all stick together, what use are we?"

EMTEZU LED THE WAY through the darkening city, his purposeful stride, and that of the twenty or thirty men matching him step for step behind me, clearing the streets. They weren't wearing uniforms, and the city was already starting to forget that black men had made up a sizeable portion of its armed forces, but there was no mistaking their military bearing. I think the guards on the gate at regimental headquarters recognized that before they realized who he was.

"Something I can help you with, Captain?" said one of them, opting for casual, while one of his colleagues unslung his rifle cautiously and nodded to another to alert the men inside.

"The city is under attack," said Emtezu without preamble. "We need access to your armory."

The sentry, a ruddy-faced man with a blond mustache and watery blue eyes, rubbed his hands absently, biding for time.

"An attack, eh?" he said at last, trying to sound interested but neutral. "I haven't heard the alarm, gunfire, anything like that."

"That's because elements within the government don't want us to fight back," he said.

"Is that right?" said the sentry, still carefully noncommittal, as if they were merely debating a point of protocol. "Which elements would those be, then?"

"The prime minister," said Emtezu, smiling openly at the preposterousness of the claim.

"Oh," said the sentry, returning his smile. "That element. Look, Captain, you know I can't help you. I understand why you are upset, and I think you know that a lot of us here sympathize with your position, but this," he glanced pointedly at the men lined up behind us, "is not the way. Go home and we'll say no more about it, yes?"

"I'm afraid I can't do that, Corporal," said Emtezu. "The government is about to hand our city over to the Grappoli, and we can't let that happen."

"The Grappoli, is it?" said the sentry, playing along, but not believing a word of it. "Well, if they have marched all the way down here, they're going to walk right into the first infantry regiment about twenty-five miles up the coast, along with a whole lot of cavalry and artillery. I don't think we need to rely on you and your, er, friends here."

"They aren't up the coast," said Emtezu, biting back his impatience. "They came around the cape by ship and are about to steam up the river mouth. The city is largely undefended."

The sentry's easy smile wavered for just a second as a note of confusion flitted through his pale eyes.

"Up the river mouth?" he said. "If that were the case, we would not be able to hear ourselves speak for the noise of the guns in the emplacements by the docks and the harbor fortress."

"The gun emplacements have already been taken by the enemy," said Emtezu. "It's up to us to take them back."

I was glad he didn't say that the coastal forts had been taken by troops disguised as circus performers and using baboons as sappers, but the sentry still made a face.

"You're joking, right?" he said. "I mean, you can't expect me to believe this."

Emtezu looked down, sighed, then looked at me and, almost under his breath, said, "This is a waste of time."

"No," I said. "It's not." I looked up at the sentry, then said, "What if they just take their uniforms? And the guns, but no ammunition?"

"What use would that be?" said the sentry.

"The man has a point," said Emtezu.

"The Grappoli are expecting the city to be undefended," I said. "We might not need an actual army to make them think twice about coming in."

"If this is real," said the sentry, "and the Grappoli are here with an invasion force, thirty men aren't going to stop them, whether they are uniformed or not."

"Perhaps not," I said. "But that sounds like our problem, not yours."

He peered at me, as if I were rock that had started speaking. "Who is this?" he said to Emtezu. "Why are you listening to this girl?"

"Right now," said Emtezu, "she is the only person in this city that I trust, the only person who might get us through the night in one piece."

The sentry seemed to hesitate, then shook his head. "I can't authorize this," he said.

"I'm sorry to hear that," said Emtezu. "I was hoping we could do this the easy way."

He stepped past the sentry, deflecting the muzzle of his comrade's rifle and kicking him square between the legs. As the man went down, Emtezu wrested the gun from his hands and turned back to the sentry, jabbing the butt into his midriff and doubling him up. Leaving the sentry wheezing behind him, Emtezu strode through the gate and into the building, checking the rifle's breach as he did so.

"Take his weapon," he commanded, over his shoulder, "but don't use it unless I give the order. I'd rather we didn't have to lock him and his friends up. Actually, I'd rather they came with us."

I stared at him as one of his men unholstered the sentry's revolver and popped its cylinder out.

"This is a court-martial offense!" gasped the sentry.

"That depends," said Emtezu.

"On what?" demanded the sentry.

"On who is in charge in the morning," called Emtezu as he walked away.

"Tsanwe!" I called after him. He turned.

"You need to go," he said, anticipating my remark. "It's all right. I'll get the Northbank Fortress back under our control. They don't know we're coming and won't expect it. If we can take it without too many losses, I'll send men across the river to the Ridleford battery, but I doubt they'll get to you in time."

"I know," I said. "Just . . . be careful."

"You too," he said.

"And thanks."

I turned quickly before I had time to think better of it, to try and find other words about what his friendship meant to me. It was, after all, almost certainly the last time we would see each other alive.

CHAPTER

30

IT WAS AFTER SEVEN by the time I reached the river just east of butchers' row in Evensteps. The Grappoli ambassador's yacht was moored in the fashionable marina just south of where the triumphal arch spanned Broad Street. The water was deep here, and the embankment was sheer and well maintained, which meant no hippos and few crocodiles. Snakes were always a danger at this time of year, but I had my good boots on, and in spite of my former exhaustion, I was suddenly wide awake.

The Grappoli flag tugged disconsolately at the yacht's mast as the evening's festivities were prepared by a small army of servants. Even before the new laws, the only Lani or blacks here were employees paid to wash down the decks or scrape barnacles off the hulls of the sleek pleasure craft that called this portion of the river Kalihm home. Since it was after curfew, I could not afford to be picked up for loitering. I watched the area from a fishing pier a little upriver for ten minutes, until I was reasonably satisfied I knew how the guards and staff operated, then ducked into the nearest alley and waited for my chance.

I suspected that the serving staff for the event itself would be all white, but Richter cared less about the servants he couldn't see. Some of the men and women carrying crates of fireworks, trays of food, and cases of wine bottles were black and Lani. I followed the returning line to the supply wagons, pulled my carefully folded maid's apron from my satchel, put it on, and joined the line. There were armed dragoons wearing the green tunics and white, feathered pith helmets I had seen outside the Grappoli embassy watching the gangway onto the yacht, but no one looks twice at a Lani servant when she is carrying things to be used by her social superiors.

I, however, did and was taken aback to recognize one of them.

Bindi. The cleaning girl from Parliament, who had apparently been allowed to continue her labors outside the corridors of power. That meant the ambassador, Richter, and his cronies weren't aboard yet. I considered staying out of her line of sight, then changed my mind. As I set down my crate of fine stemware, I nudged her in the ribs. Her eyes flicked to me and her mouth opened, but I raised a quick finger to my lips.

"Has the boat been cleaned?" I whispered.

She hesitated, thrown by my appearance, then nodded. That meant the cabins below would be unoccupied.

"Just finishing up," she breathed. "They're on their way."

"Thank you." A question I had wanted to ask occurred to me. "Bindi, when that tea chest we found upstairs in the Parliament House was delivered, did Mr. Shyloh see that it was moved there?"

She shook her head.

"He didn't know about it," she said. "Got quite hot under the collar about it taking two of the staff to move it. Waste of man hours, he said."

"So who gave the order?"

"The Heritage party secretary," she said. "Mr. Saunders."

"Now the prime minister's private secretary," I said.

"That's right," she said. "Why? What are you doing?" she whispered, glancing uneasily around.

An excellent question, and one that could have a dozen answers, several of which involved getting myself killed.

"Trying to get you your old job back," I said.

She stared at me, but her smile was doused as someone came

into her line of vision. I turned, and there was Mr. Shyloh, busily orchestrating the preparations. My heart sank. He would know I was not one of the team.

Reading my look, Bindi said, "What do you need?"

I nodded at the stairs down to the lower deck. They were only a few yards away, but I could not reach them unnoticed. Bindi's mouth set, and she gave me a short, decisive nod, then reached into one of the crates and plucked out a couple of wineglasses. As I took a hasty step to the side, she dropped them deliberately.

Shyloh was on her in a second.

"What are you playing at, you clumsy child?" he demanded.

With his focus on her, I was clear to make my dash for the stairs. Seconds later, I was below, closing the door behind me and shutting out Shyloh's murmuring at Bindi's incompetence. If I lived through the night, I'd repay her for that kindness.

If.

There were two staterooms at the foot of the stairs and then the luxurious main cabin before the carpeted hall led on to what I assumed was the galley. The doors were locked, but I had come prepared. Within a couple of minutes, I had gotten inside what was surely the ambassador's private suite. The small circular windows meant no real curtains to speak of, so my only viable hiding place was under a three-quarter-scale couch that sat in the corner beside a writing desk. My ribs ached as I wriggled into position and lay, feeling the slow rock of the boat, relieved that the nausea from the false luxorite seemed to have passed.

I couldn't have been down there more than a few minutes when I heard voices above me, followed by footsteps on the stairs and the snap of the door latch.

One set of feet. As they came into view inches from my head, I recognized the patent-leather boots of the ambassador's dress uniform. He sat heavily in the desk chair, sighed, and began fussing with something that ended with the strike of a match.

The air was suddenly touched with a curl of cigar smoke.

I didn't want to do anything. I wanted to lie there and listen, but I knew in my heart that if I had a chance—however slim—it was to act now, before the parliamentary delegation arrived. I tried to recall Madame Nahreem's neutral mask, but it wouldn't come, and in my heart I felt only the kind of true desperation that is passion without hope. I took a breath and rolled out from under the couch, standing slowly, silently, not reaching for my kukri, knowing that by the time I took my place in the chair opposite the ambassador's desk, he would have a pistol trained on me.

He did. But his alarm changed to curiosity almost immediately, the result, I think, as much of my manner as my face.

"You?" he said in bemusement. "Willinghouse's sister's maid!"

The pistol was small and decorative, all nickel plating and dainty ornamentation, but at this range, it would do the job.

"Among other things," I said.

"Yes," he said, realization dawning. "Elitus, no? You bear an uncanny resemblance to a visiting dignitary who came through the halls of that worthy establishment a few months ago." I just smiled, not bothering to deny it, and he beamed delightedly. "How remarkable! And you have come here tonight to . . . what? Assassinate me? Kidnap your prime minister in return for Willinghouse's freedom? You know there are already troops aboard and will be many more soon."

"I do," I said. "And not all of them will be from Bar-Selehm."

That quelled his smile. One eyebrow rose fractionally, and he sat a little taller, impressed, I thought, but with none of the playfulness that had been alive in his face a moment before.

"Ah," he said. "So you have fathomed our little ruse. Such a lovely word that: *fathomed*. Plumbed the depths and found out the bottom. Feldish is such a rich language, don't you think, Miss . . ."

"Sutonga," I said. "Anglet Sutonga."

He considered me, then smiled again. "You know," he said, "I do believe you are telling the truth."

"At this point," I answered. "What else is there?"

Again the smile evaporated and a heaviness descended upon him. He set the cigar down and gave me a frank look. "What do you want from me, Miss Sutonga?" he said. "I have, as you know, a busy evening ahead."

"Cancel it," I said.

"That is impossible," he replied, but not dismissively. He looked weary. Sad.

"It's not," I said.

"Diplomats serve the interests of their nations," he said. "I do not make the policies I enact. I do not even always agree with them. I rarely like them."

"Especially not this one," I said.

"As I said, I do not always get to do what I wish for. I regret that I may have been a trifle unguarded in my speech last time we met. Some things are best left unsaid. Now, if you don't mind—"

"You like it here," I said.

"Of course. That does not mean—"

"You like what the city is," I pressed. "What made it, who made it, and what it might yet be. You don't hold with your country's expansion, and you certainly don't hold with Richter's Whites First policies. The city as it is now is crumbling, and if you hand it over to the Grappoli and set Richter up as some tin-pot regent, it will cease to exist in every meaningful way. You know this."

For a moment he gazed into my eyes, then, as if unable to hold them any longer, focused on his cigar. He picked it up and drew upon it, blowing out a long stream of aromatic smoke.

"I can't do anything about it," he said. "The matter is completely in hand, the result of months of planning. What happens tonight is only the end of something that has been in the works for a long time, like a garment or a piece of equipment that emerges from one of your wonderful factories but began as seed or ore months ago."

"Machines can always be shut off."

"Not this one. It is an opportunity my government has anticipated for years."

"You could stop it."

"If I tried, they'd shoot me on the spot."

"Not necessarily. Not if you gave them information that convinced them the machine was broken, that their plan was not going to work."

"And as soon as they found out I was lying, they would shoot me and then do what they came to do in the first place."

"Not if you were telling the truth."

He frowned. "What do you mean?" he said.

"I am not the only one who knows what is about to happen here. You tell the Grappoli fleet that they are walking into a trap. That we know they're coming. That our coastal guns are about to send their ships to the bottom—the very fathomless bottom—of Bar-Selehm bay. That the streets are full of soldiers ready to defend the river-banks from incursion. That the city is united against them and they cannot take it, even with our government on their side."

"None of this is true."

"It's all true. Tell them. Stall them for an hour, and I swear you will be telling the truth."

Again the scowl, but complex now, calculating, still dubious, but wondering.

"It's all nonsense," he said. "Your troops have all marched north to fight a foe that doesn't exist."

"Not all of them."

"Enough."

"Their absence has been compensated for."

"By whom? You don't have other troops except the civilian militia, who will welcome the Grappoli with open arms."

"You make the mistake that Richter makes," I said, and now I smiled too, if a little sadly. "He is so used to thinking of the city as only the white people that he ignores the rest of us, and believe me when I say that is a grave mistake. Ambassador, we have a lot of other troops."

He breathed out then. It was almost a gasp, a slow, vocalized exhalation of realization and thought that brought with it a trace of cigar smoke. He laid the pistol down and used his free hand to rub his temples, his eyes closed. "You should be in Parliament," he said, almost smiling. "But you know what is even more eloquent than you?"

"What?"

"Music," he said. "Samosas."

He smiled again, the same sad smile as before, and reached for his waistcoat pocket. Drawing out a small key on a ring, he unlocked the drawer in his desk. He reached in and pulled out a bundle of paper bound with string, which he flipped to me. I glanced at them.

Letters.

"What are these?"

"Reading material for a later date," he said, suddenly breezy, casual, his tone a kind of audible shrug. "Keep them safe."

I stowed them in my satchel, but I was concerned.

"Does this mean . . ." I began.

"You need to go before my friends arrive," he said, rising. "Both sets. It has been a genuine pleasure." He extended his hand, and I, dazed by the speed of the transition, rose awkwardly and shook it. "Go. Quickly."

I made for the door, but turned before I opened it.

"You think you are going to die," I said.

"Everyone dies, Miss Sutonga. Not everybody lives."

He smiled, a generous if slightly strained smile, and nodded me out, sinking back into his chair.

CHAPTER

31

IT WAS QUIET ABOVE decks. The servants had all gone, and the sentries had taken up positions in the prow, on the stern, and on the gangplank, all looking out, rifles shouldered. If I wanted to get off the boat, I would have to go over the side, but I wasn't ready to leave just yet, and my brief reconnaissance before had planted an idea in my head. I skulked lightly around the hatches to where a rope ladder ran up the mainmast to a railed crow's nest.

It was open, but the only lamps other than the yacht's luxorite running lights were on the deck where the guests would soon be milling in the warm night air. I was pretty sure that if I did nothing to attract attention, I would be unseen up there.

I paused only to root through one of the open crates and withdraw a long cardboard tube and a slim metal box, both of which I slipped into my satchel. Then I scaled the rope ladder, marveling at how easy it seemed after the affair at the big top, clambered into the railed lookout post, and dropped into a motionless crouch just in time to see the guards changing position as someone shouted formal commands.

Richter was coming.

And Mandel, Saunders, and a half dozen other Heritage party bigwigs all in their paramilitary grays. I saw no one from either the Nationals or the Brevards, but then this wasn't exactly a state occasion, so no one would be on hand to ask what was going on when Richter sold the city down the river to its oldest enemy.

Unless the ambassador did as I asked.

I had no idea whether he meant to, and even less if he actually would once presented with the reality of the thing, surrounded by Richter's men—always men—and the advance guard of the Grappoli fleet.

And if he doesn't? If he just saw me as a potentially dangerous enemy agent whom he humored accordingly, what then?

I didn't know. Emtezu could get control of one of the fortresses, and then we might yet have a chance, but a bloodbath seemed inevitable either way. Even then, should I remain onboard with Richter, if he won out and I was still sitting tight here, with my kukri in its sheath . . .

Well, we'll see, won't we?

The Grappoli ambassadorial sentries went through some ritual greeting and paper checking before giving place to the parliamentary delegation, who had their own red-tunicked dragoon escort.

So if it comes to a firefight, it won't just be out there in the night, I thought. *It will be all around me.*

I wished I'd brought a pistol.

I kept very still, watching and listening as the ambassador came from his stateroom below and the speeches and drinking commenced. Moments later, we cast off, and the yacht was steered out into the channel and aimed at the Ridleford pontoon bridge, moved solely by the current of the river.

It hadn't really been a pontoon bridge for decades, though it had started as one, a way of crossing the river at its widest point before entering the ocean bay. Where it had once been simply a string of boats lashed together with some boarding for a walkway on top, it was now an imposing structure with a stone tower on each bank and another in the middle where pylons had been sunk to anchor the bridge. On either side of that central stanchion, the iron causeway still sat on barges moored together. Close to the tower, the causeway could be raised to admit vessels too tall to sneak under the metal road. The whole thing was scheduled for demolition and reconstruction as soon as the government found the money and political will to do it, but for now, the bridge was constantly being raised and lowered, lowered and raised, delaying and irritating both the traffic on the river and that which was trying to walk or ride across it.

It was open now, and would probably stay that way, though there was a walkway that stayed open for all but the tallest ships, so that if Emtezu and his men had not yet made it across to the south bank to secure the second fortress, they would still be able to do so rather than going all the way up river to the Fishwharf. I wondered if I should have been able to hear gunfire from the North-bank Fortress and whether it was a bad sign that I hadn't, and found myself gazing toward the sea for a sign that anything had happened. There was nothing. The brilliance of the Beacon on the Trade Exchange to the north did not reach anywhere near that far west, and the street lamps supplied only a sprinkling of pearly specks along the riverside.

Emtezu might be dead, I thought. *And the others. Madame Nahreem and Vestris, alone on the south bank. Tanish, Sureyna . . . They might all be dead, and I might be the last of our makeshift revolution, waiting absurdly, alone up here for something impossible to happen . . .*

I felt the moment that the boat turned into the stream. It leaned with an almost animal satisfaction as the current took it and angled it toward the open lane of the bridge. Even so, it was a slow drift, and below the party went on, a general hubbub of male voices and occasional rumbles of laughter. The serving staff wore vaguely nautical white jackets with gold trim, mingling discreetly with the guests, loaded with trays of canapés and glasses. I thought vaguely of Bindi and hoped she hadn't gotten into trouble for what she had done, though I doubted it would matter much in the morning, one way or the other.

Time passed. The river slid under us, and the yacht inched toward the towers of Ridleford bridge, everyone watching dutifully as we moved cautiously through. Ropes, cables, and ladders hung down the sides of the central tower. Somewhere ahead, in the clustering chimneys away to our left, would be the Dyer Street cement factory where I had been working the day Berrit died, the day that began my relationship with Willinghouse and the six months I had spent discovering the city I had thought I knew. It seemed fitting that it would all end there.

In fact, we didn't get that far. As we neared the bridge's central tower, the yacht seemed to drift and yaw as the current tightened. Something in the water ahead was creating a bottleneck. The skeleton crew ran to peer over the prow, and the ship slowed, skewing slightly and coming to a halt right next to the bridge's main stanchion.

"What the blazes is that?" roared Mandel, who seemed permanently outraged by the world.

"Logjam," someone called back. "Railway sleepers or something. We're going to have to clear it before we can get through."

"Isn't there someone on the bridge whose job this is?" demanded Richter.

"Personnel all cleared out, sir," said the crewman. "Security precaution."

Which probably meant that the laborers who manned the bridge and its operations were black. It was also possible that the logjam was, in some clever way, Tanish's doing. He had made a cryptic remark as we left my lodging house about slowing the yacht down. I smiled at the thought, and then immediately hoped he was nowhere near, that he was far away and would never see what was likely to become of the city.

The water in the bay ahead of us was flat, black, and unbroken, but we weren't getting any closer to it, however much the crew worked their boat hooks and spars into the mess below. A single coast guard vessel patrolled the area to keep commercial traffic away, but it was a quiet night, and I imagined the men aboard were only half watching when a slim military cutter hove into view, lightless and quiet as a spider. It was almost alongside before I heard the soft putter of its steam engine, and by then, the coast guard vessel was too far away to catch it, though it began its slow curve toward us immediately.

The coast guard boat wasn't the only thing to react to our unexpected visitors. The Bar-Selehm dragoons on deck were suddenly agitated and looking for instruction from Richter and Mandel. But when the prime minister gave his orders, it wasn't to the red-coated troops at all, but to the Grappoli honor guard, who took the dragoons' weapons and bound the men in the staterooms below deck.

As the confusion died away, I picked up the engines of two more vessels following in the wake of the cutter, broad shallow barges designed to beach marines. Even from here I could see that they were groaning with the Grappoli advance guard, perhaps a hundred men: more than enough to take and hold the riverbank until the rest arrived.

Through all this, I held motionless vigil, watching the ambassador for signs of mood or intent, but he did not react until the Grappoli vessel was moored to a cleat on our port side and four men in uniform came aboard. As they did so, I realized what I should have known earlier. I was too high to hear what was about to be said. Whatever the consequences for me—and they did not look good—I had to go down. Perhaps if I stayed just fifteen feet up the mast on the rope ladder, I could remain outside the lamplight . . .

I began the downward climb, aware that the tone of the discussion on deck seemed cordial, aware also of the two military barges jostling for position as they made for the riverbank. The invasion, for that was what it was, was about to start, and it seemed no one would notice. I looked from my place in the dark canopy of sky to the warmly lit deck below and saw the snapping bows and formal handshakes of amiable diplomacy, so that I was unsurprised when the darkness was suddenly rent by a brilliant flash of light, which left a cloud of acrid, bluish smoke. They had brought an official photographer to document the historic moment.

For a second I clung, insect like and unmoving, to the ladder, terrified that the flash had given my position away, but the laughter and chatter began again immediately, and I risked a few more feet of descent. It took me a moment to realize that the people closest to me were speaking not in Feldish, but in Grappoli.

One was the ambassador himself, and the other wore a bicorne hat and the air of a naval commander. The ambassador had turned his back on the Heritage party contingent, and seemed to be speaking in earnest, rapid terms, so that his partner became visibly agitated, looking around him. It seemed to go on for several minutes, this eager back and forth, while the parliamentary contingent looked on with an air of mild indignation.

Good, I thought. *The longer it takes, the better . . .*

But all too soon the admiral turned, advancing on Richter and pointing at him accusingly.

Suddenly, the party atmosphere was utterly gone, and the yacht was silent, save for the admiral's furious stream of Grappoli invective. The green-tunicked dragoons moved rapidly to stand on either side of him, and now their rifles were trained on the Bar-Selehm parliamentary faction.

"What is the meaning of this?" Richter demanded. "How dare you!"

"You have betrayed us, sir!" said the admiral, in heavily accented Feldish. "You try to trap us!"

"What are you talking about, man?" Mandel demanded, glaring at him through his monocle. "Marino! Tell him."

"He has already told us!" said the admiral. "Everything."

"There seems to be some mistake," said Richter, shelving his usual hectoring rhetoric in favor of something more conciliatory, now that he was looking down the barrel of a rifle. "The plan is as it was. We have prepared the city for your arrival. The coast guard vessel is of no consequence. You may destroy it with our blessing."

"And the fortresses?" demanded the admiral. "Who will they destroy?"

"They are in your command," said Richter. "I really don't see—"

"Not according to the ambassador," said the admiral.

"What? Marino!" snapped Richter. "What is the man talking about?"

"Your duplicity, Prime Minister," said the ambassador. "Your lies. You invite us here only to destroy us, to take the advantage of our fleet being directly under your guns so that you can sink them."

"Nonsense!" said Mandel. "What rot is this?"

"I believe you may drop the pretense now, gentlemen," said the ambassador, stepping forward. "Your plot against us has failed. And our ships will return to home waters before you have chance to do them damage."

Mandel was shaking his head and making a face as if he couldn't understand what he was hearing, but Richter's countenance hardened.

"I see," he said. "I always worried about you. Your tastes. Your interests. Well, now we see just how much you have *gone native*. I'm afraid, my lord admiral," he continued, turning to the man in the bicorne hat, "that your ambassador has betrayed the Grappoli Empire. Do not believe a word he says. You and your men are welcome to the city. I suggest you put this man in custody and try him according to your own laws for treason in the highest degree."

The admiral faltered, looking from Richter to the ambassador and back, and speaking quickly again in his own language. The ambassador shook his head vigorously, but I thought he looked uncomfortable.

"What is he saying?" asked Mandel. "If the fortresses are still in Bar-Selehm's control, ask him why they haven't fired a shot! Go on! Ask him that, and damn his lying eyes."

It was, I thought, an excellent question. Hooking my arms through the rigging of the ladder so that I could use my hands, I plucked the cardboard tube and the metal box from my satchel. With unsteady fingers, I opened the box, tore one of the phosphorus-dipped wooden splints from the block and struck it. It burst into sudden flame, which I touched to the fuse of the tube as I aimed it out over the bay.

The mortar went off with a bang and a dull whoosh, and the firework shot high over the river mouth and burst in an orange flare, which hung in the sky like a beacon. Suddenly the dark, flat water showed shapes mustering out to sea.

Ships.

There was chaos on deck again as the soldiers tried to track me with their rifles while Richter and Mandel shouted incoherent orders and demands, but then the guns from the north bank battery opened up, and they forgot about me entirely.

"What the hell is going on?" roared Mandel, rounding on the ambassador. "Marino, you assured us that your men—"

"Not my men," said the ambassador smoothly. "I am a diplomat. I do not control the Grappoli military."

"Who fired that flare?" Richter barked. "I saw someone. A girl in the rigging. Where is she?"

I was sprinting back to the stern, hoping against hope that I could leap clear and still reach the ropes and ladders that hung from the bridge. As I ran, I drew my kukri and hacked at a rope lashed around a hefty spool, sending chain whipping through its cleats as the anchor plunged through the water and the ship juddered and creaked. Whatever happened next, they would not simply sail away.

"To the shore!" yelled Richter at the marines in their barges. "Get them on land. It's started!"

As the barges steamed for the beach, I kept running, leaping cables and hatches, not breaking stride even as I heard the staccato crack of rifles and the zip of bullets in the air, planting one foot on the rail and vaulting with all my strength at the stanchion of the bridge and the rope ladder hanging down it.

My muscles shrieked in protest, but I caught, held on, and began to climb. Even as I did so, the light of sudden explosions in the sky showed an amazing thing: three long boats powered by black oarsmen, hide shields hung over the sides, spears sticking up, and crouching riflemen in the prow. In the back of one, standing like a warrior god in some ancient tomb painting, with his queen beside him, was Mnenga.

In the same instant, a cry came from the bridge above me: a command. A dozen black riflemen aimed and fired a volley at the closest barge. I looked up to see Emtezu, pointing and shouting to his troops. The sight of him spurred me on, and I surged up the ropes. Moments later, as the Grappoli marines returned fire, sending bullets spinning off the stone and metal of the bridge, I pulled myself over the rail and dropped into cover. Emtezu, sweating and bloodied but whole, met my eyes.

"The Ridleford fortress?" I asked.

"Not yet," he said. "But we're not done."

I nodded, then looked down to the black water. The yacht was still snagged in the gap between the pontoon causeway, but the first barge was cutting through the shallows and into the shingle bank. A few men had gone down, but dozens more were packed in tight and leaning forward as the boat ran aground. In seconds, the barge was half empty as the marines vaulted out and splashed ashore.

Only then did I see that, as Mnenga's boats angled in on them from behind, the shore was thronging with people: black and Lani laborers, dockworkers, and factory hands armed with wrenches and sledgehammers, picks and crowbars, standing feet spread, neck and shoulders rolled in grim and resolute silence. Before the marines even knew they were there, they closed fast.

On the deck of the yacht, Richter and Mandel were pointing and roaring their outrage, caught between the jaws of all they hated. The Grappoli soldiers onboard had taken cover among the wreckage of the party, but under the yacht's lamps, they were well-lit targets and could do little more than hide. They had realized what was only just dawning on the politicians: the only way they were going to live through this was by getting out of sight, either by going below decks or by getting off the yacht entirely. The former was only a short-term solution, but the latter was considerably more difficult, so I was amazed to see Richter and Mandel hurriedly making for the very rope ladder I had climbed up to the bridge.

The night was a riot of gunfire and shouting. The Mahweni attack boats had reached the second barge. The packed marines were struggling to turn and meet the lunging spears of the furious tribesmen. With the marines thus occupied, Emtezu's squad had, for a moment, free range and were picking their targets with care.

"Hold your fire! You men. Do you know who I am? I order that you hold your fire!"

Unbelievably, it was Mandel. Richter was at his shoulder. Their formal dress uniforms were smeared with oil and the greenish filth of the river, and their faces were pink and breathless, but they clearly thought their authority untarnished.

"I am your commanding officer," Mandel bellowed, "and I demand that you lay down your arms."

Emtezu did not hesitate. He strode over, drawing his revolver and aiming at Mandel's throat.

"Colonel Archibald Mandel," he said, flat and decisive, "I hereby arrest you for treason to the city-state of Bar-Selehm."

He plucked a pair of metal cuffs from his pocket and tossed them to another of his troops, never taking his eyes off Mandel, who was sputtering, "How dare you! I'll have you court-marshaled."

But Emtezu did not flinch, and a second later, Mandel was being forced to his knees as his hands were fastened behind his back.

"This is an outrage!" Richter announced.

"You're next, Prime Minister," said Emtezu.

"Oh, I think not," said Richter.

It took me a second to make sense of his smile, and then one of Emtezu's men went down clutching his belly, shot not from the river or shore, but from the south end of the bridge. A company of wild-looking gunmen were coming from the Ridleford fortress on the south bank to relieve their Grappoli comrades. Leading the charge, like something out of a nightmare, was a troupe of leaping, shrieking baboons.

The circus special forces.

Emtezu turned, roaring. "About-face! Incoming!"

His soldiers revolved, dropping to their knees and taking aim, but the attackers had the advantage, and another of Emtezu's men went down.

And another. This one with a throwing knife in his chest.

Through the smoke of the rifle fire, I saw the man who had called himself Blogvitch, clad in the outlandish leaden armor still, like some ancient knight, a goblin-man of mystical, terrible power. I stepped back in alarm and fear, shrinking away from the first of the baboons that hurled itself into Emtezu's troops, biting and flailing with its clawed paws, and saw Richter, sheltering behind an iron girder, a man nowhere near accepting defeat. I glanced down to the river where the marine barges were a boiling mass of hand-to-hand combat, but I could make no sense of how things were going.

And then, as the future of the city hung in the balance, a cry of surprise and alarm came from the far end of the bridge. Some of Blogvitch's dangerous irregulars were turning in surprise as if they were being attacked from behind. The group parted, and in the gap I saw two unlikely figures, one wild, misshapen, and shrouded, and one poised but older than anyone else in the fight, a pair of short swords whirling over her head.

Vestris and Madame Nahreem, united at last in purpose.

My heart leapt, and tears came to my eyes. It was a desperate, suicidal attack. Two fell to their blades as they cut and stabbed—Vestris animal and lightning fast, Madame Nahreem balanced, neutral, and deliberate—but the advantage of their sudden appearance had already gone, and they were badly outnumbered. I had no idea what was happening down on the riverbank or whether the regular thud of the northern gun battery would be enough to keep the rest of the Grappoli navy at bay, but I knew it was only a matter of time before Richter's citizen militia joined the fray.

Vestris sprang and lunged, and Madame Nahreem parried and spun, but the group of fighters around them tightened, grew more resolute.

We were out of time.

I glanced to Emtezu, who met my eyes, his face blank, then watched as he left the kneeling Mandel where he was, stepping forward and shooting precisely. I drew my kukri and went with him.

One last, desperate charge . . .

I stepped over a dead baboon, jostled by one of the Bar-Selehm dragoons as he fixed his bayonet and shouted his defiance. Thinking nothing, driven by the grief and rage of the last days, I matched his roar of fury and ran at the enemy.

As the troops abandoned the frenzied and fumbling reloading between shots, there was an eerie silence as body met body with blade and fist and boot. Men fell all around me, stunned and bleeding. Someone screamed—a terrible shriek of surprised agony—and one of the greenish trapeze artists emerged from the throng in front of me, armed with a sword with a curved cutting edge. I dropped into a crouch, releasing my kukri and snatching up the abandoned rifle of one of Emtezu's fallen men, bringing it up, aiming and squeezing the trigger in one fluid motion.

Nothing happened. The gun had been discharged and not reloaded. A minute smile flitted across the face of the lean and sinewy acrobat as he came on. In the madness of battle, his outlandish makeup made him demonic, a creature of death and hatred from another world. He leapt into the air, the sword high over his head, his free hand out for balance. I lunged with the empty, bayonetless rifle, striking him in the chest as he came down. It was just enough to knock him off-balance, and his wild, slicing stroke cut the air instead of my throat. He rocked back, momentarily awkward, like an elegant bird—a spirit in the air, but clumsy on land—and I shifted my grip. I turned into a tight spiral dragging the length of the rifle in a rapidly intensifying spin. The heavy butt of the gun caught him full in the jaw. He went over backwards and did not get up again.

But the delay had cost me. I looked up to see Blogvitch unleash one of his deadly knives at Madame Nahreem. She moved fractionally, not simply leaning away from it but bringing one hand up and snatching it out of the air. As he drew another, she fired the first right back at him. It caught him just left of his sternum, and he collapsed, turning toward me so that I could see the amazement in his face.

Emtezu brought another acrobat down with his elbow, then laid him out with a swinging smack of his revolver, and Vestris kicked another so hard that he spun away, collided with the low rail which ran along the side of the walkway, and went over, crying out as he made the long drop to the black water of the Kalihm.

People were running up from the south bank.

The citizen militia, I thought, despair smothering me again.

But it wasn't. It was Tanish and Sarn and twenty or thirty other gang members, mostly brown but a few white too.

I faltered, feeling the panic of the Grappoli circus fighters, as they looked wildly around them, feeling the noose close, and I looked down to where their comrade marines were fighting with the same unnerved desperation as their plans fell apart. There was no sign of further support from the Grappoli navy, and the north bank gun batteries continued to fire on the ships in the bay.

We were winning. Madame Nahreem was coming toward us like Vengeance or Justice, her black sari unfurling like a flag about her as her swords sang.

Against all possible odds, hope emerged.

The gunshot was so close it sounded like it came from right beside me, so loud and surprising that for a moment I thought I'd been hit. I winced away from it, but turned and saw Richter himself standing almost alone in the carnage behind me, the smoking pistol in his outstretched hand.

I followed his line of sight, down the barrel and across the bridge to where Madame Nahreem was crumpling to her knees, blood welling out over the black silk of her sari.

"No!"

I shouted it, but I wasn't the only one. Vestris ran to Madame Nahreem, dropped to cradle her head and neck, and my sister's face opened as she screamed her rage and sorrow. For several seconds, she was frozen there, like a mother nursing an infant, hugging the old woman to her so that I could not see if Madame Nahreem spoke or was even conscious. My sister raised her face to the sky and howled, a cry at once terrifyingly animal and profoundly human, the kind of grief and rage that can only be forged in the heart from things shared. Very slowly, the battle seeming to grind to a halt around her as the fighters became spectators at this strangest of tragedies, Vestris laid her down, and when she got slowly to her feet again, I knew that Madame Nahreem was dead.

Stricken, overwhelmed, all thought driven from my head in a tidal wave of wild emotion, all red and black and murderous, I scooped up my kukri, felt its reassuring weight, and turned to face Richter.

Time seemed to stop as the moment I had always felt possible rushed in on me, and I knew with absolute certainty what I was going to do. He was fifteen feet away. I walked slowly, decisively, my body preparing for the moment when I would seize his gun arm with my left hand as my right brought the heavy blade chopping down at the point where his neck met his shoulder. One cut would probably do it, but two or three would make sure.

I was almost on him when his revolver fired again, and again I winced, wondering where I had been hit.

I hadn't. Richter's actual target had been Vestris, who had flown at him with such wild speed and ferocity that she might have reached him before I did. He had hit her, fatally, I think, but she came on anyway, and when he tried to shoot again, she barreled into him, sending him sprawling backwards, but not down. Her knife found his chest, but still she clasped him in a furious embrace, propelling him back, and half turning to me so that her eyes met mine as they both went over the rail, and fell.

I screamed and ran to the side of the bridge, but they were gone. I think they were both dead before they hit the water.

CHAPTER

32

THE GRAPPOLI NAVY NEVER came upriver. As soon as the circus fighters had thrown down their weapons, which happened the moment they realized Blogvitch was dead, Emtezu took the remains of his men down to the Ridleford fortress, and minutes later, the south bank battery opened fire, sending those ships that had survived thus far into hasty and crippled retreat.

The marines on the north bank, pinned between Mnenga's warriors, the laborers and protesters Peter had brought to the city's defense, and a squad of armed policemen press-ganged into service by Andrews, had already surrendered. They were disarmed and chained until the regular army could arrive to take them into military custody.

The bodies of Vestris and Norton Richter were recovered from the snag in the channel which Tanish had arranged to delay the yacht.

There would be no returning from the dead for my sister this time.

I handed Inspector Andrews the letters the ambassador had given me, which I had kept safely bundled in my satchel. He sorted through them, pale and wordless as he unfolded each one and scanned it. He did not need to tell me that they laid out a lengthy correspondence between the ambassador, the Grappoli high command, and Norton Richter, an indisputable evidence train that mapped the former prime minister's treason, including the assassination of Benjamin Tavestock.

He was beyond punishment for that, though Andrews suggested he'd like to see the Heritage party leader's corpse formally tried and hanged, dead though he already was. The letters implicated Saunders and Mandel, and it looked likely that the entire Heritage party would be disbanded, their most prominent members—including the luxorite dealer Kepahler—having all been implicated in Richter's various crimes. Many would see jail time. Some would see the scaffold.

The fates of the captured Grappoli were less sure, though there was at least a code for dealing with prisoners of war. How long that war would last was similarly unsure. It was not clear whether this had been the beginning or a kind of end, but the Grappoli navy had withdrawn badly bloodied and in no state to mount a counter-assault on more open terms. The ambassador would be recalled, but it was not yet clear if he would go, and while the letters clearly tied him to everything that had happened, his part in the battle might yet win him asylum in the city he had come to think of as his second home. I made sure I went to him as he was brought off the deck of the yacht, now moored—under heavy guard—back at Evensteps. His eyes found me as he emerged, his hands shackled, his hair and clothes uncharacteristically rumpled, and he managed a bleak smile.

"I thought they'd kill you," I said, taking advantage of the moment's pause Andrews had bought for me.

"They still might," he said. "Though whether I will have to go home to face the music or stay here is not yet clear."

"You prefer our music," I said.

He laughed self-deprecatingly. "This is true," he said. He gave me a thoughtful look. "What a remarkable person you are. A true princess after all."

"No," I answered. "Just a steeplejack."

"Quite so," he said, smiling and bowing, as Andrews nodded for the dragoons to lead him away. "Quite so."

Andrews stood beside me, watching them walk through the crowd.

"I'm sorry about Madame Nahreem," he said.

"Yes," I said. It was inadequate and made him still less comfortable, but I did not know what to say.

"And the woman who killed Richter," he said. "The one they are calling the Gargoyle . . . Was that who I think it was?"

I opened my mouth to speak, but the words would not come, and he, aghast and uncertain, stood rigid and horrified as I broke down, long wordless sobs breaking from me. At last he took me awkwardly into his arms, and as everything I had held back overcame me, I wept bitterly into his shoulder for a long minute.

My sister's grief at Madame Nahreem's death had been real enough, though I knew she had attacked Richter so that I could not. I did not know what had passed through my sister's head in those last moments, or what had passed between her and Madame Nahreem in the minutes before the battle, but she had sacrificed herself so that I could live. It was, I thought, her final act of atonement, and she did it safe in the knowledge that neither it nor anything she might do, would ever be enough.

So I wept for her, and for Madame Nahreem, for Aaron Muhapi, and all those whose names I did not know who had fought alongside us, and in doing so, I wept for the city, and the world, though there were not enough tears, and would never be enough.

A few minutes later, when Andrews—assured he had done all he could to calm me—fled with relief to help orchestrate the aftermath of the conflict, Mnenga came up from the riverbank and embraced me wordlessly. It felt heartfelt and earnest, but there was a distance between us which the closeness of our bodies could not disguise. I did not need to look over his shoulder to see that Lomkhosi would be hovering close by, wearing the white spot and stripe war paint that was the insignia of the Mahweni warriors.

He looked at me, and I said, without thinking, "Lomkhosi will make you a good wife."

He looked momentarily hunted, as if unsure whether to prevaricate or apologize and then just nodded.

"I think so," he said. "And it will be good for our villages."

I wished he hadn't said that, as if the decision were political rather than personal, because I had seen the way he had looked at her as they danced, and I knew that it wasn't true, but I said nothing. He had earned that and more.

AN HOUR LATER, I was alone. I stood in the niche reserved for the sixth angel, the spot where Vestris had stood, surveying the city and oscillating between life and death. They were a hairsbreadth apart. If I leaned just a few more inches out, I would fall, and it would all be over, the work, the pain, the grief, the loss. One half step, and I would be free, unmissed, and with very few exceptions, unmourned. I thought of Madame Nahreem, of Aaron Muhapi cut down before he could lead the revolution he deserved, of my once shining and beautiful sister Vestris, and of Papa, whose death had reminded me what I was and what I was not. In my heart, I was still a Drowning girl, a Lani steeplejack, and whatever my recent employment had made me, the gulf between me and the Willinghouses of this world remained as immeasurable as ever. The gap was a chasm compared to which the fall from the highest point of the Inns of Court to the cobbled street was a very small step indeed.

Perhaps it was time for this lost angel to take her last swooping dive—

"What are you doing, you ridiculous creature?"

I didn't turn. I didn't need to.

"What do you want, Dahria?" I said.

"Well, I can tell you what I didn't want, and that was to have to yell at a deeply unpleasant custodian until he opened the doors and gave me his permission—if you can believe that—to climb six flights of increasingly dusty stairs and finally a ladder—yes, I said ladder—to a roof hatch, so I could stand up here inches from certain death while ruining whatever absurd self-dramatizing ritual you are performing. There's no one down there, you know. You aren't impressing anybody."

I sighed.

"Wasn't looking to impress anyone, Dahria."

"Are you sure about that? Because this all feels very theatrical, wouldn't you say? Or are you auditioning for the circus? I believe recent events have left them with some openings."

Now I did turn so that I could glare at her properly.

"Is it your mission in life to be annoying?" I shot at her. "To spend your days being pretty and useless so that you can spend your evenings tormenting the rest of the world with your inane babble?"

"You think I'm pretty?"

"Oh my God!" I said, to no one in particular.

"You said I was pretty."

"I also said you were useless."

"You didn't mean that."

"But I meant the pretty part?"

"Definitely."

"How can you tell which parts I meant and which . . ." I abandoned the question. "Oh, never mind. I'd like to be alone now."

"You don't mean that either," said Dahria. "And I'd appreciate it if you stepped back from that ledge. It's making me dizzy."

"Well, we wouldn't want that," I said.

"I wouldn't, no."

"Which is what matters."

"My feelings matter to me, yes, as yours do to you, which is why you are up here indulging them."

"You don't know what I'm doing up here," I said, staring out over the city again to where the Beacon I'd recovered so very long ago blazed in the night.

"My dear steeplejack," she said, with sudden tenderness, "I know exactly why you are here. You are standing where your sister stood because you know how close to becoming her you are. But you are better, stronger than she was. You refuse to let the resentments you can't outgrow master you, so you think it would be better if you fell. You see your other sister's family, and you think you will never have anything like it. You see your friends—Mnenga, Sureyna, Emtezu—who all have a place in the world, and you envy them. You thought my brother was like you because he's part Lani and he says all the right political things, but you now see that he is as far from you as the Mahweni tribes in the bush are, separated by birth, by class, and—above all—by wealth. All of which means that however well-intentioned he is, he does not finally understand you at all. You don't know how much you care about that, but you think you should, and not knowing what to think makes you sad and angry and confused all at the same time.

"Last, and most importantly, you mistake being alone with being unloved. My brother's career will get a substantial boost from his days sitting in a cell doing nothing, while you—the one who did all the actual work—will scan every newspaper for even a mention of your name, and you will come up empty. So you came here to look out over the city you held together, as if jumping from the high places where you are most at home will punish all the people who live here for their ingratitude. But you can't. Because however terrible the city can be, how much it is always on the edge of tearing itself apart, it needs you, and you, I suspect, need it. You are Bar-Selehm's unsung hero, its guardian angel. You do not know how to be anything else."

I stood listening, then thinking, feeling with the toes of my boots just how close I was to the edge, staring out over the city, which pulsed with activity as its inhabitants came to grip with what had happened.

"I'm not sure that's enough," I said.

Her voice, when it came, was frightened but determined, and it came from an inch behind my ear.

"Then you must find other reasons to live," she said. "Some of us need you." She hesitated, a moment that might have been a lifetime, then added, "I need you."

She clutched my hand fiercely, with a passion that came from more than terror of the long drop to the street below. When I turned to her, I was amazed to see her face wet with tears.

I stepped back and down, pulling her to me, and there was the embrace I had missed from Andrews and Mnenga, the one that collapsed two bodies into one, twining the minds and hearts together in strength. In love.

I kissed her then and, suddenly and unexpectedly, the world made a kind of sense.

WILLINGHOUSE WAS WAITING FOR me at the bottom. He had a police escort since it would be some time before the formal procedures involved in his release were finalized, even with the ambassador's clear and incontrovertible testimony. But he looked free, like a great burden had been lifted from his shoulders or he had been taken out into sunlight and reminded who he was.

He didn't know how to greet me, how to thank me, and he bowed and shuffled, and extended a hand as if I was an old school friend he hadn't seen for some time, and made speeches about what I had achieved and how much he was in my debt.

That was all right. I nodded and said I had only done my job, and he looked concerned that I wasn't sufficiently happy or proud. I felt calm, however, and when his confused glance fell on my hand, held tenderly by his sister, I just smiled. He made a quizzical face and opened his mouth several times as if looking to begin a series of complex questions. Dahria stared him down, and when she finally said, "What, Joss? You look like a very stupid fish who has just noticed he is no longer in the water," he just shook his head and backed, baffled, away.

She rolled her eyes at me and then I did laugh. A part of me had been dreading seeing her brother, as if doing so would confuse my feelings for her, but all I felt was surety and relief. I respected Willinghouse. I even liked him. I did not blame him for my father's death, and I understood the reasons behind his clumsy subterfuge as I understood why he was so completely useless at speaking to me as if I was a human being he had come to care for. But I did not love him.

I squeezed Dahria's hand, and she gave me a curious look.

"You all right?" she asked, as if she was holding in some lingering anxiety.

"Yes," I said honestly. "Perfectly."

FRAMED! SANG ONE OF the *Clarion*'s competing headlines the following morning, over a picture of Willinghouse. TREASON! screamed another over Richter's portrait. PRIME MINISTER SLAIN BY GARGOYLE! said another. The full account of the Grappoli-Heritage conspiracy would take days to unfold, probably much longer, but for now the news positively spilled from the papers like water from an overflowing rain barrel. It was the talk of every conversation on every street corner, in every tavern and club, the meat of every dinner. I had thought the murder of Benjamin Tavestock had created a kind of unprecedented unity of focus within the city, but that had merely been a prelude to division and rancor along all the old lines. This felt different. But how long it would last and where it would lead, I could not say.

Heritage was gone. Its existence was simply untenable, and even those members unlikely to face criminal prosecution quickly joined an embarrassed queue to profess the extent to which they had been misled, how outraged they were by their leadership's activities, how stalwart was their patriotism, and so on. It was mostly performance, but a necessary one, and it cowed those who had so gleefully embraced the government's recent policies of segregation and disenfranchisement. In the stunned silence from the Nationals, the Brevard party would make hay, not simply overturning the newest regulations, but ramming through some of their own, including an entirely new refashioning of electoral districts, which would give the black and Lani population considerably more power.

Votes for women would take longer, but a bill had been proposed, cleverly named after the late prime minister, Benjamin Tavestock, and it would officially start the conversation. Dahria felt sure that many society women had been waiting for just such a moment to lend their voices to what had been, till now, an undignified and disreputable cause.

The cancelled election was back on, though it had been postponed, to allow Parliament to draw new party lines and accommodate the sudden collapse of those on the far right. I was not naïve enough to believe that all those who had cheered Heritage on were truly gone, but their embarrassment had created an opening, and men like Willinghouse had enough pragmatism to exploit it.

Just.

Willinghouse had emerged as a martyr who had been snatched from the heretics' flames at the last minute, and he had a certain amount of what he privately called "political capital," which he intended to spend wisely. It was unclear what someone as junior as he was could do with his new celebrity, but he had already completed his transition from minor backbencher to someone of considerable power and influence. He was still too young to be considered prime minister material, but that day was not so very far away. You could see it in the way he carried himself, the way he walked, the way he addressed the House on his return, and the way he accepted their applause as if it was no more than his due.

Dahria wore a heavy veil for the cremation of Vestris and Madame Nahreem, and avoided everyone's gaze but mine, dabbing her eyes with a handkerchief gripped tightly in gloved, unsteady hands. Willinghouse stared unblinking into the fire as if forcing himself to watch his grandmother's last earthly moments, even as the heat made the rest of the crowd back away. When it was over and he joined the customarily chaotic banquet, his clothes and hair smelled scorched, his face and hands were pink, and his eyes bloodshot. His own brand of atonement, perhaps.

Dahria watched him, then turned to face me.

"She—my grandmother, I mean—said you were a good influence on me," she said. "It was the first thing we'd agreed on in years."

She tried to smile, but a sob rose in her face, and I embraced her.

AARON MUHAPI'S FUNERAL PROCESSION began at his Morgessa house and wound the long, slow route all the way to Mahweni Old Town and the square where he had spoken several times and which had been the site of the most intense intimidation by the now disbanded civilian militia. Some of the buildings were still streaked with smoke from the firebombs thrown through their windows.

The crowd of mourners—mostly, but not entirely black—numbered in the thousands. As they walked, they sang old songs, some religious, some political, some ancient tribal memories that went back a century or more before the city existed in its present form. The songs were high and plaintive, sorrow put to music, but the mood was not all sad. Several people spoke, including Willinghouse, celebrating Muhapi's life, his beliefs, and his legacy, something that had seemed impossible only a week before.

Peter stood beside Muhapi's widow, Samora, and announced that, in accord with the Brevard party's hastily cobbled mandate, he intended to be Bar-Selehm's first black member of Parliament in the coming elections, promising to adhere to the values he had learned at Muhapi's side. For her part, Samora said that she would be speaking to white women's groups to consolidate pressure on the government, which would, she hoped, bring women the right to vote within the next three years.

The city was changing, and for the better, but if the last few weeks had taught me anything, it was that progress was fragile and could always be taken away. I thought of the battle on the bridge, the way we had scrambled for every foot, and I thought that that was how things would always be. If you stopped fighting for a second, all the ground you had captured would be taken away.

And it all depended, of course, on who you meant by "the city." The Drowning was outside the walls, but on the day of the cremation, I had watched Rahvey and her family, Aab, Tanish, even Florihn and the rest of the Lani who came to the old monkey temple in memory of Vestris and Madame Nahreem. Though both had left the shanty by the river long ago, it seemed that the entire population of the Drowning had come to pay their respects, and I knew I would fight anyone who thought that Bar-Selehm did not include them. I had told Rahvey about Vestris and Madame Nahreem. About our father's death. All of it. She had wept a little and hugged her children, and given me her silent nod that was all the gratitude, understanding, and resolve that she could manage.

It was enough.

Barely.

I did not know—would never know—what kind of peace Vestris and Madame Nahreem had achieved between themselves before they had died fighting shoulder to shoulder. It pained me a little that I had not been part of that final communion, however much it had been the end of a personal history that had involved me only obliquely, but I remembered my sister's parting look at me as she seized Richter and dragged him with her down to the river. Her eyes had shared with me in a heartbeat the sorrow and remorse, the sense of love and of things lost, which she would have never been able to say.

As Muhapi's coffin was lowered into the ground, the crowd cheered and smiled, and they sang again and waved torches as if in victory, which in the circumstances, felt right. So I was at a loss to understand why I felt so strangely separate from the rest of the crowd and why I was quite unable to stem the tide of my weeping.

"It's all right," said Dahria, squeezing my hand. "He did not die in vain."

I nodded fervently, not sure what I wanted to say. I felt as I had when Papa died, like I was still a child, unmoored and drifting. Lost. It was not simply grief for Muhapi or his family, or even his cause, but something deeper and older, a grief for how the world was, how hard we had to fight for just a little fairness and justice.

"Come along," said Dahria. "I will buy you lunch."

"You mean you'll have the servants buy something and cook it for us," I said, wiping my tears away.

"No," she said. "I mean I will take you to a restaurant like a civilized person, and you will sit opposite me, trying not to eat with your hands, while we make polite conversation."

"In public?"

"I'm always polite in public," she replied.

"That's not what I meant," I said. "And you know it."

"I know all kinds of things that I do not say because that's what ladies do. We are figures of mystery and power."

"You are absurd," I said.

"That too." She shot me a grin. "Come on. We have people to scandalize."

She offered me her arm. I took it and we moved off under the smoky mantle that shrouded the city, but beyond which—high and far above—was a deep, faultless blue as near perfection as the human mind could grasp.

ACKNOWLEDGMENTS

Thanks to Finie Osako and Sebastian Hartley, always my first readers; to my editor, Diana M. Pho; my agent, Stacey Glick; to Kerra Bolton, Lee Gray, Brilliant Makhubele, and Ezekiel Bathez Sibuyi.